Friday, 2 April 1982. In Buenos Aires they're dancing in the streets to celebrate Argentina's capture of the Falkland Islands. In London, Spencer Cobbold also has nervous energy to spare because he's just given up smoking. His lunch date with Claire might help. But it's only day one and you never know how things will go.

Spencer, a headhunter, has to track down some missing files before the boss loses her temper. Gareth, Spencer's Camden Town neighbour and ex-colleague, who now works in a government department, has to track down some IRA terrorists. He also has to watch his back, because it's possible the terrorists are tracking him down.

Day One is a novel about the meshing of public and private events and the way life catches us unprepared. Masterly in its portrayal of the nine-to-five world, marvellously particular in its treatment of London and authoritative in its depiction of the corridors and lift-lobbies of power, it is a work of magnificent scope and concision.

BY THE SAME AUTHOR

PROMISE

DAY

HUGO BARNACLE

ONE

Q QUARTET BOOKS

FIRST PUBLISHED BY QUARTET BOOKS LIMITED IN 1998
A MEMBER OF THE NAMARA GROUP
27 GOODGE STREET
LONDON W1P 2LD

THIS EDITION PUBLISHED BY QUARTET BOOKS LIMITED IN 1999

A CATALOGUE RECORD FOR THIS BOOK IS AVAILABLE FROM THE BRITISH LIBRARY

ISBN 0 7043 8114 1

PRINTED AND BOUND IN GREAT BRITAIN BY COX & WYMAN, READING, BERKS

DAY ONE

Spencer Cobbold, barefoot on the greasy kitchen lino, swallowed water and ran more at the tap. He wasn't that thirsty but it was something to do. An unimpressive bell tolled three. The few cars still plying in these dead hours swished their treads through the wet of the Camden Road beyond the square. He recognised the horn that played 'Strangers in the Night', going the other way this time. The tune was out of a film; he didn't remember which.

Eight thousand miles away in a different season, the ships are closing in and before long the marines will be face down in the road while the newcomers burn the Jack; the dictator will have the islands and all his problems will be solved, but in the imperial capital nobody knows.

Spencer trudged across the living room towards the sofa. Turning to sit, he caught one foot against the thick new hardbound novel that Miles had dropped there earlier. He put the book on his knees and lit Katie's lamp on the side table. What if we cut our losses and sit up and read this here instead? But the book had won such prizes, sold such numbers that, after a couple of bravura pages which confusingly recalled another book he knew already, an obstinate wealth fantasy snared him.

First I could leave Holt Newman. Embarrass everybody with humiliatingly expensive presents: golfclubs (You could always learn, Dad), first editions, pedigree springers, oils of notable Georgian sheep. Move to Highbury Fields, three tall windows looking out front, bathroom to myself. Run one of those baby convertibles, trouble is they slash the roof to get your radio or just your goat, second thoughts car not necessary, it isn't as if you had kids to take to school. Ach.

Spencer cringed and bowed, grasping his knees; because there had been a little demiCobbold once: he called it the Rat after the size and form he pictured it attaining before, yes, well; and he hated the child for the terrible revenge it took, this downpouring of shame at the merest thought.

Love a smoke of something. Ah. Giving up, weren't we.

He killed the lights, shuffled blind through to his own room again, rolled himself up in the quilt and hunched. Would in fact commit murder for a smoke of something. He pictured his heavy hands, first throttling several girls he knew who smoked, give give, then slack in his lap in the Old Bailey dock. No, not really. Same hands caressing same girls to reassure.

Six. The awful dawn chorus was past its worst, dissipating in the breathy rush of traffic, early trains, overnight flights arriving. The luminous points of the clockface barely showed.

He wasn't asleep, just dreaming. The dashboard glowed in the dark as he was driven fast through busy streets to the station, too late, with too much luggage. The cramped minicab had full ashtrays and itchy mustard-coloured seats and the driver, weaving and braking with lunatic zest, was Orson Welles; but the bearded, massive Welles of nowadays, not the young Harry Lime figure Spencer was said to resemble. They were in the wrong lane with a bus coming at them when the engine died. 'It's been a little testimonial lately,' grunted Welles, stamping on the pedal, and it caught and whipped them on again. They veered clear across the island, ramming the oldtime keep-left bollard out of the way. Spencer, in the back, threw a panic sweat. The heater, going full blast, stiffened Welles's cigar smoke into cobweb voile which all the same was all there was to breathe; the windows were so thick with dirt and dead insects you could hardly see a thing outside, only the wings and flanks of the other crowding cars as the minicab shot and slewed towards them. It was, in fine, a bloody nightmare; but he knew he was only dreaming; for instance, the platform announcement of his train's departure as he stumbled cornily overladen to the barrier was probably in fact the forecourt tannoy of the petrol station on the Camden Road telling somebody they'd left their change. Yes.

Hell's bells. That was the signal, the blow of Paul's heel on the bathroom floor which was also Spencer's ceiling. Slept through the alarm again. He cast aside the quilt, like tearing off a plaster, only way, dropped his legs over the edge of the bed and stood in the middle of the tiny room, face to face with the movie queens above the chest of drawers: black-and-white postcards of Ingrid and Lauren, Grace and Julie, all still going strong, never could figure why people want the dead on their walls: Hendrix, Che, Dean, Marilyn, not nice somehow. Here, I'm up. What was I thinking?

He dithered over the socks in his drawer, finding none that smelt clean except an odd couple whose pairmates were long lost in the wash, dithered so that as he came to mount the stairs a minute or two late he saw Katie flit across the landing and heard the bathroom door slammed and bolted against him. He knelt and, sagging forward, brought his chin to rest on the top stair. 'Oh, Kates,' he mumbled, 'you're rocking the rote.' Head lifting from propped jaw, he yawned.

The doomladen sound of the BBC morning concert playing low in Paul's room along the landing was gingered by the skipping-rope beat of a yester hit from the top floor, where Miles's radio alarm had just tripped: 'My baby takes the morning train, he works from nine to five, and then, he takes another home again.' Thanks very much.

Spencer went to put the kettle on, dialled the speaking clock from the phone in the hallway, set his watch and sat on the stairs to wait. By the phone was the seasick-green Pytcherley Probables file. Philipson. Dealt with. Have to remember to take that in.

Paul showed lankily at the stairhead, knotting his tie. 'Hi. What's the matter, didn't I bang?'

'Yeah, you did,' Spencer rubbing his face, 'but I missed my chance.' He squeezed aside to let Paul by. 'You going home this weekend?'

'Ah — Cookham, yeah,' said Paul. Been here half his life and still thinks home's the States. Unless he means this place. No, can't do.

Paul went into the living room and paused to scoop crumbs off the tabletop into his hand. 'Jesus. Did you leave this kettle on?' He took the crumbs to the kitchen sink.

Spencer looked through. There was steam in the kitchen archway and a bloom on the windows. 'Must have. We should get an automatic one. Making tea?'

'If it hasn't boiled dry.' Paul dropped the kettle lid. 'Burnt myself in the steam.'

3

'Scalded,' said Spencer. He yawned again. Reason I keep yawn-
ing is I haven't smoked for must be twelve or thirteen hours.
Tension. Greugh. Starting to taste what my mouth's like and all.

From Gareth MacMichael's bathroom window, looking down the
mews, you could just see the trees at the bottom of Spencer's
garden. When they used to share an office, Spence was still in
Islington. The trees were always there, but they were known trees
now.

Gareth dried his face, buttoned his shirt and picked up his gun
from the top of the plastic cistern.

The gun was a military Browning automatic gloved in a large
shoulder holster. He carried it downstairs and laid it on the table.
Lynn, last of his subtenants, sharp in skirt and blazer, stood bolting
an oozy crumpet. 'Still taking that everywhere with you,' she said.
'I suppose it's a bit like wearing contacts, is it? You don't think
after a few weeks.' She'd been touring army bases over there with
the college revue troupe a couple of years back (check the show-
girl legs), staying in officers' messes, and was not, at least not
overmuch, unsettled by a loaded gun at breakfast.

'Uh, a bit the same,' said Gareth. 'Not quite, really.' He finished
the banana sandwich he'd left on the worktop.

'No ... ' said Lynn. 'So are you OK on your own for the
weekend, or have you got anything planned?'

'No, nothing.'

'Mm. Don't you think you ought perhaps to get out of London
sometime, 'cause you haven't for ages, have you? Since you came
back.' She took a last pull at her tea and slung her new hot-pink
holdall on its peppermint strap.

'Well. I could be working if the news is anything to go by.
Where are you going? Marina's, is this?'

'Yes, gang of us going down.'

'She might have asked me. I could have stood for being lost in
a crowd a bit.'

'I know, still, it'll mainly be people that you probably don't like,
people like Helga Sloman, Camilla Kenilworth ... '

'Yeah, OK.' Gareth held up a hand.

'So how does this islands thing affect you?'

'Affects all sorts of departments. You have to go into contingency measures.'

'What, I mean, like ... ?'

Gareth made the no-comment gesture she was used to, like dusting a mantelpiece.

'Ah,' said Lynn. 'Right, look.' She gave him wide eyes. 'See you Sunday, eh? Got to dash 'cause we're cutting the programme this morning, goes out tomorrow. Oh, if I get the time I'll have another word with Amanda about Prebend Street. It would be good if we could perhaps move from here, wouldn't it?'

'Yeah.' Gareth sat and lit a Camel. 'D'you think I should chase Melanie up for rent?'

'Why not? She hasn't given notice, she's still got her things here. And I doubt she's paying her boyfriend any. I don't want to pay extra to cover hers, and nor should you, she can't just run off because you're ... '

'Hit-listed.'

'Anyway, you were paying all the time you were over there, weren't you?'

He leaned back in his chair. 'Hm.'

'Golly.' Lynn checked her watch. 'I'm going to have to run. OK, then,' she said, leaving.

The house was modern and largely glass. Gareth watched Lynn cross the tiny front garden to the gate he kept hooked open (so that it couldn't be booby-trapped). One of the cab mechanics, early on the job, called out hullo from the ramp of the workshops next door. Lynn waved back and set off down the mews.

Paul had started to clean out the oven. 'Think I have time. I'm sure this hasn't been done since Miles's chicken.'

'The one we left in there that went off?'

'Yeah. Smells not too good.'

Spencer sawed bread and loaded the toaster. 'It's the maggots I don't understand. I mean the remains were in there for a few days but how does a bluebottle get in past an oven door? Unless the eggs were already in the bird when we were eating it.'

'No, the cooking would have killed them,' Paul said.

'Well, it didn't thaw all the ice. He underdid it.'

'Oh, yeah. Those icy bits.' Paul, crouching and scouring, pulled a face.

'That's why we left so much of it.'

'Yeah, but the freezing too would have killed them.'

'Wouldn't it just put them in suspended animation?'

'Whatever. None of us got sick,' said Paul.

Katie came down, hands in the pockets of her hairy blue jacket, and stood there looking cold. Spencer hoped against hope that she would break the pattern, infringe in however trifling a way, but after the predicted interval of motionlessness she did the shudder, took the sudden huge breath through the nose and said, 'Was there any post?'

Spencer shook his head. It wasn't just the daily repetition, it was her aggravatingly sublime unconsciousness of it. And now the same cars were starting in the square and the mews at the side, the same pneumatic drill was limbering up nearby, the same unknown neighbours were passing the window. Spencer felt a quick froth of murderous rage rise and spend itself, and longed with a bitter ache in the throat for the day when the sun would explode and engulf the planets.

Paul, head in the oven, said, 'Rent's due, people.'

'Right,' said Spencer.

'Right,' said Katie.

Paul took his head out. 'This morning if possible so that the cheques clear before I pay it.' The lease was in his name because he was the one with the bank references. He looked at his watch and ducked back in. 'We've got about six or seven minutes.'

Miles in jeans and thick jersey slid down the banisters and hurt himself on the newelpost. He rubbed his hip as he hobbled through the living room. 'I should have known. No point trying to start the day with any enthusiasm.' He edged into the narrow kitchen. 'Only joking, Paul.'

'Rent,' said Katie.

'OK, sure.' Miles picked his curled chequebook and a pen from the cutlery tray by the kettle. 'How much, Paul?'

'Oh,' said Paul from the oven, Miles's easiness over money a thing he never got used to. 'Er, wait. Yours is ... two forty-seven.'

' ... forty-seven. Sheesh,' said Miles, writing, and tore the cheque out. 'Here.' He held it over Paul's shoulder.

'Great. I've got this shit on my hands, Miles. Could you leave that on the table?'

'Sure.'

Spencer fetched his jacket off a chairback and went to sit on the sofa, before the hideous brass-edged coffee table with Michelangelo's God creating Adam under its glass top. A landlord item. He spread his chequebook. 'Date?'

'First,' called Miles.

Spencer looked at yesterday's paper, lying beside him. Today was the second.

Miles came over. 'So what's — ?' He trod barefoot on a dropped ballpoint deep in the shag pile of the carpet. 'I've been looking for that.' It was red, embellished with girls whose swimsuits disappeared when you held it upright. He'd once had a blue one too, given out at the same conference, but that was confiscated at Tehran airport after he tried using it to sign for some currency and got fisticuffed by a keen-eyed passing student. When they found he was proposing to change, among other monies, French 100-franc notes which displayed the breasts of Delacroix's Liberty, he was taken into detention, and when he showed his press card featuring Beaverbrook's Crusader he was forcibly deported. 'Great.' He clicked the thumbstud to advance and retract the point a few times and scribbled on his palm to see if the ink flowed. 'So what's this about you taking orders, Spence, is it on?'

'Orders from who?'

'With the Franciscans. I'm sure it was the Franciscans.'

'I — what?'

'I was going to ask you, I was with Granger and Chris Frick in the Old Eagle last night.' Miles took a turn up and down the room chopping his hands. 'They were quite adamant you were on the verge of taking orders.'

'Maybe they said I was becoming a monk. I haven't done so much lately.'

'This was quite definite.'

'I'm not even a Catholic, Miles.'

'Oh. Would you have to be?'

'I would guess so. Or at least a baptised gentile.'

'I hadn't thought of that.' Miles felt his own neck. 'Maybe I got the wrong end of the stick. Or you think they were spoofing me.'

Spencer made trumpet lips and nodded. 'Hey. Did I collect off everyone for the electric?'

'Me you did, yeah,' said Miles. Paul and Katie made noises.

'Well, I haven't paid it yet. I'll do that.' Spencer went into the kitchen. 'On the table, Paul.'

Paul dropped the used oven pad in the bin. 'Thanks. I wonder if this needs emptying again.'

'Give us the bag, I'll run it out,' said Spencer, restless with the urge to smoke. Among the rubbish he saw his last crumpled cigarette packet. It caused him a pang of grief that reminded him in turn of the Rat, and he cringed and growled as he carried the bag down the front steps to the dustbin.

Gareth warily pulled on his mackintosh, not so much against the dull weather as to cover up what the stowed pistol did to his good bespoke suit, the jacket bulking out with a suggestion of deformity or stolen library books.

Coat and jacket had to stay unbuttoned. One or two people over there had got themselves into trouble thinking they could keep out the draught and still expect to reach their best help in time if the bar went suddenly quiet, or if that unhailed cab pulled in, or if their own front door should open by itself as they were fumbling with the key on the step.

He went to make sure all the upstairs doors were shut before he set the expat landlord's finicky alarm system. It was a sorrier house without Peter's Victorian watercolours or Jo's batik hangings, but Peter had got mortgaged and Jo had left the country and Gareth was the only original tenant yet to move on. Lynn wasn't a bad replacement. Melanie was, though.

Outside, he waited until the alarm stopped its whooping. These net curtains he'd always hated were a surprisingly effective one-way screen; he could hardly see in. They had them at the office, where they were also supposed to interfere with laser sound scanners, if such things existed.

The alarm was going on too long, he'd have to get back in and check. No, it cut.

There was a blue Cortina Ghia parked on the kerb as suspect as you like, but when he'd seen it from his bedroom window earlier and rung up about it he found a patrol had reported it overnight and it turned out to belong to someone in the council flats opposite, respectably acquired secondhand this week. Once it was moved they were supposed to put out some more cones. The last lot had all been taken.

The mechanics, father and son, were running a trolley jack under a cab. Since they were around all day the law had asked them to keep an eye out. They weren't put wise, but what with the cones and the hourly patrols they must have got an inkling. Gareth doubted if it went to make him popular. They were probably worried about the insurance on the workshops and the customers' cabs. If anything did go up. And they seemed to know it was his fault, not Lynn's. They were still friendly with her, whereas they busily ignored him.

He looked around as he moved off down the cobbled mews. It would have been a bomb in the first place that took out the old houses where the low-rise flats stood now, perhaps one of the same clutch that redeveloped part of Rochester Square further down. The King's Cross goods yards were only half a mile away.

Some of the windows in the flats were boarded up, which bothered him because places standing empty had their uses to a certain sort of person. You only needed a chink in the boards to put your eye to. Ground floor, nearest block, had a genuine squatter, the upright Indian who stood in the mews at 3am shouting, 'The whole universe is against me.' The police had been to check the other vacant numbers for signs of entry, but that was a month ago.

He could place the cars parked along the mews without having to think about it. A train rumbled in the mainline tunnel underfoot and the cobbles pulsed.

Here the surviving but shabby old lockups he used to like had lately been pulled down to make way for dapper townhouses which, in a way, he also liked. They had roof gardens and built-in garages and their street windows gave on to pristine kitchens. He caught his own reflection glancing in and turned away, smiling kiddishly.

Where Davisons Street crossed — they called it that after the off-licence, its real name hadn't stuck — he turned through to the Camden Road. He never carried on down the mews past Spencer's garden wall and through Rochester Square, though he always came back that way, he didn't know why; he'd only noticed it from sometimes walking with Lynn, who ('Where are you *going*? What's the *matter*?') out of equally arbitrary determination did the opposite. He ought to be varying his entire route to and from work, but there was not much scope except to switch from bus to tube to footing it across the Park, and this bit had to be walked in any case.

On Camden Road there were numbers of others hurrying along the pavement.

It might be someone whose picture he knew, it might be someone unknown altogether. It would not be anyone who was black, or Asiatic, or Arab, or Latin. It would not be anyone under twenty, or much over forty. It could be a woman, even an apparently pregnant woman, but not a woman with children, who were great disguise but awful liabilities. It would never be anyone wearing pinstripe. When in doubt he touched his tie, to have his hand ready for the draw.

Nobody nearby earned a second look apart from the jumpsuit girl overtaking him on roller skates, and despite a satchel big enough for who-knew-what she was far and away too smart, or probably. He touched his tie as she came alongside, her Walkman hissing like cold drips on a hot pan, but without looking at him she glided on ahead. Thank you.

He kept close to the hedge, looking back every so often. There was also the traffic to mind. Rush hour was no problem for getaways, easier to lose themselves. That unhailed cab could pull in any moment, and two on a motorbike, like so, was a particularly bad sign.

Two on a motorbike came fast and grimly visored up the bus lane behind him. He touched his tie. The bike slowed, tacked past a lorry on the inside and boosted off again to catch the lights.

Thank you.

Katie came back down with her scarf on, calling, 'Ready, Paul.'

'With you in a minute,' he called from his room.

'Let's go, Spence. Have a good day, Miles.'

Spencer got his coat and stood with Katie on the front steps. They haahed at each other to see their breath.

Beyond the plant nurseries in the middle of the square, cars queued for the turning and sent up brumous exhaust.

'Electricity bill,' said Spencer, and went in to find the bill on his chest of drawers with last month's pay slip.

Miles was lengthwise on the sofa, reading.

'So long,' said Spencer. 'Is anything going to happen down there today?'

'Where?' said Miles. 'Oh, no, it's a ritual every few years, they stash their galleons to the gunwales with corned beef and cannon-balls, we send a sub, they hold a few manoeuvres and go home. Everyone knows we'll clear out eventually so honour is satisfied.'

'That's all right, then.'

'Forget about it,' said Miles.

On the steps Katie shuffled for warmth. 'What's keeping Paul?'

Spencer yawned. 'Give him a chance, he only has to do this once a week.'

'Look. There's Gareth that you used to work with.'

'Oh, yeah.' Across the mews from their corner of the square was the whitewashed false-limb clinic. You could see the Camden Road beyond it where there used to be a turning, now paved over, and you could tell MacMichael by the upmarket trenchcoat, the messy black hair and the long pace.

'What was it you said he does these days?' said Katie.

'MoD.'

'But sort of secret.'

'Everything's secret. I had that holiday job with the Post Office and I had to sign the Official Secrets Act, it means nothing.'

'I thought you were just sorting letters.'

'I was.'

'We ought to have him round. Since he found us our house.'

'He only spotted a To Let sign,' said Spencer.

'But he did ring up and tell you. And that awful place we were about to take.'

'Well, he's a good bloke. Anyway, he has been round.'

'Not properly.'

'Not five courses and all day washing up after, you mean,' said Spencer. 'Suppose not.'

'And you could ask that girl from the office.'

'Prescription,' said Spencer, and went inside again. He rifled the chit from the pocket of his other coat on the rack.

'Sorry,' Paul said, appearing with his briefcase and canvas weekend bag. 'Had to finish a memo. I need to get it typed first thing.' He held up his duffel coat. 'You been out? You think I need this?'

'Yeah,' said Spencer, brisk as possible.

'Wear it, you're wearing your overcoat, or carry it?'

'Wear it.'

'Sure?'

'Er, yeah,' said Spencer. The 'er' was a mistake. Paul was all business until it came to actually leaving the house.

'Maybe I'd better see,' Paul said, frowned, and approached the open door with caution. 'I don't want to sweat while I'm driving.'

Miles came off the sofa with surprising liveliness and into the hall. 'Going up again, Paul?'

'Nope, done.'

'So OK if I run a shower? Cheers.'

'Are we off?' said Katie on the steps as Paul banged the door reluctantly behind him a few times and got it to shut.

'Yeah. Wait. It's colder than I thought. Could you — ?' Paul gave Katie his briefcase and Spencer his bag and struggled into the coat.

Katie took Paul's arm and led him out of the gate. Someone had to. 'Why are you wearing a suit?'

'Ghastly. We've got to meet this delegation from the Indonesian finance ministry later on, for drinks. The college does a development consultancy for them, most of it's in the vac. Teach them the jargon mainly.'

'Didn't think Indonesians drank,' said Spencer.

'Probably soft drinks. But it does vary. When they're not at home. The tide of militancy hasn't fully risen as yet.' Paul smiled, found the right key and unlocked the car.

Spencer huddled into the corner of the back seat, arms warmly folded.

Paul sorted out seatbelts with Katie, who'd plugged hers into his fastener again. 'Got my bag there, Spence? OK.' He three-pointed expertly, took them round the square and joined the queue.

They were outside the spiritualist temple, a brick hut with unlit neon cross on top, faded blue woodwork, Foundation Stone Laid By Sir Arthur Conan Doyle 30th October 1926. The signboard said, Sundays: Address and Clairvoyance, Tuesdays and Wednesdays: Clairvoyance and Healing (use rear entrance), Wednesday Healing Cancelled Until Further Notice. Spencer felt sad.

'Go on,' muttered Paul, 'go on, what's — ah.' They came to the turning on to Camden Road. He nosed the car discreetly out. 'Is she going to let me go no she isn't yes — she — is.' He pulled round on to the bus lane and they rode in halting conga through the first set of lights.

Spencer saw over the newsagent's an ancient enamel sign he hadn't taken in before, Craven 'A' Will Not Affect Your Throat. He gradually felt his aches and pains come on with the last but never quite completed stage of waking and silently hulloed them each, the one in his side like stitch, the one that shot up his forearm, the curious bubbling one in his left calf, the headache and of course his chest.

They pipped the next lights and forged ahead under the blue steelboxed railway bridge with its permanent recommendation for Ferodo brake pads, engine noise squalling against low girders. Spencer's stomach contracted because he had to get out in a few hundred yards and he didn't want to.

Going over the canal Katie sang the first lines of 'Morning Has

Broken'. Paul began to hum loud and tunelessly above her, switched on the radio, wobbled the volume to make loops of sound, switched off again. 'Bastard,' said Katie. 'Anything on TV tonight?'

'*Shalako*,' said Spencer. 'Connery; Bardot; Jack Hawkins; Honor Blackman, pant pant. Western.'

'Any good?'

'Not really.'

'I'll probably be out anyway.' She tapped the window. 'There's Gareth again.'

MacMichael on the pavement turned and nodded to them, hand on heart in a strange courtly gesture.

At the disused bread factory the road narrowed, and before the big crossroads they had to turn down the one-way. Paul stopped outside the Labour Party office round the corner. 'There you go.'

'Mmh,' said Spencer, still huddled, 'right then,' and launched himself out into the noise. He slammed the door and walked on to the bus stop. Paul hooted as the car went by, revving high to gain with the traffic. He'd got Katie shammying mist off the screen.

At the stop as ever a 31 offered passage to the World's End. The crew hadn't boarded, they were nearby, talking sport till departure. Not Spencer's bus anyhow. He stood and tapped one foot heel-and-toe on the paving. A black girl in Winnie Mandela headscarf came and leaned against the railings, staring back at the corner. Spencer stopped tapping and squared up.

He took a long breath; it seemed to go no deeper than usual but the scents were keener already, diesel, rubber, tarmac, dogshit, cement dust from building work somewhere, the wool of his coat collar, the musk the girl wore. He felt a sudden joy of being, just the moment for a cigarette in fact. Heck. He gave the girl the Harry Lime smile, gave it too to an older woman who arrived smelling of hairspray and closed rooms. Both of them pretended not to notice.

When the right bus, the needed 53, sailed up clippership tall and fine, Spencer let out a happy grunt. There were four or five others waiting by now and they all avoided looking at him. What he'd forgotten till this was that not smoking makes you drunk.

By the light of the moon the first naval commandos from the mainland, a hundred of them, sweating heavily into their all-black kit, have nursed their rubber boats to shore through the prop-snarling fields of kelp and must now trek for miles across grass that grows in tussocks like basketwork stools. They've already taken their first casualty, an officer's broken his ankle.

The bus cruised Albany Street, down the Nash terrace backs, branches skirring along the roof. Spencer sat with nostrils closed to other people's smoke. Should have stayed below with the saved. He stretched his ticket till it snapped in the middle, easy, then tried the same with an old Sainsbury's receipt from his pocket, harder, and tore the pieces into smaller pieces, small as he could go. He swayed and rocked with the turns and stops as the bus manoeuvred through the filter junctions to cross the Marylebone Road. Sirens went up somewhere in the rush.

He edged out of his seat, plush moquette and real leather, continentals think we're twee but Paul thinks we're seriously kinked, and went downstairs to wait on the open platform, the grooved brown floor like a monster chocolate bar, practically smell that chocolate, yearning for it, murder. He gripped the pole hard as the turn from Great Portland Street into New Cavendish swung him outwards. Newton's First. He looked down again. Nothing like a bar of choc at all, control yourself, man.

The bus was halted. He leaned out, lights red, stepped off and began the walk, over into Marylebone Village past Ferraris double-parked and Rollers with gold doorhandles. Notices on behalf of Howard de Walden Estates threatened the removal of any bicycles chained to these railings. Bicycles were chained there in protest like suffragettes.

As he crossed Harley Street a nasty doorstop-shaped car — Lagonda is that, or a Bentley? — coming down at speed and jumping the red, hooted him. He slowed to even graver pace, august in overcoat, and turned to give the driver a Churchill as the braking car passed behind him. See if he stops to argue about it. Yes indeed. For a *right royal* wally score ten points and a cup of coffee before knuckledown and take Claire to lunch.

Why'd I never do that yet?

The car pitched to a halt and reversed up gruesomely fast, the driver lowering his electric window to yell, 'Fat sod.'

'Stick it, son,' breezed far younger Spencer from the kerb. The car's transmission thumped and it took off again, yawing wildly because the driver forgot to straighten up before he hit the pedal.

Odd, that. Not fat at all but people will take me as if I was. Spencer moved on, past marble halls with bevelled windows, bankbreaking motors outside and chauffeurs loafing as if every house hosted a wedding, recession what recession.

Queen Anne Street was a touch less flash, some of the houses only now being scaffolded for sandblasting and one or two still coated in their original steam-age soot and grime. None of the businesses here had Filipina (dressed as French) maids on show scrubbing doorsteps, they all used contract cleaners whose black crews worked at night. Spencer took out his key as he came to the tall newly-painted mansion with brass plate for Holt Newman Limited and blue plaque for Chopin Slept Here. Behind net-curtained windows the chandelier was lit in reception, so you could see in; Lowther bending over Claire's desk, Claire's head down. Spencer let himself into the hallway.

Lowther came out of reception with his mail and the ugly grin he couldn't help. 'Cold today!'

'Not really,' Spencer grumped.

'Definitely.' Lowther charged the stairs.

Spencer went in to see Claire. 'Hi.'

Claire sat with back hollowed and arms folded, large blue eyes aglare. '*Cold today,*' she said with a horrible simulacrum of Lowther's grin. She jerked her curly head at the mailtray. 'Yours is at the bottom.'

'Thanks.' Spencer tugged out the pink folder she'd marked with SPENCER and a doodle of his scowl. There were half a dozen letters. She gave him all the stuff addressed to no one in particular.

Claire hit the space bar and watched the typewriter's carriage shoot to the end and return. There wasn't any paper in.

'He says that,' said Spencer, 'depending if you come in wearing a bra. And "warm today" if not. He's a bit backward some ways.'

'Is that what it is. Don't you start.' She stuck her thumbs under her arms and yawned.

'Uh, I wasn't. Sorry. Are you not in a good mood?'

'I'm in a perfectly good mood.' She tucked her pleated white blouse in tight at the waist of her skirt and smiled sleepily.

Help. Claire was hard to take first thing, her body buxom but light, tiny-waisted, confidently sprung, and she had these unselfconscious couldn't-care-less movements. English rose by birth, reared in New Zealand though, hardly set foot indoors till she was convented. Her old man came into a farm in Rhodesia after that, so not only could she fix Land Rovers blindfold, she knew how to use an Armalite rifle. It made you think. Twice, even.

On the wall behind her she'd stuck her drawing of a tiger submerged to its nostrils in riverwater, sizing you up.

'You're very nearly late,' she said.

Spencer sat heavily on the leather chesterfield, letting his feet go up in the air and down again. 'Paul has this nine o'clock lecture with his vacation group on Fridays, he gives Katie and me a lift to our bus stops.'

Claire frowned.

'So we have to wait till he's ready,' Spencer said.

Claire put an elbow on the desktop and reclined sideways, playing with the pencils in the pencil pot. 'Oh. This your American friend?'

'Uh.'

They stared at each other for a spell. They did this sometimes.

'I'm being lazy,' said Claire. She sat up, interlocked her fingers and stretched.

Oh, Christ. Oh, well. Ask her.

The front door banged. Spencer jumped to his feet, almost to attention, because it had to be Su by the swish of the coat. He should have heard her park the whinnying Lotus outside. Claire laughed silently and shuffled paper. The phone buzzed. 'Hullo,' she said. 'Holt Newman.'

Blonde Su Holt strode in flapping her arms in the billowy designer overcoat she was favouring this week. She'd got olive leather trousers on and high grey boots. 'Morning,' she said, breathless. 'Only just on time, Spencer.'

'Well, I was here before you.'

She turned away the elegant face he would have liked a lot better if he wasn't scared to death of her.

Gaffe. Too loud. Too matey. Also, now I think of it, the car was outside when I arrived. Got to take these things in.

'I've been here since seven, Spencer,' she said, 'I've conducted three interviews and I just popped out to the chemist's if that's all right with you. That for me, Claire?'

Claire pressed Hold. 'Jock Napier, British Aerospace.'

Su pulled a face. 'I'll take it upstairs. No, I'll take it here.' She put out a gloved hand.

'You're through,' said Claire, and passed her the phone.

'Claire's been here too.' Su waved the receiver around a little, elbow on hip, to keep the man waiting. 'She's a real asset. Any other calls, Claire?'

Claire gave her a leaf from the notepad.

'Great.' Su nodded as she read it. 'Any sign of my Fionah?'

'I can just see her coming outside.'

Su raised her chin and, looking to the window, narrowed her eyes. 'Good.' She gave the receiver a last flourish, and her hair a toss to bare one ear. 'Hullo. Jock.'

Claire caught Spencer's eye a moment, then smiled down at the blank sheet she was feeding to the IBM.

'Clearly the kind of anthropology we're talking here,' Paul told the class, 'has more to do with brokerage systems, debt patterns, land tenure, wealth distribution and the whole power ratio between the neo-colonial countries and the rest, north and south if you will, than say with the marriage customs among the, I don't know, the Bonga-Bonga tribe. Oh shithouse, I'm sorry, Mr Bonga, that was crass.'

Tenka Bonga, the postdoctoral sitter-in and sensible-question asker, rollnecked and gold-rimmed, clipboard on knee in the front row, shrugged. 'It's a common name.'

'No, that was terrible, stupid, left my brain at home,' said Paul, certain that in nights to come the memory would wake him sweating.

Katie, soulsick, paused and closed her eyes before pushing at the door. Open them again: the central reservations office of the Leading Hotels Syndicate, the facing banks of phones, one lot of girls in yucky blouses talking boyfriends, one lot talking who should fetch the sandwiches at lunch. 'Me, I'll do it,' Katie said, passing. It got you out of the place. She swung her bag on to the desk and took a pad. 'Here, everybody write down.' The supervisor came in and clapped hands. Katie sat, put her headset on and straightened her booking forms. Under the windows the traffic to Holborn Circus was jamming. Michelle in translucent coral mock silk sat opposite and frowned at Katie's loose black sweater.

'That's a nice necklace,' said Katie. Her phone lit up and sounded. Hope it's French, let's talk some French.

Gareth reached the unmarked entrance on Gower Street and consulted his wallet. Swimming-pool card, library card, old NUS card he'd never thrown away, army pass, office pass. He showed the security man. 'There you are.'

'Thank you, sir.'

He never swam any more, because he could neither take the gun into the water nor leave it behind in the changing room.

His immediate boss Cath was waiting for the lift. 'Did you catch the news?' she said.

'I heard it was unconfirmed.'

'It's unconfirmed but the other side's saying it's all over.'

Eight thousand miles away the marines take up positions in the governor's house. Faces blacked, they crouch at part-opened windows. One of the radio sets has been picking up obscurely worded but still unenciphered traffic from the encroaching fleet all night and the last word from the coastwatchers was outboards gunning in the kelp. The marines set their sights on all points of approach. They wait for dawn, which is when the kind of thing that is about to happen mostly happens.

Miles clambered into the Aquascutum pinstripe he'd found under the laundry bags and news magazines at the foot of the bed. The other suit he'd found there he hung on the castored shop rail in the corner, using one of the wire hangers that tangled thick as seawrack across the floor. He looked in the mirror on his folding table and smeared the last specks of shaving foam into his skin. Damn neat shave there. He kicked ahead of him to the landing his airline zipper bag with diary, papers, tape recorder, sweets and other needfuls in, slinging it as he went downstairs. Passing the bathroom doorway he noticed his watch on the floor in there and recovered it. In the kitchen he made another cup of instant, no clean cups I'll rinse this one, drank half and lit a cigarette to see him out of the house.

His wet hair chilled as he walked through to Camden Road past the false-limb clinic. Bus or tube. Both equally lamentable when it comes down to it and honestly life's too short so when, turning, he saw a cab with its light on he yelled and flagged it. Jeez. Going to be *early*. 'Fleet Street, please.'

'No smoking,' said the driver.

'New one on me,' said Miles, but dropped and trod the cig.

On the first-floor landing, Spencer listened. Below, Su's PA Fiona came down the hallway from reception with her teetering bantam gait. He waited. She passed the stairs and kept ahead to Lillian's kitchen at the back, surely to score the first mint tea without which she could not, she always said, get going.

'Lillian, will you be an angel and save my life?'

There. Lillian asked her how was Southern Region then and Fifi puffed and blew and said how was it ever!

Spencer softfooted it spyfilm spyfilm on through Fiona's empty office, her typewriter still covered and a stack of mail left cautioning on top, and into Su's drawing room where full-length windows giving on to little balconies made the daylight seem more gracious and benign than it ever did in the mere pit of the street or in his own dim third-floor eyrie. Sadly, mind, the fragrant modern squashy leather suite was about to be got shot of for a set of mock-antiques.

He stopped just on the threshold. He could still hear Su in reception giving BAe a hard time.

I'm practically over her head here if a board squeaks. *Aber* Herr Cobalt you hef to confrond your deebest fierce.

The desk was right by the door, though, and Su's *Economist* diary, a scarlet padded time-atlas, gilt-edged, lay at the near corner, so he only had to reach. There was a copy in Fi's desk, but that would be locked, and another in reception, but that wouldn't be convenient right now. The duplicates had to be continually updated and cross-checked by Claire and the PA to avoid double-booking Su's timeslots: a sucker-trap, like that carriage clock on the mantelpiece under the Mondrian print. It had to be wound up every five days.

He opened the diary at the ribbon bookmark and scanned Su's hectic brokenstroked handwriting. There. See? Out to lunch. Worth knowing, that, if.

He slunk out and breathed normally. Through a doorway on the second floor he could hear Steve Cusson. 'Right ... because you're talking more like this area for that ... plus the tenant situation gives me some cause for ... No, I'm not disinterested.'

'*Un*,' grunted Spencer, on the next flight up. Steve's sideline. Evicting widows and orphans. Claire typed some of his property correspondence for him on the quiet and thought he was good-looking.

Spencer took the last few steps to the third landing at a spring. Hui. In the side office, spare when the accountant wasn't in, the coffee machine bubbled on a low filing cabinet. Good. He put a hand to his own door and leaned. It gave way much too quick. He lurched off-balance into Susie Stubbs who was coming out. 'Hi, Susie.' He grabbed at the doorframe.

'God, Spencer.' In a dove grey suit today and tall, Stubbs was on the cuddly swing of her diet cycle. Next she'd fast back down to svelte ranginess again. (Don't you know anyone who's not attractive, Spence? Not really. All hang together, don't we.)

'Nice suit,' he said, shouldering back the door, which Stubbs had let go in surprise, so that the piston gadget was trying to clap it shut on the pair of them. He hooked the nearby brown rubber wedge with one foot and kicked it into place. Now that really does look like chocolate. A choc chock.

'Have you been drinking?' Stubbs said.

'Course not. Stopped smoking though. Bit dizzy.'

'Oh, God, disaster. *Would* you like some coffee? I was *about* to get some.'

'Wouldn't mind.'

'I think you'd better.' She bustled out.

He called after her, 'I can fetch the mugs if you like.'

'Don't think you should handle breakables,' she called back. Two flights down and fainter she was going, 'Oh, hullo, Su, sorry, you come up. After you. I'm just sorting coffee out for Spencer who is *not* himself this morning.'

Cheers Suze. He threw the post on to his desk. Stubbs had left the newspapers there. She'd been making calls already, her desk was thick with contact forms. The third desk, clear but for the phones, best table lamp, new blotter, and glass ashtray holding only paperclips, was Patrick Goldie's.

Lowther came through the connecting door from the back office, pulled up short and stood flexing his fingers. 'Patrick. No?'

Spencer looked at the empty chair, then at the red bentwood coatstand. He shook his head.

'Ask him if he got hold of that Laing and Cruikshank bloke.'

'Sure.'

Lowther plunged back and slammed the door after him. A notepad leaf blew off the mantelpiece and a ballpoint jumped from the edge of Stubbs's desk. The artistically stacked magnetic rods of Spencer's executive toy collapsed.

Spencer went over to the window, raised the bottom sash a little and felt new air probe coolly up his cuffs. On the corner below, Jenny Prince and Les Forbert ran into each other and moved on towards the office, Les pointing out the sights with his telescoped umbrella, the cat poised on a railing, the mysterious cloud of steam from a basement area, Spencer at the high window.

Spencer adjusted his tie for them, hung his coat and sat to unlock his desk. He found the letter opener and did the post. Two more redundant ICI men wishing to hear of suitable positions (head between knees I should think), both of them young and high-ranked, it's a massacre up there, plus one redundant comprehensive head wishing similar but twenty years outside our age range at fifty-five, look up one of Gareth's diplomatic answers and copy it, plus two Pytcherley candidates bunging in their CVs, good. The CVs sent from placement agencies could wait.

Stubbs came and put a mug of black coffee on the contact forms he'd just got out. 'There. Hot fingers, ow.'

'Thank you very much, Susie.' To make room he shifted his phones, the grey keypunch direct line, the older ivory extension. He added some of yesterday's glass of water to the mug and sipped.

'That's all right! Now where was I?' Stubbs ran a finger down her master sheet. 'Niall Gregory.'

Spencer opened his bottom filing drawer again to look for some Pytcherley notes that might be in with British Aerospace. Two men both called Wright. Tended to get confused. 'What am I going to do with my life, Susie?'

'God, I don't know, Spencer. Make lots of calls. Bury the problem. Whatever it is.'

'No good at all.' Wait, Wright was a potential for shortlisting so he'd be in Pytcherley Probables, which was —

Ah.

At home. Doesn't matter for one day. As long as Su Holt doesn't want to go over it.

'Well, I don't know,' said Stubbs. 'Ask Claire out to lunch.'

Spencer sat up. 'What made you say that?'

'Uhuh? Thought of it, had you?'

'Uh ... '

'Go on, she'd like that, sincerely.'

'How can you tell? I didn't know you were that thick.'

'Thick but not entirely stupid. You just see.'

'You plural and, like, thick as thieves.'

'Oh. We-ell. Intuition.'

Never believe anyone when they say that. 'Hm.' He took an enormous gulp of hot coffee, swallowed, snatched up the receiver and dialled 21.

'Claire,' said Claire.

'Spencer.'

'Hullo, you.'

'Er, hi, listen. D'you want to come out to lunch?'

'All right.' She gave a breath of laughter. She was almost certainly tugging a brown curl down over one eye.

'Fine.'

'Where you taking me?'

'Ah, pfff,' forgot that bit, 'where you like.'

'No, you have to decide.'

''Kay, I'll surprise you.'

'Good. Thank you, Spence.'

'Right.'

'See you later,' she said, intonation turning almost creamy.

Spencer put the phone down carefully and shuddered. 'This is eerie.'

'It's your day, that's all,' Stubbs said. 'Go with it. Hullo, is that Northern Engineering? Didn't catch. You are? Great. Then can I speak to, God.' She guffawed. 'No, not Him, I've just lost my piece of paper. Oh, here. Niall Gregory, please. Thanks.'

They stiffened. Su Holt walked in, leather trousers creaking inside the high boots. Spencer, hand still on the phone, left it there, looking busy. Su said, 'Spencer, I do take it you've not been drinking, have you? You don't seem quite as usual.'

Spencer looked at Stubbs who said, 'Oh, hullo, I wanted Niall Gregory, is he there?' She covered her mouthpiece. 'I think he's just giving-up-smoking squiffy, Su, not liquid squiffy. Really.'

Spencer thought his best bet was to act dumb and to not protest too much. One, Su had no head for booze herself and feared it. Two, she had bad memories of the Kenny Thurrock débâcle. Three, she owned the place, so once she got the wrong idea you were stuck with it.

'Oh,' she said, narrow-eyed. 'You've stopped smoking.'

'Uh, yeah.'

Su leaned against the wall by Goldie's desk. 'I approve, but don't let it get on top of you. We had our fill of DTs with old Kenny last year.'

'Yeah.'

'I mean perhaps this is not the best time to give up. You'll have lots of time at your age. I stopped when I got married, easy as breathing.'

'That's nice,' said Spencer. 'People often do that, yeah.'

'So I shouldn't worry about it,' said Su. *Soudain son visage éclaira,* her face lit up, unless Spencer was completely lost you could do that one quite literally. Flaubert would use *épanouir,* but that was his thing. 'Patrick!' she said. 'Morning!'

'Hiya, Rick,' said Spencer, louder than he meant to.

'Hi.' Goldie, slight and sandy with honest smile, walked in swinging his carrier bag. 'Sorry I'm late.'

'Oh, don't be,' said Su, glancing at her watch.

'Cora being sick again.'

'Oh, no.' Su was quite genuine about this. Her near maternal fondness for Goldie Spencer found endearing.

'I don't think it's anything,' Goldie said, 'she's just turning out to be one of those babies.'

'Fran all right?'

'Getting rather tired. Scuse.' He edged past Su to his desk and unlocked. No one else of course could mutter 'Scuse' at Mrs Holt like that.

'I think we'll be staying in town over this weekend,' said Su, 'you must come to tea.'

'Fine.'

Fiona, her tininess badged by the huge floppy bow of her blouse, stood on tiptoe on the threshold and mimed knocking.

'Fionah,' said Su.

'A Mister Richard Prendergast of Anglo–Cal, just arrived,' said Fiona.

'He's late. Bring him up, then, and let's deal with him. Come on.' Su chivvied Fiona out.

Goldie put hands on hips, threw his head back and gave his long gargling first-thing sigh. 'Right.'

Stubbs, listening on the phone, frowned at him and went on, 'That's good, Niall, and what sort of region are you in, paywise, roughly? Uhuh, great. You see this job's only another five grand and it's in the south. But, er, Mrs Holt's told them they may have to go higher.'

'Right,' Goldie said again. 'What are we doing, then, Spence?' He hung his coat.

'Pytcherley,' said Spencer.

'Hell,' said Goldie wearily. 'We must have tried nearly every marketing man in the country.'

'I've got about ten new ones here, left-message-to-call, that haven't come back yet, can try again on all those.'

'All right, give me half of those.'

Spencer passed him the forms. 'And I pulled this Divitt from file, we placed him at GF last year, might know someone.'

'As a source, right, good idea.' Goldie took the forms back to his desk, tripping on the lead of Stubbs's telephone. 'Whoop. And how's Aerospace going?'

Spencer pointed at Stubbs. 'Hard at it.'

Stubbs said, 'Oh. So she's interviewed you before? Heavens. We've got a summary on you and everything, then? My file-pulling *has* let me down, I'm terribly sorry.'

Goldie winced. 'The sooner we get these files on a micro ... '

'Do you have a new CV since that time? Good, love to have that, and I'll send you the spec.'

Goldie stared at his grey phone and covered his face with his hands. 'Urrrgh. Hate getting started.'

'Yeah,' said Spencer, slouching in his chair.

'So,' said Goldie. He reached to light his table lamp. 'How's the hangover, Susie?'

Stubbs put down her phone. 'Not a trace of a one, why?'

'Thought you were out somewhere.'

'We were. The new place I told you and you said sounded nice. It was.'

'You spend a lot of time doing those sort of things.' Goldie meant that he couldn't and wouldn't pay for a nanny, whereas stockbroking Geoff Stubbs could and did.

'Oh?' said Stubbs. 'Now this man I just spoke to cold turns out to be an old contact. *Mildly* embarrassing.'

'Yes. Any good?'

'Think so. I better dig up his thingy and see what Su said about him. He was shortlisted.' Stubbs turned to the teak-veneer filing cabinets behind her desk. Spencer remembered carrying them up here after the late tenants vacated this floor. A marriage bureau. It wouldn't do. 'He was one of Gareth's discoveries,' said Stubbs, peering at drawer labels.

'Engineering A to H is bottom left,' said Spencer. 'Gareth's people were sometimes pretty good. If he'd made more than one or two calls a day he might have got on.'

'Yes,' said Goldie. 'Quite. You just have to make those calls.'

'No other way.'

'Draw the widest net.'

'Right man's out there somewhere.'

'Has to be. Somewhere.'

'You Mahomet. Him mountain.'

'That's it.'

'Just keep punching the numbers.'

'Yes.' Goldie sighed.

Stubbs, kneeling at the open drawer, said, 'If it's going to be one of *those* mornings I think I'll go down and work in Claire's new office in the basement.'

'It is Friday,' said Goldie. 'And there's no furniture in there yet.'

'I only need a phone, I can work on the floor.'

'Stop, you're making me tired.'

'Help me, Gregory isn't here.'

'Try under Niall,' said Spencer, 'it's a reversible name, someone might have put it back wrong. Next row top.'

'OK.' She looked.

'Well, I spent last night doing the baking,' said Goldie.

'Bread?' said Spencer.

'That and a carrot cake.'

'I've had your carrot cake, haven't I? Good.'

'Fran likes it. I always secretly preferred imported deep-frozen chocolate fudge cake really. Not very alternative of me.'

Spencer's salivary glands tingled. 'Don't knock it.'

'Not under Niall,' said Stubbs.

'Here we go,' said Goldie.

'If he was shortlisted try the job file,' said Spencer. 'What search?'

'Whatsits,' said Stubbs. 'Rolls-Royce. Job files?'

'End cabinet on the right.'

'You love ordering me about, don't you?'

'Um ... beats work, that's all.'

'I find it an enormous turn-on myself, to be blisteringly honest,' she said. She flipped through the files. 'Alternative baking. You university people are off a different planet.'

'I thought your Geoff was Cambridge,' said Spencer.

'Oh, but only for the sport and the May Balls. You know.'

'Yeah, I met a few like that.'

'Even at Sidney Sussex? Did you? Oh. Well, Niall Gregory isn't under Rolls-Royce either.' She banged the drawer shut. 'Not so vital, I got his address.'

'No, we have to find him,' said Goldie.

'Do we?'

'Yes,' said Spencer.

'Yes,' said Goldie. 'Not for the search, that doesn't matter.'

'No?' said Stubbs.

'No,' said Goldie, 'it's Su. She's going to want to see what you've got. It's no use saying we've lost the papers, she gets so irate when that happens and it always does seem to happen, that's the trouble. It really ... upsets her.'

'Well, what do I do?'

'I'm just thinking.'

'Mike could be sitting on him,' Spencer said. 'Les. Steve. John in the basement. David.'

'Nnnng,' said Goldie. 'Yeah. OK, Susie, go through the master job file and see which of the consultants worked on any relevant searches since that last one and then make them turn out their drawers. And if that doesn't work ...'

'What?' said Stubbs.

'Well, we'll come to that.' Goldie sat back.

'Right.' Stubbs eenymeenied before the cabinets, twisting on her toes, and went for the right one just as Spencer opened his mouth.

They heard the characteristic crack of Lowther putting down the phone next door. 'That reminds me,' Spencer said.

Lowther pushed open the door. 'Patrick. Patrick. Petersson of Laing and Cruikshank.'

Goldie, absorbed in chewing off a loose shred from his bottom lip, started. 'Wah. Oh, sure. I have to call him back, no joy first time.'

'Yeah, keep it up. Let me know. Two Ss.' Lowther pulled the door to. Goldie, Stubbs and Spencer flinched. The rubber plant shimmied.

'Hell.' Goldie loosened his tie. 'I'd completely forgotten she assigned me to him on that one. I don't like these financial things, it's absolute Greek to me. Spec somewhere.' He took some stapled pages from his desk and sniffed. 'It's surprising how few people are interested in a tax-free posting to a sunny island.'

'Kids at school, furniture storage, old mum in a home,' said Spencer.

'Yes.' Goldie ran a hand over his desktop. 'What have I done? He gave me that man's number yesterday, I've lost it.'

'That bit of paper that just blew across the floor,' said Spencer. 'You left it on the mantelpiece.'

'Where, oh.' Goldie fetched it. 'That's the one. Seriously down to it now, everybody.'

'*I'm* busy,' said Stubbs.

'Excellent.' Goldie hung his jacket on his chairback, sat and jockeyed his chair forward. 'Let's go, Spence. Five four three two one.' He and Spencer lifted handsets together and punched numbers.

Without a cigarette it was vertigo.

The big officer and his sixteen commandos scramble down the rocky hill behind the governor's house. Under the blackup their faces are red from the hike. By now the main party should have surprised the defending marine platoon in their barrack-room beds a couple of miles away and disarmed them, so this officer just has to call on the governor and accept the surrender. In the half-light he can see people moving about behind the windows. He sends six men off to either side of the grounds as cover and keeps four with him. Edging past dustbins and drainpipes, he finds a door and motions an NCO to kick it open. Guns off safety, the commandos burst in.

Small kitchen. Small lounge with stretch-covered furniture. Stairs. Small empty bedrooms. We've got the servants' quarters.

Outside again, the big officer rounds the corner of the annexe and spots the back door of the main house. Someone in intelligence was meant to have passed him the architect's plan but they decided it was too secret, or else they lost it. OK. He strides across the yard towards the door. There are some geese in a wire run. They honk.

He's on his back, hit in the thigh. His lieutenant drops too. A medic dashes from the annexe, but the defenders hurl a grenade at him and bring him down with splinters in the legs. The lieutenant picks himself up, hugging cracked ribs where the Swiss Army knife in his top pocket stopped the rifle slug, and takes cover.

The shooting breaks off. The big officer tries to stand, can't, pulls the pin on a grenade and waves the grenade where he lies, yelling at the marines in the house. They're yelling back. He's saying give me and my medic first aid and you can tie the grenade handle down. They're saying throw the grenade away and we'll give you first aid. He doesn't understand what they're saying. They don't understand what he's saying. They leave him there, rifles sighted on him. None of his own men draws a white handkerchief to help him after what just happened to the medic; they're staying put and the marines have got them all marked down, so it depends how soon the armour comes ashore. He's bleeding from an artery, in hot slops.

There wasn't supposed to be any shooting.

'General Foods, good morning,' sang the switchboard girl.

'Hi there. Charles Divitt, please. Marketing.'

'Who's calling?'

'Spencer Cobbold.'

'What?' She laughed. 'What firm are you calling from?'

'Holt Newman.'

She paused. 'No, come off it, Rob.'

'Who's Rob?' Spencer sat forward.

'You're always doing this to me.'

'Hang on, who am I meant to be?'

'I know you.' She laughed. 'Wait a second.' She went off the line.

Spencer turned his empty ashtray round and round.

'What's happening?' asked Stubbs. He shook his head.

The girl came back on. 'Now I know it's you, Rob, because you're not picking up your extension. Whose private line are you on?'

'Mine. I don't know who Rob is but I am definitely Spencer Cobbold.'

'Spell it then.'

'Look, I just want to talk to Charles Divitt. We're the head-hunters who got him for you and I want a tip on a search I'm doing now.'

'Headhunters?'

'Oh, come on. Executive search consultants.'

'I thought it meant something to do with cannibals.'

'Well, you're out of date, and you've got your tribal customs mixed up anyway.'

'So what's an executive search consultant, then?'

'That's confidential,' he thought he might as well say.

'You're the limit, Rob, you've totally lost me.'

'I'm not Rob.'

'And we don't have a John Trevithick or whatever you said. These names you come up with.'

'Charles Divitt. Been there since last year.'

'Oh. Aha. I'm going to give your line just one more go, Rob.' She was gone some time.

'Thanks for dropping me in it with Su back there, by the way,' he said to Stubbs. '"Not himself this morning".'

Stubbs swallowed a laugh. 'She'll forget it, don't you worry.'

'Right,' Goldie murmured to the phone, 'and what age are you?'

Spencer said, 'You've planted the seed now, Suze. Hullo.'

The girl was back. 'I'm most extremely sorry, sir.'

'OK. Found Rob, did you?'

'Your name was?'

'Spencer Cobbold. From Holt Newman in London.'

The girl in Banbury said, 'You must get a lot of mickey-taking with a name like that.'

'No, it's never happened before.'

She cleared her throat. 'I'm really sorry. But I have this friend, and your voice — '

'What's your name?'

'Marilyn.'

'I don't believe that either.'

'Ringing for you.'

'Thanks.'

The amphitracs, green armoured bugs the size of lorries, swim through calm dawn seas to the shoreline. One of them, carrying the rear-admiral in charge of the invasion, proceeds backwards. Its aft thrusters jammed as it peeled away from the mother ship, so that in forward gear it only steers in circles. The bow thrusters are working and the driver's flipped the periscope back to see the way but his job still isn't all that easy. Stern first, the thing handles like a brick.

Commandos flash a lantern from the beach. The drivers throttle down and cruise in one by one. Close to schedule the first craft's tracks touch bottom. The troops inside crouch, ready to drop the flaps from their weapon slits. Land drive engaged, the machine roars and crawls dripping up the white beach.

As Spencer rang off Stubbs said, 'Note how Spencer's Rutland accent *vanishes* on the phone.' He looked at her inanimately, slooshed the tepid remainder of coffee around in his mug, a yingyang whorl, and swallowed it. Did she think he ought to talk more Rutland on the phone, or less Rutland the whole time?

Goldie listened at Lowther's door, opened it a crack, peeped, went on in.

'D'you get him?' Lowther said. 'My main man.'

'Just one second,' shouted Stubbs. She bustled high-nosed to the door. 'Mike, I need to go through your drawers.'

'Bit personal, Susie,' Lowther cried. 'What for?'

'Susie,' gravelled Spencer, and pointed to Goldie's grey phone lying off the hook. She covered her mouth and went through. Spencer sat back, hands behind his head.

Goldie hurried in, took up his phone. 'Hullo. That's fine, Jon, Tuesday morning eight. And it's Mike Lowther you'll be seeing. Bring that with you, I should, save on posting. Right.' He laughed. 'Yes, it's quite busy. Bye now.' He made a note on the man's form. 'You're very relaxed, Spence.'

'Guy's about to ring me back. I hope.'

'I haven't seen you light a cigarette this morning.'

Spencer closed his eyes. 'Don't talk about it.'

'Oh, sorry. I better do some of your Pytcherley people now, I suppose.'

'They're not mine.' Spencer picked up the extension and dialled.

'I'm Jenny. Who's that?' said Jenny, next floor down.

'Princess. Morning.'

'Spencer! How are you?'

'OK. Can you do some letters? Yesterday was chaos so they've all piled up.'

'Oh. Not tried Claire?'

'She's Steve and David only now, no chance.'

'She doesn't start that till Monday.'

'No, but you know what she's like. And I mean you do do ours now, don't you?'

'Well, this is the whole bone of contention which I'm rather hoping Su will get around to sorting out because.— '

'You did those ones the other day.'

'Ah, that was just a favour,' Jenny said, smile audible. 'Strictly I do Les and Mike. Mind, strictly I was David only, back before he went part-time. It didn't stop people asking.'

'No, OK, leave it then, I'll let you know.' Spencer hung up. 'This who-types-for-who is getting ... '

'Isn't it,' said Goldie, putting down his own phone. 'Well, new girl next week.' He sniffed.

'She's for Holly and Robin. Who do you get to do yours?'

'Oh, depends.' Goldie smirked, which must mean Claire. They were mates. He held a sheet up. 'This chap's left the firm, replacement's only been there for a month, no good.'

'Which?'

'Tyler.' Goldie crushed the sheet, took aim one-eyed and tip-tongue, missed the bin. 'Damn.'

'You got no Zen, Rick.'

Goldie keyed another number. 'Hullo. Mark Kenworthy, please.' His extension buzzed and he took it while he waited on hold. 'Eeyep,' he said, and started laughing. 'What's the — ? You can't! Don't!'

Stubbs came back in and closed the door. She looked at Goldie. 'Oh, David's in, then. Mike hasn't got it,' she told Spencer. 'His drawers are practically empty. Says "I don't deal in paper".'

Goldie stopped laughing. 'Hullo, Mark?' He clapped the ivory handset to its cradle and addressed the grey. 'Ah, how d'you do. It's Patrick Goldie here, Holt Newman. I don't know if you've heard of us. That's good.' He was patting his desktop. 'I'm calling you in connection with — an assignment which we're running' — he beckoned frantically to Spencer, who brought the job spec over — 'to fill a major marketing position in the brewing industry.' Goldie went into the spiel and sat back.

Stubbs's extension buzzed. She took it. 'Because he's talking to someone,' she said, and hung up.

Spencer's direct line rang. 'Cobbold,' he answered executively.

The voice was sharp and pushy. Not that nice. 'This is Morris Lustig. My secretary tells me Charlie Divitt put you in touch, what's it about?'

Spencer began the spiel he knew by heart. His extension buzzed. David Cracknell. He lifted and let drop the handset, silenced it. Goldie's went again. Goldie killed his too and simply left it off the hook. Spencer's buzzed again immediately. Spencer did the same as Goldie this time, still spieling. Stubbs looked at hers. It started up. She took it.

'Is this Tony Pytcherley's lot we're talking about?' asked Lustig.

'We're not to say so, so I haven't said,' said Spencer.

'That's what I was afraid of. Paying what again?'

'Up to thirty.'

'It would have to be. At least. That's tricky.'

'Honestly,' said Stubbs, and hung up.

'If it's any help,' said Spencer, 'the man we're looking for — or woman — should be capable of moving up one fairly quick. That's why we're pitching it to people that bit too good for the job, you read me.'

'I begin to read you, yeah. That could make the difference,' Lustig said.

'OK,' said Spencer. 'That's for your ears only. If I can just ask you some questions.'

Stubbs dialled another extension; with a pen, to save her nails. 'Claire? *Could* you pop next door and tell him "Stop it"? He'll know what. *Thank* you.'

Spencer took down the history and the address and rang off.

'You mustn't tell them that, you know,' said Goldie.

'I know, but.' Spencer signed a comp slip to send Lustig with the spec.

Goldie strained air through his teeth.

'It makes it,' Spencer said, 'a fuck sight easier.'

'Spencer, contain yourself,' said Stubbs.

'Sorry, Suze. It's this not smoking.' Spencer cradled his extension. It stayed quiet.

'Ah, yes, mm,' said Goldie, remembering something. He slapped his desk. 'These direct lines, you know, Susie, there's no hold on them, you really can't go shouting things across the office when it's off the hook.'

'Well, I hate to tell you, Patrick,' Stubbs said, 'but you did walk in this morning and make *that* noise yet again *while* I was talking to a candidate, as I have often asked you *not* to do.'

Goldie suppressed a smile and coughed. 'Be that as it may —'

'Be that as it may, your direct lines do have a mute or swearing button, with an asterisk, which I *urge* you to consider use of.'

'Great Scott. Do they?' Goldie looked. 'This new technology. I thought that was the memory bank or something.'

'I thought chicken soup,' said Spencer; mostly, though, for form.

'And what's the sharp sign for, in that case, then? A sort of Dolby for a bad line, is it?'

'Redial last number,' said Stubbs, 'don't ask me why.'

'Sharp's American for number,' Spencer said. 'They wear Chanel Sharp 5, and don't ask me why either. The thing is, Suze, the swearing button only works as long as it's held down. You have to keep your finger on.'

'Oh,' she said. 'Well, I'm sorry but you can't expect me to be utterly au fait with all your high-tech new phones' whatsits when *I* haven't even got one, making do *as* I do with my dial-nine-to-get-a-line extension here — '

'You will have one, I'll get you one,' said Goldie.

'Well, I'd feel jolly important if you would,' said Stubbs.

'You're indispensable, Suze,' soothed Spencer.

Goldie looked down smiling. 'I always do my best for all my staff.' He laughed. They laughed.

They stiffened. Mrs Holt walked in.

'Sorry, Su,' said Stubbs, 'he just addressed us as his staff.'

'That's what you are,' Su Holt said.

'It was more the way he said it,' Spencer tried.

Su turned. 'I hope you can come up with something on the Pytcherley search today.'

'Sure. Heard of Morris Lustig at Argyll?'

She folded arms. 'I have. Why don't you try and reach him, then, because he's hot.'

'Just sending him the spec. He could be interested. I tried cold before and he wouldn't return calls, but I had an intro this time.' He sat back and risked a level gaze at her.

'You should have got him in for interview,' she said.

Ah. Should have really. 'He was cagey. Didn't want to push in case it put him off.'

'I hope you didn't tell him anything.'

'He had heard rumours.'

'All right … Well done. Perhaps this afternoon — we'll see.' Su turned away, leaving him to figure.

She wants another progress meeting. With all possibles and, natch, Probables on show. Home and back in how long. Can be done. She's out to lunch, won't know.

'Thank you for that Richard Prendergast, Sue,' said Su, 'I'll hang on to his papers.'

'Oh, was he good? I am glad, Su,' said Stubbs.

'Not for Aerospace, no. Both realised that, the first five minutes. Not hands-on enough for them. I was thinking of him for us.' She looked at Goldie.

'As the new consultant, oh,' said Goldie. 'Right.'

'Very bright, articulate, double first, bit full of himself but he'd be an interesting addition to the mixture. Anyway he's going to give it some think. A definite possible. So what else is happening with Aerospace?' Su walked round behind Stubbs's desk and took up the forms. 'These them?'

'Yah,' said Stubbs. 'One or two sound OK.'

'Forget him.' Su tossed a leaf aside.

'Right.' Stubbs cast a smile at Spencer, unreturned.

Spencer and Goldie waited for the scene.

'And him I've met before,' said Su.

'Wh — ?'

'Niall Gregory. He's good.' Su's voice was rising. 'You've got papers on him already.' She tapped the cabinets behind her.

'Ah. I did look in the obvious files, can't dig him out as yet,' said Stubbs.

Spencer glanced at Goldie who glanced back.

Su, taking breath, let her hands drop and lifted one foot. If she started to stamp and shout the day was lost and the effects could last through next week.

Goldie got in fast with: 'Susie's just tracking it back to which consultants might have borrowed it, which seems to be our problem here.'

Su, the cue spoilt, gave up and relaxed. 'I don't care where or how it's found, I want it found. And I want you, Patrick, to come with Mike and me to the computer exhibition, that's on Tuesday, which is what I also came to say. You'll be the main user of whatever system, this department, so if you'd put that in your diary.'

'Ooookeydoke.' Goldie hefted from his drawer a big red book identical to Su's except for having his initials on the cover. 'Be interesting,' he murmured.

Spencer put 'Rick off' under Tuesday in his skinny Collins.

Su went to the door. 'We have to come to a decision soon. Once we're on computer we can stop these bloody paperchases. I'm fed up with them. I'm going down before old Fionah makes a mess of something.' She pulled the door to slam it after her, found it wedged and left it.

'That wasn't as bad as I thought it might be,' said Goldie, after waiting some time sitting very still.

'Yeah, well done, Rick,' said Spencer.

'I think we came within a hairsbreadth of a wobbly there,' said Stubbs.

'Yes, you shouldn't really have said anything,' said Goldie. 'I've told you, only show her the solutions and keep quiet about the problems. She doesn't want to know.'

'Oh, well, I'm not going to lose my stuffing over it, it all bounces off of me.'

'Does it?' Spencer said.

'Sure.' Stubbs leaned forward. 'And I think she actually hesitates to take it out on me because perhaps I'm a bit more upper, which is just the thing she hasn't got.'

'Hmm.'

'And of course she knows how I'd react.'

'Get off,' said Spencer.

'No, really.'

'If she thinks you're on for a fight you're likelier to get one, I'd have thought. Winds her up, the same as most of us.'

'Ah, but unlike you I just don't care,' said Stubbs.

'No, well, you're a woman so you'd get another job more easily.'

'Anyway,' said Goldie, 'we've still got to find the thing.' He coughed. 'OK. Did you come up with something, Susie?'

'I'm going to try Les,' said Stubbs, 'and John in the basement. I'll take your mug, Spence, may I?'

'Sure.'

She went downstairs singing, to 'Strangers in the Night', 'La la lalla la, la lalla la la ... '

Goldie yawned, making Spencer yawn in sympathy.

'I thought that went Dooby dooby doo,' said Spencer.

'So did I.'

'There's a car drives up and down the Camden Road some evenings has a horn that goes like that.'

'Is there?' Goldie said. 'I've heard a Colonel Bogey horn. Not that though.'

'D'you know what film it's from?'

'*Bridge on the River Kwai.*'

'Naaao. "Strangers in the Night".'

'Is it from a film?'

'Certain. Driving me doolally. Your extension's still off.'

'Oh. Thanks.' Goldie cradled it.

They angled back their chairs and yawned again.

Rory in the café put an elbow on the counter and the Magnum hanging heavy in his zipper jacket's hidden inner pocket bumped the edge. He looked around. The eaters at the plastic-wood-topped tables didn't look back but they weren't avoiding looking either. That seemed OK. The waitress showed up from the back-room there. Rory, cute enough and tall and, in the right mood, roguish, wasn't in the right mood so he simply raised his finger at her. Trigger finger. Thinking what to have, he fancied good strong spoonstand tea and holy God he smelt a kipper. There was a feller sitting there across the aisle reading the small ads and he had it on his plate. All oaky varnish colour, smoky-smelling. Rory just did not remember when the last occasion was he had a kipper. He pointed. 'Cup of tea and one of them thanks.' The waitress, turning to the tea urn, yelled the price. He paid and took the cup and saucer to a seat and read the *A-Z* and soon she brought the fish, all oaky, salty, smoky on the plate. Rory ogling a herring.

★

'The junior ticks are slacking again.' David Cracknell, shirtsleeved, filled the doorway, the one man in the building bigger than Spencer. Twenty years ago he must have been a prefect at his grammar school; Spencer had a vague idea he'd even mentioned it.

'Oh, hi, David,' said Goldie.

'You're doing absolutely nothing! It's incredible! Appalling!' Cracknell moved into the room on strangely dainty black-brogued feet. The stout waistcoat and trousers were twilled black on electric blue. The windowlight reflected off his large celebrity spectacles and presidential teeth.

'We've been working very hard,' said Goldie.

Cracknell feinted a cuff at him. 'Why did you cut me off? There I was telling you my plans for when my office is redecorated and you hang up on me.'

'It was an obscene phone call,' Goldie said. 'The murals in particular. I certainly don't think you should mention them to Claire.'

'What do you mean? She was very flattered. I've got her doing the sketches.'

'I don't believe you.'

'Shows how much you know about women, then, mate, doesn't it?'

'Besides that, I was on the other line.'

'Well then, why answer in the first place? I'll tell you why. You're scared it might be Su and she'll think you're not at your desk. That's what it is. Hey?'

This was true so Goldie said, 'No, it's not.'

Cracknell turned. 'What's old Spencer up to? I don't believe it. Another one. A totally inactive hunk of matter.'

'Hunk's all right,' said Spencer.

'Oh, bleeeagh. Look at you.'

Spencer asked Goldie, 'Have you noticed how Su's started calling everybody "old"? I'm sure she gets it from him.'

'I had, yes.'

'All right, now, what's this bureaucratic nightmare?' Cracknell grabbed up Spencer's contact forms. 'Old Pytcherley's job, poor bugger?'

'There you go,' said Spencer.

'Pay attention. I want results on this one, matey. Now. Today.'

'I got you one. An Argyll man, Lustig. Su describes as hot.'

'Well, that's one, now I want lots more. I'm taking very heavy stick from Su for this catastrophe and so I'm simply going to have to bully my researchers till they start to make some sort of effort. Did you reach that Philipson last night? I know you didn't, don't even bother telling me.'

'Yes,' said Spencer.

'And?'

'He's coming in at three instead.'

'That's something. You remembered. Not too preoccupied with getting Katie's knickers off, then.' Cracknell had met Katie at the Rochester Square housewarming and had been incorporating her in his fantasy narrative ever since.

'He was a bit annoyed,' said Spencer, 'so I said your secretary had double-booked you and you would have called yourself but you were entertaining clients.'

'Close. It was a backer for this film I'm trying to produce.'

'Well, you didn't tell me, so I improvised. Sounded better anyway. And what came up that you can't make two today? Claire never double-books you, does she?'

'No, of course she didn't. And stop admiring *my* secretary. I can hear your great Rutland cogwheels turning, Spencer,' Cracknell clenching teeth, 'and I can tell you that you haven't got a hope. Forget her.'

'OK.' Spencer eye-smiled, mild, co-operative.

'Anyway this lunchtime I've another meeting. Also on the film. It's the only time that they can make; it could go on. Look, this is really none of your business. And where are Philipson's papers? They aren't in this lot.'

'Uh.'

'Great.' Cracknell slapped the sheaf down. 'You've left them at home. So I have to interview this man with no CV to go on, do I?'

'He'll bring it in.'

'He's already sent it in. You showed it to me.'

'Uh.'

41

'I don't even know the bloke's first name, do you?'

'Dugald, wasn't it?'

'*Dugald?*'

'Wasn't it? I thought it was.'

'I thought that was Murdoch,' Goldie said.

'No, don't think so.'

'Right.' Cracknell took one of Spencer's pens and scrawled across a contact form. 'We'll see if he answers ... to *Dugald*. What else do you remember? What's his age?'

'Ask Patrick. He contacted him in the first place, wasn't me.'

'Did I?' Goldie said.

Cracknell threw the pen down. 'This is hopeless! What?' He spread his hands wide in delight. 'You realise? This is pathetic! The two of you! I don't believe it!'

'I really don't remember,' Goldie said. 'It must be last week since I spoke to him. Claire's bound to have his first name in the diary.'

'Spencer,' Cracknell said, taking no notice, 'if you'd just copied his home number out instead of walking off with the whole file — '

'I was in a tearing hurry,' Spencer said. 'You only asked at the last minute, I was halfway out the door.'

'It only came up at the last minute, *sunshine*. What are you ever doing that's so urgent, anyway?'

'I said I'd cook, that's all. I had to catch the late-night opening at Kentish Town Road Sainsbury's. Shuts at seven.'

Cracknell bunched his face behind his glasses. 'Well, how incredibly mundane. Is this your life? Look at Patrick here. At least he procreates in his spare time.'

Spencer (hullo Rat, I know, I know) looked at the window. 'I can fetch this stuff at lunch.' I've got to anyway. 'We're only just across the park.'

'Oh, forget it.' Cracknell started for the door, heels dragging.

'So what is happening about the film?' said Goldie.

Cracknell sidestepped and dropped into the spare armchair. 'Things are moving!' He set right ankle on left knee.

'Great.'

'If I can interest this key player, that should clinch the backing.'

'Who's that?'

'Oh, you don't need to know,' fussed Cracknell.

'Still, it's going well, though, good.' Goldie curled one hand to buff the fingernails with his thumb. 'Tell me, do you know if Su is going out to lunch today?'

'Yes,' said Spencer. 'Sweaty Bennett's taking her to Simpson's.'

'Yes, he is.' Cracknell straightened glasses. 'Spencer's strangely well-informed. What's up?'

'And what time are you meeting this film person?' Goldie said.

'Around half twelve on. It depends when they can get here. Why?' said Cracknell.

'Su usually goes out about half twelve, if she's going. We may need to check her files for something, that's all.'

'Which you've lost. Is it another one of mine?'

'No, it isn't one of yours. We may need someone to keep Fiona out of harm's way for a minute, though.'

Cracknell weaved his lion head. 'Oh, all right, then.'

Goldie said, 'I think Su's lost it, but she doesn't know that and she's after us to find it. And she's building up to one of her really angry moods.'

Cracknell nodded. 'Well, we're due for one. She doesn't wear that moonphase watch for fun, you know.'

'Actually, I wish it were all that predictable,' said Goldie.

'So I'd better tell Fi my cheeseplant's looking peaky again, then, had I?'

'Don't overuse that one. Ask her something like some sensible advice on how to do your office up. These girls all fancy themselves as interior designers, that should keep her happy down there for a bit. If you're not around we'll have to wait until she goes out too.'

'If she does go out,' said Spencer.

'Mm. She only ever takes five-minute lunch breaks, that's the thing,' said Goldie. 'Can't quite sort her act out to get in here from West Sussex by the time Su wants her ever, and then continually trying to make up for it. You can tell the job's on top of her basically.'

'Well, not that many people are cut out to work for Su,' said Cracknell. 'And most of them are in the SAS.'

'Glamorising it a bit,' said Spencer.

'What? Which, Holt Newman or the SAS, Spence?'

Spencer foggily shook his head. 'Both. Either.'

'What's the matter with you this morning? You look completely out of it.'

'Stopped smoking.'

'Oh. Is this wise?'

'No,' Spencer said.

'I don't know why Su won't make Claire her PA,' Goldie said. 'She's the best secretary we've got by far.'

'Best in the West End,' Cracknell said. 'Thanks, Rick, don't mind me.'

Stubbs came in. 'God, Patrick, with their tempers? They'd be — ' she pulled a snarl and clawed the air — 'all day long. I think that's *kind* of understood.'

'Is it, oh,' said Goldie.

'Besides Claire's much much too good-looking.'

'What, so what, that would go with Su's status, wouldn't it?'

'You're so naïve. She can't have a girl who looks better than she does.'

'Why not?'

'Oh, Patrick. Hullo, David, how are you?'

'You know I'm meant to go to Chelsea for the range later on?' said Gareth.

'Yes, well,' said Cath. She was a dark, pretty, softspoken girl not much older than him. 'How long will it take?'

'Couple of hours.'

'Back by half two?'

'Can be.'

'Heads' meeting's not till two, and we don't really know if the vicar's going to be back from JIC, so you shouldn't miss anything. But once things start to move you will have to be here.'

'Yeah.' He lifted the Browning and its rig from his desk drawer and got up.

'You're not off now?' she said.

'No. The main thing about being a potential target is not sleeping. But the next thing is the constipation, so if you get one of those rare twinges that tell you when it might be easing off you have to take advantage of it.'

'I won't ask in future. Are you leaving that file up? People wandering in all the time.'

Gareth threw his jacket over his terminal. They were running case reviews on peace campaigners. 'Save keying in again. And you can watch my wallet.' He took the Browning with him down the corridor.

Parked and straining on the seat he felt a riving pain, not for the first time. Blood lately, too. Is that haemorrhoids? Yeehow. He held back. Oh, let's go or we'll only lose the chance. He laughed at himself. Shit first, arse-questions after.

Mattie in the Regent's Park walked slowly from the bandstand sorting all the notes and sketches that he'd taken in his head to put down later. There had to be enough room underneath the floor to put to use and that five-lever lock there on the access hatch was easy dealt with. The little signboard had those brackets, like for slotting in the odds at races. So they must put the performances up there, but if that only happened on the day he'd have to watch and see how regular it was and who was playing. If he got the St John's Ambulance Brigade band by mistake or schoolkids the publicity could backfire. He'd have to send it up to OC Mainland for approval first but that was OK, it'd need to wait till summer anyhow. Still, you never knew your luck because he hadn't thought of that one and he'd only really come to watch the birdies.

Mattie, wiry, smallish, black-Zapata-moustached, stopped on the path up to the bridge and then, with just the right respectful but unwary glance at a patrolling pair of bobbies going by, he drew out from his parka pocket his expensive little green pair of binoculars and trained them on the island in the lake. If the coppers asked, he was an electrician, which was true, and he was early for his next job, which meant what you liked.

But they passed him and their talk was all of patios and barbecues.

It was nesting. On the big tree there. No sign of the other one.

He watched, watched, and was suddenly rewarded. The great S neck reared, the spear bill skyward, and the great grey wings and reedlike legs unfolded, and with a beat at first heavy but soon easier, near silent, the great ungainly beauty of a bird took flight. Mattie ogling a heron.

'That one wasn't any good,' said Spencer as he hung up.

'No, nor was mine,' said Goldie, brooding over the contact form he'd just filled in. 'I need some more of these forms, have you got the original?'

'You should be *rattling* through these calls, come on,' Cracknell turned to say.

Stubbs was telling him, 'And then Geoff and Bryn began to sing, not very loud but putting on these *dire* Australian accents, and so the waiters asked us *would* we like our coats.'

Spencer, rummaging in a drawer with one hand, reached for his buzzing extension with the other. 'Yeah, it's Spencer.'

'Claire,' said Claire. 'Is he up there?'

'Yes, he's up here.' Spencer kneed the drawer shut and held out the original contact form for Goldie, who took it off to copy.

'There's a Julie on the line,' said Claire. 'Does he want me to transfer it up?'

'Someone called Julie, David. D'you want to take it here?'

'Oh, yes?' said Stubbs.

'Ah,' said Cracknell. 'Right, I'll go down to my office. Tell Claire to give it thirty seconds and then put it through. And I do want that Philipson stuff.'

'Get that?' Spencer asked Claire. 'He's just left.' The old house's joists gave little shudders as Cracknell took the stairs fast.

'Yeah, thanks, Spence,' said Claire. 'Who's Philipson? Isn't he one of this afternoon's?'

'It's all right, that was addressed to me. But in fact — '

'What?'

'Oh, hang on.' Spencer held his forehead. This isn't going to work.

'Have to wait, I can hear him coming now.' Claire went off the line.

Spencer sat with inert hands on the blotter.

Stubbs looked up from her desk. 'What's wrong?'

'I double-booked myself.' He did a tragic laugh. 'I knew I was taking Claire out to lunch and I knew I'd got to go and fetch this file from home at lunchtime and it only just clicked that there was anything impossible about being in the both places at once. I'm just not getting there this morning.'

'Oh, Spencer, why? You can't let Claire down. Mustn't.'

'I don't know. Two different things. I must have had two different todays in mind.' He looked at the receiver still in his left hand and put it back.

'What are you going to do?' said Stubbs.

'Both. Have to.'

Goldie came in with his new forms and gave Spencer the original. 'How did you get on, Susie?'

'No luck with Les, no luck with John in the basement,' she said. 'I also had a look at Holly's desk down there because I think it used to be Kenny's. No luck either.'

'It was,' said Spencer. 'That's the one I had to shift down the stairs singlehandedly when he,' tipping head at Goldie, 'skipped off on the Aerospace visit the day all the consultants' new mock-Georgian got delivered and had to be made room for.'

'Yah, but you were showing off to Claire,' said Stubbs.

'I was not. No one else'd do it. And she only watched me so I didn't chip paint on the corners.'

Stubbs cocked an eyebrow.

'She's into all that, isn't she,' said Goldie.

'All what?' said Spencer.

' ... Men lifting heavy objects.'

'Is she?'

'You know. She's always talking about some hunky builder down the road in summer, and those exercise classes she goes to at Pineapple, she's a very physical person.'

Spencer looked at the fireplace.

'Anyway, Suze,' said Goldie, 'if you've drawn a blank it's Plan B then. OK.'

'Fine. Oh, Mrs Holt's about to throw one,' Stubbs said.

'What?'

'I just passed by on my way back up. The clock stopped, apparently.'

'What clock?'

'The carriage clock. If I can't twrust you with a little thing like that, Fiona,' Stubbs said with Su Holt's funny R, 'what can I twrust you with, can you tell me?'

'Oh, no, poor old Fi. That's what happened just before she sacked the last one. Emma.'

'What Carolyn resigned for in the end, too, really,' Spencer said. 'Stuck the rest of it for years, but not once the clock-winding bit started.'

'Fair do's, Fiona is, well, pretty hopeless,' Stubbs said.

'I know,' said Goldie. 'Still. If we could make some break-through here with Pytcherley. That's what's really agitating Su. It's dragged on now since ... ' He puffed.

'November,' Spencer said.

'No, is it?'

'And if we're on the standard one-third fee, we've spent at least that on our time and David's and Claire's all added up already.'

Goldie squinted at him. 'Ten thousand. You must be right. We're actually doing this for nothing now.' He gave a tired chuckle. 'It's not going to end. I'll still be doing it when I'm thirty. Forty.'

'Generations hence,' said Spencer. 'The hereditary curse of the Goldies. Contact forms preserved in ever-deepening piles in a locked room in the west wing.'

'Don't,' said Goldie, and coughed.

'Would you like me to try making some calls for you?' said Stubbs.

'No, Susie,' said Goldie hoarsely, 'you've got other things to do. Besides ... '

'It's the one that's just called Secret on the agenda, isn't it?' she said. 'As the mere junior here I have to leave the meeting before that point. And if it started in November I was still a humble typist down below.'

'No, it's the next one under that, called Confidential,' Spencer said. 'But we still can't tell you what it is.'

'I've heard you do the phone spiel often enough. Beer marketing?'

'Not really, no,' said Goldie. His chest wheezed. *Heek.* 'Scuse.' He took his inhaler from his jacket pocket and, coughing, went out to the side office.

They heard a *Pfuit. Pfuit.*

'Are you all right, Patrick?' Stubbs called.

Pfuit.

'It's sad she can have that effect on him,' said Stubbs.

They stiffened. Su's raised voice reached them from two floors below. A door banged shut with sense-deadening force. The windows shook. A short tense silence hit the house.

Lowther, on the phone, recovering himself, said, 'Bit of a disagreement somewhere, go on.'

Downstairs Jenny Prince typed half a line of gibberish and tore out the sheet.

'Jee-sus.' Les Forbert put the phone back to his ear. 'Beg pardon. I've no idea what it was, I'm new here.'

Steve Cusson said, embarrassed, 'Things get pretty high-powered around this place,' but the chalkstriped investment banker he was interviewing only studied the table in between the chairs where Claire had set the tray of china, watched his coppery lapsang souchong leaping to the teacup rim and said, 'Well, now I've seen one.'

The Daniell prints in series down the staircase shrugged their frames.

Claire, typing to a tape of Cracknell's voice, carried on to the end of the par and read it over. Looks OK. The candidate on the chesterfield, awaiting interview, gazed up at the chandelier as its troutstream tinkling faded, then across at Claire. She felt her colour rise and said, without meeting his eye or taking off her headset, 'Someone's left the skylight open. Creates a shocking draught.'

In his office next door down the hallway Cracknell told the man in Canada, 'It means we have to creep around on tiptoe for a bit. No, as you're dealing with me it won't be a problem, George.'

Lillian, in the kitchen, filled a kettle.

Next to the kitchen at the very back, in the large quiet office of Holt Associates, strategic planners (namely Mr Robin Holt, absent this week in Japan), a honey-haired schoolgirl on her Easter break was totting international steel consumption figures with a Casio, her stockinged feet tucked up beside her in the handsome leather rocker. Her little Sony tran was tuned to Capital, playing low. Gary Moore, remember Paris back in '49, plangent guitar. She reached the bottom of the column, put the total in, pushed back her hair. 'Cheers, Mum,' she said.

In the basement, Holly Jessup was counselling a redundant textiles executive. She laughed for nerves. 'Well, that's as good an example as any.' The videocam was running. 'I'll play that back and show you how you looked. Ideally, nothing's got to faze you in an interview, if you can reach that frame of mind.'

He unhunched in his chair. 'Sorry. I thought it was another bomb on Oxford Street for a moment.'

'Don't apologise. We're only here to learn.'

'Sorry,' he of course again said then.

Running in towards the settlement the amphitracs come under fire, bullets bouncing off the armour plate with weird chirps like guitar strings breaking. The machines pull off the road and trundle into dips on either side. The commander can see the two or three small houses where the outpost of marines must be. The tracer fire is all from there and so are the smoke trails of antitank rockets, but those are falling short. He'll tell his mortar teams to have a shot at bringing down the house roofs. That might let the men inside surrender honourably without killing any of them.

Fiona stood by Claire's desk, the big red diary held against her midriff, waiting for Claire to finish the par. Claire stopped the tape with the footswitch and pulled the headset off. 'Hullo.'

Fiona, eyes fixed, said with a bobbing spasm in the throat, 'I forgot to crohosscheck the appohointments.'

Claire sighed. 'Leave that with me. Come and see Lillian, come on.' She stepped around the desk and manoeuvred Fiona out towards the hall. Get her away from the candidate.

Les came in, looking for his man, and met them in the doorway. 'I say. All right, Fi?'

Claire widened at him what she knew were her amazing eyes to say Say nothing.

'Ah.' Les turned to the candidate on the chesterfield and held out his hand. 'Peter. Yes? Sorry to keep you waiting. I'm Les.'

Claire shepherded Fiona down the hall. The tears broke. 'Can't do much right,' gasped Fi.

'You're just the nearest person handy, that's all,' Claire said.

The outside phone line buzzed.

Les, halfway up the stairs with Peter following, leaned over the banisters and stage-whispered down to Claire, 'One black, two sugars?'

'Coming up.'

'I'll fix that,' said Lillian at the ever-open kitchen door. 'Drop of mint, Fiona? I thought someone might feel like something.'

'OK?' Claire patted Fiona's shoulder. The phone was still buzzing. 'Got to get that.' She sprinted back up the hall.

Anyone could take an outside call on their extension and just as Claire got there someone did. Claire could guess who without picking it up. She balled her fists.

★

'Sorry,' said Holly, switching the videocam remote to off and reaching for the phone. 'Hello-o?'

'Holly,' Su Holt said, 'I've got your mother-in-law on the line.'

'Oh. Su. Hullo. Have you?'

'And I've forgotten how these buttons are supposed to work so you'd better be ready to ring her back if it cuts off.'

'Oh. Yes. All right.'

Patrick Goldie looked around the door. 'Is David interviewing?'

'Not until eleven,' Claire said.

Goldie coughed and went.

Claire compared diaries and made a list of all the double-bookings to be rearranged. The outside line buzzed. Call for Su. It was only the MD of the florist's apologising for this morning's late delivery. 'She's in a meeting but I'll pass it on.' Buzzed again. For Mike. She put it through.

'How long are you hiding out for this time, then?' said Cracknell. His office was the building's murkiest room, a Morris-papered den hung all about with hunting prints, Spy caricatures, plates of old cavalry uniforms. He'd tried for a gentlemen's club look and achieved, he said, only the terrible semblance of a wine bar. He'd been after the funds to have it all redone for years, since the day it was completed.

'Don't know. Half an hour should do it,' Goldie said, sprawled on his back on the ivy velvet drop-arm sofa.

'And you're just leaving poor old Spence and Suze to take the heat.' Cracknell sorted through the papers in a plastic folder to no purpose.

Goldie sniffed and gave himself another spray. 'The research department usually comes next, yeah.'

Claire marched in, put some typing down on Cracknell's desk and went out, shutting the door silently.

'Thanks,' said Cracknell.

'What's so exhausting,' said Goldie, 'is the way you never get beyond square one with her.'

'Who? Claire? That's all you know,' said Cracknell, furtive.

'I don't believe you. No. Su. You never build up any sort of credit, you're on this knife edge of approval–disapproval all the time.'

'Oh. Come on. She wants to make you a consultant.' Cracknell thumbed his red braces from under his waistcoat. 'Hey?'

'It'd still be the same.'

'Well, that's life, mate, sorry. Nobody gets any credit with anybody. I've had you in here making similar remarks about the lovely Fran before now. And how long have you two been together?'

Goldie coughed. 'God, did I? It's true you think that married means you just don't have to keep on proving your credentials with the person, but you still do, day on day.'

'There you are, then. It's quite normal, you know. It goes on in most homes.'

'Dyeugh, but — '

'It's even how the country gets run. Be good or Mrs will be upset. Now I hope you don't mind if I do some work here.' Cracknell checked his Rolex in the light of the brassnecked green-glass-shaded desk lamp.

Goldie sniffed. 'Why, you're not busy, are you?'

'What's that supposed to mean? I'm always busy. I've just got this company a hundred thousand pounds' worth of business from Canada, if you want to know, with more to come if we produce results. So you can — '

'Oh, that George Whatsisface. That came off, then?'

'He's flying over today, he just rang before he left to make the flight, he's going round the London search firms next week.'

'So you're not the only one he's seeing.'

'I'm the only one he's seeing for Sunday lunch at the Connaught, sunshine. The others are a formality. He told me.'

'Well, that is good.' Goldie folded arms and stared at the ceiling. 'The directors won't like it, though. I mean, she will, but Robin and Bryant are going to look pretty silly. They're bound to try and make sure she doesn't renew your contract this time.'

'I — '

'Since they hate your guts anyway.'

'I was aware of that,' said Cracknell, straightening glasses, 'there's no need to remind me. I quite look forward to a showdown with those two. I like to go out with a bang.' He let his arms hang between his knees. 'At least that's what always seems to happen.'

'This film better had work out, then.'

'It is working out.'

'Hope so.'

'Are you all right for cold water there, Rick? I mean let me know when you run out of buckets.'

Lillian held a coffee tray. 'Want me to take this up?'

'No, I'm just going, leave it there,' said Claire. 'How is she?'

'All right. Talking to Tara.'

Claire put the diary on the tray along with Spencer's new mail copy of *Marketing Week*, which he'd missed at the bottom of his folder. He was supposed to go through it for names.

Claire enjoyed the rhythm of a stroppily ascended set of stairs, and the tautening of the muscles of her legs. Going up, she hummed the first bars of a song she couldn't place, each tricky interval just caught.

The first-floor landing was deadly still. Claire was lightfooted in her flat moccasin shoes but as she left the diary on Fiona's desk a floorboard croaked beneath the carpet.

Around the tall white door to Su's room a hairline crack had opened up between the wall and frame. Next time round the whole shebang could pop right out and leave you squashed flat on the spot if you were standing here.

Claire stole out and up to the next floor. Jenny should be doing this, but with Les you didn't mind the odd time.

Les, and then at his example Peter, both rose part-way from their chairs. Claire blushed, murmured, 'Don't get up,' and set the tray down. She'd forgotten Les did that. The last one who always stood when she appeared was the boy MacMichael.

Spence with Su this morning, jumping like he'd sat on a scorp.

Claire carried on to the top, humming the tricky bars again, and this time placed the song. 'I'm Mandy, Fly Me'. Smiling, she stopped herself.

Spencer was on his own. Claire spun the polythene-enveloped

journal on to his desk, fluttering his papers. She hoofed idly over to the window and looked out. 'Where's Susie?'

'Took some stuff off to type,' said Spencer. 'Rick with David?'

'Uhuh.' His eyes at her back. She pressed her fingertips to the sill and lifted her heels, hup two down two. A black cat on the steps of the apartment house opposite put up its chin, spotting a bird, and saw Claire at the window. It stared in the ain't-done-nothing way that cats do stare. An overalled engineer ran up the steps with a portable air conditioner. The cat sprang to the balustrade.

Spencer looked at Claire and felt his eyes prick, she was so bravely made.

'Right.' Claire turned about, legs crossing. 'I'd better collect this Dugald Philipson's papers for this afternoon, then, David'll want them, and you've decided where we're going, have you?' Two athletic paces put her face to face with him across the desk.

Spencer had not felt such plain fright since Jacqueline in Toulouse. Hoops here to be got through. His voice was going hollow. 'On your first point — '

'Oh, come on. Where are they?' Claire reached over, took his blotter by the corners nearest him and slid it towards her, stepping back. At the point of balance on the desk edge it uptilted.

Spencer lunged to stop the heap of papers sliding off, his arms across the blotter, his head coming under Claire's chin. His nose was almost inside the open neck of her white pintucked blouse and almost within nuzzling distance of her large, firm, smoothcleft and, though pale, extremely definite young breasts, would you call that a mole or more of a freckle, with the fetchingly silly little silk bow of her bra between them, not white but sky blue, surprising for some reason; so he put his face down on the blotter, partly to pretend he hadn't looked, partly to help keep his papers still and partly because, the way he was jammed up against the desk, if this lightning erection got any further it was going to hurt.

Now he had nothing in view but paperwork.

Claire chinned his crown and straightened. He hauled the blotter back and gave her a tolerant look. Red, she laughed through her nose and, holding her eyes on his, walked backwards over to the fireplace.

Spencer sat up. Like that skirt. Sort of close-grained tweed, nice fit round the hips. Her calves in those silverwhite tights, keen-shaped as fish. 'Philipson's in the Probables file,' he said. 'Which is on the linen chest.' Her chest proud under close white linen.

'The linen chest. Fine.' Claire left her mouth open, tucked in her chin against her threadfine gold neckchain and scanned the carpet, swinging her shoulders, hands clasped behind her.

'Which is in the hall. In Camden Town,' said Spencer.

'Yeah, I had that. Oh, well, David'll just have to manage without.' Her shoulders heaved and stilled. 'Heeeuw. Never mind. Where shall we go? Jack Sprat's?' She kept her head down and prompted, 'Eh?'

'OK. Thing is,' said Spencer, 'I think Su's going to call one of her progress sessions on Pytcherley this afternoon and I'm really going to need that file,' the last few words unnaturally loud to cover up a stomach rumble.

'I see. So you're putting me off.' Claire moved and sat sidesaddle on the edge of Goldie's desk. 'Or what?' She started linking Goldie's paperclips into a chain with the ferocious concentration she gave all her tasks.

'Well,' said Spencer, should have got her away and brought this up later but let's blunder on shall we as we've started, 'it's only ten minutes by Miles's pony, flag a cab,' it's double that, 'I can go after. Su could be out till half two, Sweaty Bennett's the only man in the world who can get her to drink, oldest client and all that. We'd have a good hour before I need to dash.'

'Time doesn't work like that, you'd never do it. What makes you think she's going to want this meeting?'

'She hinted. Anyway, it's what she always does when she's in a mood, just to keep us in late.'

Claire held the ends of the paperclip chain to her nape so it hung in a necklace. She smiled at Spencer a moment, dropped the chain back in the ashtray. 'Well, I can't eat if you're clockwatching. And I'm bloody hungry.'

'You only ever have an apple normally. I've seen you.'

She walked round and threw herself in Goldie's chair. 'You made me work up an appetite. Besides I was in a rush this morning. I haven't touched a thing since I had a cream cracker in the middle of last night's *News at Ten*.'

Not that he or several million other saps had been doing any different, but the picture of her — her, beautiful sexy crosspatch Claire — mildly watching TV alone at home roused and stirred him. The oil-prospecting boyfriend last heard of somewhere hot and dictatorial. She was fumingly displeased for a bit, carrying a candle like a grudge, then seemed to have forgotten to fume lately. Which is where we came in.

And did she watch hugging her knees on a cushion, while Sandy and Selina gave her the crisis update? Surely. Ready dressing-gowned after a bath because she had to be up early? Course. And does she in such private moments wear big owlish glasses? Like the idea, but sadly she's got eagle eyesight as it is.

'Oh,' said Spencer. 'Not much use if I said dinner instead, then.' You just blew it. Way too fast.

'No, that's all right,' said Claire, 'I've got the afternoon off, I was going down to Knightsbridge anyway, I could treat myself to a salad in Harvey Nicks or something in Harrods Health Juice Bar, forget it.'

'Oh.' Did not go down all that well, did it. 'You taking your half day? Early in the month.'

'No, she's given me an extra one for coming in early to cover for Fi.'

He nodded. 'You'wre a wreal asset.' What's my next move? What's still left?

Claire laughed and jerked one of Goldie's drawers open and shut open and shut open and shut. 'So you're really going to sneak back home to Camden, are you?'

'Have to, really, but — '

'Well, that more or less settles it, then, doesn't it?' She glanced up quickly and down again. 'Unless you're going to invite me back and make me something.'

Wait a second, what *is* this? Spencer shrugged eyebrows and looked aside as if considering coolly. I'm supposed to use *subterfuge*. I'm supposed to use *guile*. I'm supposed to make *lying promises* and spend *serious* amounts of money. To slow it down to something like his natural pace he said, 'Well, you'd be lucky to get a bacon sandwich out of what there is in our kitchen.'

Claire stared down at the desk and started linking clips again. 'That right?'

'And the bacon's last week's if it's still there and the bread's a bit stale by now except for toasting. I did a shop last night but we went and ate all that.'

'Brown sauce?' said Claire.

'Expect so.'

'Mayonnaise?'

'Bit left, I think.'

'I could get some lettuce and tomatoes in Morris's. What about stuffed olives? Pickled gherkins?'

'Jars of party leftovers somewhere. Could do you those.'

Claire frowned. 'Right now for a bacon sandwich I'd sell my grandmother.'

'Would you?'

She tilted back her chair.

He sat back too.

They locked eyes, then Claire looked him over slowly.

Spencer felt skinless, boneless, weightless. He floated.

Claire held it on his feet, stuck well out from the desk. 'You're wearing odd socks.'

'Yup.'

She tipped her head on one side and hugged herself.

The outside line's repeater, on the landing, buzzed. She took up Goldie's extension and pressed Connect. 'Holt Newman. I'm afraid he isn't in today. One or two days a month, I'd have to look it up.' They must be wanting Derrick Bryant. 'I can give you the number of his own firm, where I'm sure you'll find him.' She rattled it off, said Not at all and gave the ivory set a pert drop to its cradle.

She eyed Spencer's socks again, then looked up at him and did her silent laugh.

He loved that.

They stiffened. Su Holt's booted tread was somewhere on the stairs. Not reached the next floor yet: they heard Steve and his candidate make way for her at the half-landing, and her muttered thanks and sudden speeding-up to pass them.

Claire, with a graceful forward fling of arms, came to her feet.

'Here we go,' said Spencer.

'Relax.' Claire chasséd aside to Lowther's door. 'So am I coming?'

'Yeah, sure,' said Spencer.

'OK. See you in a bit.' She tapped at Lowther's door and slipped through without waiting for an answer.

Su came in. 'Where are the others?'

'Wait a sec,' Lowther told the other end, and tucked the phone under his jaw. 'Yeah?'

'Oh.' Claire edged towards the outer door. 'Just to let you know that Jenny's in reception after lunch, so she'll be on 21 in case you need her.'

Lowther gave the air a smart tap with his pen. 'Cheers. OK, Drew, I'm back.'

'Send Rick up, David,' Spencer said. 'Su here wants him.'

Goldie broke out coughing.

'Susie I'm not sure about,' said Spencer, 'I'll just — ' He scuttled out and down the stairs.

Claire was looking in at Jenny's door.

'Thanks,' Jenny said, 'I'd quite forgotten.'

Stubbs was in there, leaning on a filing cabinet. 'Susie? Su. Upstairs,' said Spencer.

'Oh. Right. Scuse, Claire,' said Stubbs.

Claire backed into Spencer and pressed her hip and shoulder up against him for a moment. He put a hand to her waist just before she moved away. His ears were roaring. He was half inclined to give a rebel yell.

On the way down Claire passed Patrick Goldie coming up. 'You'll sort it out, Rick.'

'Thanks.'

Goldie, Stubbs and Spencer cut the mutter as they came in.

'Hullo, Su,' said Stubbs.

'Shut the door,' said Su.

Spencer shut it, kicking out the choc chock. Su waited for them to sit down and started in.

'I have the feeling things are slipping.' She settled back against the windowsill. Her leathered bottom squeaked on the paintwork. She slowly paced the room instead. Business booming, all been under pressure, no blame attached, more effort needed all the same. Million-pound turnover projected this year, new staff coming soon, meantime however. 'I think we ought to have a brainstorming today on Pytcherley. That hasn't gone at all well.'

Goldie shot a glance at Spence in case he thought of saying why.

'Now by the time I've sat through old Ron Bennett's round of jokes at lunch it could be getting on for three and I'll have plenty that needs doing after, so we'd better say we'll start at five.'

Make that six. And these things ran for two, three perspirational and mostly wasted hours on end.

'I want everything you've got so far. I want you in on this one, Susie, too. The other two can give you all the background.'

Stubbs opened wide her mouth to speak. Goldie shut it with the look.

'Sorry if it upsets your arrangements, can't be helped,' said Su. 'There's always some new avenue or other that you haven't tried. Where did you get that Morris Lustig, Spencer?'

'Mm?' Spencer switched mode from half-attentive to active. 'Divitt. Guy we placed at GF Coffee Products. They're both ex-Heinz.'

'Oh, him with the Orange-boy accent.'

Spencer felt Stubbs try to catch his eye. Su's accent goes: *He saze he'll be wring ging gus back.* Lord knows where it comes from, north-west of Rutland anyhow, halfway to Fazakerly shouldn't wonder.

'There you are, then,' Su said. 'Always other avenues.'

Spencer suppressed in turn a nervous yawn, a lust to smoke, and then an insane, salary-hazarding urge to look at his watch.

Cracknell came into reception. 'All right, listen.'

'What?' said Claire.

'This Craig Jackson.' He was holding a shortlist candidate's summary, six leaves of marble-textured paper set for binding.

'What did I do, then?'

He pointed. 'You've given him "clean-cut good lucks". It says something about the guy. It's just it's not what *I* said. So you'll have to change it.' He poked the sheets at her face.

'OK.' She took them. 'That's where the big bang put me off. I'll do that side again, then.'

'That's how Joyce produced *Finnegans Wake*, you know. No genius involved, just dictation,' said Cracknell, leaving.

'I don't know what you're talking about but I'm sure you're right.'

He closed his office door and shouted through the wall, 'This is our tragedy, Claire. We simply don't communicate.'

'The problem's not on my side,' Claire said.

'I'm surprised the rumour hasn't worked its way to Tony Pytcherley by now,' said Goldie.

'Old Tony Pytcherley can't see what's under his nose,' said Su, still pacing. 'And he couldn't smell a rat if it was farting up his nostrils. So don't imagine that'll get us off the hook because it won't. You'll have to give it all some major think before this meeting later on and then I want to hear a damn sight better answers than I'm hearing at the moment. Now then.' She stopped the pacing. Spencer felt disoriented as if the room must be moving around her instead. She turned to Stubbs. 'What happened with Niall Gregory on Aerospace?'

'Euh?' Stubbs said. 'Ah.'

Spencer felt hot.

'Well,' said Goldie, so that Su turned back, 'it's looking ... not too bad, I mean ... '

'You mean,' said Su, 'the bloody thing's still missing.' She kicked a boot heel hard into the carpet.

But Spencer heard, and so must they, the sound of someone young and lithesome running up the stairs in moccasins.

'No,' said Goldie, playing for time, 'I think we've got it

narrowed down, it's just a case of ... ' *heek,* his chest wheezed. 'Yes, right, so ... '

The moccasins reached the landing.

Goldie coughed. 'Khhrrrm. Sorry.'

Claire walked in and knocked. 'Hi. OK?' She smiled at them. 'Su,' she said, 'Sir John Smeath's just arrived, I've put him in the drawing room.'

Su said, 'Tell him I'll be — '

'And I've got Fiona looking after him.'

'I better come right down, then. Five o'clock, you three,' said Su. 'The boardroom.' And was gone.

Claire closed the door and leaned back against it. Goldie and Spencer put their elbows on their desks and looked at her. Stubbs, across the room, said, 'Claire, I *think* the boys would like to kiss your feet.'

'Well. Wouldn't mind,' said Spencer.

Claire kicked up and caught one moccasin, stuck out one silverwhite foot, 'No takers? Haven't got all day,' then dropped the shoe and stepped back into it. 'Missed your chances. I don't know.' She shook her head as she straightened and smoothed her skirt.

Spencer again could have cried to see her incurved outcurved strong upstanding figure.

'I'll have to ring Geoff now and replan *everything,*' said Stubbs. 'I'm sorry, Patrick, but I don't see why I should.'

'And lose your bonus?' Goldie said. 'Expensive night out.'

'And it's not as if it's my search even.'

'It is now.'

'Quite, so you chaps balls it up and suddenly it's my problem.'

Stubbs and Goldie argued. Claire sat on the edge of Spencer's desk, budging back his phones, and looked over her shoulder at him. 'All right, you?'

'I could do with a cigarette.'

'Why, run out?'

'Trying to give up.'

'You won't last.' She smiled.

Listen to the lady, said the drug. She loves you.

★

Willis, in his office, in the castle, over there, popped the cassette from the player on his desk.

'Elevenses,' said Margot, bowling in from the corridor with a canteen tray, two plastic cups aboard. 'One for *you* ... ? The Dashing Black Sergeant was in the canteen, chatting Rachel up.'

'Ta. Aye, well, he brought me this,' said Willis. He allowed himself a few ayes a day for Yorkshire pride and to see who took the piss. 'So I won't be in this afternoon.'

'What's that, off the answerphone?' Margot slipped a biscuit from her desk drawer and nibbled.

'Yeh, Tambourine Man wants a meet. We aren't due for one yet but the words are all in order, so either it's a set-up or he's got something.' Willis lit a Three Fives and dialled an army number. 'Morning, Captain Sutton, it's Nigel Willis. I'm going to have to ask you for four guys as back-up again, like right away, if they're not too busy.'

Spencer leafed through *Marketing Week* and noted for the card index a couple of the people mentioned. The coffee machine in the side office, primed by Stubbs just now, was giving its last snorkel sighs. He went out and poured three fresh cups, white for Goldie. As he brought them round, Stubbs said, 'Is anyone now going to tell me what the problem with the Pytcherley search actually is?'

'It's a snark hunt,' said Spencer.

Goldie looked up. 'What. Oh, yeah.' He put the spec on the corner of his desk for Stubbs to take.

She came over and looked at it. 'Fairly straightforward.'

'No, that's a blind. Tony Pytcherley's heading up the biggest subsidiary and he's on the main board of the group, and he's useless so they want to get rid of him. But they can't sack him, or they're scared to, so they're trying to squeeze him out sideways without him noticing.'

'He doesn't know we're running a search,' said Stubbs.

'No. Or he's not supposed to. And it says marketing director but we're really looking for somebody to replace him. As an executive, not as a shareholder, obviously.'

'Except we're not allowed to tell the candidates all that,' said Spencer. 'And no one wants to work for him because he's such a well-known git.'

'I see,' Stubbs said. 'So they won't be working for him, but we have to pretend they will.'

'That's right.'

'Which puts them off.'

'Yeah.'

'But I thought you didn't even tell them the company.'

'They can work it out from the spec.'

'And then they say no.'

Spencer looked at his master sheet. 'Well, three hundred and seventeen of them have so far.'

Stubbs said, 'I think I'm even less pleased that you've got me into this now, but I do see your problem.'

'Su should never have taken it on,' said Goldie. 'Sort of thing she used to tell them to stuff. But since business started to snowball she's so hyper. The recession's making her rich, all these firms revamping their management, she won't turn anything down.'

Stubbs said, 'Well, I'm not going to let this make my life a misery as well, so if we can't think of a solution to propose before Su gets the thumbscrews out at five we'd better just refuse to handle it. Tell her it isn't on, frankly.'

Spencer and Goldie said nothing.

She looked from one to the other. 'No? I'll speak for all of us if you like.'

'I don't think it'll work,' said Goldie.

'Just a suggestion.' Stubbs went back to her desk.

'But ... hm, no, well, thanks, Susie.'

'OK, up to you,' said Stubbs. 'Oh, go on, tell me what the Secret job is as well.'

Spencer said, 'It's just Su taking tea with the odd father-figure to try and find a chairman for ... a group with interests in tobacco and Worcester sauce among other things.'

'Oh, Imperial. We're always doing things for them. Is that all?'

'We didn't tell you that, remember,' Goldie said.

'I thought it was something for the government,' said Stubbs.

Spencer turned a page and went on with *Marketing Week*. 'Hey, listen, this is great. An exploration team sponsored by Smirnoff has rediscovered the dodo breeding on the Seychelles.'

'What?' said Goldie. 'That's incredible. Good grief.'

'*The* dodo?' Stubbs said. 'As in dead as?'

'Oh. Sod it, sorry,' Spencer said. 'It's a report on April Fool ads people have been running. Sod it.'

'Shame,' Stubbs said.

'Rather bad taste,' murmured Goldie.

'I remember my godson showing me a stuffed dodo in the Nat Hist, it looked rather sweet,' said Stubbs.

'This one's straight, I think,' said Spencer. 'Public relations firms looking for new gimmicks to use at press launches may like to know that the RAF is selling off its Vulcan bombers at a mere six hundred pounds each.'

'Hundred?' Goldie said. 'Not hundred thousand?'

'Nope. Minus engines. And you have to pay for towing them away. But if you're a scrap merchant, what do you think the profit on that would be? Off the graph. I bet you find you've got to have friends in the Ministry of Defence before you can buy one. Licence to print money.'

'Try asking Gareth,' Stubbs said. 'How is he?'

'I haven't seen him lately much, but he's back over here now.'

Goldie said, 'Perhaps we should send these bombers to the South Atlantic.'

Spencer, surprised, said, 'That's a bit aggressive for you, Rick.'

'No, we could hand them over as a bribe to this Argentine scrap-metal gang that's holding the sit-in on the islands. Make their fortunes, send them home happy.'

Spencer laughed. 'Yeah. Greatest empire ever known. Now held to ransom by a bunch of Patagonian rag-and-bone men.'

Stubbs said, 'Well, I think the Royal Marines should have gone round and run *their* flag down *straight* away. It'll only end in tears.'

'Yeah, but I suppose all that went out at Suez, Suze.'

Goldie said, 'What can we do down there, though, Susie, really? It said in the *Guardian* yesterday we've just sold our last aircraft carrier to the Australians.'

'Have we?' Spencer said.

'Yes, the *Invincible*, it's only just been built but Margaret Thatcher says it costs too much to run. So we can't go sending gunboats anywhere any more because we can't protect them from air attack, simple as that.'

'Are you sure this wasn't another April Fool?' said Stubbs.

'I don't think so. It was reporting a speech by whatsisface, old John Nott; I can't imagine him joining in a *Guardian* hoax.'

Spencer said, 'The Australians? You're positive it didn't say the Swiss?'

Lowther came in and snatched the certified accountants' directory from the bookshelf. 'Patrick. Got a minute?'

'Right,' said Goldie drably, following him out.

Fiona stiffened at the typewriter. Su Holt looked around the door, holding out a folded slip of paper. 'Pop this down to Claire, please, if you could.'

'Now?' said Fiona.

Su neither spoke nor moved.

'Right.' Fiona hopped up and scurried round the desk. 'Claire,' she nodded, looking at the slip. 'Mm.' The door softly closed again. Fiona took off to the stairs.

Claire, plugged in to one of Steve's tapes, fingers that seemed lazily to float tripping ten keys to the second, showed Fiona her teaplate eyes and said with barely a disturbance of her typing-trance, 'Right, leave it there.'

Fiona returned to the first floor head high and chuffed that any errand in this office could be quite so easily run. Back at her desk, though, she wondered if there might have been a catch. Perhaps she was meant to wait for an answer or see something done. She feared to ring Claire and look silly. She didn't know what to do.

Claire rang, a smile in her voice: 'What's this about then?'

'Um — I didn't read it.'

'Never mind, I think I can work it out, it's not the first time. Don't worry.' And rang off.

★

Cracknell's last candidate had left and his next was yet to come. Claire knocked as she walked in.

'Hullo, my little dervish,' he said with clenched grin. 'Now go out again and do that properly. I might have been sniffing my armpits, or picking my nose, or even peeing in the plantpot for all you knew. Go on.'

'I could hear you reading. You grunt and drum your fingers.'

'All right.' He threw down his notes. 'But it'll have to be a quick one,' struggling with the top button of his waistcoat, 'I've got this man from Mars arriving any minute.'

'No chance.'

'Oh.'

'Su wants you to go and loiter in reception. I think it's so that you can have a look at John Smeath on his way out.'

'OK. Well, what if my Martian appears?'

'Leave him for a bit and we'll hang about out here and talk shop. They won't be long.'

'That's it, dominate me, run my life. If I'd wanted this I'd have got married, you know. I wasn't short of offers.'

'Yeah, right.'

'Anyway, Smeath's a Secret, I'm not in on that job, or am I now?'

'Oh, you know, she likes a second opinion sometimes. You and him have got a friend in common, by the way,' said Claire.

'Eh?'

Seventy miles he'd driven on the high road through the mountains to this the second city of the province, a river-riven city still more northerly and if anything more drizzled-on than the one he'd come from.

Past the bridge they'd set a checkpoint up, two Land Rovers in staggered order so you had to weave between. It hadn't been there long because the tailback wasn't much. The usual sign said 'Sorry if your journey is delayed', and that pathetic last line: 'Blame the Terrorists'.

He stopped to wait his turn and flicked the wipers of the party-owned Cortina to intermittent. With the engine quiet and idling he could hear the observation helicopter, somewhere up there, like the sound of roadworks in the sky.

He'd rung the chief to let him know before he left and so he might as well assume they knew now too. But that was all right, he was clean, his car was clean, there was nothing proven on his record, his cover was good, there was nothing here to be afraid of. He felt OK. Except two soldiers got the chop in this town yesterday, which meant they'd look for any chance to shoot.

He had the radio on, waiting for the news to come at noon in ten or fifteen minutes' time, but at the moment he was listening to a storm of interference obviously caused by all the signals stuff and spy gear in the trucks and helicopters of the interfering occupying army. Well tucked-in thought. Could make a little thinkpiece for the paper, that. A little bit of O'Grady (his writing name).

The shabby car in front moved up one to the check. It cut its engine and the interference stopped.

The soldiers hardly bothered, saw the driver's licence, took his number down and waved him on. The storm of interference started crackling up again. Worn-out suppressors on the electricals. The driver looked back (out of pure reflexive habit, since for certain there was nothing going to be coming) as he pulled out past the Land Rover. It was a priest. Ah well. When he'd gone they let one through the other way.

The crackle faded. His turn now. Handbrake off, roll forward, handbrake on, and window slowly wound down as the young officer rapped curt knuckles on the glass.

The officer stooped, his close-set dark eyes quick to scan the cabin of the car and size the driver up. 'Switch off. Right off, radio as well, please. Keys out.'

'I was listening for the news. Those islands. Have you heard?'

'That's not my problem at the moment, sir, and certainly not yours. Licence and any other identification, please.' The officer talked normal, not your public-school at all.

He showed his licence and his party card. The officer took and read them, wrote down details in a Filofax thing. A squaddie behind him talked into a radio.

There was another squaddie, hook-nosed, walking backwards round the car with the mindlessly alert look of a footballer and a black nightsighted AR-15 Armalite Colt rifle which was no way standard issue.

'This your car?' said the officer.

'It's a party vehicle. I'm on official business.'

'What business would that be then, sir?'

'You really telling me you don't already know?'

The officer tapped fingers on the roof, pushed his lips out, gave the man an eyeballing. 'If you've got any sort of timetable to keep to, sir, may I suggest before you fuck it up beyond redemption that you simply tell me where it is you're going and who it is you plan to see there when and if I let you have permission to proceed?'

The driver looked ahead. 'I've an appointment at our advice centre in the free zone up the road to see the counsellor.'

'What counsellor?' said the officer.

'Martin McGuinness.'

'Oh, that counsellor. I see.'

'To discuss our policy for the assembly elections. In my capacity as deputy to our public affairs director. And in Martin McGuinness's capacity as candidate.'

The officer nodded with enlightenment. The radio guy behind said, 'Vehicle check's OK, sir, driver check's OK.'

'Right.' The officer handed back the card and licence. 'Thank you.'

The driver noticed that their berets had the bootblacked emblem of an ordinary county regiment which they might or might not in reality belong to.

They waved him on. They were only showing him who was boss. As if he didn't know.

The man from Mars was waiting on the chesterfield and reading the *Financial Times*. Claire was busy with a spate of calls incoming. Cracknell, restless in attendance for the planned chance meet, stooged down into the kitchen where he ate some walnuts and watched Lillian mix salad. 'You want to use less mayonnaise, Lils, it's only Su who likes it done like that. Go on, be your own woman.' He looked in on Su's daughter Tara, who giggled every time he showed his face. 'What is it? Why can't you take me seriously, as an interested, compassionate, caring, older man friend? Your sweater label's sticking up, look.' He decided to go upstairs and make himself apparent there. 'Fi. Hi,' he said.

'Ooh. David!' said Fiona.

'What?'

'Nothing. Just nice to see you.'

'Oh.' He fiddled with his braces. 'Listen, I hear you know a thing or two about decor. Hey?'

'Come on. Who told you that?'

'It's been the rounds. You've got the eye.'

'I suppose I could have, I don't know.'

'You told us how you did your new place down in Horsham up, it sounded great. So look, you've seen my office, what do you think I should do about it?'

'Room for improvement,' said Fiona, realigning the margin to address an envelope, 'I'll say. It's a bit of a wine bar.'

'Yes, well, you've identified the nature of the problem.'

'All it lacks is stools made out of barrels and a couple of blonde condescending waitresses who haven't paid their stage school overdrafts orf yet.'

'Yes, yes, don't overdo the mockery, Fi, it hurts.'

'Oh, whoops, beg your pardon, I thought we were sort of joking.'

'That's OK. Now look.' He leaned on her desk and lowered his voice. 'Once old Su's gone out, come down and get the feel of the place and tell me how you see it. After last time I really think I need a fresh angle on this.'

'Well, I'm going to have tons of busy things to be getting on with.'

'Never mind all that.'

Su Holt came through. 'Oh. David. I don't suppose you know Sir John Smeath. David Cracknell, one of our senior consultants.'

Cracknell shook hands and chatted as he tagged along downstairs to reception. Smeath was a tall, shouldery, longheaded man, his dark backswept hair white-winged about the temples. His tan and his walk and the rockdrill look he gave Claire were convincing evidence of power.

The Martian stood, smiling, and folded his paper.

'Not yet, sorry,' Cracknell grinned. 'A couple more minutes, OK?'

The Martian sat down, looking abashed and deflated as if he'd started having doubts about the whole thing now, the bogus dental appointment to secure the morning off, the calls that must be piling up without him at the office, the hurried sandwich on the 125 train back to Slough, the job itself, the lot of it.

Claire went and bent over him, hands squeezed between her knees. 'Let me get you some coffee.'

The Martian blinked and perked up. 'That's an idea. Black, as is, please.'

Cracknell could tell that Claire'd just given him an eyeful of frontage as well as a nice smile and a bit of attention. But she wouldn't know she was doing it, except subconsciously.

Su found herself helping Sir John on with his camel overcoat. She saw him out, came back in. 'Your office for a second,' she told Cracknell.

He gestured her to his ivy velvet drop-arm and sat at his desk, swivelling the chair and looking down at her to redress the power balance a little. 'I don't know why you get me to do this, Su — what am I meant to tell from a couple of minutes' smalltalk?'

'First two minutes the most important, David. It helps me sound my own feelings out. And you often notice a great deal whether you realise it or not.'

'Well, he's not what they're looking for; he's too smooth, too sharky, too all sorts of things.'

'He's not what they think they're looking for. We're paid to think a bit different or they could do it for themselves. And he's a bit different.'

'That silk suit? You were impressed, were you?'

'Oh, yes. With the sharky side taken into account and everything. But — '

'You'd be crazy to put him up, Su.'

'You think? This is what I want to know, see. There was a turn-off factor which I couldn't put my finger on and before I risk it I better be sure if it's just me or if it matters.'

'It's not just you. D'you want to know what Claire says?'

'No, why should I?'

'He's a kerbcrawler.' Cracknell laughed.

'How would Claire know?'

'When he got here and she took his coat, he said, One moment, and he pulls this business card out of the top pocket and he puts it in his wallet. She could read it, it was that girl Marianne from round the corner. The one who always wears dark glasses.'

'Oh?'

'I got talking to her in the butcher's once, she handed me this smart engraved card with her name and number, I thought it was the old charm working and when I rang her up I found I'd made a classic and embarrassing mistake. I mean, to look at her she could quite well be from the law firm next door, the way some of them dress nowadays, unless you know what to look out for, I suppose.'

'I should think he made the same mistake, then,' Su said.

Cracknell grinned. 'Except I've pointed her out to Claire in the street, so she knows her, and she's seen that card. She'd just recognised her strutting past outside, you know the way she sits and stares off when she's typing, and this giant silver Mercedes prowls up and Marianne stops and points at herself, Who, me? and talks to some bloke in the back, pretty obvious what's going on, Claire looks the other way, and a minute later Smeath comes in fiddling with Marianne's card and going sorry he's a bit late but his driver has to find two meters free to park this great Mercedes. Like, I've got a big one. Anyway, look at him. What do you think?'

'Hmm,' Su said.

'I expect that's where he's off to now. For a bit of executive unwinding.'

'Yes, all right, David.'

'I mean I don't have a moral problem with it. The girls opposite my place in Shepherd Market did me a very neighbourly good turn when I had the break-in over Christmas. They could see these two characters at work through my living-room windows, so when the guys came sneaking out the street door they were ambushed with whips and chains and the full armoury of today's modern well-equipped house of pleasure. They dropped all my bits and pieces in their rush to escape. I gave the manageress one of my African masks for the waiting room.'

'Tuh. Your stories.'

'Stories? But look. Right outside this building. No discretion whatsoever. If he's chairman of Imperial he's only got to stop the wrong girl once and get his personalised number taken and we've dropped a very major client in a very sticky mess. They then have to run a whole new search for a replacement, which I rather doubt that we're invited to conduct. And you try floating this company on the back of that.'

'Flotation's not an immediate prospect yet but I take your point,' said Su. 'I might ring him up and see what he's got to say about it.'

'It's something that the guys who do it don't have any real control over, isn't it? He's not going to pack it in.'

'Leave it with me, forget him for now. What am I paying Claire Tarrant out there, do you know?' Su put her feet up on the sofa and studied Spy's Disraeli.

'Eh?' Were those boots clean? 'She wasn't trying to earn points, Su, she was only gossiping.'

'Not like you. Yes, just remind me.'

'I think she's eight and a bit to nine with bonus, and I know places where she'd collar twelve.'

'Bluffer,' said Su. 'Robin and I will be going through the pay review at the weekend. No one's indispensable around here except for him and me, but I'd be sorry to lose little Miss Tarrant and we didn't give her anything for the new job, so we might see about that.'

'She occupies one of your well-spaced soft spots, does she?' Cracknell said.

'Not exactly. They're irrelevant anyhow. Except perhaps in Patrick's case, where it happens to coincide with my view of him as an investment. Your eyes just went for a walk, you disagree?'

'No, don't be so susceptible,' said Cracknell.

'I had a soft spot for Gareth, and the massed Soviet gymnastics team could trampoline on my soft spot for old Spencer Cobbold, but that doesn't mean I chuck money at them if I think they'll find that they've got better ways to spend their days than working here. Even though, unless I mean because, I wish I had as well.'

Cracknell rocked his chair. 'So where do I come in? You promoted me in the field to senior consultant a couple of minutes ago in case you'd forgotten, so what do I command for that?'

'Did I? We'll see when your contract comes up. Heard anything from George Farmer?'

'Well now.' Cracknell shifted in his chair and got comfortable.

'I rather like this room,' said Su. 'It's masculine. I don't know why I gave you funds to do a retart.'

Clocks clap hands.

The amphitracs run round and round the settlement, engines gunning so that everybody knows and stays indoors. The airstrip's taken and the first planeloads of reinforcements are arriving. The admiral stands and waits outside the church, where he's asked by radio to meet the governor and fix surrender terms — he holds a plastic waste bag from the amphitrac in token of a truce because his aide thought he was joking when he said to pack a white flag — but the only ones to show up are some mainlanders who work here. The marines have had them in detention overnight. They explain the governor won't leave the house because the commandos in the garden won't stop shooting, in fact it was a job to get out even with your hands up and a native grasp of Spanish to explain yourself in. Also the big commando leader is now halfway into coma with a live grenade still in his fist.

Distant shots are heard. This can't go on. The admiral and two other officers set off to walk up to the governor's house, their waste bags held in plain view.

The visitor bided in the outer office where a puce and meaty elder volunteer minded the phone, the chief's bodyguards loitered, keeping watch, and tight-jeaned scraggy females sat on plastic chairs and, talking loudly, smoked like trains until their turn to see the chief. They had their shopping, it was first day after giro day, and a circus of small kids with them. They'd be here to ask about plumbing leaks or broken windows the executive wouldn't get around to mending, or security force harassment, or allowances to prisoners' wives. One of them asked the visitor, 'Where you from?'

'Falls party headquarters. I have to have a quick wee business word with Martin in there, I'll try not to keep you waiting too long, OK?'

'Sure, you go ahead, we're just local.'

'Ah, come on.'

The door of the back office opened and the chief showed out the woman he'd been talking to. 'Come by on Monday, then. See where we've got.' Stocky, curly-headed, he was in his trademark cords and crewneck jumper with a tie just showing. He pugged his chin and beckoned to the visitor.

They went through the back office and out the side door to the bog. The chief turned on the taps to fox any listening devices and gave the nod to talk.

Spencer made a few calls on another search and got nowhere. He put a line through the last name on the contact list, ballpoint ripping the paper. He tilted back his chair.

'Yup, yup … and what sort of package do you have at present, roughly, I mean just to get an idea,' murmured Goldie.

Spencer swallowed. In the Dordogne they're turning the tobacco patches over to strawberries piecemeal, see them growing side by side, treats treats. Our wipers going *pluie pluie pluie*, she was driving, on a bend we hit a rabbit, just clipped the head and killed it clean, bloodspots in its ears that's all, she took it back for lovely sister Véronique to cook, *cadeau inattendu, Vévé*. She smokes. Lovely sister smokes, her husband's had a heart attack at 34 and he still smokes.

Raisiny smell when you open the pack, way it must build up under those sheets they cover the Virginia plantations with to keep the leaves moist, shame you lose it soon as you set light.

Troy Donahue kissing the girl on top of the stepladder at the end of that film, two heads in the sheeted white acres as the camera pulls back, the villain was weed baron Karl Malden in a limo with a coroneted R on the doors but he wasn't called Judd Raike the way I always think, that was Dean in *Giant*, oh no, yes he was, Jimmy Dean was Jett Rink.

Lifebelt on the Player's pack, too right. Whole chapter in, what's the one with the stolen V-bomber underwater, *Thunderball*, him and the girl discussing who the Player's sailor was, him and the girl.

Spencer swallowed and looked at his watch. Well gone twelve and it's all coming up.

He stood and pulled on his jacket.

'Going out?' said Stubbs.

'Uhm.'

'Well, you lasted past noon.'

Goldie, off the phone now, sniffed. 'I wish you would light a cigarette up, Spence, the smell of those French ones is relaxing. Reminds me of holidays. Unofficelike.'

'It is rather a *seductive* smell, I suppose,' said Stubbs.

What, said the drug, are we waiting for?

As Spencer passed reception's doorway Claire looked up and started.

'What?'

'Oh, it's you,' said Claire. 'I thought it might be somebody important for a moment.'

'No, it's OK.'

'Do you like my ocelot?' She held up the pad.

He walked in to see. He'd heard the quick scuff-scuffing of her pencil from the hall. 'Great. Anthropomorphic round the eyes though.'

'Is it? I see.' Claire looked. On the far corner of the desk was spread the *Geographic*, open at the photo she was working from. 'Well, mine always are.' She put the pad aside. 'Have you got anything to type?'

'Oh.' She's *offering*. 'Susie got some done but I'll see when I get back. I'm going round the corner.'

Claire said, 'Cracking already. Dear.'

She was never right for you, the drug said.

At X.Y. Jones on Marylebone High Street he noticed something fishy in his change. 'What's this? Irish? Goanese or something?'

The girl said, 'That's a 20p. The new one.'

He scrutinised it. 'It's feeble.'

'Can't leave things alone, can they?'

Gauloises for the office in one pocket, Marlboro for home in the other, he recrossed to the bank and there paid off the electricity account. Coming out he had to make way for a string of seven women in black burkas going in, tallest first shortest last, all fat. Probably in cocktail dresses underneath. At the kerb his favourite traffic warden, the one with the legs and the coppery bun, was having a word with the chauffeur of a monster custard-yellow Rolls that must be theirs, or their master's more like.

'Do us a favour,' said the chauffeur, 'they take these out of my wages.'

If I had a car I'd cruise the streets until I spotted her and then park on the pavement. Intro. Unless there's a boyfriend. Course, always is. Have to track the bastard down and run him over first.

Spencer patted his pockets. Still there. He walked around to John Bell & Croyden, chemist's, Wigmore Street, and left them his prescription. Call back later. He turned up Welbeck Street and unsealed the Gauloises pack. He put the thick French filter in his mouth, stood ready with a match and, as the wind dropped, struck and lit. Before the match hit the pavement he remembered why he'd quit, feeling the same sick taint in the mouth, but too late now.

Foooooled you, the drug said, works every time, I don't know why you listen to me, I really don't.

Willis, with Rachel riding shotgun or actually submachine-gun in the passenger seat of the tuned-up but decrepit-looking Ford Capri, stopped at the barracks gate and showed the card that identified him as an officer of Signals. Rachel passed hers over too. 'Captain Willis, Captain Traynor, we're here to see Captain Sutton.'

The squaddie said, 'Yeah, you're expected, sir, you want the Signals compound, yeah? You make a right past that block — '

'We know the way, thanks.'

'OK, then.' The squaddie turned and waved, the gatepole lifted.

It was a few minutes' drive around the speed-bumped roads. The base was mostly like a redbrick campus and even the Funny House, a concrete bunker short on windows, was not that different from some college libraries.

Willis left Rachel in the messroom. He couldn't take her any further because now that Gareth had got blown the only other person cleared for meets with Tambourine Man was Becky, who was on leave for her father's funeral till next week.

The captain indicated Willis's droopy parka and flared jeans. 'Is that another disguise?'

Willis said, 'I could wear my normal clothes but I feel better if I don't. These go with the car more anyhow.'

They walked along the corridor to Ops. The walls in there were covered with mugshots, charts, maps and location photos. The table was covered with automatic weapons, pocket radios and more maps and photos. Four hard men in leather jackets sat playing cards.

Bespectacled, vestigially moustached Willis felt not too tough. 'Hi.' He'd met them all before.

They nodded at him. The SAS weren't given much to sirring. Their own officers they barely rated, paper-rank civilians from MI5 they'd rather take no notice of at all.

'As we're shortstaffed I've got to make this meet alone, which you should never ever do,' said Willis, 'so this time the back-up's got to work close in, and two of you had better go ahead to check the place out first, and two go in the same time as me.'

Captain Sutton said, 'Fine. Give them the RV point, they'll do the rest, no probs.'

The men put their cards down and sat forward.

The marines, disarmed, their berets snatched for souvenirs, are face down in the road. The mainlanders have finally got the damp Jack to burn for the camera. There are cheers, the louder because the big commando captain died on the stretcher just now. The mainlanders' own flag is shaking out its creases at the head of every staff in the settlement. They've also hung it from windows and draped it over walls and announced that any islander who touches it will be shot.

The marines ignore the burning Jack and think about sleep. The general who is now the islands' governor has come ashore, bringing with him the authority to start changing all the place names, so the marines literally do not know where they are any more.

Cracknell saw the Martian out and went into reception.

Claire typed another confirmation and apology for one of Su Holt's rescheduled appointments. She'd split the list with Fi for something to do.

Cracknell said, 'The first thing that one said when I sat him down was *What a remarkable girl you've got out there.*'

'Shut up.' Claire smiled and typed the envelope.

'He was a nice guy. You do prefer the bastards, though, hey, don't you? Like that appalling Kinley you wanted me to hire instead of old Gareth.'

'Your mistake there, not mine, I'd have thought.'

'See? You haven't forgiven me for it yet. You wanted us to take this guy because you fancied him and what you couldn't *get* which I couldn't *miss* was he wasn't even seriously interested, he was wanking about, he wrote in to say no thanks without waiting to be asked in the end, didn't he?'

'You did keep him waiting. For weeks. You dithered.'

'See?' Cracknell pointed hard. '*Still* there. *Niggling* away.'

'Not Kinley again,' said Goldie, coming in from the stairs. 'I don't believe it. It must be nearly two years.'

'Yes, he could have made a consultant by now,' Claire said. 'Very good one, probably.'

Cracknell said, 'You don't know what the *fucking* hell you're *fucking* on about.'

Claire paled and said quietly, 'Get out. Get out of my sight. Go on.' She stood up and started round the desk.

Goldie backed. Cracknell turned and left.

Claire sat and shuffled envelopes into a block. 'What do you want?'

Goldie said, 'I wondered if you could give me a buzz and let me know as soon as Su goes out, please, if you could.'

'All right.'

'Why is that such an issue still?'

Claire sighed. 'I don't know. It's a thing we do, that's all. He thinks hiring the boy MacMichael was a black mark against him, and I play up to it.'

'Gareth wasn't a complete disaster. Just got fed up making calls.'

'Yes. I was quite taken with him in a way, but I don't tell David that.'

'And Su hired Kenny Thurrock if you want disasters.'

'Yes,' Claire said. 'Well, it stops us rowing over a thousand and one other things, we have a quick row over that and use up all our irritation at once.'

'So did Spencer tell you he saw Kinley in the papers the other day?' said Goldie.

'What?'

'He spotted it when he was meant to be going over the business pages. Apparently Kinley's been remanded for smuggling videos in Poland, or Czechoslovakia, might have been. *Dr Zhivago*, James Bond and things. They gave his background, it's the same guy.'

'Oh.' Claire was turning pink now.

'Still. Enterprising of him, I suppose. He said in court he's with some right-wing freedom organisation, which didn't exactly help the embassy people trying to bail him out.'

'Oh.' She frowned and shuffled the envelopes again. 'Well, that sounds brave. And cranky.'

'Mm.'

'Where do you want to be buzzed?'

'I'll be in David's.' Goldie went out.

Claire found Tara in the back office and said, 'If you take the calls till one, Jenny's got to shop but she'll be back by then, OK? And I'm just going to the loo so keep an ear out.'

On the first half-landing she met Su Holt coming down with affable, florid Ron Bennett who'd arrived ten minutes earlier. 'Evening,' Ron said.

Su was calling, 'Just do it, Fiona. And if anybody rings, say three. Oh. Claire,' she said. 'I won't see you till Monday. Can you make it in by half past eight, show Naomi the ropes?'

'Right.'

'Sorry for these early starts. It won't be unappreciated.'

'Oh, Mr Hull from the florist's rang to apologise, so the delivery people must have reported the complaint OK.'

'You should have put him on. I wanted a word with Mr Hull.'

'I ... think you were busy,' Claire said.

'Never mind, I'll get him later. Bye.'

Back at her desk Claire dialled Cracknell. 'Tell Patrick Su's just gone. I'm not waiting for your visitor.' She hung up and dialled Spencer. 'Your letters are in your folder to sign. I'll be leaving once I've cleared my desk, so, are you going to be ready?'

'Right. I'll see you down there.'

Cracknell walked in. 'Look, don't bugger me about. I'm sorry I shouted. Now give it five more minutes, OK?'

Goldie followed him. 'Come on, David, won't take that long.' He dragged Cracknell out to the hallway. 'Anyone can let him in.'

'It's not a him. And how do I look if I haven't even got a secretary?'

'Laid–back and dynamic. I suppose a lot of these money people must be women nowadays, are they?' Goldie had talked Cracknell halfway up the stairs already.

'It's not a money person, it's the person I need to get the money people interested.'

Fiona came out to the landing. 'You two. Hullo. Are you plotting something?'

Goldie chuckled, 'What?' and looked at Cracknell as if he hadn't noticed he was there.

'Fi,' Cracknell said, 'I want you.'

'Oh, but I've got to see Claire,' said Fiona.

'Later. I'm very busy too so do as *I* say, *now*, and come and give me your guidance.'

Fiona smirked and clucked. 'Oh, all right, masterful.' She followed Cracknell down.

Claire gathered up her magazines and drawing things, her box of multicoloured paper handkerchiefs and copy of *The Right Stuff*, to load her bag. She found the tiny scent bottle she hardly ever used and gave herself a touch behind the ears and inside each wrist. The entryphone sounded. 'Hullo?'

Spencer lifted his coat from the hook and went over to the window. The front door banged below. It wasn't raining and when he put his head out the air was mild. 'Won't need this, will I.' He hung the coat again. 'See you, Suze.'

'Someone's cheerful,' Stubbs said. 'Did you sort things out?'

'I'll tell you later.' Going down, he passed John in the basement coming up to the men's loo. Not often encountered, John in the basement was an ex-executive and now Su's personal researcher. 'Hi, John.'

'Is Mrs Holt gone out to lunch yet, do you know? She didn't seem to be at home just now.'

'Spose so.' On the first floor Spencer looked into Fiona's office, empty. The door to Su's was open. 'Hullo?' He craned in.

'Jeez, I thought you must be John again,' said Goldie, crawling from the kneehole of the desk.

'Hi, Rick.'

'He just came mooching round humming to himself. If he sees me she'll know.' Goldie went through a drawer. 'Her proper files are a blank so it's down to this as usual and she keeps her desk in no known order at all.'

'Should let Fi in on it.'

'You can't, she'd go and blurt something, it's not like when Carolyn was here.'

'Anyway I would keep watch,' said Spencer, 'but I've got to be off.'

'Can't you — ?'

'No, got to go. Try locking yourself in.' Spencer skittered down to ground and bulked into reception. 'Hi there.'

Claire gave him a social smile. A slim, diminutive, loose-haired blonde was looking at the Daniell print above the chesterfield. Green hessian jacket, short short black stretch skirt in last-word fashion, black leggings. The hair hid her profile. She must be Cracknell's movie mogul. She didn't look like one, not with a tapestry bag, but films were a weird business. 'We off?' he asked Claire.

'In a minute.'

'David's?' he mouthed with a jerk of the head.

Claire nodded.

'David'll be a couple of minutes while we straighten something out,' he said, half over his shoulder, to the little woman's back.

'Oh, yes. Thanks,' she said, bright shy gawky voice not unfamiliar, and glanced round.

It's —

Spencer, with whole-body pins and needles and still not quite sure why, walked over to her. He waved a finger at the picture. 'That's Jama Masjid mosque, Old Delhi. Where I was attacked by a large mob on the last night of Ramadan for being seen passing with a girl who had her hair uncovered. We had to keep running till we got the other side of a line of police with rifles.'

She turned to look at him full face, listen to yourself, and he realised how stupidly he was trying to impress at the same time as he realised who she was.

The big mouth, the strong cheekbones, the blue sharp-shaped eyes with funny gull-wing brows, the whole face like a perfect unexpected theorem. Nobody could look like that but she does. He saw double for an instant, the real face and the magazine cover he fell for aged seven. She was even better in person than in pictures, which was not the normal way of it.

'Sorry,' he said.

She turned back to the Daniell. 'I haven't been to India since I was a girl and I've got to fly out there on Monday. I'm quite excited.'

'For a film?'

She nodded, keen. 'They're making, do you know the novel, *Heat and Dust*? It should be very good.'

'I've read that. You're not the wayward memsahib, are you?'

'No, she's a new discovery. Terrific, apparently. I'm much too old.'

Say nothing flattering. Spencer sat down on the chesterfield and looked at Claire, who did her silent laugh. 'Are you?' he asked the little blonde, and worked out that she must be over forty now, which made no sense, since to look at her she couldn't possibly be more than twenty-five.

'Have you been there?' she asked Claire.

'No,' Claire said, 'too scared of diseases.'

'But you've lived in Africa,' said Spencer.

'That's why, Spencer.'

'Have you? Oh, which bit?' said the woman.

'Rhowhoooahzimbabwe.'

'Mmhm.' The woman nodded, her immense and glorious lower lip stuck out. 'Is that — where you come from?'

'No, English.' Claire lifted her hands in spirals and laughed. 'Nomad.'

'Uhuh.' The woman sat down next to Spencer.

She just sat down next to me.

She said with a muggy unsure look, 'Sorry, was it Spencer?'

'Yeah.' Don't offer a paw.

Instead of telling him her name, which would have been a nice but phoney thing to do, she cocked her head and smiled.

'I like your voice,' she said.

Spencer rubbed his face. 'Oh.'

'He has a great voice,' Claire said, 'that's what we employ him for.'

'Gareth had the great voice,' said Spencer, 'I just rumble.' In urgent need of a diversion he asked the woman, 'What's that badge?'

She looked at her lapel. 'No Cruise.'

'Uh. Have you been down to the airbase, then?'

'Yes, well, it's … ' fiddling with her bag strap, 'something that's important … Are you interested? I think I've got some leaflets.' She brought out one with the usual symbols and graphics.

'Uh, all right, thanks.' Do not ask her to autograph it.

Claire, who had nothing against nukes at all, wound hair round a finger.

'I carry them about,' the woman said, 'because if you look on the back there's a big London meeting coming up in summer, James Cameron's speaking, I think two Nobel Prize winners, you can see, anyway that's an invitation.'

'Thank you. You're not down,' said Spencer.

'I'm not an expert, I'd dry up without lines. But I should be back by then, maybe give platform introductions.'

'Yeah. So are you thinking of doing David's film?'

'It's — certainly a project I'd like to talk about, yes.'

'Are there many film producers who do ordinary office jobs as well?'

'In this country, most of them, I think.' She looked at her watch.

Spencer looked at his. 'I'll see if I can hurry things up.'

As he reached the stairs Goldie came down, waving Gregory's papers. 'Got it. I thought you'd gone.'

'I would have but it's complicated.' Spencer stepped back into reception. 'That's it, he's coming.'

She smiled again.

Cracknell, Goldie and Fiona milled in. 'It's great to see you,' Cracknell said. 'I'm sorry you've been waiting.'

'Oh, we've been fine,' she said.

Claire drew on her white cardigan, knotting the woollen belt, and over that her blue mac, one of those new ones that toned darker towards the bottom as if they were dripping dry, the only thing she ever wore that Spencer didn't like.

Fiona was asking about another diary problem. 'Check with my copy there,' said Claire, 'no clash fine, any trouble leave a note.' She grabbed her bag.

Spencer had drifted to the front door. He held it open for Claire. The film star, there in the hallway with Cracknell, did a little fluster, like where'd they go, and said bye. Claire and Spencer grinned and shuffled out.

On the step Spencer said, 'Did you know that was who was coming?' He folded the leaflet away in a pocket.

'Yes.' Claire set a good pace round the corner into Welbeck Street.

'David said a key player, I thought he meant some tax

accountant. Right, what are we doing?'

'I don't know, you're in charge, but I want to get some things anyway.'

'Right.'

On Marylebone High Street he noticed the news-stand.

INVASION 'UNDER WAY'

'They've gone and done it,' he said. 'Wait a sec.' He bought a *Standard* and they stood looking at it. Picture of a warship, emergency cabinet meeting, utmost gravity, massive land, sea and air forces employed, Royal Navy vessels diverted from exercises off Gibraltar in response, still funny when you thought what it was all about but not that funny.

'Is this how wars start?' he said.

'I don't know.'

The odd fat raindrop hit the paper.

'Shit,' he said, 'it's raining.'

'Why didn't you bring your coat?'

'I was in a good mood.'

'Come on.'

Gareth slung the shoulder holster on and stood tugging his shirt straight.

The phone went. 'Yeah.'

'Gareth. Carl. Bit of news, if you wanted to pop up.'

'I was on my way out, but a couple of minutes won't hurt.'

'Fine.'

Gareth didn't take his jacket because the stolen library book effect was too ridiculous. Cath was out so he put his wallet in his back pocket. He went down the corridor, still adjusting cuffs, past two Labour and Unions analysts who stood well aside to let him by. People didn't react like that when he was carrying the rig in his hand, only when he wore it.

Upstairs in Terrorism he passed through Middle East and into Irish Section. Carl sat back behind his terminal. 'Ah, the novelty braces.'

'I've got to be somewhere else. What's up?'

'We had Nigel on the scrambler,' Carl said. 'Tambourine Man's called, he's seeing him any time now, thought you'd like to know.'

'OK. Unscheduled, was it?'

'Quite. We may be nearer solving your little problem. If Tambo's being sent to join the unit over here, then obviously we can scoop them up.'

'Yeah, that'd be nice.'

'I'll fill you in when Nigel rings back. One thing though.' Carl tapped his keys and called the bulletin file up on his screen. 'Our friend O'Grady dropped in on his nibs.'

Gareth read. 'What's that about?'

'It could be elections, but I doubt. Assuming Tambourine Man's right, O'Grady does run Mainland, we were thinking on the lines of some spectacular they might be getting up to celebrate this small colonial event you may conceivably have heard about. Rub our noses in it sort of thing. They'd need McGuinness's approval.'

'They'll do that, sure, they'll do that anyway, or else they're off the front page, but it's a bit headless chicken, isn't it?'

'Well, it would have to be short notice. But we did wonder. Do you think the panic could be that they've blown Tambourine Man, and that's why he wants to meet? Either been caught, and he's setting Nigel up for them, or not been caught and feels like asking for protection?'

'No idea.'

'Against that argument O'Grady must still think his cover's good.' Carl cleaned his aviator glasses on his tie.

'They might not know our man knew about him.'

' Aah, mm.'

'What did Nigel reckon?'

'We haven't spoken since that turned up, he's out now,' said Carl. 'I could reach him if need be. How good was your hold on this chap? I mean there's money but he can't touch it, and you caught him shifting a tagged weapon, so we could stick him for possession with intent, I suppose, not much.'

'It wasn't that, it was the woman.'

'Which? I don't think that's on my brief anywhere.'

'No,' said Gareth. 'She was the property of a very nasty operator who's serving a tenner inside. But he could still put word out and get things done to him if we let him know the guy was seeing her.'

'Certain rules against that,' Carl said.

'Doesn't matter as long as he believes we'd do it. And since then he's in too deep, he couldn't do a deal with them. I mean they could force him to cooperate, but he knows he'd end up in a ditch with a sack on his head either way. And I think we convinced him that even if he could do a deal we'd take him out ourselves.'

'Rules again,' said Carl.

'You haven't actually worked in the field, have you, Carl?'

'Wild horses.'

'It's all you level-headed people saying no that means the one or two of us a year who do sign up for it get thrown straight in the deep end.'

'You said he's in too deep,' said Carl. 'We haven't had that much from him in Mainland, not to damage them. So this was before, in his local unit, was it? Am I allowed to know about that?'

'I don't think you need to. You can ask Nigel if he'd ask Tom, he could clear it. Shouldn't think he would.'

Carl capped and uncapped a ballpoint. 'The Battle of Shit Creek, for example, connection there?'

'Brown's Brook, they shot another guy for that,' said Gareth.

'A Special Branch asset, in point of fact. Who was nothing to do with it, according to persistent rumour.'

'Put about by Special Branch,' said Gareth.

In this greengrocer's the assistant wore a suit.

'What fruit have you got in the house?' said Claire, packing salad stuffs away in her bag.

'Shouldn't think any,' Spencer said.

'You ought to eat fruit.' She gave orders to the suited man, who brought her apples, oranges, grapes, bananas, figs and in-shell peanuts.

'It's not all yours,' said Claire, 'I'm taking some home.'

'Oh,' said Spencer. He paid and made Claire give him the bags to carry, but he still felt mothered, taken care of, warm.

They moved on up the High Street, turning to look at each

other and smiling every few steps.

'Where now?' she said.

'Druce and Craddock's along here.'

'OK.'

'Doubtful about the bacon at home. Hi, John.'

Claire looked round. 'What? Was that John in the basement?'

'Yeah, saw him coming down from the post office.'

'Did he ignore you?'

'No, he lifted his eyebrows.'

'Oh,' said Claire. 'He always ignores me. Pretends he hasn't seen me. Even on the stairs.'

'He's just shy of you.'

'I don't see why.'

Spencer said patiently, 'Because you're beautiful.'

Claire tucked in her chin. 'Huh.'

Spencer said, 'What's it like?'

'What?'

'What's it like?' he said louder. 'Being beautiful.'

'I don't know.' She shook her head.

'What percentage of it is a nuisance, for instance?'

'None of it, really.'

'No? I thought there was meant to be endless bother.'

'There is, but that's just being a woman,' Claire said, 'you don't have to be specially ... Anyway I'm not, I'm too short.'

Spencer thumbed over his shoulder with his free hand. 'She was short. Shorter than you. Tiny.'

Claire shrugged. 'That's true. Did you notice she fancied you?'

'Yup,' Spencer said.

Claire bumped him.

'Sorry,' he said.

At the butcher's Spencer got in half a pound of streaky and tried a fantasy of walking round a small French market with her, but it didn't work that well, she'd make him do the talking, she'd boggle at the Saxon stuff they hadn't got, like bacon, she'd fret over the doomed live chickens that brought back sticky childhood memories, she wouldn't wow the locals with her eye for a special fish or cheese, she'd just impress the shifty moped boys who Spence would have to give that fuck-off look to show he knew what they were saying. She'd be a tourist. The sunshine still felt good, though, and she was adorable in T-shirts.

Outside, he put his bags down on the rain-starred pavement between his feet. 'There'll be a taxi in a minute, plenty come down here.'

'Su said she won't be back till three in case you're worried,' Claire said.

'Oh uh. Well, we can't hang about.' He looked up and down the road.

'Actually, this is pretty silly, you just carry on if you like and I'll — '

'Cut that out.' He looked up and down the road again. 'Have you ever been to my house?'

'No, not yet.'

'Where were you when I had the party?'

'On holiday, I think. Everybody said it was good.'

'Nnh. Was.'

'How long does it take to get there?'

'Ten minutes with no traffic.'

Claire mulled that.

'Here's one,' Spencer said. 'No. Taken.'

They watched it go by, lamp unlit.

'I don't like white ones anyway,' said Claire.

'No, they do a lot of stupid colours now. Red, blue, brown, lilac, Benson and Hedges gold. People come from all over the world for a go in a black cab and what do they get?'

'Hey, I think it's pulling up, it's dropping someone off.'

Further down a woman in hussar jacket and pencil skirt disembarked and paid.

'Do we run?' said Claire.

'Yeah, go on.' Spencer gathered up the bags.

Gareth turned to go, turned back and said, 'What happened with the name he coughed up last time, this Louise de Cameron?'

'Ah. Yes. She does exist, oddly enough,' said Carl. 'Have you ever drunk a Château same?'

'Yes, it's a Pécharmant. I told Richard to look it up, you were skiing.'

'OK, well, those are her people. They buggered off after Bonnie Prince Charlie and made good in Frog and some of them have slithered back across the Channel since. Are you Scots?' Carl said suddenly. 'Sorry.'

'I'm from Hertfordshire,' said Gareth.

'Yes, but, ancestry.'

'I think my grandfather was Ulster Scots. But then Mac-Michael's a branch of clan Stewart, which is originally ethnic Welsh.'

'The Stewarts? So you're descended from royalty?'

'I am royalty. Unfortunately so's Rod Stewart. And so's John McMichael the UFF boss. What about Louise, then?'

'She's, oh, she's twenty-four, convent, art school, works as a photographers' agent.' Carl opened a drawer. 'Little black BMW, place in Notting Hill. One of those. Now get the pictures.' He pulled out some glossy candids taken by the watchers. In and out of restaurants and taxis, smiling often, large mane, overdone clothes. 'All that hair, apparently that's red.'

'Yeah?' Gareth looked at the shots.

'Not bad. I wouldn't mind,' said Carl.

'Are they still watching her?'

'Actually no, no funny business after two weeks, so Inspector Draper took them off.'

'That's not very good,' said Gareth.

'The Yard didn't like the overtime bill.'

'Can't we use our own people?'

'They're a bit pushed, and I've really got nothing to go on. Tambourine Man only said he'd heard the name. The phone calls aren't worth transcribing, nothing too untoward in the bank records yet, though we think she's got accounts we haven't traced. There is her FBI file.'

'Her what?' said Gareth.

'It's tolerably harmless. We asked the Washington office to ask the cousins and it appeared via Grosvenor Square the same day. They have these wonderful machines that transmit documents straight down the phone lines. She was in New York on bona fide business and she turned up at some fundraising do for the cause. About a year ago and once since. In fact, Washington office did tell us back then, because the girls at Curzon Registry have got her name down, but then whose haven't they?'

'We've had her on file for a year?'

'So it seems.'

'Was that where she got involved, New York? Someone she met then?'

'Ahm — don't know,' said Carl. 'Obviously we're talking in terms of some fiery-eyed patriot getting his tackle into her at some point. But whether it was a *coup de foudre* in Manhattan or a slow awakening of her womanly instincts while she was at art school I couldn't say. At any rate, I'd be hard-pressed. As no doubt was she.' Carl studied the photographs on his desk.

'I'm late,' said Gareth.

'Righto. Well. Shame they didn't post you back to us instead of the Trots-under-the-cot lot downstairs, but that would have made too much sense, I suppose. How is it?'

'They don't like Cath and me looking at their casework. Let alone reporting it up to Home Office. I think they think we're part of the conspiracy. Still, we're being taken off the report for a bit to try and find the people who really might lob petrol bombs into naval dockyards if war starts. Down there they don't know who that might be. Too busy drawing diagrams of how gays have infiltrated the BBC.'

Mattie looked both ways along the street and seeing no one but that coloured girl with junior in the buggy there he crossed, ran up the steps and found his keys. Last look and in. The hallway smelt like old potato sacks. A flashy try-this-offer envelope addressed to K.H. Best the downstairs girl was lying on the meter cupboard, meaning somebody had picked it off the mat. Rory wouldn't do that and the top floor two were at their jobs all day. Mattie went up to the first-floor landing quietly, listened at the flat door and let himself in.

'It's me,' she said. She was on the couch, her legs stuck out in purple trousers and a pair of cowboy boots. 'I have to go, I'm late for lunch with someone. Just as well you came back as I didn't want to have to leave a note.'

Mattie stuck the little German automatic back into his waistband, safed.

'Careful how you do that,' she said.

'Where's your car?' said Mattie.

'I left it just off Church Street, no tails, if there were I would have nipped into the Vortex Gallery.' She put a picture magazine with foreign title in her bag.

'You wouldn't see them, they work a relay so you never spot the same one twice.'

Standing up she was as tall as Mattie. She had a wet-look black belt on, so wide it came up to her paisley-shirted boobs. Her quilted satin bomber jacket changed its colour in the light, green to maroon, you got a headache just to look at her. But in this town she wasn't that unusual except the long red hair. 'Anyway,' she said. 'I had a visit at the office from a friend who has a friend who's had a phone call,' and she heaved a nervy sigh, 'and. It seems you should be making plans to leave.'

Mattie listened with a hardman stare.

Over there, young Sean with his hair and blouson silvered from the misty drizzle went into the supermarket. Miriam was sat at one checkout, the manager at the other. Sean asked Miriam, 'Where's Evie, on her dinner hour?'

'Just missed her.' Miriam entered two large Coke bottles on the till. 'There she goes.'

Sean turned. Evie in her ski jacket passed the plate-glass front as she came round from the staff door. Sean ran out. 'Hiya. Seen Liam?'

Evie said, surprised, 'Hi, no, why, should I?'

'Someone's got a job for him, he doesn't seem to be around.'

'Job?'

'House needs emptying.'

'You asked his mum?' said Evie.

'She didn't know, he comes and goes.'

'If you're trying all of that man's exes, Sean, you'll have a busy day.'

The tree by the spiritualist temple was in deep pink blossom. The rain had stopped. Spencer paid off the taxi at the corner and they walked along the narrow lane that made up this side of Rochester Square. The tendrils of the high hedge round the plant nurseries straggled overhead and almost touched the upper window ledges of the houses. 'This is nice,' said Claire. 'An arcade.'

'It just needs clipping back, they'll do it any day.'

'Which is your house?'

'End of this row facing us.'

'So ... yes, have you got brothers and sisters?' That followed. She'd spent the ride here asking all about his housesharers. It was good and womanlike and necessary get-to-know-you stuff and all the same it made him feel he'd rather be alone without the tension.

He must have mentioned Helen before but he reminded her. 'My big sister. She teaches at Brighton Poly, runs a huge motorbike.'

'That's right, you've said. Do you get on?'

'She's great. I scarcely see her though.'

'My brother's so much older than me I don't know what he's like,' said Claire. 'Well, half-brother.'

'What's he do?'

'Something in chemicals. He gets around the world, I gather.'

Better ask. 'Which one of your parents was married before?'

'My father was. I think she walked out.'

At Spencer's corner they had to wait for a police car that turned out of the mews. The hatless crew looked them over as it rumbled past.

'We get a lot of those lately.'

'Rough neighbourhood?'

'Not as far as I know.'

They crossed to the house and mounted the steps. Next door's magnolia was out. 'You've got those council blocks,' said Claire, pointing across the square.

Messing with his keys he let that go. The afternoon they heard the Oxford Street explosion kill the bomb disposal officer she was grumbling for the rope. She might think council flats should all be piped for tear gas like the miners' hostels on the Rand.

Come on, said the drug. So she's old-fashioned. Nothing you can't live with. It's your pre-match nerves at work, that's all. Talk of matches, got a light?

'Where's Gareth's place?' said Claire.

'Right along the mews there at the side,' said Spencer.

'Is it? We were at his thing there when he left but this area doesn't ring a bell.'

'It was dark.' He tripped the second lock and gave the sticking door a shove. That 'we' could mean the two of them, the office people as a body, or her and the oil-prospecting boyfriend she'd brought along. Been brought by, you'd have thought, the way she clung on meek and silent.

Which made it promising that now she stood so passive in the hallway, neck drawn in, shy, waiting for an invitation before she shed an outdoor thread or set foot further. Or she might just be being well brought up.

If she pleaded starvation and got down to sandwich-making right away he could take it that there wasn't much chance anything would happen. They always act busy when they want to block your move.

'Come in,' he said. He crowded her through to the living room and left her standing in mid-carpet while he went to dump the groceries on the kitchen floor and out of sight. Coming back he threw his jacket over a dining chair. 'I'll hang your mac.'

'This carpet,' Claire said, shaking her head at the ankle-deep green shag. 'You could graze sheep on it.'

'I like it. D'you want anything to drink, like flat Perrier? We've got about three half-empty bottles.'

'Half-full, Spence. That's all right.' As she unbuttoned the drip-dry mac she turned away from him. On the hint, if it was one, he stepped up behind her to take it. She laughed and got out of the coat with playful shrugs.

'OK. Wait a second.' He hung the mac and doubled back for the drinks.

As he passed Claire she fluffed out her hair and said in the low voice she'd settled on since coming in, 'Your file's out there, don't forget it this time.'

'Eh?'

'Your file.'

'Yeah.' He defridged a bottle and poured water into tumblers. It fizzed unexpectedly. Claire followed him into the kitchen, which he didn't want because she might turn busy. He thrust a glass at her. 'There. I could put lime juice in it, or the fag end of this white Burgundy Miles likes to make his kirs with.' Talking about fag ends, the drug said.

'A spritzer,' said Claire. 'Go on, then, just a bit.'

Accepting alcohol was positive but they could still get bogged down in lunch-fixing. Spencer was too tense to look at food, and getting tenser.

'Someone cooked chili con carne last night,' Claire said, eyeing a pan full of dishwater with telltale beans and mince afloat.

'Me.'

'Are you a good cook?' She smiled and drank, leaning back against the worktop.

'I can be but I get bored with it.'

She looked over her shoulder. 'I like the magnolia.'

'Yeah.' He went out to find the cigarettes in his jacket pocket, hoping to draw her off. She didn't follow, so she'd probably start to unpack shopping. He lit up and stared at the french windows and the back garden where the apple tree was flowering. You could hardly see the housebacks beyond the gardens the way you could in winter, and of course they could hardly see you, but that might be a useless advantage now.

Claire said almost in his ear, 'Whose room is that?'

'Through there, that's mine.' He blushed. She'd come out. She was going with it. Make time not sandwiches.

'It looks small,' she said.

'It's just a boxed-off corner of this living room.' He went and rapped the thin partition.

Claire looked round the open door, hanging on the jamb, one leg stuck out high behind her in a classical arabesque. 'Cosy if you don't want to go to bed too early.'

She just said bed. He took a drag. 'I had last pick, I'm the lowest paid.'

She swivelled on her toes to face him and brought down the high leg, planting the foot at right angles outward. 'You've got her on your wall.'

He thought a moment. 'Yeah.'

'I forgot you're a film buff.'

'I'm not, I just like films.'

'What sort? What's a good film?'

'Shit, I don't know. On now?'

She shook her head with a gentle smile. 'Just generally.'

He swallowed the last of his drink, mixed stronger than hers. '*Citizen Kane*.'

'You're a film buff.'

'*Les Enfants du Paradis*,' he said, to be difficult.

She shrugged, head on one side.

'*Goldfinger*,' he suggested.

'Oh, yes.'

'*Bad Day at Black Rock. Gumshoe. Billy Liar. The Apartment. The Third Man. Touch of Evil. Hud*.' He puffed. '*Electra Glide in Blue. Lacombe, Lucien. A Canterbury Tale. A Matter of Life and Death*.'

'David Niven, is that?'

'*Casablanca*.'

'Another one I've seen. Well, I like ... *Gone With the Wind*.'

'Never seen it. *The Maltese Falcon. Point Blank*.'

'Ahm,' she consulted the ceiling, '*Great Expectations*.'

'*If* ... '

'*Ben Hur*.'

'*Bof!*'

Claire wrinkled her nose. '*Bof!*?'

'It's French. Means yeah, well, anyway, so what. It's a black comedy.'

'Well, I've mostly only seen films at school,' said Claire, 'and some on TV since I came to live here. Like the David Niven, I remember having a late takeaway and being in a very strange mood.'

That would be a reference to oil prospectors so he made an understanding Mm but didn't pick it up.

She looked at him. 'All right, what's good on now?'

If they made a date there was a hefty possibility she'd put things off till then. '*Céleste*, here at the Camden Plaza. Great reviews,' said Spencer. 'It's about old Marcel Proust. In German. I haven't seen it yet.'

'Are you inventing this?'

'No. *Reds*, maybe. I'll look in the paper in a minute, if you like.'

'OK ... Show me round your garden?' Claire said, putting her glass on the dining table with his.

'Sure.' He guided her over to the french windows, an unnecessary hand on her shoulder. 'You didn't make this cardigan, did you?'

'No, I bought it. What's wrong with it?'

'Nothing, I like it,' he said. 'The knit's big for machine-made so I wondered.'

'Hm.'

He undid the four stiff window bolts with one sharp macho yank at each in rapid order top and bottom. He drew blood from a knuckle but not much. The key was on the bookshelf where he wanted it. The tricky under-used lock gave at the third twist. He and Miles had taken turns for half the afternoon to make it work last Saturday while Katie ferried mugs of tea, but Paul had had it out and fiddled with it over Monday breakfast.

Spencer drew the hinged frames inward crisply.

'You really know how to open french windows,' Claire said with ironic uh-huh nods but the same gentle smile.

He stepped out on to the new planked balcony. She came to the wooden rail beside him and they stood looking round and listening to the birds.

'When did you last cut the grass?' she said.

'Before winter. Paul likes doing it so he'll get around to it, but he's been away the last few weekends. You have to run miles of extension cable out from the utility room in the basement and then try not to drive the mower over it, it's tedious. I think the grass is fine like this, deep and plushy.'

'It's a good stretch of lawn. Can we go down?'

'Right.'

He felt awkward on the steps because of trouser cramp. They moved along the border and he pointed out the two yellow tulips, the white daffodils and the things that looked like hyacinths the size of bluebells. Claire gave swishing kicks at the grass and said, 'It's wet.' She detoured over to the weeping willow, parted the trailing branches and went inside the tree's tent, where there was a patch of bare earth. 'Dry here.'

Spencer sucked the blood off his knuckle, put his hands in his pockets to straighten himself up while he had a moment's respite away from her side, scanned above to see if there were any swifts around yet, but they were still in Africa, and wondered whether the cigarette he'd left burning in the ashtray would tip off and scorch the dining table.

He went in under the willow.

'Hullo,' said Claire.

'Hi.'

They considered the pattern of the branches against the sky. Their sleeves were touching and the tension hit voluptuous extremes. Spencer shivered. There was an inexorable push past his waistband and up inside his shirt. He shivered again and resisted the mock-surprise expression on his face in case Claire was looking at him. He glanced aside. She was looking at him. She smiled, so he smiled back.

'Are you going to kiss me?' she said. She let the smile fade and the blue eyes widen.

Two cars ahead, the Geordie SAS man indicated left and Willis nearly missed it. He clamped teeth on his Three Fives filter and flicked the column stalk. The wipers stopped. He wasn't used to Fords. He tried again and set the horn off. He had to brake as the next car slowed behind the Geordie's Vauxhall. He shouldn't have let it keep there but he hadn't had a chance to overtake. Near stalling, he changed down. He'd veered into the middle of the road. He hooked back to avoid a gravel lorry, changed down again, restarted the wipers and found left flash. The Geordie was in his earpiece with, 'What's the matter, are we going wrong?'

Willis switched the radio in his pocket to two-way and said, activating the throat mike, 'Nothing, sorry mate, got the controls mixed up.' The cigarette dropped out.

'OK.' The Geordie turned off, the next car carried on.

Willis scrabbled in his lap to get the cig back as he swung wide round the turn. He recovered, missing a minibus, and gunned in second to close up on the Vauxhall's tail. The tweaked Capri leapt. Willis laughed. They were fine for time and the advance pair of lookouts hadn't reported any bad signs at the rendezvous yet. Even around here you were more likely to die in a car crash than a firefight.

'Lights,' said the Geordie.

'Cheers.' Willis doused them. The wipers were squeaking dry but when he tried the intermittent sweep the screen starred over. He wished it would either pack in or rain properly.

Claire broke the kiss, catching Spencer's wrists as he let her go and pulling him out through the wet willow branches. She walked on to the apple tree, frisking her hair for bits of foliage. He wandered after her. 'Are the apples any good?' she said.

'They're, no, they're awful.'

'Ah well.' She looked up. 'I used to have a great tree house, in New Zealand.'

'Yeah?'

'With a rope ladder I could pull up. Which wasn't much use because my dad could still reach in and grab me if I didn't want to come indoors.'

'Mm.' She likes a fight. Once found her arm-wrestling the boy MacMichael on the reception desk, won too, cheated using both arms, mind.

The neighbour's cat jumped on to the wall. Claire patted her knees and made soft clucks and heys but it only sat and curled its tail around and waited. 'No? ... Bye then,' she said to it, and began moving off towards the house with a look at Spencer to see if that would be all right.

At the steps he nodded her on first and admired her as she went up. The cat mewed right behind them. It was a following cat, nuisance to get rid of sometimes. Claire looked over the rail and coaxed, 'What?' It froze, havered and bolted. 'Lost my touch,' she said.

'No, it just does that, then it comes after you again,' said Spencer. 'Let's get in.'

'What do we wipe our feet on?'

'Uh, the planks, we need a new mat.'

'I see.'

Inside, he thought of putting on a record but he didn't know what. Claire checked her bright yellow watch and said, 'Oh. Still over an hour.'

'No rush, she's keeping us in this evening anyway.' He fingered albums.

Claire gave a small sigh so that he turned to look at her. Head on one side, smiling, she untied the belt of the white cardigan. It didn't have buttons. She put her shoulders back and slipped it off, slowly, sexually, offering the smart jut of those special breasts inside her blouse. Spencer's mouth dried. Claire was making herself laugh. She dropped the cardigan on an armchair, clasped hands behind her head and asked, 'Can we eat in a minute?' with a lifting note, like maybe not right now.

'In a minute,' Spencer said.

A silence fell. They stood six feet apart, staring at each other. 'Come here, then,' Claire said, stepping up to him.

Sean couldn't see Danny so he tried the other bar and couldn't see him in there either, but when he came back Danny was sitting by an almost empty pint that had the table to itself a minute ago. 'I didn't see you.'

'I took a piss,' said Danny. 'What have you got?'

'Evie Sullivan says he goes out to see his auntie at the Island,' nickname for a Catholic town in Protestant farmland a few miles away.

'His auntie?' Danny said. 'He never had one out there. Little Evie's putting you on.'

'She's not a real auntie,' Sean said. 'He calls her his auntie

Stephens, she's Miss Molly Stephens, he used to stay with her when he was a kid. His mum used to chuck him out if he'd done something.'

'Oh, her. She didn't live there,' Danny said.

'Maybe she's moved since then. Evie went there with him once, like instead of going to meet the parents, because she's a bit of a good girl and that was part of how he got round her. The auntie's a nice old lady and she said he'd never introduced his girlfriends to her before so it was like special.'

Danny lit a Major without offering.

'No thanks, Danny,' said Sean.

Danny flicked the pack across the table. 'Help yourself then.'

'Well, is it worth checking out? Because it's somewhere he goes and people don't know.'

'Leave that to us,' said Danny. 'You get on home and stick in case you're wanted.'

Mattie stood before the bathroom mirror trimming his moustache with scissors so that he could shave it off. The light in here was good, the house backed on to a reservoir, no buildings blocking out the sky. 'So what do you think?' he said.

Rory, leaning by the door, said, 'If the girl's OK they don't know where we are, the best they're going to do is put our pictures out. There's no one sitting in parked cars around here, I don't reckon she was followed. We could sit tight.'

'She wants us moving, though. If she can fix this plane to pick us up she wants our target notes and all our dropsites to give the other guys tonight.'

'Yeah?' Rory said. 'And what do you want?'

'If they're saying do one job and then get out and that comes straight from chief-of-staff I'm not about to argue.'

'Do one rush job.'

'Yeah. We're up to that.'

'If we're such a bad risk they could give it to the other guys.'

'Maybe they've been told to do one too,' said Mattie. 'Or we're more expendable, or even we're more reliable. Anyway they want their money's worth out of us and they need to do something to kick the Brits while they're down, which is the best time to kick somebody if you're going to.'

'It'd have to be a soft target,' Rory said.

'Yeah,' said Mattie. 'Well, let's get the notes out and see.'

Danny waited on the corner feeling antsy with the nearly new five-hundred-dollar automatic that he'd just untaped from underneath the roof of Sharon Long's kid's rabbit hutch now held inside his folded local rag.

Wolverhampton Pat drove up and kerbed the Datsun long enough for Danny to get in.

'All right then?' Danny said.

'Sure,' said Wolverhampton Pat. He thumbed at the toolbag behind the front seats.

The road wound down through apple orchards with their first dusting of blossom, and once or twice Willis saw the lough far off between the hills. Pausing behind the Geordie at a small T-junction he pulled the Browning and tucked it ready under his thigh on the seat.

They crossed the ancient humpback bridge with the noisy little stream going under. They were in a pocket of republican territory here. The next village was the one with only four males under forty still alive and at liberty, steel front doors put in to stop the loyalists from down the road. At a turn there was a signpost reading 'BROWN'S BROOK 6', with a whitish spraycan splotch where some loyalist came and fixed it to '6–0' after the army's big score against the mortar gang and some republican fixed it back again.

A mile on at a crossroads the verge was piled with wilting flowers to mark where the republicans shot a gasman because he used to be a weekend soldier. More of that was going on since Liam moved from local intelligence to join the Mainland operation.

The road ran between loyalist fields again. One of these bends was where last year the loyalists shot up a minibus full of workmen going home to the mixed but mainly Catholic town ahead. The town had next to no republicans in it up till then.

The cars came into the thirty limit on the outskirts. Turning into the crabby one-way system Willis glanced down the main street, the same bomb-damaged shops still boarded up.

Danny came out of the post office and walked back to the Datsun. 'Yeah, she's in the phone book. The guy says you take a left at the end by the garage and it's the second left after. He knows her, she gets her pension there.'

Willis bumped the Capri over the rutted and puddled entrance of the corporation tip. He could see some figures moving on the trash hills in the distance. 'People about,' he muttered.

In his earpiece, Foxwell of the first pair said, 'I've got them on scope, been there a while, it's just kids fossicking.'

Willis drove by an outcrop of abandoned fridges, swung the car around and parked up facing the way out. Iffy stillness, drizzle and the call of gulls. He unbelted and got his right arm out of the parka. He took the Heckler MP5 short submachine-gun from the clip under the dash where a normal car would sometimes have a fire extinguisher and checked it over, muzzle clear, small curved thirty-six-round mag in tight and taped securely to the upside-down spare, safety snicking off OK. He pulled the cocking lever back in its slot against the spring and let it fly forward with a cold-chisel clink as the action stripped and chambered the first round off the mag. He put his arm through the sling and back into the parka sleeve. His watch showed just on RV time and by the rules he had to give it ten.

He opened the door, found he'd parked over what could well be one of the largest, deepest and most septic-looking puddles in the province, said fuck.

The Geordie came on the loop. 'What's the problem?'

'Nothing, talking to myself.' Willis fired up the Capri and bunnyhopped it forward. He holstered the Browning and stepped out on firm mud.

Old sinks, stained mattresses, sofas with springs poking, obsolete TV sets and oddities like disused giant cable drums ranged off into the prospect. Some of the fridges still had their doors on, child-traps.

He fiddled with the sling under his open parka. He pulled his hood up. Ten minutes in this drizzle and he wouldn't be able to see through his glasses.

Foxwell and Lowe's position should be that scrubby wood by the pylon. Geordie and his mate were moving in somewhere behind the row of saplings nearer by. Normally the soldiers sat in their cars half a mile from the meet. They didn't like this deployment, with the cars left on a farm track up the next turning where they could barely keep an eye on them, particularly with Fox and Lowe's car sitting there an extra twenty minutes in advance to provoke curiosity if anyone passed by.

Willis's watch hands hadn't noticeably moved. He decided to smoke.

Wolverhampton Pat was covering the back of the terrace from the alley. Danny knocked at the front door. As Miss Molly's footsteps came along the hall he rolled his black balaclava mask down over his face. He stuffed the paper inside his bomber jacket and readied the Beretta in a two-fisted grip.

Straightbacked Miss Molly opened the door part-way, saw the mask and gave him a ferocious glare. She was retired from teaching now but the glare was still in good working order. Danny barged in. 'We're looking for Liam.'

She said nothing, maybe couldn't speak yet for the shock, that often happened. Danny cleared the ground-floor rooms, no one, but two new-rinsed teacups were draining upside down by the kitchen sink. He rushed the stairs, the riskiest bit, panning the Beretta fast along the landing as he came up. All the doors were shut. He cleared the bathroom and bedrooms one by one, and the airing cupboard. From the back bedroom window he could see Wolve in the alley. He waved and shook his head, scrub it.

In the hall he said, 'He's been here.'

Miss Molly, holding her elbows, hissed, 'He's gone.'

'When?'

'Half an hour ago. Get out of here.'

'Where did he go?'

'He said he had to see someone. I don't enquire. He only stopped by for a cup of tea.'

'Did he have a car?'

'No.'

Danny saw himself out. 'If you make any contact with the security forces you will be executed.'

On the street he rolled his balaclava back up to look like a woolly hat and folded the paper round the gun. Wolverhampton Pat, with the AK assault rifle in the toolbag, met him at the corner.

'Missed him,' Danny said. 'He went about half an hour back, but he didn't have wheels.'

'He could hitch a lift. Or get the bus.'

'We've got to say we checked the area. Anywhere round here a tout could meet his handlers. Waste ground, where the brewery was, the old branch line station, the town dump, the sewage works.'

'Who says he's meeting them round here?' said Wolve.

'He's moving like he knows he's wanted. So he'll try and get them to pull him out which means he'll have to see them pretty soon, and if he called on Molly Stephens here it can't be too far out of his way.'

'Is he going to chance that if he's running?'

Danny shrugged. 'She half brought him up. And he's one of those guys keeps his life in boxes, I didn't know he was still in touch with her until Sean dug it out of Evie and I never knew she'd moved out here. That was practically a safe house.'

They climbed into the Datsun. 'We just drive around?' said Wolve. 'Left here we get to the old station and the dump first, right the sewage works.'

'Right'll put us in that fuck-awful one-way. Turn left and we can go round the outside. If we don't see him there's the quarry out at Waterdown.'

'Uh — I think I've got a hostile,' Foxwell said.

Willis didn't see anybody. 'Where?'

The one with the toolbag appeared on the great tumulus of womenswear. Willis ducked and pushed Liam down flat.

'Wolvie on the skyline now,' said Fox. 'Looking round, doesn't seem to see you. No clear shot for me, those kids are in my line of fire behind him.'

Lowe came on. 'Can do here but close.'

Geordie said, 'Can do easy.'

'Was that your red spot on his back then, Geordie?' Fox said. They used laser sights.

'That's me.'

Fox said, 'Five-One, you're OK, he's coming down again. Going after Danny boy up the path. They're both headed for the river end. You better make for the car.'

'Yeh, will do, cheers.' Willis dragged Liam to his feet. The inner path wound around the tyre hill, through banks and dunes of clutter, eventually reaching the entrance where the naff yellow souped-up Capri stood. 'It's open, get in,' Willis said. He stopped to wipe his glasses.

'They're on that heap of — old concrete bollards or fenceposts or something,' Fox said. 'I think they've seen you this time.'

Willis turned. There they were, heads and shoulders on the skyline, the kids clear to the left. He raised the Heckler, thumbing the catch to rapid, and tripped off half a mag of nine-millimetre pistol rounds, a scare shot at this range.

The figures were hunching as if to aim. Fox was already saying, 'Shooters out. Go go go.' There were muzzle flashes from the concrete heap and tracer fire leaping the dump towards it as Fox and Lowe and Geordie and Geordie's mate opened up from the woods. Rooks started out of the trees and gulls wheeled higher screeching but the kids stood and stared. The concrete stack puffed dust.

Willis lifted off the trigger. He'd been firing for just over a second. He safed the gun and ran to the Capri. Liam hunkered down in the passenger's footwell and looked extra caught out.

Willis turned the key in the ignition. Something hit the car roof hard and whined away. The Capri bounded forward and Willis almost lock-to-locked to get around the Datsun. Fishtailing, the

Capri hurled up dun spray. Willis flipped the lights and wipers on and pumped the horn as he exited the gate at an angle. A sludge green Mini estate was coming dead slow, face behind the wheel squirrel-anxious at the gunfire. Willis careered past on the verge and redlined the rev counter away down the lane.

Spencer, tucking in a clean shirt, went back to the kitchen. Claire was at the worktop wearing one of his shapeless pullovers. He hugged her from behind and kissed her neck and sniffed her hair as she pressed the top decks of toast down on the bulky sandwiches. He'd cooked the bacon and chopped the salad stuff, she'd done the layering while he got some clothes on.

They sat at the table and used cutlery, having both failed to tackle the sandwiches by hand without shooting gherkins and tomato discs across the room.

'Didn't you once say your mum was Jewish?' said Claire.

'Yeah, came from Austria. But she's not religious.'

'So the man with the knife hasn't been at you and you can have bacon sandwiches.'

'Sure. You know you don't have to rush just because I've got to. Stay on here and take your time if you like, soak in the bath or ... '

'I'd feel a bit funny in a strange house. Actually no, that's a nice idea, reading a book in a deep bubble bath in the afternoon with the place to yourself, but I'll have a shower and come with you. If that's all right.'

'I don't want you to feel hassled, that's all.'

Claire looked at her watch. 'You need to make it by three. I often fit a shower in in the mornings when there's only that much time, and I don't live any nearer. In fact I'll do it now, can I? Then have the rest of this in a minute.'

She gathered clothes from around the living room and the bedroom and he gave her his spare towel. 'I don't know if that shower attachment's any good,' he said, 'I've never used it. The others do.'

'I knew you wouldn't. Basker, you are.' She held up the sky blue bra. 'Here, you snapped the hooks. Oh, no. And this was new, ish.'

'Sorry, Claire. Nice one too, looked great on you.'

'And you don't get it as a memento.' She put it in her bag.

'Oh, why? It's no use to you now.'

She frowned. 'Damn right there.' She took it out again and threw it on the bedroom carpet.

'Well, no use to me either,' he said, 'I was kidding.'

'Tough, you're stuck with it.'

'I'll buy you tons more.'

'Men get the wrong things.'

'Do we? I suppose so, I'll buy you dinner though.'

'Not tonight, I've got a girls' night out thing.'

'Tomorrow?'

'I'm staying at my aunt's in Berkshire over the weekend.'

'Oh.'

'Next week's all right.'

Claire was showered and back downstairs, dressed and fresh, calmly finishing her bacon sandwich, in the time it took Spencer to find his shoes under the bed and light a cig.

'Right.' She pulled on the white cardigan. 'Oh, I said fruit, didn't I?' From a carrier she piled a lush still-life's worth into Katie's brass bowl on the table, arranged it a little, smiling to herself, and trickled the peanuts over it.

'You left yourself any?' Spencer said.

'Yeah, I've just lightened my load. I can fit the rest in my bag now. Anyway, you paid.'

'So I did.'

'In fact you bought me lunch. In a way.' She took his Marlboro and laid it in the ashtray before sliding her arms round his neck. 'Have you breathed all that smoke out?'

He turned aside and blew, twice for luck. 'Think so.'

'OK.' Claire snogged him juicily.

At the front door as they were leaving she said, 'Spencer.'

'Yuh?'

'What did you come back here for?'

'Well. Give you one mainly.' What did she think?

She fetched the Pytcherley Probables file from the linen chest and stuck it under his arm.

'Oh yeah,' he said. He touched her face and stroked her hair.

'Come on.'

Outside he said, 'Are you still going to Knightsbridge?'

'Might as well.'

'I'll get the cab to drop me off and leave you a fiver or something.'

'It won't be that much. I could take the bus from there anyway, it's only a hop down Park Lane.'

'You won't want to get out and wait for a bus once you're settled.'

'No, I won't, will I? Oh, I might. I like riding on top.'

'Should have said.'

Claire blushed. 'I mean — Oh, don't. Another time.'

Spencer slowly blushed himself. He hated smug gits making we've-done-it innuendoes. He'd try and fight the impulse in future.

They walked down the paved way past the false-limb clinic to the Camden Road. No cab coming yet.

'I won't see you till Monday, then,' he said.

'No, and I'll be down in my new basement office then.'

'Won't see you then either, then.'

'I am back on Sunday night but I'm not sure what time, and Sunday evenings aren't much good for mood, are they?'

Next door's cat miaowed behind them. 'What are you doing?' Spencer asked it. 'Push off. Cats don't use busy main thoroughfares. Go on.' He pointed. He didn't like to give it the usual bump start with his foot while Claire was watching.

The cat miaowed again. Claire crouched down. 'Here. What?' The cat rubbed itself against her legs, arching hightailed, purring loud enough to hear above the traffic as she stroked it.

Spencer looked for a cab. Three or four went by taken, the next he flagged with the Pytcherley file. 'Wigmore Street then Knightsbridge, please.'

'OK, guv.' Spencer absolutely loved it when drivers really said that. The cat had scuttled off. Claire and Spencer boarded.

The cab was proper trad black this time, and the traffic seemed lighter than two hours ago. They let the twists and turns of Camden's one-way system push them together on the seat.

The driver took them through Regent's Park, where the trees were blossoming in sprays. Spencer pointed out the mountain goats high on the Zoo's manmade peak. Claire leaned across him to see, and left her arm around his shoulders the rest of the way.

They sped by the immaculate cream façades of the Crown Estate, crossed Marylebone Road and bowled down Portland Place, jostling along with the red buses past the masted and portholed bulk of Broadcasting House.

As they came to the kerb on Wigmore Street, Spencer peered at the meter and gave Claire three pound notes. 'Should do it. Have a good weekend.'

Claire widened her eyes, kiss me.

They kissed, holding it a few seconds.

Spencer opened the door, hesitated, kissed her again, jumped out. He was sure there was something he should have done or said and hadn't. He smiled at the driver. 'Thanks.' That was it, he hadn't thanked Claire. Too late now.

Claire waved as the cab pulled away. Once it was lost in the traffic Spencer went into John Bell & Croyden and collected his prescription. On Welbeck Street with no one around he punched the air, laughing. He stopped to light an emergency cig, every cig's an emergency cig but some more than others, this one to cap off the sudden extreme elation. It worked quickly and feeling more controlled he dropped it and trod it out as he turned on to Queen Anne Street.

Su Holt was in reception, leaning against the wall, talking to Jenny and Goldie. 'Where have you been, Spencer?'

'Popped out to the chemist's.' He produced the small but clearly printed bag from his pocket.

'Oh.' She turned back to the others. They were laughing. 'So that was that,' she said, 'and I just picked them up from the cloakroom on my way out, put them on again, returned to the real world.'

'What?' said Spencer.

Su giggled. 'Simpson's, Spencer. The doorman said I'm afraid we don't allow ladies wearing trousers madam, so I kicked my boots off and stepped out of my trousers and handed them to him, There you are then. This shirt's quite long, I said, I'll wear this as a dress, any complaints?'

'Good on you,' Spencer said.

'Thank you.'

The entryphone buzzed. Jenny took it. Spencer heard the guy through the front door saying, 'Dugald Philipson, for David Cracknell.'

Su said, 'Why have you been walking around town with that file?'

Spencer said, 'I was bringing David some papers. He was tied up, I remembered I'd left my prescription to collect. Just had it in my hand.'

Su looked unconvinced but equally unbothered.

Philipson came in, youngish bald type, confident. Jenny, on the phone, said, 'David, your three o'clock's here. OK ...Well, he's here as well at the moment, so — Fine. OK. Bye.' She hung up and told the candidate, 'He won't keep you a moment. Spencer, David wanted some papers ... '

Spencer found Philipson's sheets in the file and passed them to her.

Philipson was shaking hands with Su. 'Mrs Holt? Yes. Pleased to meet you. Seen you on the business pages.'

Su giggled.

Goldie took Spencer's arm and said out of the corner of his mouth, 'Kitchen.'

Spencer could not believe Goldie was going to give him a ticking off, but it might be a warning. Perhaps Su had been back for ages and noticed he was missing and made comments.

In the kitchen Lillian said, 'Looking for some tea?'

'Please,' Goldie said. 'Are those biscuits going?'

Tara Holt was perched on one of the stools, smirking round a Rothmans. She always smirked when men came into the room, something to do with being eighteen and stacked.

Spencer asked Goldie, 'What did you want, then?'

'Eh? Nothing,' said Goldie, indicating Tara with his eyes.

'I know when I'm not wanted,' she said, and got down to do a flounce out.

'Just to put an end to this,' said Spencer, 'I was going to say —

116

'No, you don't, it's fine,' said Goldie, and sat her back on the stool. He was more powerful than he looked and Tara, although she was some kind of swimming champion, was too girly to struggle. She just squirmed for show and stayed simpering where she was put.

Goldie and Spencer took their mugs upstairs. 'So, uh,' Goldie said, 'where did you get to?' He was murmuring, almost without lip movement, standard operating procedure for any dodgy conversation in the stairwell except when Su was known to be out of the building or in her own suite with the door closed. They couldn't hear her voice in reception, she might be anywhere now.

Spencer murmured back, 'Why, who's been asking?'

'David wondered if you'd run off with Claire, as you left together and you still weren't back by gone half two.'

Not trouble, only gossip. Spencer held the file up and breathed, 'Home, had to get this. Claire was going shopping in Knightsbridge.'

'Oh. You didn't take her to lunch or something first, then, only you have been gone an incredible amount of time.'

They came to Su's landing and kept quiet. Through Fi's open door they could see Su's open too.

On the next flight Goldie said, 'Is that a different shirt?'

'I made a messy bacon sandwich.'

'You're lucky Su's too far gone to notice things like that at the moment, she'd be straight on to it normally.'

'She would, yeah. When did she get back?'

'Barely ahead of you, you're all right.'

In the research office Stubbs said, 'Did you have a nice time?'

'OK thanks,' said Spencer.

'See it on your face.'

'What do you see on his face?' said Goldie.

Stubbs smiled. 'Nothing.'

'He looks perfectly normal to me.'

'Ah, men don't notice these things.'

'What things? You mean he did take Claire to lunch, the bugger.'

'Just to put an end to this,' said Spencer, 'I was going to but there wasn't time, with the paperchase on, so she came along and I showed her the garden and made her a bacon, lettuce and tomato.'

'David'll go spare,' said Goldie, 'you know he has this imaginary thing with her, or I assume it's imaginary, you could have got up to anything, it'll wreck his fantasy life, well, one of his fantasy lives.'

'That's all right, David likes going spare.'

'Actually the film thing seems to be less of a fantasy than we thought, doesn't it?'

'Only dreamers ever achieve anything, Rick. I still bet it won't get made, though.'

'Oh, and I'll tell you what I do notice, Susie, despite being a man. You've put these on again.' Goldie went to the light switch and turned off the fluorescent strip lights. 'We never have those on in here.'

'We don't,' confirmed Spencer.

'That's better. You can see perfectly well what you're doing by the desk lamps and it gives a softer glow to the room, see? Those things make it feel like an office, terrible.'

'Sorry,' said Stubbs. '*As* an ex-typist I'm used to it but I don't mind, if you prefer it like this it's fine with me. Now then, shall we do some work?'

'Can if you want,' said Goldie. 'You never get hold of any of these people at this time on a Friday, though, they stop returning calls. You only have to call again on Monday, there's not much point.' He shuffled and batched some contact sheets and reached for his paperclips. 'Who joined all these up?'

Liam sat and smoked.

Willis, by the captain's vacated desk, put down the phone. 'We're on a flight from Aldergrove.'

Liam nodded.

'You've annoyed my boss.'

'Sorry,' Liam said.

'You're sitting on time-sensitive information.'

'I know.'

'Approaching from the back of the dump. Take my position as your twelve o'clock and go to ten, but you won't see him yet.'

Willis found himself facing the promontory of dead fridges. He edged out into the grass and thistles but further trash heaps blocked the view. On the other side of the dump there was no road or track, only the river. The player must have kept low along the bank for Foxwell not to spot him sooner.

Willis climbed a pile of tyres. The fossickers, a hundred yards away or maybe twice that, he was useless guessing distances, didn't see him, they carried on examining a bike frame they'd turned up.

'He's under the wire and in,' said Fox. 'Headed round the edge your way, no shooter showing yet.'

The Geordie said, 'You're skylining yourself.'

Willis scrambled down. 'What's he look like, Fox?'

'Six foot, fair shaggy hair. Wait up, I think I know this one. Haven't seen him for a bit but I know him.'

'I think it's OK,' Willis said.

'I've got it. Liam Anderson, used to be their battalion intelligence, out of circulation lately.'

'That's OK, Fox.'

'He's your Tambourine Man, is he?'

'You didn't recognise him, right.'

'You're the boss.'

The Geordie came on again. 'This our guy?'

'Yeah, we're all right,' Willis said.

'Why d'you call him that? Is he a Dylan fan?'

'No. We just wanted him to play a song for us, seeing as we weren't sleepy and there was no place we were going to. And if he buggered us about then in the jingle-jangle morning we'd come following him.'

The Geordie said, 'Christ.'

Willis dropped his Three Fives, trod it in the mud and put his hand round the Heckler's grip under the parka.

Liam walked into sight along the path that skirted the dump. He did that thing of pushing one big capable bananabunch hand through his blond Seventies non-haircut to say here I am, like Jack the Lad walking into the bar.

'Five–One to all Fives, wait for now, out.' Willis switched his pocket radio to standby so the SAS men wouldn't be in on the conversation but he'd still hear them.

Liam came into talking range. 'On your own?'

'No, the backup's around.'

Liam had two basic expressions, cocky and caught out, and at the moment it was caught out. He also looked as if he'd been up all night. 'They're looking for me. I'm going to be questioned.'

'Who told you?'

'This girl, works at the club where they were talking about it last night.'

'That was careless of them.'

'I've been keeping on the move but you better get me to England.'

'Have you heard of passing a marked card?'

'It wasn't like that.'

'There's no way your lot know what's going on.'

'Some Special Branch tout must have told them.'

'Special Branch don't know either,' said Willis quickly.

'Maybe they know enough to work it out. Everyone reckons you threw our boys a Special Branch informant to cover up for one of yours after Brown's Brook. So now they're getting their own back. I thought Roddy Deakin was clean because our security boys'll get confessions out of anybody, but maybe he really was Branch. And his handlers can tell if it wasn't down to him it was me and if I'm not with them I'm with you people.'

'And if you ask me,' said Willis, who was hardly going to admit this was the very cock-up he'd seen coming over the horizon for some time, 'it's all marked cards. So the coppers have passed one and it's got passed on to you. But they're guessing, that's all. They don't know you're ours.'

'It makes no difference. If I'm going to be questioned I end up like Roddy did. Nutted.'

'It's just a checkup before you're sent over.'

'That's not how it happens. You stick to the deal and when you get me to England I'll tell you who was in the unit I was being sent to join.'

'You don't know that, Liam, you're given contact procedures

and you wait to see who shows up, come off it.'

'You're wrong. There were three and one of them came back, his wisdom teeth went crazy and he had to have an operation. And he briefed me. Those other two are in, they're active, you need those names, I know them.'

'Look, if you're blown they're blown, they'll be pulled out.'

'You could watch the ports,' said Liam.

'Any idea what we charge them with?'

'They've been ... studying targets up to now ... I mean Oxford Street was the other unit, but ... '

'That's not an awful lot, is it? Considering you're the only asset we've ever had in Mainland and you'll be as much use as a chocolate teapot from now on.'

'I'm not even talking to you. I want to go to England and I want to see MacMichael, I'll talk to him.'

'He's not working your case any more.'

'But he knows he owes me.'

Willis took a deep breath. In fact it wasn't working out too badly. For a start he wouldn't have to do these meets any more. He might even get posted home.

The Geordie came on. 'Blue Datsun, two up, turning in.'

There was the whump, whump of a car taking the ruts at the entrance. Liam looked past Willis's shoulder. Willis pushed him back into the cover of the fridge pile and switched the radio to two-way. 'Anyone we know?'

'I didn't see,' said Liam.

Geordie in the earpiece said, 'I can't tell yet but they seem to know you.'

Willis heard the car stop, engine idling. The drizzle falling on fridge carcases made a sound like old ladies sucking their dentures.

Danny said, 'We should have parked around the bend and come in quietly. You don't think of these things, then it's too late. That was him, though, wasn't it?'

'Yeah, I'd say it was,' said Wolverhampton Pat. 'That other guy ... ' He shrugged.

'It didn't look like a Brit. Those flares.'

'Maybe he isn't up to anything, I don't know.'

'Leave it running. Let's go and see.'

Willis held the Heckler's muzzle to the back of Liam's neck, found the stolen police Walther in his waistband and lifted it.

'This is not a set-up,' said Liam.

'No, be a bit obvious, wouldn't it, thing is if you pull a weapon my fellers blow you away.' Willis pocketed the gun.

'They're out,' said the Geordie. 'You've got two hostiles.'

'This way.' Willis set Liam moving with a clap across the back and they pelted down the path, Willis bearing in mind to keep his index finger straight and clear of the Heckler's trigger, and to take a few steps facing backwards now and then. No one was in sight yet. A hundred yards' headstart? Or nothing like?

Geordie was saying, 'Wolverhampton Pat Milliken with a tool-bag and Danny Forrester with the local rag, I read that one AK one handgun but they're not showing yet. Not hurrying either.'

'Fox,' Willis said, 'I better get to your position, mate.' The wood was beyond the stretch of marshy grass on the other side of the wire fence.

Fox said, 'No. They could pick you off first. Take cover in the dump. Now.'

Willis bundled Liam off the path, into the tall weeds and then the rubbish. They jumped bales of shredded paper, stumbled up a slope of plaster rubble with old cast-iron gas pipes and shattered woodwork sticking out, ran over a vast spongy mound of fire-blackened blouses and dresses, probably from the workshops of someone who fell behind with the protection payments, and made their way down, over splitting plastic ICI fertiliser sacks full of mouldy foam rubber packing material, to where some rusted-out cookers lay by one of the dump's inner paths.

Willis took a bearing on the tyre hill.

'Down,' said Fox. 'Down.'

Willis hit Liam's shoulder. They crouched behind a bathtub that had curtains and broken tiles at the bottom and the slashed two-tone red-and-grey bench seat of a jukebox-era car wedged in it at an angle.

'We're keeping our side of the deal.'

'I don't know that. Not till you get me there.'

'I left Captain MacMichael a message, if he comes back before we have to split to make the flight you could give him the names over the phone, the Met can get the pictures out, start rolling.'

'No.'

'We'll still take you,' Willis said. 'The boss is fine about that. Someone over here played silly buggers trying to finger you. OK. We're taking your protection seriously. Nobody minds you taking it seriously, it's your neck. But what's not going to do you a lot of good is the prima donna bit, I won't sing without the right orchids in the dressing room.'

'I could tell you now and you could turn me over to our boys. You could shoot me and pin it on them. How do I know?'

'What for?'

Liam shrugged. 'I'd be no more use, like you said.'

'And you think we couldn't do the same in London?'

'You couldn't get away with it the way you could over here.'

'So what's stopping us? All you're holding back is the names of two blown guys. It's not that much.'

'They're not new faces. They're guys you want.'

Willis tried not to look too interested. 'Even if they are, the value of that information — are you listening? — is falling by the minute.'

'First the Mainland command has to check what I knew about. Then they have to get word through, it's not direct contact.'

A military tap at the door. 'Yeh,' said Willis.

Geordie came in with a slip of paper. 'Police want you to call that number about taking your statement.'

'Cheers. That can wait till I get back.'

'Did they pick up Wolve and Danny?' said Liam.

Geordie glanced at him but spoke to Willis. 'They're away. That was a serious piece of cover, fucking concrete. I would have gone for rockets if we were allowed to use rockets.'

'Yeh, well. Liam still says he wants to see Captain MacMichael, it's only his excuse for keeping his trap shut till he's made it to London, but anyroad we've got to take him to the plane now. We can't use the Capri again, they might be out looking. And the bullet gouge in the roof's a bit ... '

Geordie said, 'You asking us to run you there?'

'We need transport, yeh, I'm not so sure about unmarked soft vehicles.'

'If he stays on the floor and that bird of yours sits up front, they didn't see a woman at the dump.'

'I want an armoured Land Rover,' said Liam.

'One's no good,' said Geordie, 'you have to have at least three to look like a regular patrol and if they do take a crack with armour-piercing or a rocket they've got to play find the lady and get lucky.'

'We'll have three, then,' Willis said.

'By the time it's organised you could have had a helicopter.'

Willis snapped his fingers. 'We'll have a helicopter.'

'Captain Sutton's still around in the mess if you want to ask him.'

Spencer remembered the unsigned letters in his folder and went down to reception. He glanced over them. Soon all the form letters would be turned out on a word processor at the touch of a couple of keys, but these were genuine hand-typed Claire Tarrant originals.

'What are you smiling about?' said Jenny in a warm inveigling tone. Jenny wasn't fat, she was no more than plump, and not very plump at that, but she had a fat girl's fear of being left out of the joke, even when, as now, there wasn't a joke to be left out of.

'Nothing,' said Spencer.

'Oh. You looked as if there was an amusing mistype somewhere.'

'Nah. I haven't seen any yet.'

'I was going to say I could correct it as a favour when I get a moment.'

'No need, they're all right.'

'You're still smiling.'

Spencer laughed. 'Sorry.'

'What is it?'

'Nothing.' Of course when you were sexually active you gave off pheromones that made women start acting in an attentive and submissive manner. Which would be more use when you weren't getting any. Another one of evolution's tacky little pranks. Spencer signed the letters, enveloped them and flipped them into the post tray behind the desk one by one. The last missed and he had to go round and pick it off the floor.

The entryphone buzzed. Jenny let in an overalled delivery man with a clipboard. 'Desk, filing cabinet, two chairs, low table.'

'Oh yes,' said Jenny, 'I'll show you where it has to go. It's in the basement.' She led him down the hall. 'There's an awkward turn here at the top of the flight and another at the bottom.'

'Yeah, when isn't there? We'll handle it.'

Spencer went upstairs and from the research office windows he watched Claire's new desk wrapped in plastic come off the double-parked truck.

Once she was down there they'd hardly ever meet unless they went out of their way. First that made him sad. Holly Jessup he spoke to only a couple of times a month. John in the basement's existence was near hypothetical. Spencer didn't mind that, but he loved seeing Claire every day, in the ordinary course of things, without arrangement or pretext, and now it wouldn't happen any more. Then he saw the advantages. No getting under each other's feet. No gut-wringing embarrassment, no scenes or continual dissimulation in front of the others. Whether it worked out or not. No conflict of roles. No traps. No heavy repercussions. He was still free and in control. He could walk away from it and the worst that could happen was a very occasional frosty hullo. He was on to such a good thing here he started hardening up and wanting Claire again badly right now. Then he felt guilty about making cynical calculations. Then the truth hit him.

Claire had done the same calculations in advance. She'd said yes because she was changing offices, because from now on if she had second thoughts she could always avoid him.

He went back to his desk and stared at the blotter. It was still a pretty big yes. The way she held his eye as she shucked off that blouse. The final helpless yelps or very acceptable impressions of same. (Oh, come on, if she suddenly turns red hot and goes slick with sweat like that it's genuine, let's not be neurotic about it.) But afterwards she was so vague about the next time.

There could be plenty of reasons for that. His place was a hopeless venue when anyone else was in. He didn't know what her flat was like, or even whether she shared, he hadn't thought to ask. He didn't know what she liked doing when she went out, either, though he could take it she didn't like films with subtitles. He really had no idea where to go from here, and Claire ('You have to decide') might be expecting a firm lead, the vagueness a ruse to test his initiative. Appalling thought. He hadn't got any.

And if Cracknell hadn't told him to change Philipson's appointment, and if he hadn't been in a rush and taken the whole Pytcherley Probables file home instead of copying down the phone number, and if he hadn't left the file behind this morning in his smokeless confusion, and if Su hadn't lost the Gregory papers and blamed it on the research department as per, and if Fi hadn't let the clock stop and mucked up the diary and driven Su from bad to worse, and if the Pytcherley disaster hadn't given Su the perfect means of putting the researchers in detention for the evening, he'd never have got Claire back to Rochester Square in the first place.

And there he was thinking he was in control.

Gareth took off his mac. 'Have I missed anything?'

'Not really,' Cath said. 'No one knows what's going to happen yet. We've been given some assessments to make, but I took a couple of messages if you want to call the people back.' She handed him a notepad leaf.

He dialled the first number, got a stroppy 'Yeah?' at the other end and said, 'I was told to contact Nigel Willis.'

'You've just missed him. Is that Mr MacMichael? How's it going?'

'Oh, hi, Geordie. OK. I thought I'd seen that number before somewhere.'

'He said if you called to tell you he'll call you later. He's coming over, bringing someone.'

'Here?'

'That's right.'

'Has there been a problem?'

'Nothing we couldn't sort out with a few hundred rounds.'

'Ah. Anyone hurt?'

'No, no-score draw, like you usually get.'

'I see. I've just been having range practice with someone who knows you. Hopkins.'

'That skiver. They've got you keeping your hand in? What d'you carry?'

'Browning, standard.'

'Can't go far wrong. That's a legitimate one, is it?'

'Sure.'

'Take care of the spare anyway.'

'I will,' said Gareth, hoping the monitors didn't spot the implication there, or follow it up if they did.

The chopper banked into a turn. Liam, craning to see from the downside window, gripped his armrests as the green earth tilted up at him and the pull of gravity gained and shifted out of true, not plumb towards the ground any more but weirdly skewed with the canting of the cabin floor.

Willis said, 'Is this the first time you've flown?'

Liam nodded. 'Good feeling.'

'Never flown?' said Foxwell. He was along to keep Liam under armed guard as far as the plane. Willis would have to take a civil flight back so he'd left his weapons with Rachel.

'Why would I?' said Liam.

The machine straightened out and lost height. A road slid beneath, surprisingly close, a fence topped with barbed wire, then the concrete of the airport apron. They slowed to a dawdle, floated almost still, settled over a white-marked H and touched down.

'Are we here?' said Liam. 'Already?'

'Yeh.' Willis unbuckled, got up and leaned into the cockpit to show the pilots a palm. 'Thanks.' They showed him their thumbs.

Foxwell slid the cabin door back and jumped out. Liam and

Willis followed him, stooping in the downdraught. They crossed the apron to the military terminal building. A camouflage-drab Hercules transport was parked nearby, and a pretty little red-and-white executive jet with RAF markings. One of those was probably their flight, no prizes which.

Inside, Willis found a WRAF minding a desk. 'We're changing here to go to Northolt.' He produced his Signals cover pass.

'Have you got the flight reference, Captain Willis?'

He sorted through the pieces of paper from his pocket. 'There.'

'Thank you, sir.' She pulled a clipboard towards her. 'Plus one civilian,' she said.

'The tall one over there, the other lad's our escort. We've got to make a couple of calls before we take off, is there an office we can use? I was told to ask for Squadron-Leader Chester about that kind of thing because we need somewhere to put this feller while we're waiting.'

'I'll call Squadron-Leader Chester. Do you know you're flying with the General Officer Commanding, sir?'

'Pardon?'

'They've put you on the GOC's plane, sir. He's going over for a conference, I think.'

'I see,' said Willis. 'Right.'

'It's just that when he arrives they'll want to take off in the next available slot, so you'll ideally have to be boarded by then. Which should be anytime soon.'

'We won't need long.'

'Fine. But there are secure communications facilities in the VIP area, the squadron-leader'll show you.'

'Oh. OK. We're not exactly dressed for it.'

'I'm sure you have your reasons, sir.'

On the tube back to Hammersmith, Claire wondered if the black satin trousers she'd bought were really her. They weren't spray-on tight or anything but they were still slinky and glam, perhaps a bit obvious. She'd been thinking of wearing them with her off-white jacket tonight, a sort of girl version of men's tropical evening dress, but now she had a feeling she'd look like one of the restaurant staff. And she couldn't think what else would go with them. She hated the whole business of clothes sometimes.

She also wondered if she should have cancelled tonight and done something with Spencer, not that there was too much you could do if you both shared houses. She tried to imagine weekending at Camden as a less than proper paid-up member of the household. It might be all right, depending what the others were like, except that your only real inner retreat would be that cardboard-walled cupboard off the living room. Her own place had a better layout, but bringing a man into a girls' house was far worse than bringing a girl into a mixed one.

From the Hammersmith stop she headed up the Shepherd's Bush Road, humming to herself, and turned on to Brook Green.

Besides, you didn't want a man making himself too much at home unless it was It, and it was still early to say. A couple of days to let her mind catch up wasn't such a bad idea. If she was desperate for him by Sunday at least that would tell her something. And it would have been a little bit mean to ring her friends and cancel, saying she'd met this man. They'd go and bitch about her behind her back. But if she turned up smiling and looking great and dropped a few hints, that would be extra rich and thick double mean and they'd have to put up with it, much more fun.

She came to the corner of Luxemburg Gardens, only an ordinary redbrick terrace opposite the school but Spencer made a thing about the address because of the classy area of Paris.

On second thoughts that wasn't Spencer, that was the boy MacMichael. Spencer probably didn't even know what her address was. Of course he could find it on the Holt Newman list, if he bothered to look, along with her phone number. She'd typed that sheet herself and everyone was meant to keep a copy.

She let herself in.

She wouldn't take it too well if the weekend passed without a call. Before she went out this evening would be nice, to show he couldn't wait, but he'd still be at the office, and a sexy last-thing late-nighter after she came home would obviously be better in any case.

She threw shopping, mac and cardigan on to her bed. The

shower attachment at Rochester Square wasn't up to much so she promised herself that long hot soak in a deep bubble bath if she could get through the clothes-trying and reach a sensible conclusion without having any tantrums.

'I don't know if I'll be there in forty-five minutes,' said Gareth. 'There's a Northolt tube, but it's right out at the end of the Central Line and it's still nowhere near the aerodrome.'

'Aye, well,' said Willis. 'There must be a pool car you could borrow.'

'I hardly think so, Nige. It's not official, is it, it's not my department any more. As far as the director's concerned I'd be bunking off when I'm supposed to be at my desk.'

'Carl's coming but he was down at the Yard for a meeting, so he's hitching a lift with Inspector Draper. They'll have left by now. I don't know. Just get a taxi.'

'All the way to Northolt? It's about as far as Heathrow. What's that, ten or fifteen quid? And I won't get it back on expenses. I'll tell you what, I'll ring my mum and see if I can borrow their car. They've got two. Mind you, the second one's usually at the garage. Still, if I try that, then I've only got to go to St John's Wood and drive from there.'

'Well, whatever you can sort out. They're going frantic to put us on this plane now, so. Shift yourself. See you when we land.'

Gareth rang off and called his mother, who said, 'You just caught us going out the door. Gig managed to come home early, as promised, for once, so we're off up to Suffolk.'

'Oh, that's nice. What car are you taking, because I've got to go to RAF Northolt in a hurry, meet someone off a plane.'

'Have you? Ah. We've loaded up the Granada.'

'OK. Is the other one working? If it is, I should be insured on it for the summer half from first April, shouldn't I? I sent Gig the cheque.'

'I expect so, then. Hold on.' Gareth heard her go out through the hallway and come back. 'He says that's all right, the tank's about a quarter-full so keep an eye on that but it should be plenty, otherwise, no, it's running fine. You could put a drop more in and come up and join us tomorrow if you're not too busy.'

'Yeah. Well, that's a thought, I might. We don't know if they'll want us in the office over the weekend yet. I'll let you know in the morning, maybe.'

'I see. Yes, do. Right. I must cut along. Oh. If you could give us an idea by the not terribly late morning, I'll know how many to shop for at Mr Grice's.'

'OK.'

'Right. Car keys in the usual place. Toodle-oo.'

'Cheerio.'

Cath said as he hung up, 'What would it take to keep you here for more than five minutes at a time?'

He pulled on his mac. 'It's only today. If things run late I'll ring in.'

Squadron-Leader Chester stood aside to let Willis and Liam past down the aisle of the executive jet's tiny cabin. 'Seats five and six.' He pointed.

'At the back, yeah?' said Willis.

'Is that all right? The GOC and party will be boarding last deplaning first so it is ... logical.'

'That's fine, we don't mind.' Willis directed Liam to the right-hand seat with a push and took the left. Outside the window was the scarlet sweep of the wing. The RAF roundel was a paisley teardrop shape seen from this angle. Over on the helipad the chopper crew started the rotor again, droopy vanes flexing out straighter as they spun, Foxwell waiting on the concrete for the pilot's thumb to give the OK to approach.

'If you'd buckle in,' said Chester, 'we shouldn't be long now.' He left the cabin. A young steward in a high-necked brass-buttoned white jacket came from behind the curtain at the front and stood by the entrance.

Willis was sorry to see there was no leather upholstery in here. The seats were wide and armchairlike but they were covered with the kind of nubbly burnt-orange fabric you often saw on the furniture in dentists' waiting rooms. There were no teak and brass fittings either, no cocktail bar, no sign of a TV or a stereo.

Considering this window was only a few feet ahead of the rear-mounted engine's intake, it looked as though the bulkhead door behind the seats led to nothing but the toilet, not a bedroom or an on-board sauna. Worst of all, there were no lovely smiling WRAF handmaidens, just this kid trying not to give the two badly-dressed passengers funny looks. It was better than being stuck in canvas slings in the back of a rackety Herc with no pressuriser, but it wasn't secret-agent heaven.

Liam sat staring out, chin in hand.

Willis watched a man in earmuffs drive the electric servicing trolley out from under the plane's T-tail.

The helicopter lifted off, swivelled, dipped its nose like a musk-ox lowering horns to charge and clattered off back to base.

Chester, down by the aircraft steps, was talking on his radio. Beside him a white-gaitered RAF policeman had appeared from somewhere with an Alsatian.

Two cars rolled up, doors opening as they stopped. Chester and the dog handler came to attention and saluted. The men from the first car stood about pointing Hecklers into the middle distance. Three men from the second mounted the steps and entered the cabin.

The steward took their hats and raincoats to hang behind the curtain. The general and his aide were both in uniforms with red staff-officer tabs, but you could tell the general by his extra medal ribbons, his older face and that peculiar Establishment hairdo, slicked back flat with precise parallel combtracks. He politely ignored the intelligence contingent he must have been warned about and took the front seat on Liam's side. The aide sat across the aisle. They opened their briefcases. The other man, civilian suited, a bodyguard, gave Willis and Liam a nod and parked himself ahead of Willis, possibly figuring at a glance that Liam was the one it might be better to have in the corner of his eye.

The steward brought in the clever folding steps and shut and sealed the door. Outside the cars curved away. Chester, on the radio again, was walking off, the dog and handler were out of sight already.

The engines' whirr pitched up to a whistle. The plane shuddered, started off the mark, swung through a quarter turn and trundled rapidly forward. Liam sat up, gawping at the wing every time it wobbled as the plane bumped over a join in the concrete.

Rain shaken from the roof spilled down the windows. The plane made a couple more turns, past obscurely numbered signs that reflected the orange flashes of the belly light, and came to a stop again.

The general laughed at something the aide said. Liam was patting his hands on his thighs in a rhythm that suggested to Willis either Bernstein's 'America' or the theme from *633 Squadron*. He wondered which Liam had in mind, the joys of starting a new life in another country or the hazards of flying with the Royal Air Force.

The engines roared like a crowd. Everyone sat back abruptly and the fitments rattled as the wheels pounded over the concrete. The droplets on the windows splayed off into threads and vanished. The cabin sloped up, the rattling died and Liam grunted as the lift-off drove him harder into his seat. He leaned close to his window to see the world turn to map. 'Shite,' he said as they reached the cloudbase and the view blanked out.

'You won't see much this flight,' Willis said. 'It's pretty overcast all the way.'

'It's going to be like this?' Liam pointed at the fog outside.

'Not as such, we should be going over the top of it.'

The steward came round. The GOC and aide asked for black coffee, the bodyguard Malvern water. Liam said, 'D'you have Black Bush?'

'No, sir. Jameson, sir.'

'That'll do.'

The steward looked at Willis. 'That's OK,' said Willis. 'I'll have a cup of tea and two sugars, please.'

'Ceylon or Earl Grey, sir?'

'Well, just tea, you know.'

'That'll be Ceylon, sir.' The steward asked Liam, 'Ice or water, sir?'

Liam looked caught out. 'Straight. No, I'll have ice.'

Soon after the steward came back with the tray they lifted free of the cloud into stark, impossible sunshine. Liam shook his head

129

and smiled, and wagged his glass to make the ice tinkle.

Gareth, emerging from St John's Wood tube past the flowerbeds and the two tall palm trees, walked around the corner to Woronzow Road. The flat was the ground floor of a large villa that looked as if it might be haunted, something to do with those gables. The scent of potpourri and Antiquax indoors didn't dispel the impression altogether, though the undertone of warm bread helped. He took the keyring with the winged Aston Martin fob badge from its coathook in the hallway, found an *A–Z* on the living-room bookshelves and went out to the row of garages at the side.

Eighteen years old, bottle green with white-stripe tyres on chrome wire wheels, the Aston was a DB5 Vantage Shooting Brake, the fastest estate car ever built and almost certainly the daftest.

The engine started with the gruff throat-clearing noises of a rugby club chairman calling for order in committee and launched into a fluent, authoritative burble. Gareth let it carry on for a minute while he adjusted the mirror and the black hide driving seat and checked his route in the *A–Z*.

The gearbox was always awkward till the oil warmed through. He got reverse the second time of asking and backed out. The engine note wavered while he was shutting the garage. 'No funny stuff,' he said. He heard himself and looked up and down the road, but there was no one in earshot. Belt fastened, he gave it some choke and touched the pedal.

There was a Mercedes coming at the junction — there generally was in these parts — but having made it into second gear Gareth couldn't be bothered to stop and change down yet, so he had to turn out and cut in front, heaving at the wood-rimmed wheel and blipping the 300-horsepower throttle. He kept up the revs to grab some safety distance and held off correcting the wheel so he drifted to the centreline and the Mercedes had room to overshoot him on the inside if need be.

But the Mercedes driver had braked a little, in good time, and given way with no fuss at all.

Gareth felt shown up and embarrassed. To penalise the Mercedes man he slowed, blocked the lane and made him miss the green light at the Wellington Road junction by the tube.

With extra leeway allowed by the absence of parked cars at the lights, the Mercedes slid alongside the Aston to wait and the driver, an Arab by the looks, handsome and dark-suited, lowered his window. 'It's very nice. How much do you want?'

Gareth smiled and shrugged.

'Ten thousand,' said the Arab.

Gareth shook his head gravely, you insult me. His stepfather had bought the old chariot for two and a bit, but that was years back, and lately the market price had gone ballistic, far beyond the Arab's pretend offer, beyond even the gross tally of all the petrol-pump charges, insurance premiums, road taxes and repair bills ever paid over the whole time the car had been in the family. On paper, not only could a DB5 Vantage Shooting Brake haul wet dogs and picnic hampers at 160 mph, it cost less than nothing to run while doing so.

'Twenty?' said the Arab.

Gareth shook his head, still nowhere near.

The Arab laughed.

When the lights ambered, Gareth had the clutch just biting and the handbrake off. The four lanes of traffic on the Wellington Road drew to a halt, clearing the way, and at the first glimmer of green he did a full-dress standing start.

It must have been the new cylinder head. The club chairman gave one of his loud howling yawns and the Aston shot forward into the mouth of Grove End Road opposite, gaining speed even quicker than it used to. Gareth shifted gears like mad to keep up. The Arab had embarrassed him again by mildly turning off left.

The Aston scudded past the American school and the synagogue. Gareth eased off, let the choke in and engine-braked for the turn on to Abbey Road. Along there to the right was the Beatles' zebra crossing by the EMI studios. Gareth's mother, collecting his little half-brother Douglas from the local primary off the High Street, used to run into Linda collecting the McCartney kids. Douglas had never heard of their dad; it was before Mark Chapman sparked off the Fab Four revival.

Gareth felt prickly cold and wished he hadn't thought about doorstep assassins. He turned on to Hall Road, crossed the wide, die-straight, near-deserted thousand-yard boulevard of Hamilton Terrace with its Shamsy-Lizzy plane trees, ignoring a solitary Cadillac whose soft ballooning gait over the potholes really made it too slow to stop for, even though the lights were changing to red, and swept down over Maida Vale, catching the green this time.

The engine note echoed off the wedding-cake frontage of Warrington Crescent leading into Little Venice. Gareth crossed the canal bridge. The elevated Westway straddled the road ahead and the traffic seemed to be moving along it freely. It was that curious slack time between the first Friday rush, the one caused by people knocking off early, and the second.

As a rule Gareth got lost here and ended up in Bayswater, but a last-second glimpse of a signpost put him on the sliproad and the Aston stormed the gradient.

Rolling along with the hatchbacks and vans in the Westway's middle lane, he pushed buttons on the radio. First he found a story reading, pointless since it was halfway through, then choral evensong, fine by him.

A black Porsche overtook so fast he felt the shockwave rock the Aston on its springs. He'd seen the Porsche before, doing the same kind of thing on the Euston Road a few weeks ago. The obnoxious registration 1 5ELL was distinctive.

Ahead, a couple of cars pulled over as the Porsche threatened to ram them. If Gareth followed on quick he could use this idiot to clear a way for him and save a little journey time. He changed down and looked over his shoulder. Someone in a big orange BMW coupé was dashing up on the outside, perhaps with the same idea, but he still had a moment to get in front. He indicated and put it to the chairman. The chairman did a far-gone Dylan Thomas impersonation, the force that through the green fuse drives the flower drives my green age, and the Aston gathered way into the fast lane.

The flyover was making a long left-hand curve uphill between tower blocks. At ordinary speeds the curve was very gentle. It tightened up hard as the Aston revved towards full power and cracked 100 mph. The bodywork leaned and Gareth was pushed against the door, but the Aston held its line, tracking steadily round the arc at 120 now and still accelerating. The steering went mushy for a second, but that was only because they were cresting the incline, and it recovered straight away once the Aston settled into the downhill gradient, so Gareth stopped sweating. The curve eased and he could see the black Porsche. He doglegged the gearshift back up to fifth.

A lollipop sign reminded him the speed limit was fifty. He was doing about three times that. The middle-lane traffic was sledding backwards past him and the oncoming cars on the other side were no more than distorted flickers and short-circuit stutters.

He lifted off the throttle to keep his distance behind the Porsche and lit the headlamps in case anyone tried to pull out.

The road curved right, then straightened. He was somewhere over the Portobello area. In about a mile the elevated motorway section ended. It narrowed from three lanes to two before that and the traffic was thickening already. He cut the power and let the airstream slow him right down.

The Porsche, turbocharged if the large red letters spelling TURBO across the back were anything to go by (which they weren't necessarily), surged away, but the road was too crowded for people to keep moving over and letting it through any more. The driver had to brake drastically and Gareth caught up without touching the throttle. The fatuous number plate glowed. Gareth doused the lights. In his mirror the orange BMW was just reappearing. Flat out, the ancient Aston was 20 mph faster than the fastest current BMWs, roughly the difference between Jesse Owens and a pair of starting blocks.

He could hear the radio again, and he listened to the rest of evensong while he queued through Shepherd's Bush and Acton. Afterwards the announcer gave one of those hazy Radio 3 timechecks, 'It's just after five o'clock,' and read some news. The Marines were on their way home and the Commons were going to hold a Saturday session for the first time since Suez. Troops had exchanged fire with gunmen at a dumping ground in County Tyrone, no casualties, Royal Mail was 7–1 favourite for tomorrow's Grand National, and the Boston Symphony Orchestra had cancelled all performances of Stravinsky's *Oedipus Rex* with Vanessa Redgrave because the actress had voiced support for the Palestine Liberation Organisation. Make your mind up, Boston. D'you like terrorists or don't you?

Traffic filtered off at each junction until, after Hanger Lane, the flow freed up and the Porsche made a break for it. Gareth was listening to a wonderfully afternoony harmonica concerto by an English composer he'd never heard of and he didn't want to drown it out, but he was running late, so he tagged along. The white Deco colonnade of the Hoover factory went by, so this must be Perivale. Gareth liked to see places where things were made.

Goldie, Stubbs and Spencer sat waiting at the boardroom table. The folding doors that connected with Su's office were shut. She was still interviewing, they could hear the candidate's occasional laugh.

'What veneer's this, then, Rick?' said Spencer, tapping the table.

'Elm,' said Goldie, who was good on furniture.

'Is it? Looks too new. Unless it's imported from somewhere where they've still got elm trees.'

'No, it's mid-last century, it's just been well looked after.'

'Kidding.'

'No, look.' Goldie laid aside the copy of *Advertisers' Annual* he was looking through for Pytcherley leads, although they knew there weren't any left to try, and got down under the table.

Spencer followed.

'Little knocks in the legs there,' Goldie said. 'Been there ages. Cheaper varnish gone all black in the angles of the frame. The age of those screws. And you can see how long ago those dowels were banged in and varnished over.'

'Oh, yeah.'

'Maker's mark in the wood there. It's a Victorian mark.'

'The style's more Georgian, Regency.'

'God, repro's not a modern invention.'

They got up again.

Stubbs, reading a novel, had modestly turned to sit sideways while they were down there. 'Quite finished?'

'Sorry, Suze,' Spencer said. 'You've got a slight ladder.'

'I know about that.'

'I wonder if we should just go back and wait upstairs,' said Goldie. 'Su can phone up when she's ready.'

Cracknell looked in from the landing. 'Spencer,' he gritted.

'Hi, David,' Spencer said, 'how'd lunch go?'

'Fine. Now look — '

'Great. Philipson any good?'

'He was, actually, yes, I might shortlist him. And don't think that makes up for what you've done, because it doesn't.' He pointed.

They stiffened. Su Holt opened one leaf of the folding doors. 'I'm just going to see Mr Hyland off and return some calls, then I'll see you in five minutes. Hullo, David. What's Spencer done?'

'Hi, Su, it's, oh, it's nothing,' said Cracknell.

She made a little 'Hm' and went to escort the candidate out through Fiona's office and downstairs.

'You signed your star, then,' said Spencer.

'One of them,' said Cracknell. 'It's all subject to backing. What are you people doing in here, anyway?'

'Brainstorming on Pytcherley,' said Goldie.

Cracknell grinned. 'The man from Mars I was interviewing, he said one of his achievements was seeing through the change to a new formula Mars bar with a higher fall-off factor, I said what, he said it's a bit more aerated, so apart from looking bigger it doesn't stick to your teeth so much. I said do you ever feel you're wasting your life? He sort of crumpled and said you could put it that way, yeah.' Cracknell laughed and went out. 'Brainstorming on Pytcherley,' he muttered as he reached the stairs, so they could just hear him, and he laughed again.

Golf courses spread themselves. Stands of birch and poplar shimmered with new greenness. The Porsche had turned off for Harrow or Pinner, so Gareth slowed down. The harmonica concerto had reached a lyrical, expansive bit.

He knew when the aerodrome was coming up because the streetlamps halved in height. He glanced across the other carriageway. The boundary fence ran alongside, with an inner brick wall nowadays to deny terrorists a sightline. At the main gate sat a Spitfire on a plinth. There was no turning lane and no gap in the central reservation so you had to carry on for a mile to Hillingdon Circus, go round the roundabout and come back the other way.

The RAF corporal on the gate was in camouflage gear and carrying a rifle.

Gareth showed his Ministry of Defence cover pass. 'I'm supposed to meet a flight from Aldergrove. You should have had some Scotland Yard people through earlier, I'm with them.'

The corporal talked to another corporal who sat in the gatehouse. Gareth turned down the concerto, which had gone folkish. The guardhouse corporal talked on the phone, the one in camouflage came back. 'All right, sir, go left and follow the signs for VIP Reception.'

The barrier lifted. Gareth drove on and found a low block with dark cars parked outside. He added the Aston to the rank.

Now that he came to listen properly with the engine off the folk element wasn't badly done, like Dvorak only English, and he could tell he was about to miss the finale, but he took the key out and walked to the building's glass doors where a guard in blue asked for identification.

In the lobby a needled-looking officer was standing about. 'You're Mr MacMichael, are you? I've put them in there, end of that corridor.'

Nice carpet, blue with yellow RAF crests woven in. Gareth pushed at the cinema-style double porthole doors and found he had to pull instead.

The lounge had wide windows looking out towards the runways. Paintings of old aircraft hung on the walls. Liam and his considerable retinue were sitting dotted around on a huge horse-shoe sofa. The sofa was upholstered in a shade of turquoise that might have been chosen to set off the travelling outfits of one VIP in particular.

Carl got up and said, 'Ah!', Willis waved, DI Draper of Special Branch nodded, the other detectives just looked, and Liam pushed his hand through his hair. Liam was red-eyed and white-faced.

'The altitude didn't agree with him,' said Willis.

'I was fine for about ten minutes,' said Liam, 'then I got this headache, right behind my eyes and nose here, I've never had anything like it, I thought I was going to die. The paracetamol didn't work. And when we came down again it got worse.'

'How is it now?' said Gareth.

'I feel lousy, it's still hurting.'

Draper said, 'We asked someone to find a flight surgeon but I think it's just his sinuses playing up, he'll be all right.'

Gareth didn't take off his Burberry or sit down. 'So you've got some names for us, Liam.'

'I just — ' Liam turned to Draper. 'Is this safe house anywhere near? I just need to lie down, you know?'

'That's not the deal,' said Willis. 'Come on, or you can forget about seeing a doctor and I'm putting you on the first Hercules back to Aldergrove. They don't fly as high, but that's because they've got no cabin pressure at all. And they take quite a lot longer.'

'Who told you the names, then, Liam?' said Gareth. 'Look at me.'

Liam looked up and said, 'That was Steve, Steve Hinch, he was in the unit. I was sent to see him, he still had a face like a football from having his wisdom teeth out.'

'So he was briefing you on … '

'Money, contact procedures, things you do and don't do … '

'Was he meant to tell you the names?'

'I don't know, I think he just thought, I knew him now, so he said you'll be with, I mean he mentioned them while he was talking about what it was like.'

'And it was people with history. That you'd heard of. We've probably heard of.'

'Yeah.' Liam leaned forward on his knees and said to the floor, 'Rory Kite. Mattie Ball.'

One of the detectives went over to a white phone on a nearby table.

Willis knuckled Liam's arm, 'All right, mate,' and went out.

The detective on the phone asked the Yard end to order up the pictures, place an all-ports watch, arrange an overnight print run for posters and alert the armed support group.

'But there's the other unit in too,' said Liam. 'And I don't know where they are. Or even who they are.'

'Sorry?' said Gareth. 'You mean you do know where Kite and Ball are?'

'That's not what I'm saying. I mean ... well, Steve said the house backed on to a reservoir, if you're interested, because Mattie's a birdwatcher and you could see a lot of birds out there, so he liked that. Yeah, and the street was named after the Queen, Steve thought that was funny. Tells you nothing in a city this size.'

'He didn't say the actual street.'

'No. I said what sort of area, he said you'll see.'

Gareth said to Draper, 'I've got an *A–Z* in the car, unless anyone's got one with them.'

The detectives looked at one another, shook heads.

Willis came in with a bald RAF officer who wore a white coat over his uniform and carried an attaché case.

Gareth went out to the Aston. The street atlas was the new colour edition and the blue of reservoirs stood out well. He sat and looked through the maps page by page while he listened to the end of the concerto. It took a couple of minutes. He went back in.

The doctor was closing his case. Liam swallowed an enormous pink-and-white pill with some water. The doctor said, 'Even flying in a pressure cabin, it's still like being catapulted halfway up the Matterhorn. So if your nasal sinuses are congested and the blood vessels in the linings swell up with the decompression it's quite painful. But that'll work in a minute.'

'What are sinuses?' said Liam.

Gareth smiled, not that he really knew either.

'They're places where the bones of your skull are hollow,' said the doctor.

Liam said, 'What have I got them for?'

'They make your skull less heavy to carry around, but they're mainly there to cause problems and keep doctors in work. How many years have you smoked, roughly?'

'Twenty, maybe.'

'You must have started around age five.'

'Right.'

'Oh. Well, if you can't cut it out, the next time you fly you'd better buy some of those pills at the chemist's first. Now. Am I done here? Good.'

'That's great, thanks,' said Willis.

Gareth sat beside DI Draper. 'There are only two streets with queens' names that back directly on to reservoirs in the whole of London. There's Queen Elizabeth Walk in Barnes, there, which is drawn so narrow I don't think it's residential, it's just the access to Barnes Common playing fields and tennis courts. And I can't picture Liam's people holing up in Barnes, anyway.'

Draper gave a half-laugh.

'Why?' said Liam, slumped with his head back while he waited for the pill to work.

Gareth said, 'It's kind of ... owner-occupied. And middle-class, and accent-sensitive.'

'Goodbye,' said the doctor at the door, and because he was a doctor everyone returned the farewell dutifully in full voice as he left.

Gareth said, turning pages, 'The other one's almost the same name, Queen Elizabeth's Walk, Stoke Newington.'

Draper bent to look.

'It's long, but most of it's up the side of this Clissold Park, there's only the short stub at the end where it turns right and goes along by the reservoir. That side of the street you've only got about twenty or thirty houses to pick from, I should think.'

'Yeah,' said Draper. 'Good call. Andy, you see this?'

The Anti-Terrorist Branch detective who'd been on the phone came over. 'Right.'

'D'you want to get Stoke Newington to see if they know any nosy neighbours, might help pin the house down?'

Gareth said, 'Mind you, it's practically in Stamford Hill.'

'A lot of orthodox, yeah?' said Andy.

'I don't think they like the police bothering them. Specially getting on for sunset on a Friday.'

'Local boys'll know a rabbi who can liaise if need be. And there'll be other people. Worth a shot.'

Draper said, 'Make sure you tell them no uniforms on the street. Carl?'

'Yes?'

'John?'

'Boss.'

'John, talk to Tracey at the Yard. House and flat numbers for this side of this bit of street. Utilities, voters, the usual, for those numbers.'

'Boss.'

'Carl, if we could cross-check those with any names you've linked to the redhead, that might be a help.'

'I'll call the desk and they'll send the Yard what they can, I'm afraid it's mostly rather raw.'

'OK. Are there enough phones in here, or shall I ask Flight-Lieutenant Perry for office space?'

'No, they're everywhere you look,' said Willis, sweeping a finger round.

'So, Kite and Ball, what's their form? Dave, flick through this A–Z, make sure Gareth didn't miss anything.'

'Kite's done a stretch for extortion,' said Willis, 'but he's supposed to have killed, is it thirteen people?'

'Think so,' said Gareth.

'That's one more than Martin McGuinness even. Half a dozen with the same Magnum handgun, very cocky, big reputation, not a nice guy.'

'Some of those jobs were informers,' said Liam, 'he used to be in security, I wasn't looking forward to sharing a flat with him.'

'Ball,' said Willis. 'Nicer guy. But as he's a bomb maker he might have killed even more people than Rory. There's not so much intelligence on him. Did a few years for possession of oven timers. RUC'll send you the stuff.'

Liam sniffed. 'He's meant to know more than anyone about corncrakes. They're extinct over here because you've screwed up your countryside but we've still got a few, only they live in areas where you don't go lurking about if you're not one of us or you get blown away, so he's the world's expert. But it's probably all shite, anyone who's been in the organisation a while gets this sort of myth that builds up. Maybe he saw one once, I don't know.'

'You met him?' said Draper.

'Me? No, neither of them.'

'Well, there you go,' said Willis, 'put your men in the long grass by the reservoir, play the right birdcall from the BBC sound archive and he'll walk into your waiting arms.'

Draper said, 'Andy's department handles the arrests. Ready to move in a minute, Liam?'

'OK.'

'Once you're safe-housed there'll be a lot more we want to ask you but most of it can wait for today.'

'You won't need me, eh?' said Willis.

'No, if you're going back in-province you can't be wise to his location. But get Carl to copy you the debrief tapes, and you, we'll need comments.'

'Sure,' said Gareth.

'Right.' Willis stood up. 'Can you give us a lift into town, Gareth, and I'll go on home and have a bath.'

'What about the money?' said Liam.

'You can't spend it when you're under protection. I'll tot up your pay so far and we'll double that for your payoff and Carl'll show you the accounts. Relocation expenses, Mr Draper sorts that out.'

'Can I get a green card?'

'It's possible,' said Draper, 'if you've got Irish nationality. But State Department might want to have a think about it.'

Dave the detective gave Gareth back his *A–Z*. 'You're right.'

'OK, Gareth.' Draper held out a hand to shake. 'Much obliged.'

'See you.'

'We'll keep you posted.'

'Sure. So long, Liam.'

'I'll be all right,' said Liam, and gave his nose a blow.

In the corridor Gareth said, 'That's an original threat, Nige, talk or we put you in a Herc.'

'Well, you go with what you've got,' said Willis.

'Did the doctor agree to wait till he co-operated?'

'That wouldn't be Hippocratic so I told Flight-Lieutenant Perry to hold him at the door while we concluded the secret bit.'

They passed through the lobby where Flight-Lieutenant Perry was still looking needled. 'Bye, thanks,' said Gareth.

Perry gave an inverse nod, putting up his chin.

Gareth pushed, and then pulled, at the glass doors.

Outside Willis saw the Aston. 'Whose is *that?*'

'It's my stepfather's.'

'And he lets you drive it?'

'I passed my test in it.'

Willis walked around the car, admiring. 'I didn't know they made estates, or is it a conversion job?'

'They farmed the work out to a coachbuilder, but it was a proper factory listed option.' Gareth unlocked.

When the radio came on with the ignition there was operatic singing, which Gareth hated. He switched it off quick.

Willis leaned over to see the speedometer. 'A hundred and how much? *Eighty?*'

'Oh, it won't really do that. It comes close, but now I'm not on urgent business I haven't got Crown Prerogative, so I can't show you.' Gareth backed out and headed down the access road at the regulation 15 mph.

'That's all right, I'd rather you didn't. Sorry for dragging you out here, he's a manipulative little beggar, but it seemed the best thing to play along with him.'

'I don't mind.'

''Cause he was frightened, and maybe he really does reckon he can trust you, one good turn.'

'He must think I'm stupid.'

'How?'

'What, if I don't know why he warned me I was blown? It wasn't me he was worried about, he was worried I might lead them to him. I don't blame him, he had to cover himself, but that's why it was hardly a favour.'

'No, but you know how he thinks, he'll have convinced himself it was.'

'So I'll look out for him?'

'Something like that.'

'You think the police marked his card?'

'I wouldn't put it past them. I don't know if they really believe we did the same to them or if it's just their way of holding a demarcation dispute.'

'He seems relaxed about working with our police, considering.'

'Different country, everyone knows that. It's whatsitomatic.'

'Aut? Idi? Axi?'

'Axi.'

'These chaps who turned up at the dump, I hope that was just unfortunate timing, you weren't followed?'

'No, what happened, they called on Miss Molly and found he'd been there so they did the local rounds. I wouldn't give too much for her chances now, she won't take any kind of protection, she only wants to know he's all right. And the girl who tipped him off's disappeared, lifted from her place by four guys in masks. Hey. Spitfire.'

They came to the gate. The barrier lifted, the corporal called, 'All right then, sir.'

Willis said, 'What's he doing in battledress with that sodding great rifle? The general went ages ago, he drove away straight off the tarmac.'

'I don't think it's to do with that.' Gareth waited to turn out. There was a slow queue for Hillingdon Circus in the other direction by now, but the cars coming their way were at full tilt. 'They're going to have to move this gate round to a side road, this is lethal. You haven't heard the news all day, then.'

'No, what? They haven't, have they? Invaded? This is a war footing we're on? What happened?'

'The garrison surrendered. They're all being put on a plane back to Heathrow.'

'Oh, no. That's it. That's done it now. Poll ratings like hers, worst on record, she can't afford to let it go.'

'Maybe not.'

'I can see it. We fight them, we win, when did we ever lose lately?'

Gareth said, 'Well, does Suez count?'

'Get off. Overnight success. We just had to pull out because the Russians and Americans didn't want us playing in their sandpit and winning.'

'All right. Irish independence.'

'If only we bloody had lost that one.'

'Sorry, the treaty was on our terms, wasn't it? Um. Afghanistan, no, our terms again ... I know, American war of 1812.'

'The one where we took Washington and burnt down the White House, you mean.'

'And then got kicked out.'

'Punitive raid, fulfilled its purpose.'

'OK, American war of independence, then.'

'Wasn't the British army,' said Willis.

'Wasn't it?'

'It was not. Hanoverian militia, London wouldn't foot the bill. I do have a degree.'

'Well, when did we last lose a war, then?'

'I'm blessed if I know,' said Willis.

'This is ridiculous, we must have lost one sometime, we're supposed to be good at losing. War of Jenkins' Ear.'

'Yeh, that might be it. Fiasco, that was.'

'But it was donkeys ago, it was under Walpole. We're over-looking something, we've got to be.'

'Maybe. But what have this lot ever done except for massacre left-wing students? So, we blow them to buggery, lucky old Argentina gets rid of the junta and we're stuck with — I can't stand this, I really thought she was on the way out, is there a lighter in this dash?'

'There, look. Hold on.' A heavy lorry gruffed past. The Transit van behind it was just far enough off. Gareth turned out. His mirror showed the Transit hurtling into close-up as he made second gear. He kicked the throttle flat and with a raging lycanthropic snarl the Aston crouched, twitched its tail and sprang down the straight towards London.

'Stone me,' said Willis. He struggled to right his head. The acceleration had thrown it back.

'I'm only doing eighty, well, ninety now.' Gareth overtook the lorry in third.

'It was the time you took to do it, or rather didn't take. Hell fire.'

Gareth snicked through to fifth and eased off. 'I'm sorry, but we'd have been stuck there all day. It's like if I hadn't pushed it earlier you'd still be waiting for me, I'd have got caught up in that lot leaving town.'

'Yeh, look at it, depressing, well, she doubled all the tube and bus fares last week, didn't she?'

'What, you mean this is the knock-on already? I think this is still the before picture, not the after.'

'You said affter.'

'Ahfter,' Gareth corrected himself. 'I pick things up from whoever I'm speaking to, take no notice. Here's the end of the Hillingdon tailback, see. It could be worse.'

'It will be. Or maybe not, the rate she's putting people out of work.'

'Look on the bright side, Nige. Perhaps the defence staff say it's no go, too far away. Or the Americans hamstring us again, it's their hemisphere, or the navy's oil tankers are all torpedoed and they have to come home, and it's too late for another try because it's nearly winter down there. Anything could turn up. We get humiliated, she gets the shove.'

'I don't fancy that,' said Willis, 'not as a good bet. No, we'll have to plant someone else in a mainland terror unit, that's it, slip them a few hints how to get at her.'

'The trouble with that is, apart from the fact that most of their jobs fall through, and assuming they buy the idea coming from you in the first place and you manage to keep your name out of it when they're caught, you still find the law of unintended consequences sets in.'

'Sympathy vote for the government?'

'State funeral, commemorative stamps, Trafalgar Square renamed, landslide sympathy vote.'

'I could put up with that,' said Willis.

'Strewth, I couldn't.'

'As long as I didn't have to put up with her actual existence.'

'The lighter's popped out.'

'Cheers.' Willis lit. 'Shall I open a window? Save a stink, keep your old man's ashtrays clean?'

'That's very kind, yes. Switch is on the dash there.'

'So. Any other ideas. Come on. Spencer,' said Su Holt.

Spencer felt clammy and seedy.

Goldie chewed his lip and played with file sheets to look thoughtful. Stubbs sat forward to look interested.

'Expand the age range? Otherwise, I don't know,' said Spencer.

'That's what you said last time,' said Su.

'Well. We still haven't tried it.' In fact he had, with no luck, but he had to say something.

'Who else could we bring into the equation, then, if we moved it up from thirty-five? Hm?'

'I can't remember.'

'Come on. I want to have ten new possibles before I call it a night.'

They had one so far. Spencer trembled with the effort of holding back a scream. He shook his head stubbornly.

'Patrick. Any useful over-thirty-fives on file?' said Su.

There weren't, but Goldie made a show of checking through. They had to wear her down. 'I'll just, erm ... '

Su's phone rang in the drawing room next door. Fiona had left for home so Su went to answer it.

'This is dire,' said Spencer.

Goldie coughed.

Stubbs made a blowing noise.

Goldie looked up. 'Sh.'

They heard Su in the drawing room say, 'Don't you try accusing my staff, if there's been a leak it's your end. Because I know my people. That's up to you, you're paying. Fine. No skin off my nose.' She hung up clatteringly and looked round the folding doors. 'All right. Search scrubbed.'

'Just like that?' said Spencer.

'Tony Pytcherley's found out. No surprise. They've lost their nerve, they say they want to put the search on hold while they talk to his lawyers, but I can't be bothered any more. So. Off home, go on. Oh. Not you, Spencer, in here a minute.'

Goldie and Stubbs, packing up their papers, looked at him. He could suddenly feel his pulse in his tongue. She must have noticed the different shirt and maybe even clicked to what Cracknell was on about. Following her through to the drawing room he calculated that he could admit the trip home for the file and simply bluff her on the timing. What he did with his lunch hour was his business. The messy bacon sandwich explanation would still do for the shirt and she couldn't disprove it. Unless someone had told her how long he was out.

'You live in Camden now, don't you?' she said. She sat down on the squashy leather sofa, leather trousers squeaking, and poured herself some mineral water.

'Yeah.' Instead of the Mondrian over the fireplace there was a signed Russell Flint print of girls lolling on a beach. When did that happen?

'Quite near Gareth, is he still there?' said Su.

'Couple of hundred yards away, he's up the mews.'

'So it's not that far to go.'

'What, from here? Or our place to his?'

'Something I wanted to ask you.' Su put her glass down and reached over the far arm of the sofa. She lifted up the Mondrian in its stainless steel frame. 'Wondered if you'd take him this. He always liked it and I've had to get another picture for that wall.'

'Had to?' Spencer said.

'This won't go with the new furniture I'm getting next week. And the people I interview always take it as some sort of intellectual put-down, I've got sick of hearing their inverted-snob reactions to it. I could hang it up at home but I thought Gareth might appreciate it.'

'I expect so.'

'Could you do that, then? Here.'

Spencer took the picture from her. It was reproduced much

larger than the tiny original, you could tell by the size of the cracks in the paint.

'What d'you think of the replacement? Just arrived this afternoon,' said Su.

'It's nice to look at.'

'Cost enough, it's signed.'

'Yes, I saw.'

'Of course that Mondrian's only a Tate Gallery poster in a plain frame.'

'Yes, no, he'll be pleased with it.'

'Oh, good. How is he doing?'

'Glad to be based back here, I think.'

'I know I would be. All right, then. Have a good weekend.'

'OK, and you, Su. Bye.'

Upstairs in research Goldie said, 'What was it? What's that?'

'She just wanted me to give this to Gareth.'

'Oh, she's gone ahead and bought that Russell Flint thing. She was showing me the dealer's catalogue the other day.'

'Yeah, it's not bad.'

'A bit dreamy, niminy-piminy, idealised.'

'Easy on the eye.'

'If you like that kind of thing, the lingerie-ad style.'

'Oh, you know.'

'Odd choice of Su's.'

'It's there for visitors.'

Stubbs, on the phone, said, 'I'll see you sooner rather than later after all, then, Régine. Don't let me keep him from his bath. Mm? Oh yah?'

Coated up, Goldie and Spencer switched their desk lamps off and left.

'She wasn't suspicious of your movements, then, that's good,' murmured Goldie on the stairs.

'No. Or else she doesn't care, it hasn't caused a problem.'

'She also seemed convinced it wasn't us who let the word leak out on Pytcherley.'

'Did ourselves a favour if it was. And the firm keeps the fee, presumably.'

'I should think so.'

'Something else she doesn't care about, then. I wonder if old Carrington'll take the fall for this invasion.'

'Does it matter?'

'Secret job. Odds are he won't be interested but she loves adding a lord to her contact list. So shall I mention it? Because if he's picked up his cards by Monday then it won't look such an on-the-ball idea, research department get less credit, she might even think of it herself.'

'OK, go on.'

They came to Su's floor. Spencer looked into the drawing room. Su was still on the sofa, reading interview notes. 'Yes?'

Spencer said, 'If the Foreign Secretary has to resign, he's chaired boards before, he'll be looking. Secret job.'

'That's a good thought. Can you pass the *Who's Who* there? Excellent.'

Back on the stairs, Goldie murmured, 'Shame it wouldn't keep, really.'

'Eh?' said Spencer.

'Slight waste, because with Pytcherley cancelled she's in a good mood anyway. So when something upsets her on Monday we'll need a rabbit we can pull out of the hat to distract her with and that one's gone. It gets us points now but they won't count then. It's like Alcoholics Anonymous, so last week you were sober, what about today?'

'Perhaps she'll contact him on Monday, get a nice hobnobbing buzz then from that.'

'Her credit not ours though, for that bit. Never mind.' In the hallway Goldie tapped at Cracknell's door and went in for a fat-chew. Spencer carried on.

Tara Holt had her pixie-booted feet up on what was no longer Claire's desk in reception.

Spencer stopped and tilted his head.

Tara said, 'Yeah, well, she's expecting a call and Jenny's gone, so muggins has to do the Holt Newman cneye helpyeew? What did happen to Newman? She never talks about it.'

'Before my time,' said Spencer. 'There are supposed to be

bloodstains that never came out of the boardroom carpet but I haven't noticed them.'

'D'you like my legs?'

'They're all right, why?'

She blew up her fringe. 'What's that you're making off with, then?'

He turned the Mondrian round to show her, put a finger to his lips and quit the building.

He waited at the Portland Place bus stop for a couple of minutes, then decided to walk. The Mondrian might be awkward on a crowded bus, the corners could poke people. The newly-doubled fares were meant to put you off using public transport, the PM had some strange doctrinal axe to grind, so Spencer was perversely happy to pay the difference if it helped to keep those fabulous Sixties buses rolling, but he'd have to forgo the pleasure this time.

At the top he crossed into the park and took the Broad Walk between banks of tulips. Little green nameboards fixed on pegs in the soil identified each vivid breed, Cliff Richard, Abu Hassan, John F. Kennedy.

Two tall black rollerskater guys bore down on him going backwards. Just in front of him they did a nifty crossover manoeuvre and swopped tracks at speed. 'Watch it, coonface,' said one to the other, who said, 'Clumsy black bastard, out of my way.' They laughed and shot narrowly past Spencer either side. A young black woman with a briefcase, walking by, cast Spencer a sullen eye as if he'd started it, although she'd obviously started it herself by being there and looking neat, which of course made the guys want to impress and irritate her.

Rory Kite and Mattie Ball were sitting in the front room with their bags packed but their target notes still out. In the street below the window, cars were turning up and rooting into spaces as the neighbours all came home from work.

Rory slurped his sweet white instant coffee from his mug and said, 'I vote we make the Forces TV girl the primary and if we have a problem then the MoD civilian personnel feller. If that's what he really is. You never know if any of these files are cover. OK, she's real, we've seen her on the box.'

'When you said soft targets,' Mattie said.

'Sometimes the more they're so-called innocent the better. I did that census taker last year, wife and mother, picture of respectability, nice looker, and the dividend was massive, big news.'

'Sure. TV Jane, I'm guessing, but the pattern is she should be here in town another week before her next month on assignment starts, the difficulty is she, like, she gets around at weekends, goes and stays with friends I think, not every time but that could start from Friday evening.'

'OK,' said Rory. 'She'd be great to do, remind her fans before they go off and recapture any islands we'll be here and waiting for them when they come back, if they make it, but supposing she's not around, the personnel guy, he's fine, the tabloids'll splash with why-him, only everyone'll know why, if you work for the government of occupation you're the problem and the answer is we blow your fucking head off. And we know the poor sad bastard hardly ever goes out anywhere except to work. And that office block with no sign up, I've got a feeling.'

'There's plenty of government offices with no sign up,' said Mattie. 'Looks like he's permanently posted back here since a month or two now anyway.'

'That doesn't rule him out, it's are you now or have you ever been, you know.' Rory psyching up.

'I wasn't disagreeing,' Mattie said, 'I'm just making sure you're happy with the targets, you're the trigger man. I should be doing it with plastic but there's no way we can recce it and place a car bomb in the time, not guaranteed same-day, and with our pictures maybe out.'

'We'll do fine. They're always on the watch for bombs, we haven't tried a gun hit over here in so long it's the thing they least expect.'

'Only we have to be right there to do it, harder getaway.'

'I don't mind. Did you clean that PPK or could you find the time with racing on all afternoon?'

'I cleaned it, you were sleeping.'

'They jam unless they're just right. If we do have any trouble and I need you to back me up I don't want sorry got a jam. Louise is coming when?'

'She couldn't be exact. Not too long. She has to pick up keys, we'll go to this place she's got empty, later on she'll drive us if we want.'

'Not all she'll do from what I hear.'

'Don't kid yourself.'

'It's what she's in it for.'

They heard the phone ring in the flat downstairs. The front door banged, the phone stopped ringing.

'Oh, is that Ms Karen Best?' the woman's voice said.

'Yes, who's this?' said Karen, wary, fearing telesales or market research from the formal sound of it.

'Sorry if it's a bad time to ring.'

'I've just come in, ran up the steps.'

'I thought you sounded out of breath. It's Detective Constable Heather Fuller, Stoke Newington CID, we spoke about your stolen car a few months back, I don't know if you remember.'

'Of course, hullo, how are you, it was found, in Tottenham, should I have told you, I assumed you'd know.'

'We did, yes, that's all right.'

'Oh. Have you caught someone?'

'I think we may have done, but when they ask for matters to be taken into consideration they can't always remember all the cars they've stolen.'

'I see. Well, thank you.'

'I was actually calling on another inquiry, it's quite routine, regarding individuals who may have moved into your street recently, the past two, three months.'

'Well, it's such a long street.'

'Your particular part of it, backing on to the reservoir. We believe someone may have noticed them because it would originally be three men, late twenties early thirties, sharing a flat, now only two of them. They would have quite strong Northern Irish accents, hard to disguise.'

'Oh good Lord.'

'So can you be of any help to us at all?'

'They're my upstairs neighbours. I heard them laughing up there a second ago, am I in any danger?'

'No, nothing like that. Can I ask you to try and not raise your voice? If you can hear them — '

'Oh no sorry sorry was I shouting?'

'No, not at all, just a word of advice.' There was a muffled pause and when DC Fuller came back on there was a tumble of other voices in the background. 'Would you be prepared to look at some pictures, Ms Best?'

'I've, I was about to change and go and see a film, I — '

'To help us decide if these might be the individuals we're concerned with? If you leave the house now and walk to the, to the Lordship Road end of the street, a colleague and I will be there by car in a couple of minutes, we can bring the pictures. We'll show you identification.'

'All right. Yes, all right. Oh. It's. You know. Half an hour ago the worst I had to worry about was the layout for an article on country kitchens.'

'Well, we've all got to make a living, haven't we? The pictures have just come over the wire so they're not too high quality, they're all lines like old black-and-white television, but you should be able to tell us if it is your new neighbours.'

'You know it's a sort of a joke I tell my friends, IRA living upstairs, saw one of the IRA in the hall this morning and he gave me a wink, but I never really thought, oh good Lord, er ... '

'Now if these are the individuals, Ms Best, nothing to worry about but I'd suggest in that case perhaps you should go straight on and see your film after we've spoken to you, not go home, so you might want to bring whatever you need when you leave the house, and we would prefer it if you didn't take the time to change, I'm very sorry about that.'

'You, right, well, I suppose, oh, what, you're, what, you're sending in the SAS.'

'No, nothing like that.'

★

In the mess at Chelsea barracks Sergeant Roger Hopkins, London duty troop, Counter-Revolutionary Warfare Squadron, 22nd Special Air Service Regiment, was watching the news when one of the lads came in and said, 'We're on.'

'Falklands? Fucking A! I thought we were stuck here.' Hopkins put up his hand for a high five.

'Stoke Newington. We're on standby if the filth can't handle it but they want some input anyway.'

'Oh well, a shout's a shout. Let's push off and collect some gear.'

Mattie wadded the target and dropsite notes into the bottom of the Golden Virginia tin. They were fair-copied very small on phonepad paper. The loose tobacco lay on the *Standard*, ready to pack back on top. Louise would give the tin to some runner to be passed on to the other unit. 'You want us to leave out the ones we picked? You know, in case? The guy gets stopped tonight they'd have it down in writing where to look for us.'

'Yeah, put a match to them, you might as well,' called Rory from the kitchen at the back. He'd unloaded the Colt Python revolver on to the table to give it a check and was now loading it again. The extra-long brass Magnum cartridges held twice as high a charge as normal pistol ammunition and could throw the .357-inch calibre copperjacket hollowpoint slugs hard enough to punch holes through the engine blocks of cars.

'There's not a lot of room in here,' said Liam, squashed between Carl and a large detective in the back seat as the Rover made its way from suburbs into countryside. 'My head's hitting the roof.'

'They copied the design from a Ferrari,' Carl said, 'perfectly ridiculous idea, but there you are.'

'You what?' the driver said. 'They never. British Leyland?'

'When you put it that way,' Liam said, 'a four-door stretch Ferrari, sounds cool. I still don't reckon anyone past puberty should have to try and force themselves into the back here.'

The radio spoke up with callsigns and then, 'Message for Inspector Draper,' female tones.

Draper, in the front, picked up the mike. 'That's me, Trace, what you got?'

'Local CID think they've identified the house, they should be able to confirm that in the next few minutes, suspects may be on the premises, CID and Andy's people hope to get an OP set up to confirm that too. Utility subscriber for the flat, the name won't click with Box 500 sources yet but the bills are paid cash, so the name could well be quite fictitious. No voter registered. Accommodation's rented, three flats in the house, CID are in touch with the ground floor tenant so we can expect some progress on the owner.'

'That's coming good, that it so far?'

'Box 500 have an intercept, in fact there's more than one, the calls were made at lunchtime, just been processed. They're regarding plans to charter a light aircraft.'

'OK, I see, have we got take-off and landing points?'

'We don't know where it's taking off from yet. The destination Box 500 are aware of. That's on neutral soil.'

'And it ain't in Sweden.'

'No, sir.'

'We making any overseas arrangements? View to welcoming committee?'

'We've established contact, yes. That's all I have for now, sir. But the intercepts are still ongoing. Chief Superintendent Bone requests you to return here ASAP, sir.'

'OK, will do when we've dropped our friend off, out.' Draper hung the mike up. 'Well done your lot, Carl, catch that?'

'O'Grady or someone's ordering a Descant,' Liam said.

'It's a codeword Liam here acquainted us with,' Carl said. 'I imagine the computer pulled it from the Irish Sea phone cable and just for once it wasn't somebody discussing choral practice.'

'Anyway,' said Liam, 'him or maybe someone calling up his people from the redhead's network this end must have said we want a Descant. Then I guess you have the numbers, tap them, see who they call next, and who *they* call ... ?'

'Pretty much so,' Carl said. 'The computer does it by itself whenever a keyword crops up, it's wading through the transcripts that's laborious.'

'That's right, fill him in,' said Draper.

'Oh, if Liam has a change of heart and goes back, and tells his former comrades all he's seen and heard, they'll still blow his brains out afterwards, and if his information makes them even more inclined to paranoia than they are already that does us no harm.'

'If that's your attitude,' said Liam, 'I'm thinking there is no such computer and you're feeding me a line.'

'What I don't like,' said Draper, 'is the thought of leaving this one to the Garda. If Kite and Ball have skipped it from that house before our mob move in we need to know this one grass strip, of all the places in the south-east that could take a light plane, that they happen to be making for. This charter outfit, what we got on that?'

'I only know they work from Europe mostly and they're mostly Brits,' said Liam.

'I expect we've traced them from the phone calls now,' said Carl.

'But it's the pick-up point we need,' said Draper.

Liam said, 'I gave you all the landing sites I knew in Ireland, I don't know any English ones.'

'So unless,' said Draper, 'someone goes and says it straight out on a tapped line, half past midnight, Pidcocks Farm near Steeple Bumpstead, be there, we've got no idea, we don't know where the hell to look. If all they say is rendezvous at Biscuitbarrel, usual time plus thirty, we might know where the aircraft's coming from or even who's the pilot but we're really none the wiser. Then the best we've got to hope for is the Garda meeting them the other end and I can just imagine how it goes from there.'

The driver said, 'Oh dear, they had a car there waiting and it drove them off so quick and we forgot to mount a block on that farm track they took and would you know we never caught the number in the dark at all at all.'

'Or else they get them and they find a flyspeck on the extradition papers so they let them go.'

Carl said, 'I expect you'll find them very shortly at the flat and none of this arises.'

Phil Cropley, at the Bar du Sport, saw that the *Malouines* affair was breaking big in the French evening papers. They still had their own island colonies to worry about, so it struck a chord, plus they were in the middle of delivering brand-new attack jets and Exocet missiles to the Argentine navy, so they needed to consider their position, plus they were all obsessed with the Queen, so the story had the same *schadenfreude* factor as if some quaint little trinket from the Crown Jewels had been pinched.

Phil asked Marc behind the counter for the phone. Marc brought it out and whacked it on the brass bar top and went on shouting about whatever it was he was shouting about to Thierry. Phil dialled Ibbotson and said, 'Just calling in.' He tapped ash. 'What's the status on this, then?'

'Oh, it's go,' said Ibbotson, which meant that somewhere, probably in Belgium, an IRA runner had handed over enough of the Provos' not-so-hard-earned drug and racketeering income to Ibbotson's man to bring the charter operation into swing, so Phil would, as agreed, be flying the twin-prop Piper over to a field in Essex in the middle of the night, collecting two passengers and heading on to Ireland. 'But can we make it Soylent now instead of Ivy?' said Ibbotson, a change from the original brief, which meant that either the Irish farmer had suddenly refused to clear his sheep off the Ivy landing site, or a reliable friend in the Garda had rung to say Ivy would be crawling with coppers. 'Apple as weather alternative still.'

'Right,' said Phil, 'I'll call in later.' He rang off and waggled fingers at Marc, which always meant a café cognac unless words to any other effect were added.

It wasn't tulips all the way. Most of the Broad Walk's monumental length ran through a tract of open grass. Towards the north end there were fewer people on the scene, more squirrels though. One sat down in Spencer's path to scratch its ear. He thought for an affronted moment he might have to go around it, but when he came within a stride's length it jumped to and fled. He turned to watch it clamber up the post that held a sapling straight. In the distance beyond, among the trees at the park's far rim, the dome of the mosque glinted evilly. Spencer felt his face souring at the sight of the thing as always and looked away, tightening his grip on the

Mondrian. A duck flew over with a drake in pursuit, mallards. They made a steep turn at the next copse and came back. Above the copse he saw the slender paper-dart-like shape of Concorde drifting in from the Atlantic, low and slow on its final circuit. When he was making lunch with Claire (Claire!), that machine was still on the ground in New York. Whoosh. He smiled.

Just short of the Zoo he struck across to Gloucester Gate and came out at the head of Parkway. He checked his watch. Twenty-odd minutes since he'd left the bus stop.

A Routemaster was waiting at the lights with not too many heads in its windows. He stepped on.

'It's only down the road and all change,' said the conductor.

'Yeah, I know.' Spencer sat on the endways bench next to the platform, hugging the Mondrian to his chest. It came up past his face. He didn't have the room to shift it round beside him without elbowing his neighbour so he angled it a little to see past it as past a door ajar. The people sitting opposite considerately forbore to stare.

The bus moved on, past the Henlys car showroom where a classy old Alvis stood on display, shame they only make tanks these days, and down the slope towards the Camden Gate flicks. Spencer craned to find out what was showing, good grief, *I Live in Fear* by Kurosawa, black-and-white posters of Toshiro Mifune going yikes against a mushroom cloud. On the whole he thought he'd rather tackle Proust in German at the Plaza round the corner.

Over the much patched surface of the great fiveway junction the driver took them at a lick, slowing up for the zebra by the tube in Kentish Town Road. The felt-tipped announcements on the white board in the station entrance normally concerned delays or captious escalators, but this evening, Spencer saw, the message, formed in letters of a size and rigour well past normal, ran thus:

H.M. FORCES
ALL
LEAVE
CANCELLED
RETURN TO UNITS
IMMEDIATELY

His breath left him, in a sigh rather than a gasp, but all of it, and at one go. He shuddered and drew some back. Even now, this might not mean the full disastrous works. In any case he wouldn't have to do the job himself, and no one else he knew would either. And those who did perhaps would take a lesser risk than Spencer took by smoking, never mind by crossing roads, which he'd be doing in a minute. Still. Cold sea hurt, and so did fire, and so did flying metal.

The bus pulled in. This was the last stop on the route unless you wanted to be carried round the back of the disused bread factory to the terminus. Spencer burrowed a fist in his pocket for coins as he made the platform. He asked the conductor, 'What's that, forty, fifty now?'

The conductor refused payment with the gracious, weary gesture of an envoy declining the eleventh course at dinner.

'Oh. Thank you very much,' said Spencer.

The conductor accepted the thanks with one of those small, eloquent motions of the head that ranked high on the list of things white people couldn't do.

Spencer walked back to the crossing by the tube. He glanced again at the crisis notice in the entrance behind him as he waited.

A tall, slightly Oriental girl came down the station steps, looking round in a lost sort of way. She had stackheeled boots on, black jeans and a designer combat jacket, with a smart leather holdall slung from her shoulder. Making up her mind, she sauntered leggily to the kerb beside Spencer. The traffic stopped at once.

They crossed to the Halfway House pub in the fork of the Kentish Town and Camden Roads. Spencer usually stuck to the wrong side of the Camden Road from then on, at least as far as the Ferodo bridge, but the girl, looking round again with a toss of her long black hair, decided to take the second crossing right here, over to the Mother Red Cap, and the traffic had already freeze-framed for her, so Spencer, after wavering a moment, followed.

On the pavement the other side she turned and set off towards the High Street. Spencer's way home was the opposite direction.

Fifty yards up the road, of course, he had to wait again to cross at the turn-off for the one-way system. The traffic swept on round the corner, ignoring him and the Belisha beacons and the Highway Code, for some time, then suddenly jerked to a craven halt.

The girl stepped out across the zebra stripes beside him. 'Excuse me. Hi. I'm totally confused,' she said in a husky French voice. Obvious now he thought of it. She was part-Vietnamese. Or did she look a bit more Indian? In which case she might be something to do with Mauritius or Réunion. Or then again Tahitian?

'Hullo,' he said comfortably, as if his mouth were not turning dry. He gave a nervous cough and spoilt it.

'I'm looking for a pub called the Falcon, you know it?' she said. 'Is it this way?'

They reached the kerb. 'Yeah,' said Spencer. He pointed ahead.

'Ah, great. I've never been in Camden before, it's so confusing.'

'It, is, yes.'

'This agency sent me.'

'Oh,' said Spencer. The Falcon looked an ordinary pub from the outside, which was all he ever saw of it, but Katie had been in there with someone once and they left quick when a strip show started. 'Well, you turn left at the railway bridge.'

'Railway bridge?' the girl said, worried, seeing none.

'You'll see it in a minute, round the curve after the traffic lights.'

'OK. Good, so, you know the place I mean.'

'I've been past it.'

'I'm a dancer,' she said.

'Oh, yes? Isn't it a bit early?'

'It's past the hour of opening. And I have to see the manager, I have to see the stage, sometimes not much room, it changes what kind of act, and I like to arrive before much of the crowd or they think we just saw her, outdoors coat, big clumsy bag she was carrying, then there's no illusion.'

'No, right, I'll remember not to turn up and embarrass you if I'm out for a drink later.'

'Ah no, if you like, I don't mind!' She laughed. 'That's OK. It's just when you know the whole audience recognises you.'

'Ah.'

'But, I perform, I'm good, people to watch, of course I want.'

'I think I'd be a bit embarrassed now.'

'Yeah?' She gave him that puzzled you-English look. 'Maybe you should get a little drunk first, I do.'

'Do you?'

'Sure.'

They reached the next junction and waited for the lights. A small redfaced man, stained check overcoat flying open, dodged and lurched through the traffic towards them. Horns blew. The man milled his arms and shouted 'Up the IRA' at passing drivers. Near the kerbside he crabbed over to the girl, gave her the finger and shouted 'Up the IRA' again. She shied back. He cackled, turned on Spencer and gave him a finger with each hand. 'Yahaagh! Up the IRA!'

'Up U2,' suggested Spencer.

The man sneered and started waving his fists and muttering.

'No, you're right, they're crap, I take it back,' said Spencer.

The lights changed. 'Let's go,' the girl said, and stepped out. Spencer followed. Halfway across he felt the man punch him rather feebly in the small of the back. He slowed, stopped and turned.

The man cowered, tripped over his own feet, got up and ran away, cackling again.

The girl noticed Spencer wasn't with her and mooched slowly on the far pavement till he caught her up. 'So, that was witty, but why don't you like U2?'

'I've never heard them. What music do you dance to?'

'For work? Euh. Mostly not much good, that's the style, good music would be crazy, I couldn't do it.'

'Are you studying or anything, daytimes?'

'Yeah, I'm at the Courtauld Institute.'

'Right. Are you?'

'You know, art history? I'm not going to be a professor, but it's good to do.'

'Yes.'

'Aaand I'm on vacation but I don't want to go back to Paris,' she turned up her nose, it was odd that some Parisians hated the place but they did, 'much better here, and I make money. This is the bridge? Ferodo?'

'Yeah.' The ad was painted both sides so you saw it coming as well as going. It was some way up the road yet.

'Weird word.'

'Make of brakes.'

'Ah? So, you like Mondrian?'

'This? My boss is chucking it out of her office, she wants me to give it to a friend who lives near me. It's good, isn't it?'

'It's pure, it's cerebral, absolutely, yeah. You live this way?'

'Not far.'

'So. You can come later.'

He assumed she was kidding. 'Yeah. What's your name?'

'Sandrine. But for work, Suzie Wrong.'

'Wrong?'

'Yeah, because I'm not Suzie Wong, I'm imitation, but, like, bad girl.'

It didn't really come off, but he quite liked it all the same. Her own idea by the sound of it. 'Where was she from, in the movie?' he said, although he knew.

'Hong Kong, I think,' she said, then fielded his real question. 'Of course, I'm not, but my grandmother was from Saigon, so, the look.'

'Yes. I'm Spencer.'

'Spensair? That's unusual, first name.'

It still made him uneasy, that 'Spensair', a Jacqueline thing, even though everyone else he knew in France said it just the same way. 'I think my mother was a Spencer Tracy fan although she doesn't admit it. She's Austrian, I don't know if he was big in Austria, but she's been here since she was about ten anyway.'

'Ah, everyone comes from everywhere, you know.'

'Eh?'

'Everyone is mixed.'

'I suppose so, apart from Australian Aborigines, weren't they completely cut off for about ten thousand years?'

'But plenty of them are part-white now, part-Chinese, whatever, it's the strongest thing, you can't stop it.'

'No.'

'Hey, this place is famous.'

On the corner of the junction that lay aslant under the railway bridge was the avant-garde frock shop Swanky Modes.

'Is it?' said Spencer. 'I never see anyone go in.'

'Sure, very famous, very chic, everyone knows, look.'

In the window, at the feet of the headless black dummies sporting asymmetric moss-green or cerise dresses, stood picture cards of models wearing much the same with 'Featured in *Vogue*' printed underneath.

The girl shouted, against the rumble of a North London Line commuter train on the bridge, 'But I never knew it was out here,' and swung an arm to take in the generally shabby area.

'Oh, Camden's fashionable. God knows why but it is, and it's getting worse.'

'You think I will have a fashionable audience?'

'Nnn, I couldn't say.' He pictured beerbellies in purple Crimplene, but perhaps it was lean young graphic designers and copywriters. They might think strip was a kitsch art form or somesuch insufferable postmodern twaddle. He shifted his feet.

'I get the idea,' said the girl.

He felt he'd put her down by acting awkward. 'It's just, I go to the Old Eagle, it's only a few doors down across the way but I expect they're completely different places.'

'Ah, you mean that one is the fashionable one. Perhaps I take a look later, I finish nine o'clock.'

'Do you?'

'I do enough shows by then, I make enough money, later I don't like the audiences so much.'

'The lights are changing. If you cross here, down that street, two hundred metres, it's just around the first turning on the right.'

'So close. Thank you, you're kind. OK, ciao. See you later.'

'Good luck.'

She wove between the cars still shuffling up against the red. Each of them in chain stopped dead like next door's cat when startled, blocking the junction so the charge of cross traffic had to go around them.

She made the island, took the other lane at her sexy saunter, and paused on the corner by the shuttered premises of A. Brilliant & Son, Tobacconists and Cigar Merchants, till she could go over to the other side of Royal College Street for the pub.

The cross traffic yielded at first glance. Spencer saw the brake lights flash back down the line and the cars bow, bob and nod to a standstill.

Waving but not looking in his direction, she was so confident of his gaze, the girl sauntered forth into the road and the back of a Transit van hid her from sight.

The main road traffic got the green now but nobody could move, she'd gridlocked the junction.

Spencer wondered if Claire could do that and decided as rule not, it took long hair and a certain bearing. You didn't have to be tall and mannequinlike, though: he'd seen a five-foot-two woman cause a minor smash-up at the Angel once. Or tightly clothed: Sandrine's combat jacket was open so he'd noticed she could pack a sweater out impressively enough, but none of those drivers would be able to tell from where they sat.

He made his way through the jam and under the bridge.

Had he just arranged to meet her later on without quite meaning to? Her English was at least as good as his French (which he gave himself a large helping of points for not trying out), so when she said 'See you later' she must know that meant nothing in itself, but she'd planted on him certain details as to her intended movements, which women did not do except to score a meet.

He didn't see why she'd want to, though. When they looked that good they already had boyfriends, it was a law on a par with gravity. The boyfriends were total tossers, by another law of similar infrangibility, but that was a side issue.

The only explanation he could think of was that when some people went abroad they made a point of getting pally with total strangers all the time for no real reason.

At home in Crouch End, Willis lay on the sofa while the living room slowly dimmed around him. He ought to put the boiler on for some hot water, then go round to Mr Patel's and buy coffee, eats, soap and all the other bits and pieces he didn't have in the cold, dead-smelling flat, then ring British Airways about the shuttle flight back to Aldergrove on Sunday, then ring some friends and see if there was anything doing Saturday night while he was here, then dig out towels and spare clothes from the cupboards, by which time he might be able to run a bath.

But he either couldn't be bothered to get up or just plain couldn't. After-effects of being shot at. While he waited for the weakness to pass he found his Three Fives in his parka pocket and lit up. The hunt for an ashtray might have got him off the sofa, but there was one to hand on the floor already, with six-week-old butts in it.

Spencer pulled the plug and let the washing-up water run out while he dried his hands on a teatowel. Birds sang. On the radio, Carrington of the FO and Nott of the MoD were holding a press conference, answering in low guilty voices to reporters' questions. Argentine assets were being frozen, resolutions were being filed at the UN, more ships were getting ready to sail. Carrington said he wasn't resigning, but that meant nothing.

Spencer decided to go and fetch a bottle from the offie. He'd smoked so much less than usual today he still felt twitchy. Besides, knocking back some wine would lessen the temptation to wander down the pub later on. Yes. He did a short tap dance on the kitchen lino, grabbed his jacket off a chairback in the living room and went out.

At Davisons on Murray Street round the corner, the radio behind the counter was tuned to pop, playing that strange live version of 'Are You Lonesome Tonight?' where Elvis kept cracking up.

'Quietest we've been in here since opening time,' said the thin, polo-shirted manager as Spencer stood at the shelves of reds deciding.

'Yeah?' said Spencer.

'Had a rush on earlier. Don't know if people are celebrating or drowning their sorrows.'

'Bit soon to celebrate.'

'Ooh, I don't know, I think she's blown it good and proper this time.'

'Nah, devil looks after his own.'

A statuesque blonde girl in tight white trousers and black spangly boob tube looked through the doorway at the back. 'Norrere yet?' she said in Northern, perhaps asking after a promised minicab. Spencer hadn't come across her before.

'They did say twenty minutes,' said the manager, 'it's not due. Don't worry, I'll call you.'

'Hiya,' she said to Spencer.

'Hullo,' said Spencer, puzzled for a moment — had they met before, then? — till he remembered people from the north were like that, same as travelling types, always being friendly when you weren't friends at all.

'Soph, the wife's girl,' said the manager. His wife's daughter from a previous marriage, that must be. 'Down from Manchester.'

'Oh. How are you?' said Spencer.

'Bored,' said Soph.

'Are you?'

'Nothing to do down here.'

'Isn't there?' Spencer picked up a bottle of the only known Lebanese claret and took it to the counter. The manager rolled it in a sheet of tissue.

'No, it's dead dull,' Soph said. 'Manchester I'm always out clubbing Thursday through Sunday every weekend, there's nothing down here.'

'Been to the Camden Palace?' said Spencer.

'Yeah.'

'Dingwalls down at the Lock?'

'Yeah.'

'Well then.'

'That was last weekend. They're not as good as back home.'

'If the streets were paved with gold you'd complain about your heels sinking in. So what's on tonight?'

'Me and my friend Patricia are going to go up the West End and get ripped off. I don't know why people move down here, I can't wait to go back next week.'

'Ray of sunshine,' said the manager.

'You're not young forever,' she said. 'Another couple of hundred weekends, that's all, and I'm past it. Time's wasting.'

'I hate being young,' said Spencer, and took his change. 'Thinking you've got to fit things in or it's too late.'

'You're not young,' she said, 'you must be nearly twenty-five.'

'Not yet. Cheers.'

'See ya. Have a nice evening.'

'You too.'

'I doubt it. If you're having a dinner party can I come?'

'Sure,' said Spencer at the door. Unlike with Sandrine, you knew when she was kidding.

'I told her not to take a job with the Inland Revenue,' said the manager. 'I said you'll be frustrated and restless.'

Outside, the shamrock sign on the Irish Centre opposite was lit up to show the bar was open, but the streetlamps weren't due on for hours yet. The daylight still seemed unnaturally prolonged since the clocks went forward.

Spencer, heading home, stopped, crossed and turned up Camden Square instead. He might as well see if Gareth was in, although the MoD were quite likely working overtime.

The square was a much bigger and once grander one than Spencer's, a park in the middle with tall trees and a playground. The old houses Goering had managed to miss were ornate and many-tiered, carriage trade, some tatty now, a few gentrified again.

Halfway up, a footpath led off between two of the low-rise council blocks. You could see straight through to Gareth's house across the mews at the back, and he must be in because that was his stepfather's incredible old motor in the carport.

As Spencer reached the front door he could hear Gareth whistling somewhere inside the house. Not many people whistled any more and no one else at all would whistle Lennon's 'Across the Universe' in an upbeat tempo that made it sound like something by Disco Tex and the Sex-O-Lettes, to horribly sad and eerie effect.

There was a spyhole in the door, which didn't use to be there. Perhaps some rape case had sent the girls paranoid. Spencer rang the bell and the whistling stopped, but he didn't hear anyone coming. He was wondering whether to ring again when the door opened. He jumped.

'Sorry about that,' said Gareth, boyish grin to the fore. 'How's things?'

'All right. Are your folks here?'

'No, I borrowed the car. I see you've done Davisons.'

'Yeah. I've got something for you back at the house. Su's old Mondrian. She's hanging up a Russell Flint to replace it and she thought you'd like it.'

'Oh. That's nice of her.'

'So if you want to come down the road.'

'Right, hold on.' Gareth took his trenchcoat from the hooks in the minuscule hallway. 'He's OK in his way, Flint. He could do great girls. And his Arthurian illustrations are terrific.'

Spencer said, 'I don't know what you've got in your inside pocket but it doesn't half bugger up the fit of that suit. Waste of Savile Row tailoring.'

Gareth pulled on the coat and tugged his shirt cuffs down. 'I know, I hate it, but it's something I have to carry with me.'

'One of those Filofax things?'

Gareth stood shaking his keys. 'I'm trying to think if I should set the alarm.'

'I didn't know you ever bothered with it.'

'I do at the moment.'

'Have you been burgled or something?'

'No. Oh, well, never mind.' Gareth came out and locked the door. 'I can't be all that long anyway, I've got to go back to the office. Bit of a flap on, I expect you've heard.'

'Yeah. What, are we walking?' said Spencer as Gareth led the way out through the carport's open double gates.

'You don't want me to get the car out to go three hundred yards?'

'I've never been in it.'

'Come on, I hate backing through gateways. And trying to park in the sort of fiddly little half-spaces you have to make do with on Rochester Square by this time. It'll take longer than going on foot.'

'Save you humping the picture back.'

'It's not that heavy.' Gareth had gone a few yards along the cobbled mews. He waved his arms, spun and strode back. 'All right, stand over there, watch for anything coming.'

Spencer went to the other kerb.

In the carport Gareth did a sort of press-up on the concrete beside the Aston, looking for something underneath, as if the car'd been making funny noises lately, but he didn't seem too bothered. He got in and brought the loose end of his trenchcoat belt aboard before he shut the door. The engine fired with a deep note from the double-barrelled exhaust. The reversing lights shone.

Spencer looked up and down the mews, shouted, 'OK', and beckoned with his free hand.

The Aston launched itself out at him tailfirst alarmingly fast, slewed round and stopped parallel to the kerb beside him. Gareth threw open the passenger door.

Spencer joined him in the cockpit. Nice leather seats but no flash woodwork, except the rim of the big steering wheel. The dashboard was black crackle finish. 'So have you done a stunt driving course, then?'

'You have to if you're going to drive around over there, in case of ambushes. But also the mechanic's done something to the engine, it's a lot quicker on the uptake suddenly and I'm not used to it, sorry.'

'That's all right.' Spencer stuck the wine of Lebanon between his thighs.

A car turned into the mews from the Murray Street end. The roadway was narrow for passing, though it looked doable if one of you went up the kerb where nobody was parked.

Gareth trickled the Aston slowly forward over the cobbles. 'And it's not all stunts exactly, it's more like I don't know that purple Escort and there's two men in it so I want to pass it where I've got the most room for manoeuvre.' He let the other car come on till they met by the ramp of the council flats' parking area. He used the ramp to go around the other car and accelerated away.

'Only you're not over there now, you're over here,' said Spencer.

'Mm.' Gareth braked for the junction and nosed the Aston out to take a look. There were cars coming from both directions. 'Oh well.'

Spencer said, 'Erm — .' He seemed to have mislaid a few seconds of his life. The Aston was across Murray Street already and bounding on down the mews with a growl.

Gareth pulled round the corner of Rochester Square at the end. 'Space, great.' He parked right outside the house, the spot Paul usually bagged. He got out. 'Are you coming?'

'Nn? Hm,' said Spencer.

'If you'd seen in the mirror, we were well clear before those cars came by. They weren't moving much really.'

'In relative terms maybe. You said the mechanic had done something, you didn't say he'd fitted warp drive.'

'I expect he's only put it back like it should be.'

Spencer found his legs and stepped out. He shut the door behind him, said, 'I think I'll do that again,' and did it again, to hear the wonderful clunk it made one more time. 'Brilliant. Thanks.'

'We'd still have walked it quicker.'

'We wouldn't.' Spencer let Gareth into the house and showed him the Mondrian propped on the sofa. 'There it is.'

'Ah.' Gareth held it at arm's length. 'Remember to say thanks to Su for me, that's good.'

'Sure. D'you want some of this red?'

'I'm not really supposed to, but I'll have a glass if you're opening it.'

Spencer, rummaging for a corkscrew in a kitchen drawer, called out, 'Not supposed to? You been ill?'

'No, but for one thing I've got to get the car back up the road without bending it, and for another thing I have to carry this weapon these days and I think drunk in charge of a government firearm's fairly serious.'

Spencer looked round the kitchen archway, doubting his ears.

'You what?'

Gareth had slung his trenchcoat over one of the dining chairs. He patted the great bulge in the jacket of his ridiculously good steel-blue suit. 'I've been given a concealed weapon permit, but they make you responsible for the thing so you have to have it with you at all times and be in a fit state to handle it.'

'You're having me on. That is a Filofax in there, isn't it?'

'No.'

'It's a gun? Type thing?'

'Yes.'

'What d'you want one of those over here for? I thought concealed weapons were all banned anyway.'

'No, there's a couple of hundred people around London with permits. It's usually if they're at risk from terrorists.'

'Jeez. So what have you done to annoy the terrorists, or is that a secret?'

'Simply working for the civil service over there. As a rule they'd never have heard of me, but someone with a galloping personality disorder who worked in our pass office sold them copies of some of our ID reference sheets. When you're issued a pass your picture and details go on file on a reference sheet. Mine had a false job description but they know my name and my face and anyone working for the Crown's fair game. So I had to be posted back.'

'This bloke got caught, then.'

'Well, an informant showed us the copies and it soon became pretty obvious who'd done it. Silly thing is I still have to watch out because they've got my home address and there's at least two of their units in London just now.'

'That's appalling,' said Spencer. 'Wait a minute. When you got down beside the car before you got in, you weren't checking it for ... ?'

'Yes.'

'Eurck. How do you live like that?'

Gareth shrugged.

'Shouldn't you have police protection, or go in a safe house?'

'No, cost too much. Only important people get that. Rest of us get a Browning and best wishes. Still. It'll probably never happen.'

'But, so you really thought the blokes in that Escort might be them?'

'No, but in case it was, I made it hard to block me.'

'And this is what you think about all the time.'

'No, I just do it, I'm used to it.'

'What do Lynn and whatsname make of it?'

'Melanie? She's moved out. Lynn's OK, though.'

'Melanie. She always was a bit ... '

'Yes.'

'You definitely ought to have a slug of red.' Spencer went back into the kitchen to uncork the bottle. He wouldn't quite believe this until he saw the gun.

Gareth came through. He looked round the kitchen and said, 'Your central heating timer's still on GMT.'

'You would notice a thing like that. Reset it if you like.'

Gareth twiddled the dial on the wall by the boiler.

Spencer pulled the cork and poured. 'Here.'

'Thanks.' Gareth gestured at the bottle.

'What? Oh.' Spencer showed him the label. 'Musar.'

'Great.'

'Be twenty quid if it was French.' Spencer gulped some. He took the bottle through, put it on the hideous coffee table and flopped into an armchair.

'Are the others not around?' said Gareth. He went over to the french windows.

'Katie's seeing some married man she can't decide whether to do it with or not for dinner, at least I think that's what's up, Paul's gone down to Cookham, Miles is probably still at work. Although he usually stays at Christine's in Islington over the weekend anyhow.'

'Your apple blossom's nice. You can see it from our bathroom window.'

'That's funny, you can't see your house from here.'

'No, but you could from the top of that tree.'

'I'll take your word for it. Show me this Browning.'

Gareth put his glass on the hideous coffee table and took an imposing black pistol from under his jacket. He kept his index finger straight, clear of the trigger.

'Good grief, it's big enough,' said Spencer.

'Small ones jam. I'll have to unload it.' Gareth released the magazine from inside the handgrip. It was a steel box the size of a Mars bar, at its top end a crimped aperture that held a bullet, gold with bronze snout. Gareth laid the magazine by his glass, turned, pointing the gun at the bottom of the french windows, and yanked back the breech. Another bullet flew up, spun aside glinting and landed on the carpet. Gareth let the mechanism snap shut with a harsh, chill noise. He held the gun out by the barrel. 'It's heavier than it looks.'

Spencer still nearly dropped it. 'It is too. Sorry.'

'Don't try and fiddle with it.'

'No.' Now he'd got it in his hands he didn't like it. It was beautifully sculpted, solid, lustrous, a brutal elegance about it, but all the same. He read off the small capitals engraved on one side. 'Browning FN 9MM.'

'Millimetre.' Gareth found the bullet in the carpet pile. He dusted it with his fingers and pressed it into the magazine.

'Course.' Spencer clucked. 'FN's the Belgians, isn't it?'

'John Browning did a lot of work for them.'

'The top half's a separate part.'

'The slide. That blows back and recocks it when you fire.'

'What are all these widgets?'

'The stud in the root of the trigger guard is the magazine release. The tab up by the hammer is the safety. The little bar thing on the side is the slide stop, you press the end down to unlock the action after you reload. You also pull it out when you want to dismantle the thing.'

'If it's an automatic, does that mean it keeps firing if you keep your finger on the trigger?'

'No, there's a pre-war version that will, you can switch it to rapid, but it's a terrible job to hold it steady, even with the shoulder stock. Which in your case you have not got.'

'They made these pre-war? It looks modern.'

'So does Mondrian. Modern goes back a long way.'

'You'd better take charge again.' Spencer held the gun out by the barrel, which seemed to be the etiquette.

'Thanks.' Gareth fitted the magazine and worked the slide, k'shlak k'ching, aiming at the window. 'That's now live. Don't do anything startling while I uncock it.'

Spencer sat very still.

Gareth eased the hammer slowly home with his thumb. 'OK, safe.' He put the gun away under his jacket.

Spencer drank and said, 'Shoulder holster then.'

'Yes. With a good one properly adjusted the weight's not so bad, but it always looks awful.'

'You could have your suits altered.'

'I'm hoping the situation's not permanent enough to warrant it.'

'Yeah. I don't know. I mean the terrorists are going to be around for ever, aren't they?'

'They'll lose interest eventually. In me, anyway. In the whole thing at some point.'

'They shot that bunch of them, when was it, couple of months ago, doesn't seem to have put them off.'

'Brown's Brook, you mean.' Gareth took out his plain Camels. 'Would you like one of these?'

'Thanks.'

Gareth flicked the soft pack's base so the cigs stuck out like organ pipes. 'It wasn't meant to put them off, it was only meant to stop that mortar attack.'

'Yeah, but there must be better ways of doing it, they just make propaganda out of that.' Spencer took the most protrusive Camel.

'Can't be helped sometimes.' Gareth took the next and tapped it on the face of his watch.

Spencer, remembering it was better to avoid a mouthful of loose tobacco but not wanting to look too imitative, tapped his on the foot of his wineglass. 'I suppose.'

'And it wasn't planned for.' Gareth lit both cigs and dropped the match in the butt-strewn saucer Miles had left on the table, which might as well carry on being the ashtray for now.

'Sounded like it was.'

'No, ambushes are off for our side at the moment. Till the brass say different.' Gareth sat beside the Mondrian on the sofa.

'So what happened?'

'Things went wrong. There was a surveillance team in the farmyard because they heard some weapons were going to be hidden there, stuff coming up from the south, but they didn't know exactly what or when. It was only an MI5 technician along with one of their field agents to take turns on watch and a couple of SAS to mind them.'

'They're all pretending to be bushes.'

'Sort of. You wear camouflage and bring your own vegetation to some extent, but there was plenty of disused agricultural machinery and fallen-in pigsties, good existing cover. So they go in, dead of night, and the idea was, as long as the farm dog didn't sniff them out, to get pictures of the couriers, they had starlight scope cameras if necessary, bug the hiding place once they saw where it was, doctor the weapons. But the next afternoon a car comes up the track, then the lorry with the mortar tubes on the back, Provos pile out, AKs everywhere, they take the manhole cover off the septic tank and haul up a container, and at this point the team realise the drop's been made before the surveillance even began and this is the collection. At least, the MI5 men realise, the soldiers don't because they're in another hide a few yards away, and earlier on the farmer stacked a vanload of secondhand roof tiles for repairing his barn right where it blocks their view across the yard.'

'Not on purpose?'

'No, if he'd known they were there the Provos would have known.'

'But the MI5 blokes can tell them what's going on by radio, presumably.'

'Yes, mutter mutter. And they've got to do something because the Provos are loading the shells from the container and in a few seconds they'll be ready to rev up and go and mortar the local police station, at a guess.'

'Well, they could warn the police. Call up some armoured cars to head the lorry off.'

'The SAS did call the mobile support, which was based at the local station as it happens. So they were on their way. But they only had Land Rovers, there's a choice of back roads round there, the lorry had been virtually turned into a battering ram, great girder bumpers welded on for taking out roadblocks, and a confrontation on the public highway's dangerous to the public. Once you let the convoy pull out of the yard you've surrendered control of the situation.'

'Hm.'

'The terrorists are still panning these Kalashnikovs about, they're always very edgy on a job. The soldiers need time to break cover and move up behind the tile stack and the spare MI5 man's the senior officer, youngest person there but senior on paper, so they let him start a diversion by giving the challenge.'

'What, drop your guns and put your hands on your heads or something.'

'I don't think it got any further than "Halt, security forces", if that, because of course all the terrorists do is start blazing away in the direction his voice is coming from.' Gareth took a drink. 'He had a short submachine-gun so he fired back, but it's difficult to aim those at the best of times. Let alone when you're being shot at, you go clumsy and useless. The technician with him couldn't even get his gun cocked. The terrorists bundled into the vehicles, firing wild. And then the SAS opened up.'

Spencer drew on his cig. 'And that was pretty much that, I imagine.' He felt stupid for not realising sooner that the senior officer was in the room.

'Yes. They had proper high-velocity assault rifles, G3s, pushing out tracer and armour-piercing and explosive at twenty rounds a second, no more powerful than Kalashnikovs really, but the tile stack was good cover and the vehicles were no protection at all. The terrorists started to take hits as they got rolling, the car's fuel tank blew, the lorry's blew, the mortar shells blew, the self-destruct charges they'd put on the lorry blew, and the manhole cover was still off the septic tank. Some sort of burning debris fell down there and there must have been a build-up of sewer gas that hadn't had time to vent.'

'Oh,' said Spencer. 'They never reported that bit.'

'I don't think they did, no. It was a fairly low-pressure explosion, it could have been worse, but there was a flash and a whoomp and a few square yards of concrete were blasted up on this rising column of cess.'

'Ah.'

'The concrete didn't lift very far and it fell back without any big chunks hitting anyone, but the actual raw sewage went sky-high. And it took quite a while for all of it to return to earth. Nothing to do but curl up tight and tuck your head in. When it did finally stop and there was just the sleet coming, the team moved in to check the terrorists, but they'd all had it.'

'Anyone would think you were there,' said Spencer.

'Anyone can think what they like, Spence, as long as they mind what they go round telling people.'

'Yeah, sure. But I don't remember seeing shit everywhere in the pictures.'

'I expect once CID finished they got some poor bloody infantry to clean the place up before they let the press in, it must have been a health hazard. That's the period when Gerry Adams says the SAS were interrogating and executing the gang and rigging the evidence to make it look like a straight fight.'

'Yeah, well, pinch of salt.'

'Siberia's entire annual output where that man's concerned. There have been cases where soldiers have given wounded terrorists one in the head for luck, but you can't fake a whole crime scene, it doesn't work like that. The only thing the army PR people did put out that was rubbish was the crater being made by a mortar shell. I don't know if they got it wrong or if they just decided an exploding cesspit sounded too symbolic.'

'Ulster, the exploding cesspit in Britain's back yard, a *Guardian* special report.'

'No, I can't quite see it either, but the army's over-sensitive sometimes.'

'But when you shouted the warning, that wasn't to give them a chance to surrender, it was to make them look the other way while the SAS were in the open, is that right?'

'It's called drawing fire. But it could have been done by firing at them first. So they were given a chance.'

'And if everything had gone according to plan, what would

have happened then?'

'I expect the mortar attack would have gone ahead only with dud shells and an empty police station. They have so many duds anyway a few more wouldn't be that suspicious. What you try not to do is give away that you had an informant. In fact the police had one as well, which they didn't tell MI5, and he was afterwards tortured and shot by his Provo mates. The only good thing was it left the MI5 source in the clear, but the police are hacked off, they think MI5 orchestrated it.' Gareth gave a snort.

'What?' said Spencer.

'What, MI5 orchestrating anything? Successfully?' Gareth picked up the no-nuke leaflet from the table. 'Did this come through the door? I haven't had one.'

'No. You'll never guess who gave me that.'

'You're almost certainly correct, I doubt I ever shall.' Gareth turned it over, reading the small print on the back, seeing who published it.

'I'll show you. Here.' Spencer got up.

Gareth said, 'Eh?' and followed on into Spencer's room. Spencer put a finger on the postcard. Gareth said, 'No. What? You met her? How?'

'She came to the office.'

'Oh, David's still trying to make the film. And she handed out these pamphlets? Actresses, aren't they sweet?'

'No, she only gave me one, we got talking.'

'Sod it,' Gareth said, charmingly on the ball as to the sick-with-envy response that Spencer wanted. 'What was she like?'

'Fine. There's something a bit intense about her but she's nice. Girly in a way.'

'Sod it. How's she looking?'

'Incredible, specially when you get that smile.'

'Oh, for Pete's sake.' Turning away, Gareth seemed to notice something on the floor behind Spencer and decide not to look at it.

Spencer looked. Claire's leftover light-blue bra lay by the bedleg. You couldn't tell it was broken. He said, 'That's what happens when people don't make sure they've taken all their washing out of the machine before you put yours in. I'll have to let Kates have it back.' He'd never thought of himself as an accomplished liar but this lie came to him the way tunes came to Mozart, out of nowhere, fully formed. He felt a surprised and guilty pride.

'Good for Katie,' Gareth said. 'Not enough girls wear light-blue underwear any more. It was a mid-Seventies thing, the same as blue mascara, wasn't it? The only one I've come across in ages was Claire Tarrant.'

Spencer's pride evaporated in the sudden heat of awful apprehension.

Gareth said, 'And that's only if you count guesswork based on the partial translucence of white shirts.'

But Claire said it was new, she can't have had it when Gareth was still at Holt Newman over a year ago. No, hang on, she could have had a previous one the same. Spencer did it with favourite shirts and pants, went out and bought identical replacements, it saved thinking. He didn't associate her with that colour that far back, not even a glimmer of it, but Gareth was more observant than he was.

Spencer's Camel had burnt down. He went out to stub it in the pub ashtray on the dining table. 'Nice colour, yeah. That's made my head go round. Why's yours lasting longer than mine?'

'I talk too much,' said Gareth, and drew. 'How is she these days?'

'Claire? OK. You know her boyfriend went abroad. You had to be quite careful with her for a while, but she seems to be over it now.'

'I expect he'll reappear,' said Gareth.

'Nah. D'you think?'

'She just strikes me as the sort who might stick with her first man. Look around to make sure, maybe, but then stick.'

'Not much of a goer?' Spencer said with a fresh attack of the smugs.

'Aiming to settle down, not put it about. Wouldn't you say?'

'I know what you mean,' said Spencer, smugless again. He did know, and it bothered him.

Gareth said, 'Although I'm sure she goes like a locomotive in the right circs.' He stubbed his Camel. 'She says she does.'

'She what?'

'Talks about it. Well, she used to. How she only went to keep-fit class to be better in bed. The use of cuddly toys in foreplay. How many times over the weekend. She was always on about it.'

'The cuddly toys you did mention once.'

'Used to fill me with helpless chagrin something rotten.'

'She's never talked to me like that,' said Spencer, wondering why, and what was wrong with him.

Gareth said, 'Well, perhaps she fancies you, so it'd be too embarrassing.'

You see what we mean about the charm.

Spencer laughed.

Gareth pulled the *Standard* over the table towards him. 'This doesn't look good, does it?'

'That, no. No. But they can't let it come to a real shooting war. It's too idiotic.'

'Do you know when we last lost one? My friend Nigel and I couldn't decide.'

'Kenya, the Mau Mau?'

'No, they were hammered into the ground. I had that on my counter-insurgency course.'

'Boer War?'

'We did not lose the Boer War. It only seems that way. Nigel wouldn't even let me count American independence because it was the king's private German army.'

'Was it? Wait up.' Spencer almost saw and smelt the sunlit class-room, chalk dust, wallcharts, buddy desks, horrible pine-scent floor cleaner, crewcuts and ponytails, Captain Scarlet badges. 'We did something in primary with Miss Dawson. Our local regiment was out there.'

'What, the Rutland Light Infantry?'

'The Royal Leicesters, they don't exist now, or they're part of something else, but they made this great bayonet charge all on their own against Washington's entire army.'

'Crikey. No wonder they don't exist any more.'

'Oh, they got through. They had to rescue a German garrison

that was cut off. Seemed weird to me, us helping Germans fight Americans. May be why she taught us it.'

'All right, Nigel overstating his case, never trust an historian.'

'Afghanistan,' Spencer suggested.

'I'm having second thoughts about that, I think we did lose one there, even this century.'

'It can happen.'

The front door banged and Miles came in. 'Hi, Spence. Gareth. Main man. Hi. What happened to your jacket?'

'It's his Filofax,' said Spencer. 'Fetch a glass. The bottle's on the hid.'

'Cheers, thanks.' Miles dropped his bag and fetched a glass from the kitchen. 'I called your switchboard today and they'd never heard of you.'

'Me?' said Spencer.

'No.'

'Me?' said Gareth.

'That's right. No one of that name.' Miles held up the bottle. 'Produce of Lebanon?'

'It's good, we've had it before,' said Spencer.

'Yeah?' Miles poured. 'That's one grape-picking holiday I will not be taking. You'd need safe-conduct passes from the Druze, the Maronites, the PLO, the Israelis, and you still wouldn't get travel insurance ... Ooh. Is good.'

Gareth said, 'If you called MoD main switchboard they don't know me, I'm in an annexe a mile away.'

'I've got his office number, you should have rung me,' said Spencer.

'I never thought of that,' said Miles. 'What sort of department?'

Gareth said, 'It's to do with human resource management.'

'Personnel.'

'Sort of.'

'I wanted to ask you, they're putting this task force together, at the moment there's not much competition for press places on board ship because everyone reckons it won't come to anything. If I wait and it turns out to be serious they'll probably give it to someone else.'

'Oh, well. Go for it,' Gareth said.

'You mean it? That is the hot inside poop?'

'So far as I know it's on. It's not a bluff.'

'Obviously the drag is I'll be spoonfed navy PR for weeks on the way. And in the end there'll only be the odd shot across the bows like the Cod War — '

'Lost that one,' Spencer said.

' — then some eleventh-hour trade-off works out, all go home. But it could be fascinating to see how close it gets.' Miles took a turn up and down the room. 'Potentially great copy. It's got farce with menace, or like Gilbert and Sullivan meet Frederick Forsyth. And the TV pictures are going to take days, no satellite links, it'll be a print-led story for once.'

'I wasn't quite with you,' Gareth said. 'I thought you thought it was serious.'

'Right! Everyone else reckons the fleet's bound to just turn back halfway. I think it'll go right up to the line.'

'What if the worst comes to the worst?'

'What, if the worst comes to the worst, the Pope's lovechild turns up in Brixton and I'm still stranded in mid-ocean with nothing to file.'

'You don't see any actual sinking ships or people stepping on landmines.'

'Naaao, it won't come to that. Will it?'

'Which side backs down?'

'We do, we're the grown-ups. Talk tough, point made, let it pass, forget about it.'

'Your kids,' said Spencer, 'are going to run rings round you.'

'Maybe,' Gareth said.

'So you think I should put in for it,' said Miles.

'As long as you really want to. I just wouldn't rule out the danger aspect.'

'No, this day and age. And the Americans won't let it get out of hand. The Mansfield Doctrine?'

'Monroe?'

'Could be. Is that your untipped Camels I can smell? I love those.'

'Yes.'

'I might bum one when I've had a shower.' Miles took his bag and went upstairs.

'I've got to go but I'll leave you one,' Gareth called.

'You off?' said Spencer.

'Mm, better.' Gareth tossed a Camel on to the dining table.

'You're putting in overtime.'

'Yes, have to. Last-ditch paperwork.' Gareth pulled on his mac and got the Mondrian from the sofa. 'This is nice, remember to thank Su.'

'Sure.' They went to the front door. 'Katie's thinking of doing one of her big dinners, I'll let you know.'

'OK. And thanks for the Musar.' Gareth's brogues clicked down the steps.

In the living room again, Spencer heard the Aston growl off round the houses to save a three-pointer. He refilled his glass.

The funereal weight of that Browning. But then Gareth said lots of people had them, and you never heard of anyone having to use one, not over here. Pure precaution. Besides, the terrorists thought he was something like he'd told Miles, personnel. Even they must have better things to do than bump off penpushers like that. Even they must.

Miles eventually came down, looking puzzled. He lit Gareth's Camel, ran upstairs again and came down looking more puzzled. 'The bath's not emptying out.'

'I thought you had a shower.'

'Yeah, but the bath filled up. Halfway to my knees, and it hasn't gone down. I'd better ring Dyno-Rod.'

Spencer went upstairs to the fog-windowed bathroom. It was much as Miles said, an open plughole but the water not visibly going anywhere. Spencer rolled one sleeve. With a finger you could feel a very slight draw down the hole.

In the living room Miles had the Yellow Pages out. Spencer said, 'There is a bit of movement, it'll probably clear itself.' Something caught his eye through the kitchen archway. 'Or else not.' The washing-up water had reappeared in the sink, only deeper and cloudier, mixed with the run-off from Miles's shower, the level still rising. Spencer rolled his sleeve again and rammed the plug in. As he took his hand away it popped straight out. He put it back and held it there against the pressure from beneath. The pipes grumbled.

'Sheesh,' said Miles over his shoulder. 'We're about to get flooded.'

'Can you chuck us the weights off Paul's poncey antique scales?'

'What for?'

'Hold this down with.'

'Ha. Here.'

'Cheers. That's done it.' Spencer dried his arm. 'I don't see why the water's coming up here.'

'The drain's blocked.'

'Yeah, but it's water. Always seeks the lowest outlet. Why this sink, not the basement one? Unless the basement's flooded already.'

They took the back stairs. The basement looked no more of a mess than normal. This could be because Katie had left some handwash-only clothes to soak in the scullery sink last night and they were still there, so the plug was in and the weight of water and waterlogged laundry was stopping it popping; although, considering the twenty-foot drop from the bathroom and the hydraulic pressure that created in the pipes, it must be a damn tight plug. Come to think of it, not that Spencer wanted to think of it, the same must go for whatever was blocking the drain.

'Washing machine's dry,' said Miles, a hand in its open door.

'The valves are shut when it's off. Or perhaps the block's isolated this set of pipes.'

'OK. Well. Better call Dyno-Rod.'

'Hold on. I've got a plan.' Spencer ran up to the bathroom, put the plug in and turned the cold tap on full.

Miles came up. 'What are you doing?' he shouted over the roar of water.

'I'm going to fill it right to the top. Then when I pull the plug I hope the sudden extra pressure clears the block,' shouted Spencer.

Miles flicked Camel ash down the loo. 'What if it doesn't?'

'I don't know. The whole place will go under in five minutes.'

'You're not serious.'

'I've never been more serious in my life.'

'Oh, right, bad films, um ... But it's madness, I tell you.'

'It's our only chance, there's no other way.'

'At least let the girl go.'

'That doesn't really apply, does it?'

'I couldn't think of any others. The bog looks OK.'

'It's a different system.'

'Uh. I hope so.'

'Well, they join up somewhere, depends if the block's before that point or not.'

'What do you think it is? I can imagine years and years' worth of cooking fat and hair and soap and old spit and toothpaste all solidifying in a bend in the pipe and ... '

'That kind of thing, yeah.'

Loudly the bath filled, the water turning blue-green as it deepened.

'Isn't that enough?' Miles shouted.

'I want it right, right up.'

It was taking some time. The tap was pounding away but the quantity of water required was huge. You could never run a bath this deep for real because the hot tank wasn't big enough, and in any case you'd send cascades down the stairs when you tried to get in.

Miles opened the window, stubbed his cig on the brick ledge and threw it into the garden. 'Those are amazingly strong, I don't know how he smokes them all the time.'

'He doesn't,' Spencer shouted. 'He alternates them with Sullivan's Sub Rosa, which are even stronger. Haven't you had one?'

'No, don't think.'

'They're a trip. You can only get them in the Burlington Arcade.'

'Can we — ?' Miles indicated the brimming tub.

'OK.' Spencer turned off the tap. The quiet was dense. He pushed his sleeve up to his shoulder, reached in and gripped the short broken chain of the plug. There was only an inch or two to get hold of. He tugged. 'It won't come out.'

'It's stuck?'

'The water's too heavy.'

'Well, if we let some out — no. Sorry. What if I get some saucepans and we bail it down the bog?'

'No, I'll have it in a minute.' Spencer went on hauling. The plug lifted. He pulled it dripping out.

The water surface oscillated, slipped and held. The overflow vent croaked at them. The bath went still again.

'It doesn't seem to have worked,' said Miles.

They heard the crash of brass weights in the kitchen sink downstairs.

'This is going badly wrong,' said Miles.

Then they heard a low hollow boom that travelled up the pipes towards them. The water shuddered. The boom turned to a mighty retching bark and the plughole vanished in a white surge of turbulence. The water surface burst, thrashed and plunged, the bath swiftly and silently emptying. A bright silver vortex formed over the plughole, proof of the free and lusty suction of the new-purged drain.

Spencer dried his hands.

'Amazing,' Miles said. 'It never used to go out that fast in the first place.'

'No. The drain must have been part blocked since before we moved in. That's cleared it.'

'Fantastic.'

'And saved fifty quid on calling the men in.'

'I'm due at Christine's or I'd buy you a drink.'

'I've already got one.'

They went down to the kitchen. The weights and the plug were scattered over the bottom of the sink, but the water had gone.

'Great,' Miles said. 'Wait a second, what is that — ?' His face buckled. 'What is that awful stench? Auwagh.'

'Methane and, uh, sulphuretted hydrogen, H_2S, I think,' said Spencer. 'And it's combustible, so don't strike a light.' He opened a window. 'It'll go in a jif. Well, sooner or later.'

'But what is it?'

'Just a bit of drain smell that escaped in the confusion. It won't last. Or I don't think it will.'

Miles made for the french windows, undid the bolts and stumbled out to the balcony.

Spencer brought his still half-full glass of red out to him.

'Thanks,' Miles said. 'That was ... phaw. What about the boiler? It's on. Flames.'

'I shouldn't think there's enough of the smelly stuff to make a bang, not really.'

'Two die in mystery blast.'

'What were you covering today?'

'Oh, the demos at the Argie embassy. Tins of corned beef being thrown through the windows. It got subbed into someone else's story. But it was funny, all these angry people, when most of us thought the Falklands were somewhere near the Hebrides up till a few days ago.'

'Get off,' said Spencer. 'Everybody always knew exactly where the Falklands were. It's Argentina nobody can ever quite place.'

The plainclothes SAS man who identified himself as Rog looked round the door of the darkening bedroom. He'd come in through the back garden. 'Andy. OK?'

'Sure.' Andy had taken the stool from young Mrs Grossman's dressing table and put it by the corner of the bay window, where he could sit and watch the house across the road without showing himself too much. The Grossmans were letting the police use the place as an observation post partly because the liaison officer made the request through the head of their children's school, partly because the rabbi said it was all right, and partly because the IRA spied for Hitler's SS in the time of the Shoah.

Rog, given permission, came over and squatted beside Andy in the shadows. 'No sign?'

'They're not there, are they?' Andy said.

'People don't all put their lights on by now. But it doesn't look too promising.'

'I can see through that front room, two open doors, daylight in the kitchen window at the back.'

'Yeah.'

'There's nothing moving. No one's at home.'

'The plane pick-up's going to be late, isn't it, probably after normal air traffic shuts down. So they've either gone somewhere near there to wait or they've just gone for a takeaway and they'll be back for their stuff after.'

'Hn,' said Andy. 'They were here. The neighbour said. Laughing. We must have missed them by ... ' He made a thumb and forefinger sign. 'If this Gower Street bloke had got to Northolt five minutes quicker we'd have them by now.'

'Well, your men are well-positioned if they do turn up. Front and back covered, not too obvious, containment groups where they should be. One or two needed moving, you'd see them as you came down the street, but that's all sorted out.'

'Thanks, Rog. I expect we're all wasting our time, though.'

'They could be in there having a kip. They're planning on a long night.'

'None of our equipment's even picked up a snore or a sign of body heat. Any curtains closed at the back?'

'No, but when it's neither light nor dark that doesn't tell you much.'

'Supposing the flat is abandoned, what's the chance of booby traps? One of them's a bit handy in that line.'

'It's never happened over here.'

'That's why I'm asking, we've got no experience to go on.'

'Well, if they've cleared out in a hurry it's most likely they've had to leave some gear behind, timers and detonators under the floorboards, so on. Far as they're concerned, the next person through that door's going to be one of their runners coming to collect it, they don't want to blow them up. Of course if they know that location's compromised it's different, but why would they?'

'I think we'll give it till nine and go in.'

When Miles left for Islington, Spencer ran a real bath. He was gungy from the office and from conquering Claire, and it wouldn't be a bad idea to let the drain have another sluice-through. Apart from anything else it might help the remains of the smell fade faster.

He lay back in the water with another glass of wine, watching the steam rise in the dusk light from the window and practising his bass Roman-emperor laugh with hilarious bathroom echo effect.

Basker, Claire said. He could have given her a ring. But she wouldn't mind, she thought he was still at work. She'd be gone for her girls' night out now, so no point trying till late. And maybe not then either, since he hadn't thought of anything to fix up. He hated dates. The timetabling, the public places, the palaver. But he'd have to offer some suggestion or other. Still, tomorrow morning might do, if he caught her before she went to her favourite aunt's in Berks was it, or Sunday night when she came back, or even Monday, which would give him a happy reason to visit her new basement office. In fact it was better he hadn't called at the first opportunity. Once they were sure of you they turned difficult. Supposedly this never happened with the right one, but that must be because the right one was the one you could keep guessing indefinitely.

Tomorrow would do. See how it goes. He could stop smoking again tomorrow as well. Or, if that failed, next year when he'd found a less soul-destroying job. Or at least by the time he was say forty, in 1998. But they might have a cure for cancer by then, which would weaken the motivation. Yeah, well. See how it goes. Every day is day one, the day you start over, the day you make your break, your fresh amends.

Gareth, back at his desk, rang Carl's extension. 'How's it going?'

'Ah, I was trying to reach you earlier.'

'Yes, Cathy said.'

'No activity at the house yet, I'm afraid. We've had some intercepts, there's a plane coming over from France, we know the somewhat literally fly-by-night operators involved, and the destination because Tambo gave us the codenames for the Irish end, but we don't know the pick-up point unfortunately. They've changed the destination once, a wayward Garda chappie tipped them off we'd compromised the first one.'

'Fffff.'

'But they haven't twigged how, and the leak's been stopped, so we're now promised a ring of steel around the fallback site.'

'You've given up on catching them over here, then.'

'By no means,' Carl said, 'no, but if they don't materialise at the house our options are narrowing. Customs and Excise, blessem, have let us have a list of possible sites for the pick-up but we can't send people out to watch all those, the manpower's tied up at Stoke Newington and it wouldn't stretch in any case, so the local police are going to have to do their best.'

'OK. Did you see Tambourine Man settled in?'

'Yes, I think he was expecting something grander, but he perked up when he found he could order anything he wanted for dinner.'

'What did he want?'

'Spag bol for some reason.'

'He'll be refusing everything but Ulster fry in a week and begging to go home the week after. Was there any word on his girlfriend?'

'No,' said Carl. 'Of course they may put off killing her and let her go as a way to lure him back, and then do both of them.'

'That would be my guess. I wanted to ask you about something I'm working on while I've got you.'

'Fire away.'

'There's a group of people who used to be in a radical touring theatre company. They're believed to have transported some explosives for the Provos in their van back in 1974. I've got a report here from earlier this week says that one of them, she now runs a wholefood shop in Somerset and performs in a lesbian mime troupe, was discussing a plan to break into the Fleet Air Arm base down that way, in the event of war, and castrate the military machine by chainsawing the radar nosecones off the country's entire force of Sea Harriers before they're flown on board ship. This was Tuesday, the *Invincible* and the Harriers were still meant to be going to the Australian navy then, she didn't seem to know that.'

'Or else she guessed that No.10 was going to change its mind. One mustn't underestimate people, Gareth.'

'Yeah, I try not to. It would certainly be best to avoid a showdown between armed Marine sentries and chainsaw-wielding lesbian mime artists, I just want to assess the threat and see if it's really likely. We've got the recent material on her, throwing rotten fruit at the British Legion parade in Glastonbury last Remembrance Day for example, but the 1974 stuff's Access F5 Only and that's you.'

'Oh, just tap in — no, tell you what,' said Carl, not disclosing his password after all, perhaps spotting a senior colleague in earshot, 'come up here and we'll take a look.'

Spencer turned out the fridge and the kitchen cupboards. A couple of eggs, some spuds beginning to sprout, an onion, a tin of tuna.

Tuna fish omelette. Gareth, who knew everything except what was what, once said tuna fish omelette was Brillat-Savarin's favourite dish, so you couldn't call it slumming.

Spencer found a saucer and broke the eggs, which, as another Frenchman observed, you could not make an omelette without doing, although Spencer was buggered if he could remember which Frenchman this time, or what the fuck it was supposed to mean.

You can't beat eggs in a saucer. He tipped them into, no, hold on, not the frying pan yet, into a teacup.

Not that it mattered who said it or what for but it was incredibly annoying he couldn't remember. He lit a cig, went round turning lights on, found his address book, which was a pile of paper on his chest of drawers, and dialled Gareth's office number. Stupid, he couldn't have given it to Miles today if it was back here. Yes he could, he had it in his desk diary too. Unless Miles had called during that wildly extended lunch hour while —

'Ministry of Defence.'

'Hi. Gareth MacMichael please, it's Spencer Cobbold.'

Whirrs and clicks. Silent spell. More whirrs and clicks. Gareth must be away from his desk, they were trying another extension.

'Hullo, Spence.'

'I was doing an omelette.'

'Yes ... ' said Gareth.

'Who said you can't make one without breaking eggs? And what was he on about?'

'Marshal Pelissier. French commander in the Crimea, too fat to ride a horse, went everywhere by dog cart. He meant you can't wage war without losing men. Which the public sometimes think you can.'

'I'm not surprised I'd forgotten him now, I've never heard of him. Heard of his brother Roman of course. Or is this the same one who said, *C'est magnifique mais* — '

'No, that was General Bosquet.'

'Was it. We lost in the Crimea, didn't we?'

'No. We won.'

'Well, I never. Why's it such a byword for a cock-up then?'

'Heavy losses, lack of point.'

'I take it you just mix the tuna with the eggs.'

'Oh, tunny omelette. Might as well. Brillat-Savarin used to fry it up with the onions first but he was using fresh. The canned stuff spits like mad if you do that, you have to scrape half of it off the ceiling.'

'Yeah, well, French chefs, what do they know?'

'He wasn't a chef, he was an appeal court judge.'

Spencer felt stupid. 'Was he?'

'Yeah. OK, I'd better get on.'

'Right, cheers.' Spencer hung up. Damn. Should have asked him what film 'Strangers in the Night' came from, he'd be bound to know that and all.

Spencer sniffed the eggs. There was a faint whiff, but when he went and stood in the hall he found the whiff was the same out there, so it was drains not eggs. Fine. Only he was doing this all wrong, there was no sense starting on the omelette till the spuds were nearly ready, and that was going to take, phuph, twenty minutes.

He desprouted, rinsed and quartered the potatoes, put them on to boil and looked at the TV page in the paper. Missed most of *Shalako*, seen it before anyway. Otherwise, a documentary on 'Is Pornography Dangerous?' or an old *Hawaii Five-O* followed by 'genial sitcom set in engineering works'. So roll on Channel 4.

It looked like he was doomed to go and meet Sandrine in the pub, and he was not feeling up to it. He must be drunk because he had snatches of two different pop songs running through his head, both of which he couldn't stand. 'It ain't what you do it's the way that you do it, Till the day I die, Till the day I die.' Bananarama with the Strawbs, nightmare billing.

He picked up some of Claire's fruit from the fruit bowl and handled it, smiling, then went to see how the spuds were.

Another thing about being drunk was you did ten seconds' worth of thinking and then realised you'd spent half an hour doing it. Or not quite that, the spuds were only beginning to soften. He whipped up the omelette and fired the ring under the pan. No bleeding butter, hardly any marge. Bottle of vegetable oil in the cupboard.

The omelette didn't come out fluffy and golden exactly, but it wasn't as shoeleathery as usual either and it tasted surprisingly OK. He drank lots of water while he ate. He also put on Miles's Robert Palmer album but forgot to listen to any of it and only noticed when it stopped.

It was knocking on for nine already, or it would be by the time he'd walked down the pub. If he didn't go he might be standing Sandrine up, which would be cruddy. Chances were she wouldn't show, but he wouldn't know that and then he'd feel guilty. He changed into jeans and sweater. He'd never got round to acquiring one of those blouson things you were meant to wear and the old Harris tweed jacket didn't work on the French, they couldn't tell it was supposed to be shabby like that, so it had to be the office overcoat.

Outdoors the sky was blood-red with the glow of streetlights. In Rutland it actually got dark at night and when it was clear you saw a million times more stars than here. Sod all to do, though.

He crossed Camden Road and went down St Pancras Way. At the bottom, where it met with Royal College Street, the Falcon stood, crowd noise and music behind masked windows. He hurried past, around the corner and over to the Old Eagle.

The lights in the bar were bright and warm yellow like the lights in a Routemaster bus, and the atmosphere was usually good. You sometimes saw people off the telly because they could come in and not get hassled, even Rowan Atkinson the other day and he was mega just now. (He didn't live round here, but according to *Time Out* his scriptwriter did.) Perhaps no one else recognised him with his glasses on and otherwise they'd all have been going Do the Trucking Song, do the Kinda Lingers one, come on, but Spencer thought not. What chance does an alternative comedian stand of not being recognised in Camden Town? About as much as Simone de Beauvoir in St Germain.

Celebrities notoriously avoid all pubs on Fridays, though, for reasons simply too too obvious darling as soon as you push through the frosted-glass doors. The place was heaving. Spencer scused his way past the blousons and jumpsuits to the bar. He couldn't see Sandrine so unless she was hiding away at the back she wasn't here. A face like that you'd spot straight off in any crowd. Relief. He wouldn't know what to say. But she could still turn up.

That nice fortyish blonde was serving. He got an elbow on the counter and only then grasped that he was going to have to drink more alcohol. True, that was what pubs were for, but coming here was so routine you didn't think. He was too full and muzzy to want a pint and soft drinks were out of the question so when his turn came he asked for a Jack Daniel's. One pub measure wouldn't make him that much drunker, and it wouldn't last long so he could run away soon, duty done.

Better not to down it too quick, even so. He sipped and let it mostly evaporate on his tongue.

He thought of the sleepy distillery town in Tennessee, the Musar vineyards on the shell-raked Lebanon hillsides, the holiday job Miles wouldn't want, the fireball in the barnyard, the job Gareth did that no one in his right mind would want, the Birmingham pubs and pubgoers gutted by the bombs of '74, the wrong men in the slammer, appeal court judges, Claire's fondness for hanging.

A finger touched the nape of his neck and a husky French voice said, 'So. I have the right place.'

He shouldn't be here. But what the hell, MI5 reckoned Claire was still linked to the oil prospector and even if she wasn't it might not work out and you had to explore all the avenues. 'Oh, it's you. Can I get you something?'

'Of course. I doubt they have good wine, so, I think, a cognac with soda.'

At the Archduke, a glazed-in railway arch on the South Bank, a jazz trio played. Heather said, 'It's not bad for Aussie plonk, is it?' Briony waved the empty bottle at the waiter and Penny went 'CoonawarraCoonawarraCoonawarra' like a didgeridoo for Claire's benefit, the old school line being that Claire had spent her early childhood in Australia. New Zealand didn't sound crude enough to be taunted with.

'So what's he like?' said Heather.

Claire moved her glass back and forth on the tablecloth. 'He's sort of, I don't know, he went to Cambridge but he's not too snobby or brain on legs, he's quite ... big, and — '

The girls hooted. 'What, like where it counts?' said Penny.

'That's not what I meant,' said Claire, 'but ... well. Aren't they always.'

'No!' the girls shouted, making the sax player falter for a moment.

'Ah?' Claire shrugged her shoulders. 'Perhaps I've been lucky.' After only two men she was in no position to tell, but that was not a thing you said.

The girls made miaow and hiss noises.

Claire was glad she hadn't come in the off-white jacket. She really would have looked like staff. This slate-blue one was short and couldn't cover up the fact that satin trousers made your bum look bigger, which might account for the wolfwhistle behind her on the way to the tube, but if you were an hourglass you were an hourglass and you just had to live with it, no use wanting to stay a skinny tomboy, there was something sick about that if you let it get hold of you.

★

'Ah, there you are,' said the switchboard girl when Gareth answered his line, 'I thought you were still with Carl Jenkins.'

'Back ages ago.'

'I have Inspector Draper.'

'OK. Hullo.'

'Gareth,' Draper said. 'Couple of things. We contacted regional Special Branch. They said thanks but the lady and her friends were in custody already, they were arrested in the past hour by MoD police as they were cutting the wire fence at the air base.'

'Oh.'

'They did not have chainsaws but they did have pickaxes and spraycans. They were subdued by the use of dogs, it seems they would have been willing to use the pickaxes on the men, but they didn't want to hurt the dogs. No serious injuries.'

'I should have got round to it sooner, sorry.'

'No, best to catch them at it or where's your evidence? The background you gave us should help MoD obtain injunctions if they get off with a fine, as seems most likely. And they'll have their day in court to sound off, so, everybody's happy. Now. You up to speed with Operation Corncrake?'

'I hope you aren't calling it that over unsecured channels, it's a bit of a giveaway.'

'No, they're using Catamaran or something. Andy's boys have gone in. It's pretty clear the targets have moved on. No toothbrushes. But they expect to find bomb-making materials when they strip the place.'

'What happened in Dublin?'

'That's been fixed. We had a tape of the intercept flown over there and the leaker was identified by voice. I think they'll try and make a professional job of it after that.'

'So it is down to them now?'

'Not for certain yet. Local forces are looking out. And the RAF are putting an old Shackleton early-warning plane over the Channel with a couple of Phantom jets to follow up any contacts. I wouldn't have thought Phantoms can go slow enough to keep track of a little Piper, but still.'

'Famous for it,' Gareth said. 'The technical term's "loitering".

They can throttle back to about 150 and still stay up.'

'If you call that loitering,' said Draper, 'which I'll come to in a minute. The Russians use helicopters and light planes for Spetsnaz saboteur units, so the RAF could do with the practice, they're quite keen.'

'What are they proposing to do?'

'Well, once this charter pilot makes the pick-up they move in and force him down at an RAF airfield, which, with the defences on full alert, Kite and Ball will not be shooting their way out of in a hurry.'

'Sounds very dicey. Messing about at low level in the dark.'

'Sounds berserk. But if they lose him, or they have to break off because it gets too dangerous — they are under orders about that — yes, our opposite numbers in Dublin will be doing the business. Or say they will, we'll see. On another matter, Traffic Division have been on to me.'

'Have they?' Gareth said.

'You passed one of their Q cars on the M40 westbound this afternoon at a speed so grossly excessive the crew thought their equipment must be faulty when it registered the figure, but they've had it checked out and it ain't. I did warn them we'd got something on at Northolt and as you have the use of that car the number carries a security tag on the computer so they came to me first.'

'Sorry about that.'

'I gave them he's-with-me and all that game and I only wished you'd made it even faster so we'll say no more about it, except for Christ's sake don't ever do anything like that again, all right?'

'Hmh.'

'And you broke the scan they were doing on a Porsche in front of you before the set could give a readout and he's got no immunity but now they've got no evidence so they're double not pleased, losing a good collar like that.'

'Nnh.'

'They were thinking of calling you as a prosecution witness, seeing as they've got your speed and you were keeping pace with him.'

'What if I don't remember his number?'

'Oh, I think you do, it's a very conspicuous plate, very conspicuous. And if he's sole insured driver, which they usually are, Porsche types, and he hasn't reported it stolen, it's a nearly watertight case.'

'I'd feel a bit of a shit.'

'That, Gareth, was the intention. But I had to tell them that your Director-General would never wear it in a month of Sundays.'

'I don't suppose he would, no.'

'So that's that. Just remember what I said.'

'Yes. Thanks.'

'Or the next time I shall tell your old man.'

Gareth had had enough of this. 'If it's in connection with my work, and I wouldn't be speeding for any other reason, then, under the Official Secrets Act, you can't.'

Draper breathed deep and said, 'Not to pull rank or anything, but remember you're talking to a detective inspector of the Metropolitan Police, eh?'

'Well aware of that, Colin. I hold rank equivalent to chief inspector myself.'

After a pause, Draper said, 'How old are you, son?'

'Me, I'm twenty-three, why?'

After a longer pause, Draper said dryly, 'No reason.'

Spencer had forgotten the tedious aspect of making friends, especially with foreigners. You spent rafts of time talking like simpletons or five-year-olds about whether certain things were 'good' or not. Jack Daniel's was good, apparently. Rowan Atkinson was good. Paris cafés were good but the place was as dead as a doornail after 8pm when everyone was sequestered in the flicks and the restaurants or at home, you could walk right across town and it was like the bomb had dropped, no one about, and that wasn't good. Tonight's audience at the Falcon was good for numbers, not bad for enthusiasm, you could sometimes find yourself performing to a silent crowd and that was absolutely not good. In a way it was good that Spencer hadn't come to cheer along but came to meet her here instead, nice, what a gentleman would do.

'If you like gentlemen you're wasting your time with me,' said Spencer. 'I could introduce you to a friend of mine, though.'

Sandrine said roughly what he hoped she would. 'I'm enjoying wasting time with you and anyway I wasn't meaning that I like aristocrats,' with Yank-type emphasis on –ist, 'some of my relations are aristocrats, they are no good.'

'No, I didn't mean that either, my friend isn't one, he's just a nice guy and wears handmade suits.'

'Ah. Rich.'

'No, but his tailor is.'

Sandrine smiled. 'That's what we say, you know, like you say *la plume de ma tante*, for us it's "My tailor is rich".'

'I know, I had to teach English in Toulouse for a year, part of my college course.'

'Oh, so you must speak good French, it's very kind that you don't use it to impress me.'

'Yeah, I thought that.'

'I'm so bored with men who do that, like I can't speak English. Did you have a French lover?'

'Um, you're upfront, aren't you? Yeah. You got an English one?'

'From time to time perhaps. OK, say something in French.'

'*C'est combien, ce petit chien-là dans la vitrine?*'

'Your accent's not bad.'

'Nor's yours, don't lose it.'

'Ah, but you mean I sound French, I don't mean you sound English.'

'Yeah, yeah.'

'But of course you do, and it's the same for us, we like that. Actually, we prefer if you are not so good.'

'*Shitoyens de Franche. Sh'est moi. Churchill. La nuit. Shera longue. Mais l'aube. Viendra.*'

'That's much more sexy. Did he say that, on the BBC, the dawn will come, I like that.' Sandrine picked up Spencer's empty glass. 'So, another?'

'No, thank you but I better not. I had some wine earlier that went straight to my head. Did you say you get drunk every time before you go on stage?'

'Not much, I always drink a quarter bottle of champagne, I have a friend who works for Air France so I accumulate them cheaply.'

'That's good.' Spencer wondered what to do. It seemed a bit too soon to clear off yet. He couldn't ask her back for coffee this quick either, that might be insulting, and even if she said yes there was no way he could bring himself to make a pass, not on the selfsame day he'd scored with Claire, and to get her alone and then not make a pass might well be more insulting, so the whole idea was best ruled out. 'Shall I give you my number?' he said.

'Sure!' Sandrine stooped and took a square black notebook from her holdall. 'I love exchanging numbers, such a ceremony. You have a pen?'

'No, you?'

She flagged the barmaid, who brought a ballpoint over from the till. She opened the book at a clean page, so Spencer didn't see any other names, and he wrote down his with his number.

'Cobbold?' Sandrine said.

'There is a Lord Cobbold but I'd have to kill an awful lot of people if I wanted to inherit the title.'

She added 'Sandrine Cazalet' and her own seven figures and tore out that half of the page to give to him.

'Whereabouts d'you live?' said Spencer, pocketing it.

'Pimlico, you know?'

'Yes, not a bad area. Shall I walk you to the tube?'

'Oh no, it's fine, you don't have many perverts here compared to us.'

'I doubt it, you just prefer being abroad.'

'You think? But it's a nice busy road and anyway I have a shriek.'

'What, a special shriek that you can do?'

'No, it's a small thing in my pocket.'

'Sorry, course.'

They pushed out to the street. He would have liked to take his short cut up St Pancras Way but he walked her to the lights under the railway bridge.

'OK, great to see you, Sandrine.'

'Great to see you. I have to cross?'

'No, down this side. We only came up that side because I live that side and you didn't know where you were going.'

Sandrine unslung her bag and swung it idly in both hands. 'Your house is close that way?'

'Yeah, you could stop and have some coffee if you like.' Oh, bugger.

'Thanks, that's kind, I'd love to.'

Sod, emergency.

'But another evening maybe?' Sandrine said, a line she must get lots of chance to practice.

Spencer had a go at the Harry Lime smile. 'OK, I'll give you a ring.'

'OK,' she said. She put down her bag and tilted her face up, turning it aside, to invite a formal smacker on one cheek, then the other one. While Spencer did the kissing she let her breasts nudge lightly up against him.

He wondered how deliberate that was.

'Ciao,' said Sandrine, shouldering the holdall, and sauntered off.

'See you.' Spencer went home feeling pretty clever. He'd roped in a real star possible that he could mentally hold in reserve in case it all fell through with Claire — nowhere near a probable but the sense of possessing alternatives was the important thing — and he'd avoided straying into duplicitous-bastard territory.

(Who was it who called Carrington a duplicitous bastard? That's why people say it. Haig? Our peacekeeping troops in Sinai painted 'Lord Carrington's Own Duplicitous Bastards' on their armoured cars when whoever it was came round on an inspection tour. Must have been Haig. He'll be on our case again now, what time's it in Washington, just coming up for five, not even close of play.)

When he got back he poured himself another glass of wine to celebrate his savoir-faire and Sandrine's breasts. It was safe to drink some more now he was on his own, he wouldn't start saying stupid things, or not so's anyone was going to know.

He did the standard square search for the TV set's remote

control and, finding it between the sofa cushions, flicked on *News at Ten*.

They're dancing in the streets in Buenos Aires, they think it's all over. Perhaps it is, and nothing to be done. An amphibious landing against a bigger army on the far side of eight thousand miles of ocean doesn't sound too practical. And whether it comes off or not, the mayhem could be out of all proportion to whatever is supposed to be at stake, unless you factor in the principle of not allowing fascist governments to go round making landgrabs any time they feel like it. That's not what it's about, what it's about's the PM and El Presidente trying not to get the boot for all-round laughable incompetence, but perhaps the principle asserts itself in spite of them, or over and above, in which case there's some sense to it, although how many of the boys who come back blinded, burnt, on crutches or in wheelchairs take the point I wouldn't care to say.

Towards the end of the extended bulletin they mentioned that the IRA had claimed responsibility for murdering two soldiers yesterday in Londonderry. The terrorists said the men were undercover SAS. The army said they were a Signals engineer who'd been installing radio equipment at the police station nearby and his driver-bodyguard, and they'd been targeted because they had to drive the same route at the same time three days running, which an SAS patrol would hardly do. Martin McGuinness of Derry Sinn Fein said he regretted all violence but the British Army presence was the cause of it.

Nice one Mart, like toilet germs are caused by Harpic, right on, well-known fact.

Spencer played his Hall and Oates and danced a bit to try and cheer up.

What am I doing dancing? This is piss-artistry of grave dimensions, this is, man my age. Next thing'll be the sickly rush of universal love for all humanity (except the Ayatollah, Begin, Galtieri, Mrs T, McGuinness there and Gerry 'Tombstones' Adams, obviously, *va sans dire*).

He went to clean his teeth, came down, shelled and ate most of the peanuts and took his pills. Two red, two green. You could very nearly still call it an early night so if the pills worked, unlikely but not inconceivable, he could start to catch up on the stack of unsawn logs left over from months of life-going-nowhere insomnia.

It was only as he put the caps back on the bottles after swallowing that he noticed the bottom line on both the labels: AVOID ALCOHOLIC DRINK. Yeah, well, they all said that, and he hadn't had that much.

Clothes dumped on the bedroom floor, he curled up under the quilt in the lampless dark. Good if Claire was there to hold, but the bed was effing narrow for two people, the old student squash, and she'd only keep kicking him awake for snoring.

Nice safe darkness, blank. Though blank meant white not black, like point blank, white dot in the centre of a target. When did they get rid of the white dot that used to linger when you turned off the TV? Good, that was, winding-down motif, put you in the bedtime frame of mind.

It ain't what you do it's the way that you do it, Till the day I die, Till the cut it out.

Sandrine's long legs. Shame Claire hasn't got long legs, although nor's Julie Christie.

Claire's lovely springy lightness.

Different kinds of breasts, keen puppies, dopey puppies, melons, grapefruits, seabags, socks half-filled with egg custard ...

It was odd, he could feel his consciousness coming apart like a dandelion clock in the breeze but how could you be conscious of it happening? Was it like this normally and you forgot straight after as you slept, or was it the effect of pills?

Cars hooshed past on the Camden Road more softly and more rhythmically than seemed quite kosher.

He heard, in the distance, somewhere up in Holloway, the novelty horn play 'Strangers in the Night'.

I remember the film!

A Man Could Get Killed.

The blue Ital, never used before on operations, carried the same number plates as another blue Ital one of the scouts had spotted parked in a respectable driveway in the Prime Minister's constituency of Finchley. But the three of them had sat in it for so long now, in the crescent street in Shepherd's Bush, that if they stayed much longer they'd attract attention. And the Forces TV girl had not showed up, and the top-flat windows of the stucco house remained dark.

'Girl about town,' said Louise, behind the wheel.

Rory grunted.

'Friday nights,' Louise said.

Mattie, in the back, said, 'What do you think, Ror? She could come home at half past midnight or she could be gone the whole weekend, if we wait too long to find out there'll be no time left to try the other one before we have to make the plane.'

Rory grunted.

'If we're going to try the other one,' said Mattie.

'Yeah,' said Rory. 'Let's abort here.'

'Your wish ... ' Louise said, starting up.

The snag with contact lenses was the fiddly chore of taking out and cleaning them at night, which Gareth tended to put off. It meant he stayed up later now than when he still wore glasses.

He went to the washbasin, telling himself to make a start. He rubbed his face and felt a pain in his jaw like a wasp sting. The mirror on the cabinet showed only a minor-looking spot but the slightest fingertip pressure hurt enough to make him flinch. He took a deep breath and squeezed. The pain peaked and was gone. The spot ejected a dead bristle, which stuck to his finger, and a quantity of blood-orange pus, which sprayed the mirror. He hadn't expected quite such a messy outcome. Spiders and snakes he didn't mind, but spots gave him the creeps. He was particularly appalled by the ingrown bristle's surreal resemblance to a leek, bulbed at the root and frayed at the top. He'd never be able to look at the insignia of the Welsh Guards without a shudder in future. Shaken, he got some toilet paper and Dettol and cleaned up. The contact lens procedure could wait. He needed a cigarette.

The bathroom featured a pretentious connecting door to his room, the only bedroom really intended for adults when the glass house was built. At most times the door was kept locked, but the girls weren't here so Gareth opened it up and went straight through. Saving the five-pace trip along the landing was a nice and pointless luxury.

He lit a Camel and sat at his desk, idly brushing dust from some of his ornaments, the Russian doll, the little pottery figure of a Robertson's golly on double bass, the Dinky Toy model of a Mini-Moke from *The Prisoner*, the bronze paperweight bust of Clement Attlee.

The Trimphone extension on the bedside table trilled, though you could hardly hear it over the fierce bell of the proper phone downstairs. Gareth picked it up. 'Hullo.' Wary of terrorists calling to see if he was in, he didn't give his number these days.

'Oh.' Like most people who weren't family or friends of his, and some who were, the woman expected a longer cue and took a moment to crank up and speak. 'Is that Gareth?'

'Who's this?'

'It is you, that moody voice. It's Claire Tarrant.'

'Claire? What can I do for you?'

'I've just noticed the time, sorry, I hope I didn't get you up.'

'No.'

'I was going to ring, uh, Spencer. But I see on my Holt Newman list I've only got his old Islington number.'

'I haven't got his new one either. I should have, but he's never remembered to tell me it and if I want to speak to him I just go and knock on the door so I've never remembered to ask.'

'Oh. Doesn't matter, never mind. Men.'

'I could walk down there in the morning and get him to ring you. Or now, if it's urgent, I've still got my shoes on.'

'Don't worry, it isn't.'

'Or there's directory enquiries, except the phone's probably in one of the others' names, trouble with shared houses.'

'No, it's all right, thanks anyway.'

'I hope it's nothing to do with work at this time of night.'

Claire made a laughing noise.

'How have you been?' he said.

'I'm fine. I wasn't sure if you were in London at the moment.'

'I'm working over here again now, yes.'

'Right. Well.'

Gareth couldn't ask Claire if she'd left any underwear lying around anywhere lately, but it looked as if he'd gone and said the wrong thing to Spencer. Several wrong things, perhaps.

When Katie arrived home she couldn't find her keys. She rang the doorbell and went on searching her bag while she waited for Spencer to come and let her in.

Which he didn't. The lights were off, she noticed now, so she leaned on the bell a good long time to wake him up. He still didn't answer. He must be out. Till when? She sat on the steps and put her head in her hands. 'This is all I need after the evening I've had.'

She tried to read some more of her Anthony Burgess book by the light of the streetlamps, but all she wanted to do was get indoors and go to bed. After a few pages she rang the bell again, uselessly again.

She kicked the door, an inch of woodwork between her and the freedom of the house, and went back down the steps. 'Please come home, Spence, please.'

She could make out the ironing board and the ping-pong table skulking in the basement. That window was nailed shut, though, she'd never shift it even if she slipped the catch with a nail file, and the kitchen window on the raised ground floor above was out of reach, unless she tried jumping to the ledge from the top of the steps. Not bloody likely.

She walked round the corner of the house into the cobbled mews. The side door in the garden wall was locked, of course. She looked up at the top of the wall. There was no broken glass, and she could get a handhold if she jumped a few inches, so she could scramble over. Smashing a window she wasn't so sure about. Paul had cleared away the useful old bricks and whatnot that used to litter the garden. She might end up having to wrap her jacket round her fist, and still breaking her hand. And all the downstairs back windows had modern frames with catches you couldn't slip.

She heard the unmistakably offbeat footfalls of a drunk

approaching. He turned into the mews past the whitewashed false-limb clinic, a small tough man in a stained check overcoat. She thought of hurdling the wall right now, and in trousers she might have done, but not in this short skirt, not with him watching. And anyway what if he came over after her, to corner her where nobody could see?

He pulled up, staring at her, and did an exaggerated shake and shiver to mock the unease he rightly thought she was experiencing. Then he crabbed rapidly nearer.

She turned and walked. Fifty yards ahead up the mews, the cobbles were spread with light from the open front of that little garage where they worked on cars at all hours.

The man capered round in front of her, smirking, and blocked her when she tried to sidestep.

She stopped. 'Excuse me, you're in my way.' She was taller than him but he was like a little boxer, he could beat her to pulp. If he got a hand over her mouth fast enough he could do almost anything and the mechanics wouldn't hear. Jack the Ripper struck in circumstances not so different.

He began to mutter, his eye never quite meeting hers. She got the Irish accent but not a word of what he was saying except 'London', 'bitches' and 'take a woman like yourself now,' which all recurred on a short loop.

The fact that he was Irish made him a little less frightening, and he wasn't being aggressive so much as being a bore, but that could change.

'I don't want to seem rude,' and her voice was far more choked than she would have liked, 'but you can see I'm on my own and you really shouldn't be bothering me.' It was no good, he'd probably been pissed since long before the dawn of feminism and he'd never heard of all that stuff.

He put his face closer and his voice lowered.

Katie nodded as if she was listening and began to edge around him. He turned with her. She kept face-on to him until she was walking slowly backwards up the mews, with him lurching forward after her. He didn't seem to have realised that she was now progressing in the direction she wanted. He cackled a bit to see her apparently backing down scared, and he didn't move to head her off.

He was raising his hands to chest height in a gropey way she did not like the look of at all. Before he could lay them on her she swung her bag, weighted with the big paperback slab of Anthony Burgess, in a lashing overarm blow to the side of his head and ran like hell for the garage.

'Hello?' she called. 'Hello?'

One of the mechanics was respraying a patch on the side of an old vermilion Cortina. The other two were examining the underside of a car that was up on the lift. They looked round.

Katie had to grab the brick pillar in the middle of the workshop's double entrance to bring herself to a stop. 'Can I, can I use your phone please?'

The youngest mechanic, the one in the turban, said, 'Sure, over here, look. You all right?'

'I'm, I hope so.'

The grey phone was on the wall amid fact-lists, charts and girlie calendars. Trembling, Katie dialled 999 and put her back to the calendars while the line rang. 'If a man comes in after me can you stop him?'

The lad in the turban picked up a gigantic wrench and stepped into the mews. 'I can't see anyone.'

'He might be hiding in a doorway. Oh God, how long does this take? Oh hi, hi, I — '

'Emergency,' the voice said. 'Which service?'

'Police,' said Katie.

The line rang some more. Katie waited again, walking on the spot. The mechanics carried on with their work or pretended to. The smell of grease in here was strong.

A man at the other end said, 'Police, how can we help?'

'Oh, this sounds stupid,' Katie said, 'but I'm locked out of my house, I've lost my keys, my flatmate's disappeared and this man's — *bothering* me.'

'We can't have that, madam, what's the address?'

'It's 28 Rochester Square, off Camden Road, but I'm phoning from a garage place up Camden Mews. I don't think he's dangerous but — '

'And your name, please?'

'Donnelly, two Ns two Ls, Katherine.'

'Are you able to hold the line a moment?'

'Er, I suppose.' Katie walked back and forth in a short arc, leashed by the flex, glancing all the time towards the entrance. She heard a distant siren and wondered whose call it was answering and how long before they got around to hers. There must be all those Friday-night fights to break up.

'We do have a car in your area,' the man said. 'We'll be right with you.'

'Oh, thank you, thank — '

'Can I have the number you're calling from?'

Katie read it off the dial.

'All right, madam. The crew in the car estimate their time of arrival about ninety seconds.'

'What? You mean it's the one I can hear already?'

'Quite possible.'

'Shit! I do beg your pardon.'

'That's OK, madam.'

The team in the Ital, waiting for the lights to change at the St Pancras Way junction, heard the siren heehawing towards them and saw the blue flashes up ahead.

Rory told Louise, 'It's not for us.'

'No reason why it should be,' Louise said tightly.

The patrol car rushed into view down the middle of the Camden Road, but before it reached them it peeled aside, power-swerving low on its wheels, and turned off.

'Isn't that our turning?' said Louise.

'Yeah,' said Mattie from the back seat.

'It doesn't have to be a problem,' Rory said. 'We'll take it easy and we'll check it out.'

The car behind them hooted.

'Go, it's green,' said Rory.

'Oh.' Louise half-stalled, but got them going with a bandsaw wail of revs on a dipped clutch.

The siren still seemed to be coming nearer till it cut.

'Look,' said Mattie. The blue flashes played on the side of a whitewashed building to the right as the Ital passed by. There was a paved-off turn with bollards. Beyond the building the slippery-shaped police Rover was drawn up on the corner of Rochester Square, coppers getting out and putting on hats.

'It's OK,' Rory said, 'it's just a burglary or something domestic.'

'You don't want to cancel,' said Louise.

'I do not. We'll be away and gone before those guys can do anything. Follow the plan.'

She turned right on to Murray Street. 'Is this the mews that crosses here?'

'Yeah, but you go on. And take the next left. Camden Square.'

'Mm mm mm.'

Mattie glanced down the mews. The blue flashes at the far end showed the silhouette of a tall girl running.

Katie called, 'Hello? Hello?', the same as when she'd run the other way.

Two policemen met her on the corner with unexcited faces. She hoped she wasn't going to be in trouble for wasting their time.

'It was me who rang,' she panted.

'All right? Where's the bloke?' said one. He had out-of-date sideburns.

The other one, who had freckles noticeable even in this light, shouted back towards the car, 'OK, we've got her.'

'I can't see him now,' said Katie.

'Heard us coming,' said the sideburned one. 'D'you want us to drive you round, see if you spot him?'

'Oh. I don't know. I think he might have been headed for the Irish Centre, they put people up, don't they?'

The policemen braced. The sideburned one said, 'Irish accent? Have you got a description?'

Katie was glad of her second-generation London vowels, though not proud of the feeling. 'Well, he was short … '

'Moustache?'

'No, only stubble, going grey, he had this red face, bashed about a bit from sometime ... '

'Wearing?'

'A ... check overcoat. Undone, no belt, quite grubby.' The policemen seemed to relax and looked at each other with eyebrow-shrugs. The freckled one said, 'Drunk, was he?'

'Oh, yes.'

'OK.' He told the sideburned one, 'We can have a word up the Centre.'

'Yeah. Did he threaten you, take any physical action?'

'He stood in my way,' said Katie. 'I did hit him with my bag when he got really close.'

The sideburned one said to the freckled one deadpan, 'Reasonable force?'

'Yeah, right,' said the freckled one. 'We can try and follow him up, or we could just see about getting you safe indoors.'

'Well, now he's gone,' said Katie, 'I think I'd just like to get in and leave it.'

'Yeah? OK. We'd better go in a back window. Can you show us something with your name and address on? Driving licence?'

'I ... don't have a driving licence.'

'Gas bill?'

'The gas isn't in my name.'

'Anything, long as it gives your name and address. Or else we can't break in. You understand.'

'Yes. Oh, God. There must be something in my bag.' Katie looked. She was going to burst into tears in a minute.

The Ital stood double-parked on Camden Square, its engine idling. 'That's the house there? Down that path?' Louise said. 'At least the lights are on this time.'

'I've never seen the car,' said Rory.

Mattie leaned forward. 'Me either. Visitors?'

'Well, if there are it's going to be their problem. Louise.' Rory pointed ahead. 'Callbox. Keep going round the square. Left past the Centre when you're back to Murray Street.'

'Right you are,' Louise said. 'Sod. It is such a *sod* trying to get first gear on a *fucking* British Leyland car. Sod. Go *in*.'

'Don't keep stirring it, smack it.'

She smacked the lever. It went in.

Katie said, 'There's this,' a private letter from the man she'd seen tonight and decided or agreed not to see any more.

The freckled one took the bent white envelope. 'Handwritten. Needs to be official.'

Katie, eyes and nose about to run, sniffed miserably.

'Don't worry,' said the sideburned one. 'Is it postmarked?'

The freckled one held the envelope close up, tilting it to catch some light. 'Yeah, local, 26 ... Mar.'

'You haven't moved out in the last few days?'

'No,' Katie said, eyes down.

'Because people do split up and try on all kinds of revenge, you see. And you will be able to show us proof of residence inside?'

'Sure,' said Katie, though she wasn't.

'Fine.'

The freckled one gave back the letter.

'Thank you,' Katie said. 'Erm, if you look ... ' She led them along the side wall.

The sideburned one tried the garden door. It was still locked.

'You'll have to go over,' Katie said. 'Then, the basement windows, you might find you're locked in down there, so ... up on the balcony, see, the french windows might be easiest.'

'Give it a go,' the sideburned one said bouncily, sizing up the wall.

'Want a boost?' the freckled one said.

'Nah.' The sideburned one jumped, pulled himself up, swung his legs over the wall and dropped into the garden.

He reappeared at the top of the balcony steps and tried the handle of the french windows. 'Nope. Always worth checking, though,' he called down. He stooped to the glass. 'There's a fold in the curtain so I can't see if the key's in. Bolts as well?'

'Ah. Yes,' said Katie in a shouted whisper. 'They could be done up.'

'We'll see.' He brought a truncheon out from under his jacket flap with a practised flick. Seen at twenty feet in bad light it still looked to Katie like a nasty weapon. 'Are you alarmed?'

'No, I'm fine.'

Behind Katie's shoulder the freckled one said, 'I think the officer meant is there a burglar alarm fitted to the house?'

'No, there isn't, no.'

'You want to look into that,' said the sideburned one. He stopped laughing and put the truncheon through the glass.

Because the fragments mostly fell on carpet there was less noise than Katie had been fearing, but she looked round guiltily all the same. The mechanic in the turban came to the front of the workshop and someone in pink came to the lit dormer window of one of the Murray Street houses that backed on to the gardens.

'Key's in,' said the sideburned officer, reaching through. 'Got it.' He took his arm out and tried the handle again. 'Won't budge. I'll do the bolts.' He clubbed the glass at top and bottom, great shards of it crashing down inside on shards that had gone before, till there was next to none left in the frame. He could have stepped through, but he reached in to free the bolts and pushed the frame open. 'Yes! Is your front door on a deadlock?'

'At the moment, I don't know,' Katie said. 'Depends how my friend left it, if he's been in.'

'You go round, then, and I'll see if I can open up for you.'

The red telephone box was at the other end of Murray Street by the curving smoke-blacked wall of a used-tyre depot. Beyond the junction loomed the gasholders of King's Cross and the clocktower of St Pancras in the auburn skyglow, with nothing from here to there but a mile of empty railyards.

If the man answered, Louise was meant to hang up straight away. If it was the girl, she had to ask her whether he was in, and if he was she had to do the 'Hullo, I can't hear you, can you hear me, look, I'll try again' routine, and then hang up.

All of which was academic, as it happened. She left the box and walked to the Ital. 'Engaged, engaged, engaged. So. Shall I try in five minutes?'

Rory said, 'It doesn't matter. Let's go ahead.'

'And if it's just the girl at home — '

'She'll do.'

'Ah?'

'She'll do. BBC.'

'Is she BBC?'

'Matt followed her to work.'

'Broadcasting House,' said Mattie.

'We're allowed to do anyone in the hostile media.'

'Mm. Uhuh?' said Louise.

'So take us back to where we were, then,' Rory said.

'OK, Caroline,' Gareth said, 'thanks for ringing.'

'I didn't,' Caroline van Oldenborgh said, over party noises, 'Lynn did, I got her to put me on.'

'Oh, yeah, well.'

'Are you as pissed as we are?'

'No, time of night, that's all.'

'She wants to say goodnight again. No, she's being dragged off for a bop.' Caroline giggled. 'We haven't had one for a while.'

'Haven't we? No.'

'Next party we're both at ... '

'Yeah, whenever that is.'

'Well, you miss out on invites cause you're such a damn recluse most people don't know you've come back. Put yourself about.'

'Tuh.'

'Harris, stop that.'

'Oh, hi, Jerry.'

'Gareth says hi. Jerry says hi. Caroline says byee.'

'Cheerio.' Gareth put the Trimphone down.

The sideburned officer budged pieces of glass aside with his boot. 'Fetch a glazier in the morning, he'll take that away for you, best not put it in the rubbish. Bin man might cut himself and sue.' He drew back the curtain. 'If we lean that coffee table up here for the night it'll block some of the draught out. Won't stop a burglar, but ... '

'I think the chance is small enough to take,' said Katie.

'You'll be all right.'

The policemen moved the bottle, glasses, ash-saucer and papers from the hideous coffee table to the side cupboard. 'Gordon Bennett, what's that about?' said the freckled one.

Katie said, 'It's God creating Adam, from the Sistine Chapel ceiling. It's the landlord's.'

'Looks like What's this, nail varnish?'

The sideburned one said, 'We're not having your sort in the Garden of Eden. Out of it.'

'Rule one, no poofters, Bruce.' They carried the table between them to the french windows. 'Up your end.'

'As they say.'

Upended, the table was pushed into place against the black jagged man-high hole in the glass. The sideburned one closed the curtain round the table's stumpy outthrust legs. 'Do for tonight.'

Katie had seen a folded paper on her shelf of the bookcase. 'Here's my Access bill. With the address on.'

The freckled one gave it a glance without taking it and nodded.

The sideburned one said, 'Any dripping taps to fix, then, while we're here? Loose stair carpet wants tacking down?'

'No, you've been brilliant, I'm really grateful,' Katie said. 'I don't know what I would have done. And you were so quick getting here.'

He waved that off. 'We were coming right by anyway, it's on our rounds.'

The freckled one said, 'We're supposed to be on armed response, but you get a 999 distressed lone female and you're practically already there you pick it up, you don't go, Oh I'll check my diary.'

The sideburned one saw Katie's look and said, 'The gear's kept in a locker in the car, it's all right, we don't carry it. Well. We could stick around and have a party but the bottle's nearly gone, shame, so, we'll love you and leave you.'

'I could make some coffee or something,' Katie said.

'No, it's OK,' said the freckled one. 'We'll have to report this in and be moving along.'

'I suppose, well, thanks again. I wonder what happened to — ?'
Katie, from curiosity, opened Spencer's door. 'Spencer?'

Camden Square was quiet. Rory and Mattie stepped out of the
Ital, masks rolled up like woolly hats, Mattie shouldering the
sledgehammer with its shaft bound in non-slip black tape. Louise
switched on the radio, to make her waiting seem more innocent
to any passer-by, and caught the hammy riff of 'Layla', Derek and
the Dominos' golden oldie, a big hit again just now. Rory and
Mattie walked unhurried down the path that cut through to the
mews.

Two policemen took up nearly all the space in Spencer's tiny
room. Katie stood back on the threshold. 'He isn't snoring,' she
said. 'He always snores, you can hear him from upstairs.'

The freckled one switched on the bedside lamp. 'Wake up,
mate.'

Spencer didn't wake up, stayed peacefully inert.

'I don't understand it,' Katie said. 'The doorbell, then you
breaking in, us talking and the light right in his face, I mean I
know he was starting on a course of sleeping pills but — '

'He's overdosed, don't tell us.' The freckled one patted the side
of Spencer's face. 'Come on, mate. Oi oi. Wake up.'

The face showed no response.

'Here a minute.' The sideburned one changed places with the
freckled one and took over at the head of the bed. He put the back
of his hand close to Spencer's mouth. 'Dah, he's breathing all right.'

'Are you sure?' said Katie.

'Come here.'

The freckled one moved out to let her in.

'Can you reach? Uh? Put your hand there,' said the sideburned
one.

She felt Spencer's steady breath warm her skin. 'Oh, yes.'

'I'll — ' With a thumb he lifted each of Spencer's eyelids. 'See
the pupils shrink then? In the light?'

'Yyy ... Did they?'

'Yeah, there's nothing wrong, he's not used to the pills, that's all.

He'll come round in the morning. Boyfriend, is he?'

'No, no, there's four of us who share the house, we used to be at Cambridge, just the other two aren't here. Parents', girlfriends'.'

'Cambridge. That explains it.' They shuffled from the room.

'What?'

'Absent-minded intellectuals, losing doorkeys, mixing drink and pills, I don't know.' His tone and smile were friendly, or were meant to be.

'There might be something in that,' said Katie. 'Except that Paul who isn't here's the brightest, got the best degree, and he's quite organised. In a way.'

Cuffs turned back and hands washed, Gareth popped his left lens out into his palm and sauced it with the cleaning solution. Twenty seconds rubbing it around with his finger was the programme. The right lens was done, rinsed and stored in the case to soak.

The front door resisted the first blow of the sledgehammer. It splintered open with the next. The glass house shook, or seemed to, but Gareth held helplessly still.

As Katie saw the men out to the hallway they stopped and turned their heads. The freckled one said, 'What was that?'

The ground floor was open plan. Gareth heard the spare loo door thrown wide and that was all the clearing that they'd have to do. The only light down there was what spilled from the staircase, which more or less told them he was up here anyway. They were coming now.

Gareth unfroze, swiped the lens into the basin, gave his hands one pass at the hanging towel, turned and, snatching up the holstered Browning from among Lynn's bubblebaths and shampoos on the cistern, went through the connecting door to his room.

The first terrorist was thudding up the stairs.

Gareth tripped the bedroom light switch off. His vision was blurry but the spill from the open bathroom and landing doors and the reference point of the Trimphone's luminous dial let him find his glasses on the bedside table first try no fumbling. He slipped them on and punched the large red button on the wall behind the table. The alarms would sound at Scotland Yard and at divisional control, for what that was worth. The single car he'd heard attending to some minor bit of trouble down the road ten minutes back had probably moved on, and even if it hadn't it would come too late.

The terrorist was halfway up.

Gareth faced the landing door and watched the stairhead at the far end as he put his arms into the holster rig and pulled the gun.

Katie said, 'What? That banging?'

Gareth pressed the safety off. He thumbed the hammer back against the robust mainspring in the spine of the Browning's handgrip. The hammer snicked and held.

He had to have racked the first round up into the chamber when he took the Browning back from Spencer. He didn't remember but he had to have, because he couldn't afford the time to work the slide now and he couldn't afford the giveaway noise it made.

He clamped his left hand tighter round his right and took aim at the stairhead. The balustrade along the landing didn't have soldiers, it had varnished plywood panels. He wouldn't see the terrorist coming much before the top step.

Glasses made everything look too small and far away when you were used to contacts.

A black mask bobbed up at the stairhead.

Gareth's heart was sprinting and he broke sweat. His face prickled. His legs weakened under him. But he didn't mind physical fear. It was a primitive, limited reaction you could hold a little of your thinking self apart from.

Louise, nodding and pouting to the Clapton riff, looked at her Swatch.

'Yeah,' said the sideburned officer, 'it came from — '

*

218

The terrorist put one foot on the landing. It was the usual amateur bodybuilder in the usual subfusc jeans and olive anorak, but the mask was no disguise because the huge revolver's six-inch barrel had the ventilator rib along the top which was peculiar to the 1955 Colt Python .357 Magnum. Therefore Rory Kite.

Gareth held his fire and waited for the other foot to come up. If he loosed off now and failed to drop Kite with the first few rounds the terrorist would duck back down the stairs. Once both feet were on the landing it was much more likely Kite would go for cover in the bathroom only one more step ahead. The doors of Lynn's and Melanie's rooms, side by side at that end, were both shut, but the bathroom's outer door was open, Gareth didn't bother closing it when he was on his own here, and the connecting door was in the corner where Kite couldn't see it from the landing.

The other foot was coming up and forward. As it did so, Kite performed the standard quick pan round with the revolver to assess the layout. The masked face and the six-inch barrel turned this way. Gareth knew his ivory shirt would stand out from the shadows but he had to be at least in partial view to give himself a decent field of fire. He saw the terrorist's eyes latch on to him, their whites expanding. The foot, at full stride, touched down with a stomp as Kite recovered balance. The Colt Python, nearly dead-on, twitched. Kite's index finger was convulsing to exert the ten or more pounds' trigger pressure that the cocking mechanism of revolvers needed.

Gareth didn't have that problem. It would only take a light dab now to set the Browning off, and since the instantaneous automatic action cocked itself on recoil he could keep on doing five dabs to the second, not a rate of fire you'd ever get with a revolver.

All he had to overcome was natural inhibition against shooting at a human target, and the mask helped there.

Katie jumped. The banging had started up again, but this time louder and faster, and it went on.

Louise held her breath and tingled with the thrill of transgression.

*

Gareth counted away the rounds, onetwothreefourfive. He might not have hit Kite with any of them but he hadn't been hit either. Sixseven.

Kite, outline fuzzed by smoke and rippling heat, dived, reeled or fell into the bathroom.

Gareth stepped aside and lined up on the connecting doorway. His ears rang. The burnt-bacon stink of the smoke filled his nose.

Kite, in a teetering crouch, had noticed the connecting door and half-turned. The Python swung.

Eightnineteneleventwelvethirteen. The Browning locked open on empty.

Kite jerked and sat down heavily.

The Python flew across the room and tumbled to the bottom of the bath with what was probably a drastic noise. Gareth was too deaf to tell.

Kite's shoulders bumped the open outer door against the rubber bung intended to protect the wall behind it. The door rebounded and gave Kite a shove that sent the masked head pitching forward so it hung between the splayed knees.

Gareth moved to the landing doorway again. As he went he thumbed the Browning's magazine release stud, let the empty mag fall out, drew the first spare from the pouches in the holster rig, slotted it inside the handgrip and depressed the slide-stop bar. The action unlocked and the slide snapped forward, chambering the top round. He'd been made to practise all that till he could do it in two seconds.

Louise stared at the mews house. Too many shots to be quite right somehow.

The policemen ran down the front steps. The sideburned one told Katie, 'Stay inside.'

The landing was clear. Gareth went out to the balustrade. The next terrorist was at the foot of the stairs below, rooted, gazing up into the light, maybe wondering what to do. The long black weapon seemed to be an Armalite.

As Gareth opened fire the illusion passed off and he realised he was looking at a sledgehammer, not a gun of any kind. The Armalite shape was created by the merging of the black-taped handle with the warped undershadow it cast across the front of the terrorist's anorak. The jut of the magazine was the shadow of a gripping fist. The steel glint at the top end, in the darkness over the terrorist's shoulder, came from one edge of the hammerhead, not from a slender muzzle.

The terrorist was hit and dropped like a puppet with its strings cut. Gareth ceased fire after four rounds. In normal time he would have scarcely finished with his left lens now.

The policemen reached their car. Katie, at the kitchen window, saw them scramble into the back and pull a box from behind the armrest. The car reversed up to the line of bollards, then tyre-squealed forward round the corner of the false-limb clinic into the mews. The siren sounded.

Louise had been expecting to hear that. As Rory said, it didn't have to be a problem. She patted the gearstick and waited for Rory and Mattie to come running.

The curtains across the upper front of the glass house parted in the middle.

There was a car double-parked on Camden Square at the gap in the flats, the tactical place to put one. Gareth couldn't hear the engine but he could see the blowing tufts of exhaust lit red by the rear lamps and he was sure it was the getaway vehicle. Annoyingly he couldn't do anything about it and nor could the crew of the approaching police car, who were on the wrong street to give chase even if they spotted it. By the time they'd gone around the block it could be anywhere.

He turned back to keep watch on the two doors. From this side of the bed he could cover both, admittedly at rather extended range for his marksmanship.

He doubted there'd be any more terrorists, but it wasn't impossible. And he had a feeling that Kite, who'd collapsed sideways on the bathroom floor in a sort of foetal curl, was alive. Dead men fell in clumsier, odder ways than that, like the other one downstairs, Ball presumably. Despite the blots on the anorak Kite might be conscious, playing possum, waiting for the moment to pull a spare gun. Gareth wasn't going close enough to take a look.

Katie found Miles's grisly collection of duty-free liqueurs in the side cupboard and poured a large Blue Curaçao.

Spencer's door was still ajar and he was still quietly asleep in there. Things come in threes. So, first the break-up scene with Alastair, then locking herself out and getting more or less molested, then gang warfare or terrorism going on in the neighbourhood, made three. Spencer was safe. Four wasn't allowed. She closed the door.

Away up the mews the siren stopped, but more of them were coming from all directions.

Gareth called out, 'Hi.'

The voice that drifted up the stairs was indistinct.

Gareth needed to be careful here in case it was the armed patrol. He didn't move. 'Say that again, I'm a bit deaf from shooting.'

'Armed! Police! Who's! There?'

'MacMichael. I'm all right but there's a — sorry?'

'Code! Word!'

'Oh. Grimsby. I'm in a white shirt, well, off-white. At the top, doorway smack in front, you'll see a terrorist I hit. No more up here.'

'See him!'

The copper must be squatting a few steps down, where the stairs turned, barely out of Gareth's view.

Gareth called, 'I haven't checked the body.'

'Where are you?'

'Dark doorway far end.'

'Are you hurt?'

'No.'

'Are you armed?'

'Yes.'

'Leave! The gun! Walk! Out here! Slowly!'

'Are you covering the terrorist?'

'We see him! Out here! Slowly! Stop when I say!'

Gareth put the Browning on the bed and walked out to the landing, hands lifted as when reasoning with an angry woman.

There were two coppers at the turn, holding a .38 Smith apiece. They hadn't taken the time to kit up in armoured vests, which showed a certain bravery. One, frecklefaced, was aiming at the bathroom doorway. The other, who had sideburns of a *Sweeney* kind unusual these days, was aiming at Gareth. 'Stop there.' Same voice.

Gareth had stopped already, a pace short of the bathroom door so as not to break Freckles's line of fire to the terrorist. He said, 'I don't have glasses in the file picture.'

Sideburns raised the Smith to the safe position pointing upwards. 'All right. I recognise you. Were you alone?'

'Yes, my flatmate's away.' Gareth put hands in pockets. One of his knees wouldn't stop vibrating but his hands pushed the trouser crease forward so the vibration didn't show as much.

Sideburns talked to the radio clipped on his jacket. 'Yeah, Mr ... MacMichael's OK, he's OK, he's OK. We've found a second hooded suspect down, he looks a mess but we're about to check.'

Both coppers came up. Freckles opened Lynn's and Melanie's doors to clear the rooms, Sideburns moved to the bathroom threshold. Gareth leaned to see around the doorframe, though all he saw was the back of Kite's head. Sideburns stooped to check the body.

Freckles said, 'Watch his hand!'

'Got it,' Sideburns said. He tossed on to the landing an automatic you could almost fit inside a cigarette packet, probably an old Baby Browning or an East Bloc copy.

'Where did he have that?' Gareth said.

'Must have palmed it from this ankle holster,' Sideburns said. 'Too weak to use it.'

'He thinks you're going to finish him off.'

'Now keep still!' said Freckles.

Sideburns holstered his Smith and talked to his radio. 'Yeah, this one's alive but he needs an ambulance now, like right away.' The radio quacked. Sideburns said, 'Multiple gunshot wounds, upper body, at least one of them's air-venting, it's very very serious. Gunshot wound to hip. And part of his ear's been blown away, I think it's superficial not a head wound but we'll cut the mask off and look.' He sat back on his heels. 'Mr MacMichael?'

'Oh yes?' said Gareth.

'Funny thing to ask you, sir, could you fetch the first aid kit from our car outside? Ask our driver, he's there, keeping people back.'

'Sure.' Gareth made for the stairs.

'Mind the body at the bottom.'

'Is that one dead?'

'Very much so, I'm afraid, yeah. Could you hurry now, please?'

Gareth meant to hurry, but still had to pause at the foot of the stairs to look at the other terrorist who was lying there. The mask had been removed. The cleanshaven face was slack, the open brown eyes skewed different ways, and there was a big puckered purple mark under the chin, the only hit. The sledgehammer lay alongside, a gouge showing in its metal head where the round had glanced off.

In the mews, the police driver was talking to a wide-hipped black girl who had a baby in her arms. The baby grizzled. She rocked it.

'Sorry, madam?' the driver said. 'You're in the flats, yeah?'

'Ground floor. End of the path, see. Ooh, Oliver, you hush, all right now, there's my boy, mmm. A car stopped outside, where you see the gap, and left the engine running, all my windows buzzed, you know, and woke my baby up, hush now.'

'That can be aggravating. Hullo, Oliver, ay? Ay?'

Gareth said, 'We need the first aid kit.'

The driver turned. 'One moment, madam. You the resident? You got a recognition code?'

'Grimsby. Can we have the first aid?'

'Coming up.' The driver walked to the Rover's tail-end to lift the hatch. 'Carry on, madam.'

The girl came with them. 'That's my boy. I was so angry and I looked out, right, it was a blue saloon with a woman in the front, she had long hair and a beret on. I thought, you inconsiderate ...'

The driver handed Gareth the green plastic picnic box with the white cross. The nearing sirens cut as more police cars turned into the mews.

Gareth ran indoors.

'Thanks,' Sideburns said, and pulled white strips and wads of dressing from the box. Freckles took scissors and began to cut the back of Kite's wet anorak up the middle. Both policemen had red hands from trying to stop the terrorist's blood and breath escaping through the wounds.

Sideburns pressed and bound the first wad to the chest. 'Have we got an exit for this one?'

'Which? Yeah, think so,' Freckles said, 'I'll ... wait, I'll cut the sweater, OK, give me a dressing.'

'Here. Now this one, that's basically shoulder muscle damage, do that in a minute, this one ...'

'Got another exit low between the shoulder blades off-centre.' They both took fresh dressings.

'This should be the entry,' Sideburns said, 'not venting and the blood's quite slow, it must have sneaked through and missed the heart and lungs, so quite a lucky one. For him.'

'Come out very near the backbone.'

'Could have cracked a vertebra? That close?'

'Well ... maybe.'

'OK. Um. We don't need to move him, keep him on his side, tell the medics to watch that.'

''Cause you don't want fragments jabbing the spinal cord.'

'Nothing they haven't dealt with before.' Sideburns glanced up at Gareth. 'You don't seem to have ruptured any of his major arteries, you'll be pleased to know, or perhaps not.'

Gareth said, 'Is he conscious still?'

'Semi. He blinks, now and then, and sort of squirms. He said something while you were out, he's deeper into shock now.'

Freckles said, 'He said, We'll get the fucking redhead, tell her.'

Gareth said, 'Perhaps she was the driver. He's decided someone set them up'.

'Yeah, we called it in. We didn't see a vehicle, though.'

'She was on the square.'

'On ... ?'

'Camden Square. There's one point with a line of sight to this place and a perfect runback. I never have liked cars I don't know parking there. Double-parking and I hate them.'

Freckles cut the mask and peeled it from Kite's head. 'You saw it? Steady, I've got to do this, try and keep still.'

Gareth said, 'Yes. And she is supposed to be with Kite's gang.'

'Do you recognise him? We were going by the Magnum in the bathtub.'

'So was I.'

Freckles put a bandage on the mauled ear. Kite convulsed. 'All right, didn't mean to hurt,' said Freckles, brisk.

Sideburns, cutting away the jeans to bandage the hip, said, 'The ear's going to be the painful one even if it's the least dangerous.'

'The round's grooved the side of the head as well but I think the skull deflected it, very shallow angle. All right now mate, all right, we've got to put a bit of pressure on that, I'm not hurting you on purpose.'

'That's it, that's it, easy now, ambulance here any minute.'

Freckles wiped away some of the weave-print of blood the soaked mask had left on the face.

Sideburns told his radio, 'I think we confirm the emergency is Mr Kite, Mr Ball believed dead, no moustache on him but nothing stopping him shaving.'

Freckles was feeling Kite's neck. 'He's getting cold, Tony.'

'Are you losing the pulse?' said Sideburns.

'No, but he's turning cold, it's the internal bleeding.'

Gareth said, 'I'll find some blankets.' He went out to the cupboard on the landing. It was only by the door. The near corner was holed where he'd fired rounds six and seven to drive Kite right into the bathroom. He gave the policemen a couple of peach-coloured blankets.

'Thank you, sir, I'm sorry they may become stained,' said

Sideburns as he and Freckles unfolded them over Kite, red hands staining them already. 'Do you mind going out again, sir, ask our driver to keep the road clear for the ambulance if he hasn't done that? I expect he has, but there could be a dozen police vehicles blocking it by now otherwise, it's a very narrow lane.'

'Sure.' On the stairs, seeing Ball again at the bottom, Gareth called back, 'Did you find a gun on this one?'

'PPK, yeah, down his trousers. I had to lift it in case of like a miracle.'

'OK.' Gareth stepped over Ball and out. He'd need a new front door. Where did you buy front doors?

The police vehicles were moving into the parking area of the flats, or on to the apron of the taxi workshops next door where the first Rover had now gone. The driver was at the carport gate, talking Oliver's mother through her statement again, with his notebook out this time. Opposite, a policewoman was stretching Do Not Cross tape between the posts at this end of the path. More police were chivvying neighbours away along the path and the mews.

'Did they want something else?' said the driver.

'It's all right,' Gareth said, 'you seem to have ... Is this the ambulance?'

A large white van with blue lights turned in from the Murray Street end.

'No, another one of ours,' said the driver. 'All right, madam, then you heard the shots, how many would you say?'

'I don't know, ten?' she said. 'I couldn't count them, it was too quick, and the echo off the flats. Ask him.'

'We will, but this is your impressions I have to take down at the moment. Ten?'

'And then a minute later two or three more.'

'Long as that? So how long then before you heard the police car arrive and the other vehicle drive off?'

'Nah, you're right, that was more like a minute, so five, ten seconds, put.'

The driver scribbled. The police van pulled up. He told the crew, 'If you park at the side there, we're securing the area, talking to people who can fill us in. Yeah, there. Push on, here's the ambulance.'

Another white van arrived, cutting its siren. The two medics in their luminous waistcoats jumped out and brought the trolley from the back.

'It's upstairs,' Gareth said. He led them in and switched the ground floor lights on. They immediately knelt beside Ball. 'Not him, he's dead,' said Gareth.

'Has anyone tried resuscitation?' said one medic.

'I wouldn't waste your time on him, he used to plant secondary bombs especially to kill you people.'

'You never know, someone has to try it.'

Freckles shouted from the stairhead, 'Oi! Up here!'

'I'll have a go,' said the police driver, coming in.

The medic said, 'There'll be another ambulance team in a minute to take over.' The medics lifted the stretcher off the trolley and carried it upstairs.

The driver knelt by the body. 'Oh, dear. Eyeballs out of whack, it's major brain trauma. Is that the entry wound here?'

'Yes,' said Gareth, 'it went in off the hammerhead, look.'

'Then again you can't be sure it is a bullet entry, that's where shitheads have their arseholes. Sorry about the bad taste, but frankly when you end up kissing Provo corpses it's a bad taste evening. Urh. Some of the roof of his mouth's gone at the back, tongue's nearly off, there's still an airway below that but — ' He pounded the chest and blew into the mouth by turns. 'No exit wound?'

'Doesn't seem to be.'

'The round lost too much energy dinging the hammer, it's just bounced around inside his skull, totally scrambled his brains.' The driver blew again. 'If we gave him massive adrenalin shots and electric charges it still wouldn't make a difference.' He kept going.

A woman outside yelled, 'You! Leave this area! Now!'

Oliver's mother's voice yelled back, 'The other one told me not to go away!'

'Hey! Shut it and go! You mess me around you'll find I turn very nasty!'

'No doubt in my mind on that score,' said Oliver's mother, walking in. Oliver was quiet.

A low-built policewoman came in through the hall and grabbed Oliver's mother's arm.

Oliver's mother said, 'Get her off me!'

'She's a witness,' said the driver.

The woman let go and grabbed Gareth's arm instead. 'And who's this?'

'He's the resident.'

Several male officers ran in and got hold of Oliver's mother.

'No, no, no, you can leave her,' said the driver.

She shook herself free. Oliver grizzled.

'What about this one?' said the woman officer.

'Him as well.' The driver blew again. 'Be a big help actually if the rest of you could stay outdoors and not disturb the crime scene.'

'Yeah, but, what, is this one a suspect?'

Sideburns came down the stairs. 'No, that's Mr MacMichael.'

'He's been carrying a weapon.' She pulled at Gareth's shoulder holster.

Sideburns made his way past the driver and the body. 'He's a licensed shot, he's Box 500.'

'They don't have licensed shots over here,' said the woman.

'It's for his own protection. She's not up to speed, sir.'

'Yeah?' she said. 'With what exactly?'

Andy walked in, followed by a couple of other detectives in pale macs and some overalled flak-jacketed Blue Beret commandos wielding Hecklers, Brownings and rifles. He held up his warrant card. 'DI Garstang. What's happening and why's that dyke trying to arrest you, Gareth?'

'Hullo, Andy.'

'Is that Ball minus the moustache?'

'We think so,' Sideburns said.

'Kite?'

'Upstairs, the medics are seeing if they can reflate his lung before they move him.'

'Who took the targets out, did you?'

'No, it seems Mr MacMichael did.'

Andy told the woman officer still hanging on Gareth's arm, 'There you are, darling, that's what Mr MacMichael does to people who get in his face. Now I want to see you, and all these spare uniform hag-fags you drag around with you, start to practise your formation pissing-off. Right now, this instant. If I'm sufficiently impressed I might fix you a spot in the next Lord Mayor's Show, if I'm not I'll fix you full stop. Get your clumping great Doc Martens off my crime scene. Do it.'

The woman and her reinforcements left, muttering, 'Sir,' 'Boss,' 'Understood.'

Andy asked Oliver's mother, 'Are you the lady who reported the vehicle?'

'Yes,' she said. 'I'm only here to give a statement, right, and it was me she started on, and that fan club with her, I can't believe it.'

'Do you want to make a formal complaint?'

'I'm not that stupid. Now how am I supposed to reach my flat across the way with all them still out there?'

'One of my detectives is going to see you home. How old's the baby now?'

'He's coming up for three months and my arms are dropping off, I've got to sit down a minute first.'

'Do,' said Gareth.

She hooked a chair out from the dining table with her foot and rested Oliver on her lap. 'Thanks. He's seen your glasses, that's why he's gone quiet again, he's fascinated by people in glasses at the moment. Aren't you?'

Andy said, 'Nick? Take some details and accompany the lady when she's ready.' He went over to the driver. 'How's it going?'

'No luck at all,' said the driver.

A second pair of medics had come in. 'How long have you been giving resus?' one said.

'Few minutes. Nothing to show for it.'

'He does not look good. Can we move him now? We'll try some gear in the ambulance.'

Andy said, 'Yes, once the officer's turned his pockets out.'

The driver made a quick search. 'Loose change. Key ring with no keys, cloverleaf fixed in clear plastic on the fob, or shamrock perhaps.'

Sideburns held out a Walther PPK in a plastic bag. 'This in the waistband.'

The driver said, 'Piece of paper. It's a betting slip. He had two hundred and fifty on a horse called Grittar to win the Grand National tomorrow. Fair odds.'

'A lot of smart money's going on Grittar,' a Blue Beret said. 'He could start favourite.'

'Never mind smart money,' Andy said, 'he's been gambling with organisation money. Two-fifty? If it doesn't win his own side would have given him a bullet in the head for thieving. You can move him,' he told the medics.

A Blue Beret with no weapon drawn, perhaps the leader, said, 'Escort?'

'Wait for them to bring the injured one down, send four, six men along with him. Up to you how many, long as we keep some. UCH?'

'Yes,' said a medic as they lifted Ball on to the stretcher.

Gareth said, 'Andy, I'm going up to get my cigarettes.'

'OK,' Andy said, 'I'll have to see you don't disarrange the evidence, spent cartridges and suchlike, accidentally.'

'I know.'

Upstairs, Kite was lying on a stretcher under a new red NHS blanket, tubes in his mouth. One of the medics was asking Freckles, 'Do we know what kind of ammunition?'

'Parabellum,' Gareth said.

'What's that?'

Freckles said, 'Standard nine millimetre, solid roundnose, nothing tricky.'

'With you. Thanks. Surgeons ask. OK if we get him on his way?'

'Go ahead,' Andy said. 'There'll be a police vehicle with you, he's under guard from now on.'

'They're scrubbed up in theatre waiting.'

'You won't be delayed.'

The medics carried Kite away downstairs.

Gareth switched the bedroom light on, tiptoed through the litter of ejected cartridge cases and found the pack of Camels on his desk.

Andy sniffed. 'The haze in here, I thought you must be a dedicated chain smoker but it's gun fumes.'

'Mostly.' Gareth lit up.

Andy considered the pattern of cartridges on the floor and the view through both doors. 'I see. I'm not sure how well your bathroom carpet's going to clean.'

'The whole place is wrecked, I'll lose the deposit.'

'From the holes in the doors and walls, your back bedroom windows must have gone. We know people who can deal with all that, I wouldn't get worked up about it.'

'There's a house backing on to this, over the garden fence.'

'We'll knock and see they're OK. If you'd killed a sleeping kid with a stray round we'd have heard by now, you might have chipped the brickwork, that's all.' Andy went through to the bathroom and asked Freckles, 'Was this revolver here fired?'

'No, stone cold,' Freckles said. 'He never got his first shot off.'

'Or the little gun out there? Right.'

The phone trilled. The other end said, 'Gareth. Carl. You're all in one piece.'

'Yeah.'

'Very happy to hear that. Not too, er ... ?'

'No.'

'And your visitors are *hors de combat*?'

'Yes. It was them.'

'So, we'll tell High Wycombe to let Catamaran run to the last port of call.'

'Why, is there a cargo?'

'Yes, it now seems there is, the trip's paid for, they wanted full value so they threw in some goods.'

'Uhuh.'

'And, ah, this way we can make a point to a certain landowner. After that High Wycombe step in. I must be off and see to things. Talk to you tomorrow.'

'Yes, thanks, bye.'

Andy came back in. 'Your weapon on the bed, Gareth? Heavy duty. Did you shoot Ball from here as well and he fell all the way down?'

'He never came up. I leaned over the rail. The empties should be near the phone table under the stairs.'

'Did he make a move to draw his gun?'

'No. I mistook the sledgehammer for an Armalite, I thought he was carrying it like a rifle. The lights were off down there.'

'What about the landing light?'

'That was on.'

'Are those glasses new?'

'No, they're a four-year-old prescription, my contacts are sharper.'

'If you had seen it was a sledgehammer would you still have opened fire?'

'I hope so. I did see what it was just before I hit him, but I assumed he had a gun somewhere. If I hesitated he could sidestep out of sight, drop the sledgehammer, pull a gun, fire up through the floor.'

'This is where the brief says, And you thought all that out in a split second?'

'I didn't have to, I knew it, like I know your face, I don't have to measure all the features with callipers and match the results with a chart, I just know.'

'All right. The inquest won't be like in Northern Ireland, you have to turn up, you can't send in a written statement. No London jury's going to bring in anything except justifiable homicide but the straighter you are the less chance you give some Provo brief to play the angles for the media. So, Armalite or sledgehammer didn't matter, Ball was in your house, he was masked up and he wasn't a gorillagram. And stick to that. Same when CID take your statement, which I don't think'll be till tomorrow now.'

Freckles looked in from the bathroom. 'Mind if I wash my hands? Covered in blood. But there's a contact lens in your basin.'

'Hold on.' Gareth went through, rinsed his left lens and put it in the case to soak.

Andy, at the connecting door, said, 'Is that what you were doing when they broke in?'

'Yes.'

Andy told Freckles, 'Remember in your statement. For when they claim it was a set-up.'

Gareth went back and sat at his desk to finish the Camel.

Andy said, 'Do you have some friends nearby who can put you up for the night? We'll have a lot of people in and out of here.'

'I know someone on Rochester Square, end of the mews. Is that too close?'

'Not if we're discreet about it. Put your jacket and tie on, look like one of us, and pack an overnight bag. Care to give your friend a ring?'

'I haven't got the number.'

'Know them well, do you?'

'They shouldn't mind too much.'

'No, they might be away, though.'

'I don't think so, I was round there earlier.'

'OK. When you're ready.'

Gareth took his flight bag from a cupboard. He put in a change of socks and underpants from the drawer in the base of the bed. The bag already held a small flat steel case. Inside that was his unofficial Browning, bought from Geordie. He couldn't leave it in the house with the police nosing about, and besides he didn't want to go anywhere unarmed. Agents and special forces nearly all kept unofficial guns, because your official one had to be handed in if you used it and the terrorists might try to get to you again before you were cleared to be issued with another. The penalty if caught with an unofficial gun was about five hundred pounds, the penalty if caught without one was sudden death, so it made reasonable sense.

Gareth went to collect his toothbrush, the lens case, a throwaway razor and a can of foam from the bathroom. When he turned round, Roger Hopkins, in civilian blouson, was outside at the stairhead talking to Sideburns and Freckles.

'Quite a few went wide,' said Sideburns, pointing at the holes in the wall and the girls' doors.

'Yeah, so?' said Hopkins, pointing at the blood on the bathroom carpet. 'We don't do your Olympic bull-in-one stuff, it doesn't work when you're scared, we do speed, aggression, firepower, that works.' Hopkins nodded to Gareth. 'Sir,' he said, unprecedentedly, the hypocrite. 'Who wears bins?'

'Sar'nt,' said Gareth. 'It's late, I haven't got my eyes in. How did you get here?'

'I was up Stoke Newington. I should have tried you in glasses.'

Gareth heard Andy call, 'You know him, Rog?'

'He trains with me,' said Hopkins.

'Oh. Took your time. Run into traffic?'

'I haven't got a blue light on the Range Rover.'

Gareth went back to his room and re-linked his cuffs. He put on a different tie for tomorrow, plain red, but left his top button undone. He shrugged into his jacket.

Andy said, 'These officers'll run you down the road and they'll be parked outside your friend's house. I'll place some Blue Berets in the garden if there is a garden, is there?'

'Yes. I'm a bit worried about leaving my parents' car here.'

'We'll have an armed guard here as well, high profile.'

Downstairs there was nobody around for now.

'Wait till the car's at the gate,' said Andy. Freckles and Sideburns went out.

'The betting slip,' said Gareth. 'Is it void now, or can Ball's family collect the money if the horse wins? They're not bad, they're not like him.'

'I don't know, void I expect. Do you do the horses, Rog?'

'Do I look like a mug?' said Hopkins.

'And supposing they could present it. At a Belfast branch? Who do you think would get to hear and pay them a visit?'

'Yes,' said Gareth. 'Oh, well.'

'We'll lose it in an evidence cabinet for a while.'

Sideburns came to the front door and nodded.

'Good,' said Andy. 'What's the house number?'

'Twenty-eight,' said Gareth.

Sideburns said, 'Not Katherine Donnelly and a bloke called Spencer?'

'How do you know them?'

'She lost her doorkey, that's why we were in the neighbourhood.'

'And then Gareth loses his door,' said Andy. 'There must be something going round.'

Hopkins said, 'Good night, sir.'

'Good night, sarn't,' Gareth said. 'Are you down to fly south?'

'I haven't heard yet, I'll let you know. Your pass'll be good for the range whoever's on. Still in touch with John B?' The B was for Browning, the unofficial one.

'Yes.'

'You want to keep in with him.'

'OK. Thanks.'

Gareth took his Burberry from the hall, followed Sideburns to the gate and got into the cramped back seat of the waiting Rover. Sideburns told the driver, 'It's the same house.'

'I can believe that,' said the driver. The car slid forward with a lazy V8 chug.

'Were you at Cambridge too, then?' Sideburns said.

'No,' Gareth said. 'I was a Cambridge reject so I went to Durham. I used to work in the same firm as Spencer before I joined the civil service.'

'Probably wish you'd stayed.'

'I wouldn't go that far. The job wasn't dangerous but it was pretty deadly in its way. Cold calling.'

'See your point there. Is he still doing it?'

'Yes.'

'Perhaps that's the trouble.'

'What?'

They crossed Davisons Street.

'Nothing, really,' Sideburns said, 'only when we did gain entry he was sleeping like a top, he never heard the bell. Miss Donnelly said the doctor had him on pills.'

'The shots might have woken him up, we didn't wait to see,' said Freckles.

They rounded the corner and stopped outside the house. The kitchen window was lit. Sideburns said, 'If you'd stay in the car till

I signal.' He went and rang the doorbell. Katie in her loose black sweater showed at the window a moment and after a marginal delay — Gareth had an idea she was checking herself in the hallway mirror, the others said she couldn't help it whoever was calling, even meter readers in clearly marked gas board vans, she still had to fluff her hair and pick lint off her clothes and make model faces — she answered the door. Gareth saw her head give a little buck as she noticed Sideburns's gesturing hands. He hadn't washed the blood off. The .38 on his belt might be disconcerting too. Her head nodded and shook as he talked to her. He looked back at the car and beckoned with a sweep of the arm as if directing traffic.

'OK, go,' said Freckles, jumping out. He hurried Gareth up the steps.

'Are you all right?' said Katie.

'Sure. Hi. Sorry about the noise,' said Gareth. 'What's up with Spence?'

'He's just completely passed out. He must be the only person who's asleep within a mile after that. And it was you?'

'Can we all move inside and have the door shut, please?' said Freckles.

'Yes, come in, come in.'

'We'll take another look at your friend if you like.'

'Well, it is a bit strange, I'm sure you're right there's nothing wrong, but ... '

'No bother.' The policemen went through to Spencer's room.

Katie hung Gareth's trenchcoat on the rack. 'Why not leave your bag by the stairs, you could have Paul's room if you like, or Miles's, they're both away, but Paul's would be more inhabitable.'

'The sofa would do.'

'No. Come and have a drink.' At the side cupboard she knelt and made some chess moves with the bottles. 'Having said that, everything we've got's disgusting except for Spencer's wine and there's not enough there for a glass. Ah. No, I know.' She got up, holding a matt green bottle of Remy Martin VSOP. 'There's this brandy Paul's been hoarding at the back which a very nice African student of his brought to dinner and he never opened.'

'Won't he mind?'

'No, he does love to hoard, but, you know. He'd mind a lot more if I didn't let you have some.' Katie whisked out two balloon glasses from the upper shelf of the cupboard, bumped the doors shut with her hips and poured. 'Americans in America who don't know anything and think the IRA's so great drive Paul round the bend. He got some press photos of one bombing off Miles that were too sick to publish and sent them to Ted Kennedy with a stroppy letter, because he's registered to vote in Ted's constituency, the family still have a house there.'

'What did Ted say?'

'Bwugh, flannel. Cheers.'

Gareth, whose notions of tone forbade salutations when drinking, did what he always did in these circumstances and made a low vague noise in his throat instead. As ever it came out unintentionally sounding sexual. One day he'd have to grow up and simply echo the given word unless he was on a date.

Sideburns and Freckles emerged from Spencer's room. 'He's comfortable,' Sideburns said, 'healthy pulse, nice colour, not sweating. All right if I run my hands under your kitchen tap?'

'There's the bathroom upstairs if you want soap,' Katie said.

'Blood you only need cold water. Second thoughts, I wouldn't mind a leak while I'm here.'

'Of course, you'll see at the top, I think I left the light on.'

Gareth rattled the little brown plastic pill bottles on the dining table. 'Anybody counted these? I will, be on the safe side.' He sat, emptied the first bottle on to the table and forefingered the capsules singly from the pile into a new pile.

Freckles asked Katie, 'Have you got a key that opens the side door to your garden?'

'We do keep things like that somewhere.'

'With your permission we'd like to put some men to watch the back of the house for tonight. Obviously they can scale the wall but if we can open up that door things would be easier.'

'Yes. Is Gareth still in danger?'

'Routine precaution, that's all.'

Katie went over to the bookcase. 'Where does Paul leave that key?'

'The kind of men we're talking about prefer to scale walls, I should think, only it attracts less attention if you stop a van in front of the door and they can slip in and out pretty much unseen.'

'It's behind my *Grand Meaulnes*, that's it. Here.'

'I'll nip round, bring it right back.'

Gareth said, 'Twenty-eight, thirty on the label and it says take two.'

Katie said, 'I'll count the other lot while you're trying to put all those ones in again.' She sat in the next chair and emptied the second pill bottle.

Sideburns came down. 'Are you due at work tomorrow, sir?'

'Yes,' said Gareth.

'We'll have gone off shift but I imagine they'll arrange for our relief to drive you in. Is it Curzon Street or Gower?'

'Gower Street.'

'One more thing, if I can have a daytime number. This may sound odd but there's a shrink they like to put in touch with us if we've fired on suspects.' He brought a pen and notebook out. 'As I gather you're a DCI in Special for liaison purposes we ought to follow the same procedure. He'll call you up, you're not obliged to go and see him, actually I think it's her these days, but if you play along for at least one visit you keep the bosses happy, then they don't think you've got some mental upset that you want to hide.'

Gareth recited the Gower Street switchboard number.

'Thank you, sir.'

'He only took two of these as well,' said Katie. 'So hopefully that's all right.'

'The doctor probably meant to write down one of each the first night to kick off and forgot. It happens,' Sideburns said. 'But it won't do him any harm, except he'll feel woozy for a day or so till he's used to it. Does he drive?'

'He can but he hasn't got a car.'

'No problem then. If he'd really drunk too much on top he'd be waxier, stickier, breathing faster. And three glasses to one wine bottle's not exactly evidence of a binge.'

'I was out,' said Katie, 'Paul was driving straight from work to

Cookham, I don't know who was here with Spence apart from Miles.'

'Me,' Gareth said, 'around seven-thirty.'

Sideburns tactfully said nothing about drink and firearms. He had time off duty, agents didn't. 'In good shape at that time, was he?'

'Yes, fine.'

Freckles came in again. 'Slight problem. Here's your key.'

'Wouldn't the lock work?' Katie said.

'Not that. There was a couple of young guys outside taking too much interest in this house. Followed the car down here. They said they were on voluntary night duty at the Centre and they heard the shooting, wondered what was up. Frankly they could have guessed, it's more than likely they helped do surveillance on you, sir.'

'Are they the ones we know about?' said Gareth.

Freckles nodded. 'Dellow and McBrain. I saw their student cards, driving licences. I had a quick word with them about the drunk,' he told Katie, 'they recognised the description, they say their boss'll read the rulebook at him. For a gentleman in his position to lose his hostel place is pretty calamitous so that might make him watch his behaviour.'

'Have they moved on?' Sideburns said.

'Oh, yeah, they could hardly wait.'

'DI aware?'

'He is, yeah, his blokes are going to go and question them as witnesses but we'll have to find another place for Mr MacMichael. Just tonight till we know how we stand. Any more friends you can call on, sir?'

'This is dreadful,' said Katie. 'But you must have. Lots. Not that I'm keen for you to go, that sounded bad.'

Gareth pulled his tie down looser. 'Nigel in Crouch End, but he's had enough disturbance for today. Can't remember his number anyway. Jo's living in Paris now. Peter and Helen are on research in Sri Lanka. David Weld's south of the river and I am not going south of the river. Sheila's doing postgrad in Oxford, or on holiday in Outer Mongolia at the moment. A few people are down at this party with Lynn in Surrey or Sussex or somewhere, I don't know why she said I wouldn't know anyone, they were all there when she rang just now.' He stood up and swallowed some brandy. 'The last person I spoke to who I think should be at home's Claire Tarrant. Where does Spencer keep his numbers?'

'All over. But mainly on his chest of drawers,' said Katie.

'I need the Holt Newman list.'

The policemen had left Spencer's door open. Katie came to help Gareth sort through the papers. 'We can put the light on, it won't wake him up.'

'Oh. No, it doesn't, does it? He looks quite contented. Apart from ... ' Sideburns had left bloody fingerprints on the face and neck.

'I must remember to give him a wipe. Now, it was his big A4 office list, wasn't it? I'm always seeing that about. It's very creased up. And scribbled on. Is this — ? No, it's the bill for the new central heating pump.'

'No, I've got it.'

'Oh. Fine.' About to turn and go out, Katie said, 'What's that?' She was frowning at the carpet by the foot of the bed. 'Oh. Well, it's not mine because I wouldn't wear that naff colour.'

Gareth took the list out to the hall, sat at the bottom of the stairs and dialled Claire from the green phone on the linen chest or blanket box. He didn't like using telephones, and if asking a girl out was bad, asking yourself round to her place at gone midnight was atrocious. His knee started to vibrate again. He ran fingers through his always untidy hair.

The other end picked up fairly promptly for this hour. Claire's voice said, 'Hello, 603 9587?' with a cautious curiosity. She'd be thinking it was Spencer, or bad news, or a flatmate's tiresome admirer, or even one of her own, or else maybe her old boyfriend in another time zone.

'Hello, Claire — '

'Gareth,' she said in a sighing way that could either be relief or, far more likely, let-down.

'Have I got you out of bed?'

'No, not quite, I'm sitting around in my dressing-gown drinking cups of water. I had dinner with some friends from school and alcohol always leaves me parched and much too wide awake. So don't tell me. You did go round to Spencer's and the man was out, well … '

'No, I'm there now, he's asleep.'

'You sound grave, is something … ?'

'He's fine. Do you want the number?'

'Er … hold on, I'll find a pen.' The other end clunked as she put it down. It hissed to itself, then whuffled as she picked it up and tucked it under her chin. 'Right.'

Gareth read the number off the dial.

'Thanks. OK then … '

Gareth thought of letting Claire get rid of him and waiting out the next few hours at the police station while the duty office down in Gower Street attempted to locate an empty set of military married quarters, which could well turn out to be in Aldershot or Rochester. 'That wasn't why I called,' he said.

'Nn hn? Um … so what's the matter? … Hello?'

'The reason I'm here is the IRA broke my door down a few minutes ago.'

Claire said nothing, and then said, 'What?'

'Only two of them. I'm OK, I have to keep a gun in case of things like that, so I've put them both in hospital.'

'This is real?'

'Yes. The police brought me here while they go over the scene at my house, but they want me to find somewhere else to stay the night. This place is too near if the press or sympathisers are hanging around.'

'Right. What are you planning on doing?'

'I thought about my parents' flat, but if I've been under observation in the last few weeks then anywhere I go to regularly could be known to the other side. Maybe in a day or so it won't matter, if the gang's been mopped up, but for now we're not sure.'

'You don't want to come and stay here, do you?'

'That'd be great if I could, yes.'

'I didn't realise that's what you meant. I haven't seen you for … '

'That's the point, you're what's called a latent untraceable contact.'

'Am I. This sofa opens out, it's not the expensive kind, just foam blocks you zed up to sit on and unzed to sleep on, you know? People say it's OK as a bed.'

'Jo's got one in Paris, they're fine. We'll have to keep you up another half an hour till we get there.'

'The water I've had to drink, if I went to bed now I'd be up again by then anyhow. Do you know where I am? Not quite Paris, but — '

'Yes, I've got this list here.'

'All right, well, I'll see you ... in a bit,' Claire said, sighingly once more.

Gareth showed Sideburns the list, underscoring Claire's place with a thumbnail. 'It's off Brook Green.' Sideburns made a note.

Freckles came out of the kitchen. 'The back-up's here, ready to follow.' He told Katie, 'We'll be off now but you'll still have,' he thumbed at the kitchen end and pointed at the french window end, 'protection, the inspector'll ring the bell in a mo and explain things, see you're happy about it, then everyone'll leave you in peace. Nice meeting you again, sorry about the intrusion.'

'Yes. Thanks, Katie,' Gareth said, taking his bag and trenchcoat.

'Good luck. Give us a call,' said Katie.

In the back of the Rover, Gareth waited while Sideburns ran to speak to the crew of the Blue Beret van assigned to follow them.

Sideburns got in. 'I'd forgotten to give them the address in case they lose us.'

The Rover took off round the square, attacked Camden Road with lights and siren, ignored the one-way system at the end to cut straight across the junction and up Parkway and dragstered the length of Albany Street. So far the van was still distantly in sight behind.

On paper, Phil was now landing at the Breton airfield after a routine flight from home base in the Ile-de-France to keep his night hours up. The bent manager would log his arrival time to agree with the fake flight plan. What Phil actually did was drop off radar and hedgehop from there to the coast. This was, of course, dangerous. He had to navigate without radio beacons, on dead reckoning and visual fixes, maintaining his orientation and avoiding high ground, trees and power lines by the light of a barely risen moon. But, when younger, he'd been trained to fly giant Vulcan bombers under the Soviet Union's defences day or night at speeds way beyond anything a twin-prop Piper Navajo could do.

Mont St Michel came up on the right, pinnacled, unmistakable. He crossed the salt meadows, then sand. Always that pleasant shock and sense of liberation when the last of the land twanged back underneath and you were over sea. You felt safer, which was a complete delusion because you could much more easily fly into the water than the ground. The size of wavelets was not such a good guide to your height as the size of trees, and the patterns could send you all *2001*.

A good rule of thumb, though, was that the cattle-grid judder of your compression wave hitting the water, plus the appearance of spray on your windscreen, meant you were too fucking low. Phil eased back the column a little. The plane lifted gradually. She'd get livelier as the long-range fuel tanks shed weight. The consumption was fairly avid at low altitudes.

So, he was feet-wet on time on course in the Gulf of St Malo, where the sailors who named the Malouines came from, with Jersey somewhere on the horizon. Fair distance visibility out here, light wind behaving as predicted, cloud patchy and breaking and nothing much lower than 5,000.

He'd wiggle between Jersey and the French Cotentin peninsula, up the Passage de la Déroute, into the Channel. At two hundred feet he should pass over the harbour and shipping radars but under the air traffic scans.

Aboard the RAF Shackleton, orbiting off Portland Bill, three operators took turns to sit behind the blackout curtain and watch the obsolete look-down radar's murky little seven-inch screen. One of those off duty was making everybody corned beef hash in the galley. He used the instant-potato recipe from Katharine Whitehorn's *Cooking in a Bedsitter*, but with the addition of tomato purée and sliced carrot.

The controller had already plotted the bandit's probable course, given the Breton airfield named by MI5 as the starting point. The duty operator reported a trace near Mont St Michel in roughly the expected quarter, and Strike Command HQ at High Wycombe confirmed that the trace did not belong to any legitimate civil or military flight.

The blip kept on coming. If the bandit was using a radar receiver it didn't seem to be tuned to the Shackleton's search band, or he would have reacted by now. He was more likely to be monitoring the coastal transmitters marked on his charts, and perhaps the shipping frequencies.

He could reach England in half an hour and the Shackleton's equipment only worked over water, so the controller needed to guide the Phantoms on to him well before that. They should be able to keep track of him over land, either with their precision close-range radar or with their infra-red seekers, but they had to be helped to find him first.

The small problem was, the Phantoms were nowhere near. They were out past the Lizard, heading rapidly towards the open wastes of the Atlantic, hooked up to their Victor tanker, taking on fuel.

The controller talked to the Victor. The transfer wouldn't be completed for another few minutes. As the Phantoms were not carrying the usual three external tanks, only the two under the wings — the third, centreline pod was for something else — they needed all the confidence fuel they could get at every prod, so the controller decided not to order them to break the transfer early. He plotted course predictions. To reach the best interception point, the Phantoms, once refuelled, would have to cover nearly two hundred miles in under ten minutes. He called Strike Command to ask a favour. Strike Command consulted and said yes.

The refuelling chief aboard the Victor shut off the pumps as the required totals came up on his meters. The strips of small orange lights under the tanker's cavernous armpits, flashing in sequence to show fuel running, all came on at once and glowed steadily to show transfer complete.

The Phantom pilots throttled down a fraction and stirred the columns to make the refuel probes break seal and disengage from the baskets on the ends of the Victor's trailing hoses. Probes retracting, the fighters dipped gently away from the tanker, wheeled east the way they'd come and began to sink towards the clouds. Behind them the Victor swung around as well, to resume its orbit.

The controller gave the Phantom crews their vector and flight level instructions and told them, 'Go Mach Two.'

The lead Phantom pilot said, 'Say again?'

'You are cleared to go Mach Two.'

Together the pilots lit the afterburners and pushed the throttles to full military thrust.

The Victor's captain saw the jetpipes shoot flame, then with a thunder-roll the Phantoms weren't there any more. Just clouds and the rising moon.

Marylebone Road, Sussex Gardens, Lancaster Gate, Bayswater Road, Notting Hill Gate.

Louise's taxi pulled over as the sirens gained fast. She told herself they couldn't be on to her and she touched the front of the Maquis-chic dark blue rollneck sweater she'd changed into earlier, feeling for her gold cross through the weave, but she was suddenly all shivers and in terrible need of a pee.

A police Rover streaked past with that melancholy drop in the siren's braying tones. After a gap, a van did the same. They bore on towards Holland Park. Nothing to do with her. She'd made it.

She remembered she'd left the swop car in Lisson Grove. Just dumped the Ital at King's Cross. Utterly slipped her mind.

The traffic shuffled about its business. The taxi turned off and set Louise down in Ladbroke Square, where the detectives watching from the dark-windowed Ford Granada on the corner observed and reported her arrival and the number of the cab. She glanced up and down the street before she let herself in, but she didn't notice them.

While they were on the radio they asked about the sirens

which could have frightened her off. They were told those vehicles had absolute priority.

Holland Park Avenue, Shepherd's Bush Green, Shepherd's Bush Road, Brook Green, Luxemburg Gardens.

The Phantoms rolled inverted for the long pull-out from the dive, slowing, slowing, still fifty miles from target so as not to make the bandit jump as they let their shockwaves catch and re-envelop them.

Second boom.

Phil felt something, didn't so much hear it, not with his engines buzzing, his slipstream hissing and his headphones on, but felt it in his stomach.

No, never. Combat aircraft going supersonic, here? Almost off Bournemouth? Home to thousands of blue-rinsed old dears who all kept the local Tory MP's phone number to hand and wouldn't dream of troubling him on their own behalf but Binkie, Reggie or Archie was such a *sensitive* little dog and it simply wasn't *fair*?

Impossible. Phil knew what must have happened. The last Concorde of the day must have been delayed getting away from New York by some glitch or security scare and was only now decelerating inbound over the Celtic Sea three hours late. Keyed up, he'd sensed the last dying ripple of the boom, but there'd be no broken glass ashore, no doggy frets, and there were no fighters.

Right side up a thousand feet above the sea and still going ten miles a minute, the lead Phantom searched, found and locked on. The navigator confirmed the trace with his opposite number in the other Phantom.

The controller slowed the fighters down again to slot them in at a discreet shadowing distance behind the bandit.

Claire was in a pure white towelling dressing-gown with what looked like one of those big T-shirts underneath, the sort girls used to wear knotted up at one side over jeans a couple of summers ago but now wore only to bed. This one was striped pink. 'I opened the sofa out and put a sheet and pillow on, but I thought instead of messing about with blankets the sleeping bag would do, all right?'

'Thanks,' said Gareth. 'Are your flatmates, housemates still out?'

'Oh, they're away till Sunday night, they always spend the weekend out of town.'

'The done thing.'

'Yes, their friends would laugh at them otherwise. Mind you, I'm going to stay with my aunt in Berkshire tomorrow.'

'I'll be gone, so — '

'Oh, not that, I was just thinking I used to stay with her in school holidays. When I couldn't go home, because of Mugabe's bunch on the warpath.'

'Ah.'

'My parents didn't want me leaving England, they only let me visit for a week at Christmas and a week in summer, and even then I had to sleep with a gun beside the bed. So, I know what it's like in a way, although nothing ever happened, well, not to us. Were you expecting some kind of trouble, then?'

'I was told they'd heard of me so I ought to watch out, I didn't really think they'd bother.'

Two Blue Berets armed to the teeth nodded as they passed the open door of the room, heading down the hall to the kitchen and the back way out. The one who knew about horses said, 'D'you want to do the locks after us?'

'You're not coming through again?' said Claire.

'No, when the shift finishes we'll use the gardens. Over the walls to the end of the street, we've had a look, no problems. Unless there's any bad dogs you know about, left out overnight.'

'I don't know, I don't think so.'

'OK, cheers. We'll be out of your way now.'

Claire moved the table lamp to the floor by the sofa, then turned the room's main light off. 'How's that?' She went to do up the locks, came back and leaned in the doorway. 'All right?'

Gareth hung his jacket and tie on a chair. 'Yes. I'm really sorry about all this rumpus.'

'Don't be silly. Anything you want?'

'I wouldn't mind a glass of water.'

Claire slipped out and returned with a jug, a glass and an ashtray. 'The bathroom's on the half-landing. What time do you need to be up?'

'About nine, I'll go in late.'

'I've got a train, so I'll put the alarm on and give you a knock. I hope you get some sleep.'

'I'll try.'

She ran a hand up and down his arm. 'Night then.' She went out.

'Good night.' He smoked a Camel and took his bag up to the bathroom, which had silk-matt brown woodchip walls and avocado fixtures, to clean his teeth.

When he came down he emptied his pockets on to the table. The keys and loose change made him see the dead man again, though he didn't have any thoughts on the subject yet. Sitting on the sofa bed he opened the steel case, loaded the Browning, chambered the top round and put the gun by the pillow. He zipped himself into the sleeping bag, superstitiously keeping his watch and underpants on because the place was alien, and smoked another Camel.

The bookshelves in here didn't have many books on them. Most of the space was taken by framed photos of chaps in uniform, evening dress or sports gear, and by silver cups, shields and miniature equine statuary with rosettes attached. The pictures on the walls were chocolate-box family portraits and the sort of specious semi-abstracts that trust-funded art students called Piers and Rhodri painted for their friends. None of it was very Claire. Presumably the place belonged to one of the done-thing gels, in which case the previous owner's middle-class bathroom must be a major embarrassment, the more so since their friends would notice there wasn't the dosh to alter it.

He wondered what Claire's room was like. Alphonse Mucha and wildlife posters, a mosaic of snapshots under glass, her own drawings, some Maori and Shona knick-knacks and the famous cuddly toys.

Plants. She'd have something living, like marantas that folded up their leaves at night with a friendly rustle.

He took off his glasses and felt under the lampshade for the switch, scorching his fingers on the bulb before he found a brass thing you had to turn like a gas tap.

The darkness made the ringing in his ears louder. For a while he thought it was a burglar alarm at the end of the street.

He was too wound up to sleep, or to do anything else like read a book from the shelves or think of an excuse to knock on Claire's door and have a conversation. And the police wouldn't let him go for a walk round the Green.

But he got cramp in his left foot and had to keep flexing it, which helped to pass the time.

At the edge of Lyme Bay Phil turned in on 040 and went feet-dry near Abbotsbury. He now had an hour's intensive cross-country work to do, throwing a two-hundred-mile curve south of London and up over the Thames estuary into Essex. Simpler, of course, to start from Calais in the first place, but there was so much high-powered radar covering the eastern end of the Channel that the risk of straying into contact outweighed the savings on time and petrol.

Fuel state was all right. With stiffened spars to take underwing and tip tanks, the Piper should manage the collection in Essex, the delivery in Wexford and the hop back to Brittany before he was down to the emergency reserve.

The Phantom crews, strolling at safe height a few miles behind, approved of the way the bandit used land contours to hide himself, but even when the radar returns went vague the infra-red was good. Staying away from built-up areas he left a heat signature that stood out like a karzi in the Kalahari.

Louise rolled over and answered the phone. It might be the boys, still OK somehow and running, angry she'd gone without them.

It wasn't, though. 'It's Sean from the Centre.' John McBrain. He insisted on calling himself Sean but he talked Norf Lahndun. 'The bloke I tagged for you now and then, something's gone down at his place, lot of shooting and we saw an ambulance. The cops questioned us, we didn't tell them anything but we can't find out what happened. Did you get him?'

'I think you must have the wrong number,' Louise said, and hung up. The phone rang again. The idiot really did think he'd dialled a wrong number. She let it ring.

Phil took visual fixes on, among other things, the rude prehistoric man carved into the chalk hillside at Cerne Abbas, the River Stour, the Shaftesbury escarpment, the spires of Salisbury and Winchester, the Itchen, the Rother and the Arun.

Bypassing Horsham he didn't disturb Su's slumbering PA Fiona in her flat above the camera shop, although a couple of minutes later the Phantoms made her dream of tenpin bowling. He skirted the southern edge of the Weald, in radar shadow from Gatwick airport's point of view, and knew he'd reached Kent on track when he saw the Lamberhurst vineyards. He didn't like Kent, it was a steeplechase of power lines. He wormed through the gap in the North Downs and with Canterbury on his right wingtip he set the compass to strike for the estuary shore between Herne Bay and Margate, being careful not to overfly RAF Manston even if it was closed at nights.

Again the big rush as he skimmed water. He flew a hoop out to sea, around the Sheerness harbour radar's arc of horizon, so he could go low enough to be certain he kept under the Southend airport radar. Southend had a feed to the London control room, the operator only sat ten feet from the military desk, and he was highly exposed here over water.

It wasn't such a wide diversion, because harbour and ship radars could only see for about twenty-five miles before surface reflections obscured the picture. It didn't bring him within range of Harwich, because the Naze headland was in the way. And it had the added advantage of putting some space between him and the notoriously unpredictable inhabitants of the Foulness bird sanctuary.

He curved in again towards the Blackwater inlet on the Essex coast and lined up on the south tip of Mersea Island for the final stopwatch-and-compass run to the landing field.

The field was owned by a thick young sir of libertarian opinions who took his landing fees in white powder and thought these occasional night stop-bys were all to do with the same stuff. When Phil arrived there were lights in the big house a mile away but no headlamps or flares in the field, therefore no show. He circled once. Fuel was too tight to hang about and so were the Southend and Stansted radar envelopes. You needed more height to circle.

The Phantoms had ascended into cloud and zigzagged to fall further behind. The lead navigator told his pilot, 'If he goes round again we'll have to break and orbit or we'll be on top of him.'

No show. The passengers knew the rules. Phil set course for the vale that would lead him up past Stansted airport in cover. He'd cross the M11 beyond Saffron Walden and begin the slog through the Midlands to Wales, St George's Channel and Ireland. He still had to deliver the boxes in the aft baggage compartment. He didn't like the look of those. They were the right sizes and weights for the components of a portable SAM launcher, and although army helicopter pilots weren't exactly real pilots, brothers in the mystery, Phil was not dead keen on helping shoot them down.

Louise heard the house door go, then the flat door, then there were torches and shouting in the bedroom. The duvet was pulled away. She curled into a ball in her mauve silk pyjamas. 'Please don't hurt me I panicked that's all I panicked!'

'This is the police, Louise,' a torch said. 'Who did you think it was?'

McBrain answered the night bell again. The same Scottish detective constable who'd questioned him before was on the doorstep, but this time he didn't say, 'Sorry to trouble you,' he said, 'That's him,' and uniformed heavies dragged Sean from the doorway and threw him on his face on the Murray Street pavement and cuffed his hands behind his back. The Scottish detective said, 'John alias Sean McBrain, I'm arresting you for conspiracy to murder, you don't have to say anything but anything you do say will be taken down and may be used in evidence against you. Mind, you said it all to Miss de Cameron earlier really.' Along the street, by the door of the other hall of residence, Chris Dellow also lay cuffed with the police standing over him pointing revolvers.

From Stratford-upon-Avon Phil followed the river — the second Avon on tonight's itinerary, and he'd crossed two Stours as well — into the Vale of Evesham, passive feminine landscape lying back and thinking of England in the moonlight, then he nipped over the M5, hung a right past the dormant brontosaurus shape of the Malvern Hills and took up the thread of the Teme, which led him into Wales. He cut across the Tenbury and Ludlow loops.

He was impressed to see how long it took the Welsh sheep to hear his custom-silenced engines coming. But perhaps they'd been deafened by RAF jets on low-level exercises.

Beyond the pass he found the headwaters of the Severn and the vast reservoir. He sidled past a towering, unpronounceable summit to the next reservoir, about three minutes from the coast, where he set his stopwatch and compass for the sea transit to Ireland.

Leaving Cardigan Bay he went very low out of respect for the air traffic radar on Strumble Head, again linked to London control, but he'd gain a little height on the Irish side to avoid making too much impression on the Arklow harbour radar. He could go to four hundred feet there without Dublin airport or Strumble seeing him.

The Shackleton took over while the Phantoms rendezvoused with the tanker off Milford Haven.

Gareth woke to find himself sitting bolt upright gasping 'Uuurh' as he felt the awful plosive sensation between his ears and saw the room lit by a dazzling flash.

The light faded to purple. He knew it was only in his brain. As he slept, the tension his conscious mind suppressed during the day built up till his heart missed a beat and restarted with that sickening thwock, the surge of blood creating the illusion of light in the visual part of the cortex and his memory supplying the furniture, shelves, pictures and curtains, as well as the view of his own sleeping-bagged knees, because if there was light there must be something to see.

It was dark again now, but his heart was trying to fight its way out of his chest and the sweat was coursing off him in actual waves.

He shook, groaned, lay down and did some deliberate and even breathing. His heart corrected itself and proceeded at a relatively stately, sober measure.

He looked at the luminous face of his father's old watch. It was about three-twenty. The attacks always happened in the hour between three and four, the most derelict tract of the night.

The sweat congealed and chilled. He went up to the bathroom, borrowed a sponge and swabbed himself clean. He wondered if the Blue Berets in the garden, seeing the blinded window glow, would think he'd been up to something with Claire. He forced back the embarrassment. As firearms specialists they should know that shooting people was a damper. There was even such an expression as shooter's droop. Provos seemed to get a rise out of homicide, but then Provos were scarcely normal.

Headlamps shone on the turf and petrol-soaked rags were burning in tin cans to provide flares at each end of the landing area, though there was plenty of space outside those. Horse gallops offered more ground than clandestine airstrips needed. Phil passed, circled back to come in upwind, selected flaps and wheels down and switched on his landing-light.

The shape of the light's cone on the ground was the best way to judge when you were about to touch. Phil chopped the throttles and let the Piper's reinforced tricycle undercarriage take the weight. He braked his way to the upwind end flares, gunned the starboard engine, turned, taxied back to the downwind end and turned again ready for take-off. The engines would not be cut while on the ground.

He got out, opened the baggage hatch, unstrapped the boxes and stood there with the company's Sterling submachine-gun magged and cocked to protect the plane. The terrorists brought their Subaru pick-up and Peugeot estate car alongside. Four of them handled the boxes, two of them considered the view with Kalashnikovs pointed well away from Phil or he'd blast them out of their cheesy Fenian socks. All of them were masked so he couldn't identify them from a police mugshot album if he happened across such a thing.

'The passengers didn't show,' he said.

None of the terrorists said anything. Uncool of him to state the obvious. And no point them asking him for details because he wouldn't know, so they just stowed the boxes in the vehicles and drove away to douse the flares. He sealed the hatch, safed the gun, returned to the cabin and fastened his belt. Light on fuel now as well as cargoless, the Piper took off like a startled pheasant.

Phil egressed over the south coast at maximum speed, using the company-fitted turbochargers. If Waterford Harbour did scope him they'd think he was an Irish Air Force C-12 on fishery patrol.

Peugeot in front, the cars bumped down the sunken track from the gallops. At a slow bend the tyres punctured. The gardai had laid spikes. Lurching round the bend, the Peugeot was confronted by a large, stationary digger, parked there under cover of the plane's arrival, the deep bushy banks funnelling the racket skyward so the aero-engines along with the idling French diesel and Jap flat-four had drowned it out, though barely.

The men with the Kalashnikovs, one behind the Peugeot driver, one in the left seat of the Subaru's cab, stuck their gun muzzles through their open windows and raked both banks with fire as the Peugeot slithered to a stop and the Subaru rammed its tailgate.

The detectives lying atop the banks kept their heads down, but one of them got some flying dirt or root fragments in his eye.

The terrorists baled out, those with no assault rifles pulling pistols, and ran off past the digger, firing all round.

Some of the detectives held their Uzis over their heads and

fired a few token bursts.

A quarter of a mile along the track the terrorists climbed one bank and escaped across the fields.

The inspector in charge of the Garda team ordered his men to clean up. The digger was reversed down to the road, the limping terrorist vehicles driven down after it to await the lowloaders, and the spikes and cartridge cases were recovered from the track by torchlight.

The inspector and the MI5 liaison officer opened the boxes at the roadside, had a look at what was in them and closed them again. A Volvo estate drew up and two more MI5 men put the boxes in the back.

Fifty miles off Milford Haven, heading due south at a more comfortable 240 knots and waiting for the Scillies to come up in half an hour, Phil saw a big, dark, mean shape slide into prospect from the top right corner of his windscreen. Shark nose, kinked-up wings, downturned tailplane, it was only a sodding Phantom. Its navigation lights winked at him. It was close enough for him to see the crew swivel their two helmeted heads in tandem and study him.

But Phantoms didn't work this side of the street. They did the North Sea. Generally. Had he blundered into an exercise, affiliation with the Nimrod unit from Cornwall or something? It was too much of a coincidence if they'd found him on their own, there must be a Nimrod out here directing them.

And they'd read his tail number now, and he wasn't even supposed to be here, let alone below legal height — there was a five-hundred-feet rule after dark — with his radio and transponder off. He was comprehensively stuffed. Unless he hacked on to France regardless and did a quick disappear to Rio with the alternative passport he always carried in his moneybelt.

The Phantom positioned itself a few hundred yards ahead and above and rocked its wings, follow me.

Phil throttled down obstinately and fell behind, make me.

The Phantom broke away in a left turn.

Phil kept straight on. Phantoms were designed to land on

carriers and they could go very slow for jets, puffing air out the side of each engine over the wing to kid the wing it was flying faster, but Phil's Piper could still outstall them. They'd have to circle him, feeling complete prats, as he moseyed at 110 all the way into French airspace, where they'd have to leave him alone. France wasn't a military member of NATO and not much of a diplomatic member either, and he was French-registered. The Armée de l'Air weren't about to send up a Mirage. All he had to do was bluff Brest control about an impromptu flight to test his inertial nav gadget, which wasn't working, and say he'd forgotten his transponder was off and radio interference stopped him filing an airborne flight plan or hearing any calls, so he'd turned back. Then as soon as he touched down he could do a bunk. The company had a car at the Breton airfield. He'd make the first Rio flight out of Paris before any gendarmes came calling.

A second Phantom overshot him and broke left. They always worked in pairs. There'd be a lot of this for the next hour and a half. He thought of punching the interception channel on the radio and telling them to foxtrot oscar, but he didn't want to get into conversation.

The first Phantom made another pass overhead, and as it drew in front of him Phil decided Rio could wait and Cornwall wasn't so bad this time of year, because the fighter's underbelly fuel pod spewed a lurid, rule-straight line of sparkles into the distance with a bullfrog noise and it wasn't a fuel pod, it was an M61 six-barrelled rotary cannon and that mere half-second warning burst would have used fifty rounds of high-explosive twenty-millimetre ammunition, which was not enough to shoot Phil down, it was enough to vaporise him and his aircraft instantly and leave no identifiable wreckage or remains.

Which meant they knew what he was doing and who he was working for.

The Phantom rocked its wings and broke left, climbing. Phil throttled up and followed. The other Phantom closed in behind him as he looked over his shoulder. He switched on his transponder, selected full Mode C with altitude reading which wasn't even compulsory in UK airspace yet, and squawked his callsign, to show the controllers how co-operative he was being.

If Ibbotson had sprung for some military all-bands radar receivers Phil might not be up this particular creek. Another reason you should never work for a tightwad. But at least Ibbotson was up the creek as well.

Phil put his Stones tape on. Side One lasted to the Cornish coast, where he recognised Newquay's surfing beaches and, not far inland, the illuminated runway of the Nimrod base at St Mawgan.

The Phantom led him into the circuit, easing past the field to the right, curling round into the wind and lining up on the approach lights. Phil could see the control tower, the maintenance hangars and dimly the pea-soup-green shapes of the great Nimrods standing ever ready to go and search for shipwrecked trawlermen or, as the case might be, to go and nuke Russian submarines.

The Phantom wouldn't be landing. It drew further ahead as Phil lowered wheels and flaps. The second Phantom overtook as well, unable to keep behind at this speed. But they'd stay in the circuit till he parked and deplaned.

He only needed a fraction of the runway's length, so he left it a while before he lost some more throttle and floated down. To the Piper, concrete didn't offer a much better landing than Irish turf did. Different if you were a jet. He rolled to a stop halfway along, by the tower at the top of the airfield's hump, where he could see the sea again. A truck with dayglo orange chevrons on the back and yellow flashing lights led him off down the crossway, past the tower's grass island and over the taxi track to the hangar apron.

A couple of Land Rovers spilled RAF Regiment troops who surrounded the plane. Phil cut the engines. He opened the cabin door, dropped to the concrete and stood with his hands up against the fuselage while two squaddies searched him and removed his moneybelt. The clean air smelled of holidays.

A black soldier the size of a wardrobe, with US MARINES over his top pocket and a .45 automatic in his hand, talked to the RAF men and examined the moneybelt. Making sure it wasn't Semtex. The Nimrods' nuclear depth bombs, stored on the base, were American navy property, so the wardrobe had to satisfy himself that Phil wasn't part of any threat to their security. Here was one United States Marine who really did guard the pearly gates in a not very funny old sort of a way.

An officer and a gentleman walked over from the tower. The gentleman was a fey individual in aviator specs and a dark blue cashmere overcoat. The officer, face shaded from the arclights by the peak of his cap, proved on close inspection to be Tom Tolland, one-time Vulcan pilot. And Phil had been hoping not to meet anyone he knew.

'Hullo, Phil.'

'Tom.'

The grumbling of the Phantoms died away as they turned home for Lincolnshire. Tom took the moneybelt from the wardrobe, looked at the passports and currency in the belt's compartments and gave it to the civilian.

'You the CO here now, then?' Phil said with a nod at the epaulettes on Tom's sweater.

'This is Mr Jenkins,' Tom said. 'He's come from London.'

'Are you Five?' said Phil. There was an Andover turboprop parked across the apron, sporting the Northolt VIP squadron's red-and-white colours.

'If it helps,' Carl said. 'Does it?'

'Well ... I'd just like to say I intend to co-operate. Anything I can tell you about my employers and their clients I will. I don't know if the Irish'll try to extradite, but — '

'No, they won't.'

'Oh, you've heard. The racehorse gallop.'

'It's owned by a Dublin business syndicate.'

'Which includes ... '

'Yes. There won't be any extradition proceedings, he and his friends will want to keep the matter very quiet, he has a certain history in the gun-running arena already. We'll oblige if he's a good boy in future.'

'What about the reception committee?'

'They were allowed to take to the hills, death involves the courts and public paperwork. But the gards did recover the rocket launcher for us.'

'I wondered if it was a SAM.'

'Yes, only three rounds to go with it and a manual in Russian and Arabic, but quite dangerous if they ever learnt how to use it.'

'I'm not told what the cargo is on black ops.'

Tom put in, 'It's still carriage of weapons and munitions of war. To add to all the other violations.'

Carl said, 'You were lucky, though, a friend of mine shot your passengers. Had that gone the other way you would now be an accessory to murder and I couldn't do anything for you.'

'What can you do?'

Carl said, 'The Civil Aviation Authority and Customs don't know who you are. If you've been sufficiently helpful to us, they needn't find out.'

Fire and ambulance trucks drove past along the taxi track.

Phil asked Tom, 'What's happening? Has your boy got a problem?'

'It's not one of mine. Listen.'

From upwind came the drumming of the Shackleton's engines.

'They've got a bad boost reading on number three,' Tom said. 'It's probably the gauge but they asked to put down here instead of risk taking it all the way back to Lossiemouth.'

A cluster of navigation lights progressed around the circuit and came in on the approach, where the antique outline of the Shackleton, with four churning props and twin-finned tail, the image of the wartime Lancaster it was bred from, showed against the moon.

'Which one is it?' Phil said.

'Ermintrude,' said Tom.

Carl said, 'Are there others with names like Florence, or Zebedee?'

'That's right,' said Tom.

'Yes … ' said Carl.

Lowering enormous balloon-tyred wheels, the Shackleton settled to earth and ran up the hump towards them. Its exhausts back-poppled and snorted blue flames as it slowed.

Gareth felt as though he'd only been asleep five minutes, but it must have been five hours because there was daylight through the curtains and Claire, whose knock had woken him, was placing a mug by the sofa bed. 'Black no sugar,' she said, straightening, and folded her arms across the front of the white dressing-gown.

At home he drank tea first thing, not coffee. Still. 'Thank you.'

'Do you want scrambled eggs?'

Scrambled brains. His eyes watered. 'No, thanks.'

'I thought you liked those. I was going to spike a clove of garlic on the fork to beat them.'

The Escoffier method. It was surprising the things she remembered him saying at the office a year and a half ago. 'I'm not up to anything cooked.'

'Have some Alpen or whatever when you're ready.' She went out.

Gareth unzipped the sleeping bag, rolled on to the carpet and did his forty push-ups. He'd trained to sixty for his field course but found it was more effort than it was worth. He made a neat pile of the bedding, folded away the sofa bed, dressed except for jacket and tie and went up to the bathroom.

When he came into the kitchen, lensed, he noticed how fresh Claire looked. Once, he could manage late nights that well himself, but in the mirror just now he looked like a hostage photo.

'The men in the garden have gone,' Claire said, and bit toast.

'Perhaps they've made some arrests, they can scratch out the threat for the time being.'

Claire pushed the muesli packet at him. 'I've never seen you without glasses.'

'I'm wearing contacts.'

'Improvement. Did you sleep?'

'Off and on. What time's your train? We can give you a lift if you like.'

'No, that's all right. I haven't even picked out my clothes for the day yet. Haven't found them, to be accurate.'

'Ah?'

'I think the girls have gone off with my things from the airing cupboard. They've got so much stuff and they're always borrowing each other's, they don't know whose is whose. It's happened before but they've made a really clean sweep this time. They've got cars so they pack these great suitcases, throw in everything. My good weekend sweaters have gone, my plaid cotton trousers I was planning on and my nice natural linen ones ... '

'Oh, Claire.'

'All I seem to have left is things I haven't taken out of the drawer for ages. And look at you.'

'What?'

'You still haven't got the hang of ironing shirts, have you? Never could.'

'Well ... '

'You buy these Jermyn Street shirts and then look like you've slept in them. Or is that one yesterday's?'

'Yes, it is. I didn't sleep in it, though.'

'We've got a steam iron if you want to let me have a bash.'

She'd made him go shy. He bowed his head and shook it. 'Doesn't matter.'

'All right. I'm going to finish getting ready. That toast in the toaster's yours.'

He ate the toast with honey, stacked crocks next to the sink, went to the living room for his jacket and tie and drew the curtains. Quite nice day, almost sunny. The view was dustbins, gravel, the hedge and, through the gateway, the haunch of the waiting police car. The school playground opposite was deserted except for courting pigeons.

He sat on the sofa and smoked a Camel.

Claire came down wearing a pepper-and-salt rollneck sweater with light brown needlecord jeans tucked into red leg-warmers. She dropped a fake-leather travel bag on the hall floor and stood in the doorway, fluffing her hair. 'How are you doing?'

Gareth sat up. 'What's wrong with those clothes? I don't see what you're on about.'

'Don't you? This,' she tugged at one side of the sweater, 'has got moth, here. I hope the pattern camouflages it. And these,' she rubbed her snugly corded thighs, 'are flares.'

'Oh, well. I've still got flares I wear. Most people have. And Abba still make records.'

Claire wrinkled her nose. 'Well, I thought I'd tuck them in.'

'I must be off. Sure you don't want a lift to Paddington?'

'I'd get there too early, I'll take the underground in a while.'

Gareth carried his bag into the hall and pulled his trenchcoat on.

'I have to let you out,' said Claire, unlocking the eye-level Bramah and the waist-height Chubb on the front door.

'OK. Thanks for everything.'

Claire replied in a wordless singsong on descending notes, opened the door and looked round it. 'Oh, they are there.' She hugged him. 'I'm really glad you're all right. Take care.' She swayed him in her hold.

'Thank you.'

She let go and he slipped out to the step.

'Bye then, Claire.'

'Lots and lots of love.'

The door shut.

'Oh,' he said. 'Yeah.' The thing with Spencer must be making her feel all warmed up.

Claire listened to the car drive smartly off. She did a slow cartwheel into the living room, lay on her back, touched her toes in the air, pedalled, rolled forward and stood, arms spread and one foot lifted and pointed behind.

They took a different route. This was Hammersmith Road. Gareth slumped low in the back seat to give himself some headroom and closed his eyes.

He went down the ten York stone steps into his imaginary garden. The sun had westered below the tops of the elms now, but the old iron handrail was still warm. He walked the lawn and sniffed the roses. He tossed thumbnail-sized stones into the lily pond to hear the tiny splashes in the quietness. He sat on the inflatable clear plastic bench by the marble table where his Earl Grey and fruitcake were waiting. A Red Admiral drowsy with buddleia nectar rested in a fold of his shirt.

He opened his eyes a moment and saw the tower of the Knightsbridge cavalry barracks.

After tea he walked down the lane, poppies and tall grasses waving from the verges. He climbed the stile and followed the path to the beach. The tide was a mile out and the breeze was fair so he rolled the yellow sand yacht from the tar-scented hut and let rip across the empty bay, tacking in wide zigs and zags to the water's edge. With his trousers rolled and his sock-stuffed shoes laced together and hung round his neck he waded in the shallows. The wind rippled his shirt. Sand and water streamed between his toes as each wave backed.

Spencer had been at work for hours, cold-calling his fruitless way into the usual state of despondent nausea, when he began to suspect that today was Saturday, in which case the whole thing could turn out to be merely a real nightmare rather than the waking kind.

He couldn't, obviously, ask any of the others if it was Saturday. They'd think he was bonkers. He had to get out of the office, go round to X.Y. Jones and look at the newspapers. While Goldie and Stubbs were talking babies he crept out to the stairs, but two flights down he ran into Su. She was wearing her navy-blue culotte suit and he could make out in detail the pseudo-heraldic design on the metal buttons, which didn't bode too well for the dream theory. 'Spencer,' she said, predatorily.

'Oh aye?'

'I was just coming to see you.'

'What can I do for you?'

'You can fetch me the papers on Wright from the Aerospace file, save me a trip up. Someone was talking about him.'

Worryingly, when he returned with Wright's papers Su wasn't in her office. He could run into her again. He left the stuff on her desk and went down to reception, where there was a candidate on the sofa but no Claire, of course, since she'd be in the basement if anywhere. Tara, having a boyfriend gripe to Lillian in the kitchen, was probably meant to be filling in. He was about to drift to the front door when Su came out of Cracknell's room, saying over her shoulder, 'See you do.'

'On your desk,' he said and strode purposefully down the hall to take cover in the basement stairway till she'd gone. He didn't want to visit the basement itself because he hadn't thought of anything to say to Claire, so he waited a few steps down. Su was in reception making polite conversation with the candidate, one of Les's but she was heading that search.

Tara leaned against the wedged-open door at the top of the stairway and asked him, not for the first or last time, 'So come on, which bit of me d'you really most want to lick whipped cream off, then?'

He didn't think he'd better use 'The stump of your severed neck, you spoilt trollop' again; she'd got quite upset by that and Claire had later frogmarched him to the kitchen where the girl was crying and he'd had to cuddle her and appeal for forgiveness, since when the flirting had predictably worsened. He said, 'I never use whipped cream, only champagne sorbet.'

'Frozen? That'd hurt a bit, wouldn't it?'

'Not me it wouldn't.'

They stiffened. Su looked round the doorpost, gripped Tara's arm and said, 'Back to your desk.' Spencer, cringing, trotted on down the stairs as if he were going to see Claire about an interview time or something.

Claire, in her flowerprint dress, was emerging into the corridor at the bottom. 'I heard that. You are disgusting.'

'Busy?' he said.

'Course I am, this is work. Did you want me?'

'Well ... '

'You can wait your turn.' She ran upstairs with some papers.

He followed, not closely, and heard her giggle behind Cracknell's door. But from above came the sound of Fiona having a strip torn off by Su, which told him the coast was clear, and he gratefully left the building.

The *Standard* kiosk on the corner of Marylebone High Street was locked up and still had its INVASION 'UNDER WAY' bill from Friday, but as the *Standard* didn't come out on Saturdays that would be there till Monday lunchtime.

With mounting dread he realised this could be a perfectly normal Monday morning. The new girl Naomi should have been in reception, but maybe she was at the copier, in the loo, in the stationery cupboard, seeing Holly or Robin on secretarial business, host of possibilities. Su only told Tara, 'Back to your desk', not 'reception'. If Robin was in today Tara could be using the accountant's office.

He stumbled into Barclays Bank. The expected queue of Middle Eastern types was in place, no long-lost friends or cartoon characters, nothing dreamlike going on. He looked at the calendar clock on the wall. It said it was Monday.

He stumbled out again. Halfway across the zebra to X.Y. Jones he decided he wasn't having it, none of this could be trusted, the newspapers would simply follow the illusory consensus.

One way he could often wake himself up was doing something fatal, but there wasn't a cliff to jump off and since the traffic had stopped for him it would be no good throwing himself under that Jeeves of Belgravia drycleaner's van. Besides he wasn't confident enough. He got to the kerb, flagged a cab, went home, went straight to bed, slept through till next morning and woke to hear a radio ad for discount carpets and a low conversational patter that strongly suggested workmen on the premises.

The drains must have blocked again and Katie had called Dyno-Rod. He pulled on jeans and sweater and went into the living room.

Two blokes were fitting a new pane of glass in one of the french windows. Their tranny, on the balcony rail, launched into Chas and Dave's 'Ain't No Pleasing You'. They saw Spence and said hiya.

He smiled weakly. He couldn't ask them how the glass got broken, they'd think he was bonkers. 'Cup of tea?' he said.

'She just made us one, thanks.' They pointed at their mugs on the balcony planking.

Katie wasn't around. Bathroom, or doing her face in her room, or round the corner at the shop. He put the kettle on. Outside there was a carload of police sitting at the kerb not doing anything.

The doorbell rang. It was another workman bloke, holding out a bunch of new and shiny brass keys. 'OK then, cheers, mate.'

Spencer took them. 'What are these?'

'Keys.'

'Yeah, granted, but — '

'For 57 up the mews. Told to drop them off here, he'll pick them up.'

'I'm not even going to try and make sense of this.' Spencer left the keys on the linen chest by the phone and went upstairs. Bathroom vacant and, when he tramped up to the top floor, Katie's room also vacant. He tramped down again. The kettle had boiled dry and the safety cut-out had ejected the plug. Par. He refilled and reboiled.

Through the steamed window he saw what might be Katie coming up the path with one or more of those red-striped plastic bags they gave you at the shop round the corner.

He let her in. 'What's going on?'

'Oh, you're up. Tell you in a minute.' She took the bags to the kitchen, hi-ing the glaziers. 'Who bought all that fruit in the bowl out there? Because you never do.'

'Well, I did. Why are they fixing the french window and why has Gareth changed his locks?'

'Has that chap been? Mind you it is gone eleven.' She put things in the fridge.

'Is it?' He looked at his watch.

'Can you make me some coffee too?'

'OK. We haven't been burgled, have we? To start off I thought, broken glass, she's locked herself out and broken in while I was in a drug coma, I'm starting to feel hung over, actually, my head feels like a marrow.'

'A marrow.'

'What? No, what are those orange pouffe-shaped things people hollow out and cut faces in and put candles inside at Halloween?'

'Pumpkins.'

'Course. Like one of them. Gone rotten and liable to burst and shower putrid clods of matter over a large radius any minute. But then I thought if Gareth's had a break-in, perhaps some gang did the rounds and we've been burgled as well.'

'Nnno. The two things aren't connected, except those guys are off to do his windows next. But I got the police to break ours,

Gareth broke his own.'

'I've just made two cups of hot water, hold on.' Spencer stirred in coffee granules. 'I see, he was locked out as well and he still can't find his keys so — I'm with you.'

'No, you're not. He broke his windows from the inside. Oh, and before you look in a mirror, I forgot to wash your face.'

In the conference room Gareth signed the five pages of his statement for the cubic, ruddy-faced, velvet-headed CID man, resisting the urge to correct the detective's uneven grammar and spelling. It was still a better and clearer account than he would have come up with on his own. He saw the detective down to the front desk by lift and went back up to the cubbyhole he shared with Cath, who said, 'Spencer Cobbold rang.'

Gareth called Rochester Square.

'I gather I missed you last night,' Spencer said. 'Kates says while you were making sure people can sleep safe in their beds I was the one doing the sleeping safe in bed bit.'

'Well, somebody has to, or where's the point?'

'Sorry to hear what happened.'

'Thanks. I'm all right. Done now anyway. Although one of them's in intensive care at UCH right across the road from here and the other's in St Pancras Morgue not far away either, which is ... '

'Yeah. We've got your new keys.'

'Oh, fine, I'll be round sometime, then. The police say I can move back home tonight. They've finished taking pictures and measuring and it's all being tidied up, the Under-Secretary here says the government's paying, which is good. I expect I'll still lose the deposit for putting a couple of rounds through the dining table when I missed the second one.'

'I thought you got both of them.'

'Not with every round, Spence.'

'Oh. Do you want to move back?'

'It'll do till somewhere else comes up. Shouldn't think the other gang'll come after me in a hurry because the lab says Kite and Ball burnt my target notes, there was some ash in the kitchen bin with flakes big enough to analyse. And they don't like second attempts much, it reminds people they blew it the last time.'

'But, associations, living in the place.'

'Yes. Well, I'll see how I feel about it.'

'Stop here if you like.'

'Thanks. I'm a bit more worried about Lynn.'

'Why, where's she?'

'Stopping down in Surrey.'

'Have you spoken to her?'

'Not yet. I was thinking, you come home from a weekend and the house looks all right but you know someone's just died there, and it might be worse if you didn't see it yourself, your imagination works on it.'

'Better tell her he died in hospital. Transfers the spookiness out the front door and down the road. Some of it.'

'That's not bad thinking.'

'Do your mum and stepfather know?'

'No, I just rang and said I was working so I can't go up to Suffolk.'

'What, you didn't tell them?'

'No, I didn't know how to put it. Same reason I always stick the gun in a briefcase if I'm round there and pretend it's office papers I have to keep within reach, which amuses them.'

'I know it's a rule you should never mention anything bad to your mum, but — '

'Well, I only had a fright, I wasn't hurt.'

'Hm. Has it been on the news? I haven't heard any.'

'No. The Provos can't claim it, you see. Because one of them was caught at the scene, it'd ruin his silent defence if he comes to trial.'

'He's pulling through, is he, sod.'

'UCH say critical but stable, he survived the first operation, he probably won't die now. And the police aren't saying anything for security. So there's no big story, one man killed in a shooting's nothing on its own, not while the Falklands coverage is filling all the space.'

'But how d'you stop your mum hearing about it if you have to give evidence at the Old Bailey in a few months?'

'More than a few. Oh, I can't be named in court.'

'Are we supposed to keep Miles out of the picture, then? Only what else have me and Kates got to talk about when we see him? Apart from life in general.'

'Tell him if you like, but all the security aspects including my involvement are D–Noticed, so he can't make a story out of it.'

'Poor old Miles. No exclusive.'

'Not unless he's particularly fond of Dartmoor, no.'

'How was Claire?'

'She seems to think you owe her a call.'

'Gah, I'll see her Monday. Has she gone to her aunt's?'

'She was about to when I left.'

'Can't very well ring her, then. What's her place like?'

'The house isn't bad, the women she shares it with sound ... ' Gareth trailed off as he heard Katie in the background.

Spencer said, 'OK. Oh, if you're around early evening for these keys then, Kates wonders if you can eat.'

'If I can eat? I'm very slightly queasy but — '

'Timewise.'

'Um, expect so, I can always skive.'

'Queasy myself.'

'When did you surface?'

'Late. Head like a, fuck, 's gone again. I went to shave and I had this bloody handprint on my face. Provo blood, unclean or what.'

'Katie meant to wipe that.'

'Half the Met slapping me round the mouth and I didn't even know about it.'

'Why would you want to? OK, I'd better do some work, I might see you about seven.'

Spencer, lying on the sofa while Katie cleaned the glaziers' puttyprints off the new french window pane, said, 'That's not too much trouble, then.'

'No, why?'

'Never mind. D'you want to go round the Lock after lunch?'

'What for?'

'Something to do. I thought girls liked the old-clothes stalls, Schiaparelli ballgowns for a tenner.'

'There is that man who has some good things.'

'I wouldn't mind the walk. If we go slowly. It's not bad out.'

'No, it's not.'

'Shall we eat at Tilley's tonight?'

'The place where they do those pies?'

'On the High Street. Gareth likes it.'

'Mm hm. Sure.'

'We can go in and book while we're down there.'

'You're smoking.'

'I know. This was a definite split with Alastair last night, was it?'

'I think so.'

'Better off out of it.'

'Who've you had in your room? Apart from all of us last night?'

'How d'you mean?'

'Someone's left her rather mistressy pastelly underwear on your floor.'

'Could be yours, white, been in the wash with jeans.'

'The colour's a fuck of a lot drabber when that happens. But I'll have it back if you insist.'

'Wait a minute.'

She went through to his room and called, 'This is not my size.'

'Could have shrunk, on the hot cycle.'

'I don't think that would change the label to read 34C. Lucky bitch, I hate her already.'

'Mind your own business.'

Katie came out. 'What intrigues me is when.' She sat on the arm of a chair. 'No one's been to stay, have they? It can't have been early evening if Miles and Gareth were here. Did you take one of those half-days off you get yesterday?'

'No.'

'I don't believe you. Is it that girl from the office?'

'What girl from the office?'

'The one you go on about.'

'I do not go on about her.'

'Ha.'

'I'm not enjoying this.'

'Why, is it all still doubtful?'

'What isn't?'

Katie curled up in her chair. 'Chuck us a cigarette.'

He sent the pack sliding her way along the hideous coffee table with a swat of his hand.

She lit the cig from the disposable lighter she wore on a leather thong round her neck. 'I'll make this salade niçoise in a minute.'

After lunch they walked through Saturday streets to the canal lock.

Spencer said, 'Would it be a good idea to get involved with someone if you're sure that one day she'll walk a cuddly toy up your chest in bed and say Pink Rabbit says can we have some sex please?'

'Is that so bad?' said Katie. She searched her bag. 'I'm going to put my sunglasses on.'

'Where's the sun?'

'There, look. And I want to wear sunglasses, I haven't for ages.'

'What I mean is, if you think in the long run you probably won't get on well enough or you'll lose interest.'

'It hasn't happened yet, has it?' said Katie. She put on the dark glasses, which she was unable to do without pouting.

'No, but in the meantime you might be, sort of, conning her.'

'Would that stop you?'

'Shouldn't think so.'

'And what if she got tired of you first?'

'I'd fall head over heels then and suffer.'

Katie linked arms with him.

The market seethed gently with young couples in little-worn free-time clothes. On the hour of three the stallholders' radios played news jingles and broadcast the word from the House and the curious excited voxpops from the crowd of foreign tourists massing in Parliament Square.

A thousand miles away to sea already, exercises over, the first ships, the tanker *Tidespring*, the frigates *Brilliant*, *Arrow* and *Plymouth*, and the destroyers *Antrim*, *Glamorgan*, *Glasgow*, *Coventry* and *Sheffield*, head on south, towards the winter.